S0-BYD-963

Acclaim for *Super-Cannes*

"One of his finest."
—*San Francisco Chronicle*

"Ballard's prose is seductive and pellucid and his stories compelling. . . . Spiked with . . . gnomic dialogue and black, black humor, this book is also a captivating Chandlerian mystery."
—*The Washington Post Book World*

"Ballard's fictional world [is] like no one else's."
—*The Atlantic Monthly*

"Rarely has his vision been so total, his creation so complete. *Super-Cannes* is as good as anything that Ballard has done before, and considering the work which that bland statement encompasses, it's the highest possible praise."
—*Star Tribune* (Minneapolis)

"Ballard is back with a vengeance."
—*The Oregonian* (Portland)

"*Super-Cannes* is the first great work of social theory of the twenty-first century."
—*Portland Mercury*

"Ballard's most commercially viable (novel) yet."
—*Publishers Weekly* (starred review)

"A magical hybrid that belongs to no known genre, a masterpiece of the surrealist imagination."
—*New Statesman*

"More than any other writer Ballard understands the transformation technology may effect on human desire. This is his most potent statement yet of the outcome of that transformation, an elegant nightmare with all the internal coherence of an Escher engraving or a Calvino fable."
—*The Observer* (London)

"From the febrile mind and pen of J. G. Ballard, instigator of perhaps the only project in post-war British fiction to fully engage with the modern age in all its blasted glory."
—*Time Out* (London)

"Ballard is a writer for whom anything is possible—a prose surrealist drawn to extremity and stylized representations of modernity, in which ordinary experience is never what it seems: it is always capable of being transformed into something remarkable."
—*The Times* (London)

"Ballard loves to go that bit further out than anyone else; to nose around the outer limits of human behavior and to rub up against the inconceivable. . . . *Super-Cannes* is prime Ballard—weighty, potent, and extraordinary."
—*Evening Standard* (London)

"One of the most important, intelligent voices in contemporary fiction."
—Susan Sontag

Also by J. G. Ballard

J. G. BALLARD

———————

SUPER-CANNES

Picador

New York

www.picadorusa.com

Picador® is a U.S. registered trademark and is used by St. Martin's Press under license from Pan Books Limited.

For information on Picador Reading Group Guides, as well as ordering, please contact the Trade Marketing department at St. Martin's Press.
Phone: 1-800-221-7945 extension 763
Fax: 212-677-7456
E-mail: trademarketing@stmartins.com

Library of Congress Cataloging-in-Publication Data

Ballard, J. G., 1930–
    Super-cannes / J. G. Ballard.—1st Picador USA pbk. ed.
        p. cm.
    ISBN 0-312-28419-5 (hc)
    ISBN 0-312-30609-1 (pbk)
    1. High technology industries—Fiction. 2. Industrial districts—Fiction. 3. Women physicians—Fiction. 4. Married people—Fiction. I. Title.

PR6052.A46 S87 2001
823'.914—dc21   2001133035

First published in Great Britain by Flamingo, an imprint of HarperCollinsPublishers

10 9 8 7 6 5 4 3

Contents

Foreword

A NOTE ON the local geography. Frequent visitors to the French Riviera will be familiar with Marina Baie des Anges, the vast apartment complex that lies like a second Colosseum under the Nice Airport flight path. The Pierre Cardin Foundation, at Miramar to the west of Cannes, is difficult to find but well worth a visit, and must be one of the strangest buildings in Europe. Port-la-Galère, nearby, is another architectural oddity, with its honeycomb facades worthy of Gaudi.

Antibes-les-Pins, at Golfe-Juan, is part of the high-tech Côte d'Azur that is rapidly replacing the old. An even better example, and the inspiration for Eden-Olympia, is the landscaped business park of Sophia-Antipolis, a few miles to the north of Antibes.

Super-Cannes is a luxury enclave on the heights above the Croisette, but the term might well refer to that whole terrain of science parks and autoroutes on the high ground above the Var plain. Together they make up Europe's silicon valley, a world away from the casinos and *belle époque* hotels that define the Riviera of old.

Nostalgic Aviation, a cheerful museum of aircraft memorabilia, stands at the entrance to Cannes-Mandelieu Airport, and is a haven for flying buffs. On the new Riviera, even aviation is now consigned to a fondly remembered past.

J.G. Ballard

PART I

1

Visitors to the Dream Palace

THE FIRST PERSON I met at Eden-Olympia was a psychiatrist, and in many ways it seems only too apt that my guide to this 'intelligent' city in the hills above Cannes should have been a specialist in mental disorders. I realize now that a kind of waiting madness, like a state of undeclared war, haunted the office buildings of the business park. For most of us, Dr Wilder Penrose was our amiable Prospero, the psychopomp who steered our darkest dreams towards the daylight. I remember his eager smile when we greeted each other, and the evasive eyes that warned me away from his outstretched hand. Only when I learned to admire this flawed and dangerous man was I able to think of killing him.

Rather than fly from London to Nice, a journey as brief as a plastic-tray lunch, Jane and I decided to drive to the Côte d'Azur and steal a few last days of freedom before we committed ourselves to Eden-Olympia and the disciplines of the Euro-corporate lifestyle. Jane was still unsure about her six-month secondment to the business park's private clinic. Her predecessor, a young English doctor named David Greenwood, had met a tragic and still unexplained death after running amok with a rifle. By chance, Jane had known Greenwood when they worked together at Guy's Hospital, and I often thought of the boyishly handsome doctor who could rouse an entire women's ward with a single smile.

Memories of Greenwood were waiting for us at Boulogne as the

Jaguar left the cross-Channel ferry and rolled its wheels across the quayside. Going into a tabac for a packet of Gitanes – illicit cigarettes had kept both of us sane during my months in hospital – Jane bought a copy of *Paris Match* and found Greenwood's face on the cover, under a headline that referred to the unsolved mystery. As she sat alone on the Jaguar's bonnet, staring at the graphic photographs of murder victims and the grainy maps of the death route, I realized that my spunky but insecure young wife needed to put a few more miles between herself and Eden-Olympia.

Rather than overheat either Jane's imagination or the Jaguar's elderly engine, I decided to avoid the Autoroute du Soleil and take the RN7. We bypassed Paris on the Périphérique, and spent our first evening at a venerable hotel in the forest near Fontainebleau, spelling out the attractions of Eden-Olympia to each other and trying not to notice the antique hunting rifle on the dining-room mantelpiece.

The next day we crossed the olive line, following the long, cicada miles that my mother and father had motored when they first took me to the Mediterranean as a boy. Surprisingly, many of the old landmarks were still there, the family restaurants and literate bookshops, and the light airfields with their casually parked planes that had first made me decide to become a pilot.

Trying to distract Jane, I talked far too much. During the few months of our marriage I had told my doctor-bride almost nothing about myself, and the drive became a mobile autobiography that unwound my earlier life along with the kilometres of dust, insects and sun. My parents had been dead for two decades, but I wanted Jane to meet them, my hard-drinking, womanizing father, a provincial-circuit barrister, and my lonely, daydreaming mother, always getting over yet another doomed affair.

At a hotel in Hauterives, south of Lyons, Jane and I sat in the same high-ceilinged breakfast room, unchanged after thirty-five years, where the stags' heads still gazed over shelves stocked with the least enticing alcohol I had ever seen. My parents, after their usual bickering breakfast of croissants and coffee helped down by slugs of cognac, had dragged me off to the dream palace of the Facteur Cheval, a magical edifice conjured out of pebbles the old postman collected on his rounds. Working tirelessly for thirty years, he created an heroic doll's house that expressed his simple but dignified dreams of the earthly paradise. My mother tipsily climbed the miniature stairs, listening to my father declaim the postman's naive verses in his resonant baritone. All I could think of, with a ten-year-old's curiosity about my parents' sex-lives, was what had passed between them during the night. Now, as I embraced Jane on the parapets of the dream palace, I realized that I would never know.

Cheval might have survived, but the France of the 1960s, with its Routier lunches, anti-CRS slogans and the Citroën DS, had been largely replaced by a new France of high-speed monorails, MacDo's, and the lavish air-shows that my cousin Charles and I would visit in our rented Cessna when we founded our firm of aviation publishers. And Eden-Olympia was the newest of the new France. Ten miles to the north-east of Cannes, in the wooded hills between Valbonne and the coast, it was the latest of the development zones that had begun with Sophia-Antipolis and would soon turn Provence into Europe's silicon valley.

Lured by tax concessions and a climate like northern California's, dozens of multinational companies had moved into the business park that now employed over ten thousand people. The senior managements were the most highly paid professional caste in Europe, a new elite of administrators, *énarques* and scientific entrepreneurs. The lavish brochure enthused over a vision of glass and titanium straight from the drawing boards of Richard Neutra and Frank Gehry, but softened by landscaped parks and artificial lakes, a humane version of Corbusier's radiant city. Even my sceptical eye was prepared to blink.

Studying the maps, I propped the brochure on my knee-brace as Jane steered the Jaguar through the afternoon traffic on the Grasse road. The stench of raw perfume from a nearby factory filled the car, but Jane wound down her window and inhaled deeply. Our disreputable evening in Arles had revived her, swaying arm in arm with me after a drunken dinner, exploring what I insisted was Van Gogh's canal but turned out to be a stagnant storm-drain behind the archbishop's palace. We had both been eager to get back to our hotel and the well-upholstered bed.

The colour was returning to her face, for almost the first time since our wedding. Her watchful eyes and toneless skin were like those of an over-gifted child. Before meeting me, Jane had spent too many hours in elevators and pathology rooms, and the pallor of strip lighting haunted her like a twelve-year-old's memories of a bad dream. But once we left Arles she rose to the challenge of Eden-Olympia, and I could hear her muttering to herself, rehearsing the risqué backchat that so intrigued the younger consultants at Guy's.

'Cheer me up, Paul. How much further?'

'The last mile – always the shortest one. You must be tired.'

'It's been a lot of fun, more than I thought. Why do I feel so nervous?'

'You don't.' I pressed her hand against the wheel, steering the Jaguar around an elderly woman cyclist, panniers filled with baguettes. 'Jane, you'll be a huge success. You're the youngest doctor on the staff, and the prettiest. You're efficient, hard-working . . . what else?'

'Slightly insolent?'

'You'll do them good. Anyway, it's only a business park.'

'I can see it – straight ahead. My God, it's the size of Florida . . .'

The first office buildings in the Eden-Olympia complex were emerging from the slopes of a long valley filled with eucalyptus trees and umbrella pines. Beyond them were the rooftops of Cannes and the Îles de Lérins, a glimpse of the Mediterranean that never failed to lift my heart.

'Paul, down there . . .' Jane pointed to the hillside, raising a

6

finger still grimy from changing a spark plug. Hundreds of blue ovals trembled like damaged retinas in the Provençal sun. 'What are they – rain-traps? Tanks full of Chanel Number 5? And those people. They seem to be naked.'

'They are naked. Or nearly. Swimming pools, Jane. Take a good look at your new patients.' I watched one senior executive in the garden of his villa, a suntanned man in his fifties with a slim, almost adolescent body, springing lightly on his diving board. 'A healthy crowd . . . I can't imagine anyone here actually bothering to fall ill.'

'Don't be too sure. I'll be busier than you think. The place is probably riddled with airport TB and the kind of viruses that only breed in executive jets. And as for their minds . . .'

I began to count the pools, each a flare of turquoise light lost behind the high walls of the villas with their screens of cycads and bougainvillaea. Ten thousand years in the future, long after the Côte d'Azur had been abandoned, the first explorers would puzzle over these empty pits, with their eroded frescoes of tritons and stylized fish, inexplicably hauled up the mountainsides like aquatic sundials or the altars of a bizarre religion devised by a race of visionary geometers.

We left the Cannes road and turned onto a landscaped avenue that led towards the gates of the business park. The noise from the Jaguar's tyres fell away as they rolled across a more expensive surface material – milled ivory, at the very least – that would soothe the stressed wheels of the stretch limousines. A palisade of Canary palms formed an honour guard along the verges, while beds of golden cannas flamed from the central reservation.

Despite this gaudy welcome, wealth at Eden-Olympia displayed the old-money discretion that the mercantile rich of the information age had decided to observe at the start of a new millennium. The glass and gun-metal office blocks were set well apart from each other, separated by artificial lakes and forested traffic islands where a latter-day Crusoe could have found comfortable refuge. The faint mist over the lakes and the warm sun reflected from the glass curtain-walling seemed to generate an opal haze, as if the entire business park were a mirage, a virtual city conjured into the pine-scented air like a *son-et-lumière* vision of a new Versailles.

But work and the realities of corporate life anchored Eden-Olympia to the ground. The buildings wore their ventilation shafts and cable conduits on their external walls, an open reminder of Eden-Olympia's dedication to company profits and the approval of its shareholders. The satellite dishes on the roofs resembled the wimples of an order of computer-literate nuns, committed to the sanctity of the workstation and the pieties of the spreadsheet.

Gravel tore at the Jaguar's tyres. Waking from her reverie, Jane braked sharply before we reached the gatehouse, sending the old sports saloon into a giddy shunt. Two uniformed guards looked up from their electronic screens, but Jane ignored them, readying a two-finger salute that I managed to conceal.

'Jane, they're on our side.'

'Sorry, Paul. I know, we want them to like me. Open your window.' She grimaced at herself in the rear-view mirror. 'That cheap perfume. I smell like a tart . . .'

'The most gorgeous tart on the Côte d'Azur. They're lucky to have you.' I tried to settle her hands as she fretted over her lipstick, obsessively fine-tuning herself. I could feel the perspiration on her wrists, brought out by more than the August sun. 'Jane, we don't have to be here. Even now, you can change your mind. We can drive away, cross the border into Italy, spend a week in San Remo . . .'

'Paul? I'm not your daughter.' Jane frowned at me, as if I were an intruder into her world, then touched my cheek forgivingly. 'I signed a six-month contract. Since David died they've had recruitment problems. They need me . . .'

I watched Jane make a conscious effort to relax, treating herself like an overwrought patient in casualty. She lay against the worn leather seating, breathing the bright air into her lungs and slowly exhaling. She patted the dark bang that hid her bold forehead and always sprang forward like a coxcomb at the first hint of stress. I remembered the calm and sensible way in which she had helped the trainee nurses who fumbled with my knee-brace. At heart she was the subversive schoolgirl, the awkward-squad recruiter with a primed grenade in her locker, who saw through the stuffy conventions of boarding school and teaching hospital but was always kind enough to rescue a flustered housekeeper or ward orderly.

Now, at Eden-Olympia, it was her turn to be intimidated by the ultra-cerebral French physicians who would soon be her colleagues. She sat forward, chin raised, fingers drumming a threatening tattoo on the steering wheel. Satisfied that she could hold her own, she noticed me massaging my knee.

'Paul, that awful brace . . . we'll get it off in a few days. You've been in agony and never complained.'

'I'm sorry I couldn't help with the driving. Cannes is a long way from Maida Vale.'

'Everywhere is a long way from Maida Vale. I'm glad we came.' She gazed at the office buildings that climbed the valley slopes, and at the satellite dishes distilling their streams of information from the sky. 'It all looks very civilized, in a Euro kind of way. Not a drifting leaf in sight. It's hard to believe anyone would be allowed to go mad here. Poor David . . .'

David Greenwood's death dominated our time at Eden-Olympia, hovering above the artificial lakes and forests like the ghosts of Princip over Sarajevo and Lee Harvey Oswald over Dallas. Why this dedicated children's doctor should have left his villa on a morning in late May and set out on a murder rampage had never been explained. He had killed seven senior executives at Eden-Olympia, executed his three hostages and then turned his rifle on himself. He had written no suicide note, no defiant last message, and as the police marksmen closed in he had calmly abandoned himself to death.

A week before our wedding, Jane and I had met him at a London reception for Médecins Sans Frontières. Likeable but a little naive, Greenwood reminded me of an enthusiastic Baptist missionary, telling Jane about the superb facilities at the Eden-Olympia clinic, and the refuge for orphaned children he had set up at La Bocca, the industrial suburb to the west of Cannes. With his uncombed hair and raised eyebrows, he looked as if he had just received an unexpected shock, a revelation of all the injustices in the world, which he had decided to put right. Yet he was no prude, and talked about his six months in Bangladesh, comparing the caste rivalries among the village prostitutes with the status battles of the women executives at Eden-Olympia.

Jane had known him during their internships at Guy's, and often met him after she enrolled with the overseas supply agency that recruited Greenwood to Eden-Olympia. When she first applied for the paediatric vacancy, I had been against her going, remembering her shock on hearing the news of Greenwood's violent death. Although she was off-duty for the day, she had taken a white coat from the wardrobe in our bedroom and buttoned it over her nightdress as she laid the newspapers across my knees.

The entire London press made the tragedy its main story. 'Nightmare in Eden' was the repeated headline above photographs of Riviera beaches and bullet-starred doors in the offices of the murdered executives. Jane hardly spoke about Greenwood, but insisted on watching the television coverage of French police holding back the sightseers who invaded Eden-Olympia. Blood-drenched secretaries, too speechless to explain to the cameras how their bosses had been executed, stumbled towards the waiting ambulances, while helicopters ferried the wounded to hospitals in Grasse and Cannes.

The investigating magistrate, Judge Michel Terneau, led the inquiry, reconstructing the murders and taking evidence from a host of witnesses, but came up with no convincing explanation. Greenwood's colleagues at the clinic testified to his earnest and intense disposition. An editorial in *Le Monde* speculated that the contrast between the worldly power of Eden-Olympia and the deprived lives of the Arab immigrants in Cannes La Bocca had driven Greenwood into a frenzy of frustration, a blind rage at inequalities between the first and third worlds. The murders were part political manifesto, so the newspaper believed, and part existential scream.

When the case at last left the headlines Jane never referred to Greenwood again. But when the vacancy was advertised she immediately called the manager of the supply agency. She was the only applicant, and quickly convinced me that a long break in the Mediterranean would do wonders for my knee, injured in a flying accident nine months earlier and still refusing to mend. My cousin Charles agreed to take over the publishing house while I was away, and would e-mail me copy and proof pages of the two aviation magazines that I edited.

Eager to help Jane's career, I was happy to go. At the same time, like any husband from a different generation, I was curious about my young wife's romantic past. Had she and Greenwood once been lovers? The question was not entirely prurient. A mass-murderer had perhaps held her in his arms, and as Jane embraced me the spirit of his death embraced me too. The widows of assassins were forever their armourers.

On our last night in Maida Vale, lying in bed with our packed suitcases in the hall, I asked Jane how closely she had known Greenwood. She was sitting astride me, with the expression of a serious-minded adolescent on her face that she always wore when making love. She drew herself upright, a hand raised to hit me, then solemnly told me that she and Greenwood had never been more than friends. I almost believed her. But some unstated loyalty to Greenwood's memory followed us from Boulogne to the gates of Eden-Olympia.

Baring her teeth, Jane started the engine. 'Right . . . let's take them on. Find the clinic on the map. Somone called Penrose will meet us there. Why they've picked a psychiatrist, I don't know. I told them you hate the entire profession. Apparently, he was hurt in David's shoot-out, so be gentle with him . . .'

She steered the Jaguar towards the gatehouse, where the guards had already lost interest in their screens, intrigued by this confident young woman at the controls of her antique car.

While they checked our documents and rang the clinic I stared at the nearby office buildings and tried to imagine Greenwood's last desperate hours. He had shot dead one of his colleagues at the clinic. A second physician, a senior surgeon, had suffered a fatal heart attack the next day. A third colleague had been wounded in the arm: Dr Wilder Penrose, the psychiatrist who was about to introduce us to our new Eden.

2

Dr Wilder Penrose

A ROBUST, BULL-BROWED man in a creased linen suit strode from the entrance of the clinic, arms raised in a boxer's greeting. I assumed he was a local building contractor delighted with the results of his prostate test and waved back as a gesture of male solidarity. In reply, a fist punched the air.

'Paul?' Jane sounded wary. 'Is that . . . ?'

'Wilder Penrose? It probably is. You say he's a psychiatrist?'

'God knows. This man's a minotaur . . .'

I waited as he strode towards us, hands raised to ward off the sun. When Jane unlatched her door he swerved around the car, displaying remarkable agility for a big man. His heavy fists took on an almost balletic grace as they shaped the dusty contours of the Jaguar.

'Magnificent . . . a genuine Mark II.' He held open Jane's door and shook her still grimy hand, then smiled good-naturedly at his oil-stained palm. 'Dr Sinclair, welcome to Eden-Olympia. I'm Wilder Penrose – we'll be sharing a coffee machine on the fourth floor. You don't look tired. I assume the Jag sailed like a dream?'

'Paul thinks so. He didn't have to change the spark plugs every ten miles.'

'Alas. And those twin carburettors that need to be balanced? More art than science. The old Moss gearbox? Wonderful, all the same.' He strolled around the car and beckoned to the clouds, as if ordering them to listen to him, and declaimed in a voice not unlike my father's: '*Peeling off the kilometres to the tune of "Blue Skies", sizzling down the . . . Nationale Sept, the plane trees going . . .*'

'*Sha-sha-sha* . . .' I completed. '*She with the Michelin beside me, a handkerchief binding her hair* . . .'

'Mr Sinclair?' Leaving Jane, the psychiatrist came round to the passenger door. 'You're the first literate pilot here since Saint-Exupéry. Let me help you. They told me about the accident.'

His strong upper arms lifted me easily from my seat. He wore sunglasses of pale plastic, but I could see his eyes scanning my face, less interested in the minor flying injuries to my forehead than in whatever strengths and weaknesses were written into the skin. He was in his late thirties, the youngest and by far the strongest psychiatrist I had met, a giant compared with the grey-haired specialists who had examined me at Guy's for the Aviation Licensing Board. His welcoming banter concealed a faintly threatening physical presence, as if he bullied his patients to get well, intimidating them out of their phobias and neuroses. His muscular shoulders were dominated by a massive head that he disguised in a constant ducking and grimacing. I knew that the tags we had swapped from *The Unquiet Grave* had not impressed him as much as the Jaguar, but then his patients were among the best-educated people in the world, and too distracted for vintage motoring.

When I swayed against the car, feeling light-headed in the sun, he raised a hand to steady me. I noticed his badly bitten fingernails, still damp from his lips, and backed away from him without thinking. We shook hands as I leaned on the door. His thumb probed the back of my hand in what pretended to be a masonic grip but was clearly a testing of my reflexes.

'Paul, you're tired . . .' Penrose raised his arms to shield me from the light. 'Dr Jane prescribes a strong draught of vodka and tonic. We'll go straight to the house, with a guided tour on the way. Freshen up, and then I'll borrow your wife and show her around the clinic. Arriving at Eden-Olympia is enough culture shock for one day . . .'

* * *

We settled ourselves in the car for the last lap of our journey. Penrose climbed into the rear seat, filling the small space like a bear in a kennel. He patted and squeezed the ancient leather upholstery, as if comforting an old friend.

Jane licked her thumb for luck and pressed the starter button, determined to hold her own with Penrose and relieved when the overheated engine came to life.

'Culture shock . . . ?' she repeated. 'Actually, I love it here already.'

'Good.' Penrose beamed at the back of her head. 'Why, exactly?'

'Because there isn't any culture. All this alienation . . . I could easily get used to it.'

'Even better. Agree, Paul?'

'Totally.' I knew Jane was teasing the psychiatrist. 'We've been here ten minutes and haven't seen a soul.'

'That's misleading.' Penrose pointed to two nearby office buildings, each only six storeys high but effectively a skyscraper lying on its side. 'They're all at their computer screens and lab benches. Sadly, you can forget Cyril Connolly here. Forget tuberoses and sapphirine seas.'

'I have. Who are the tenants? Big international companies?'

'The biggest. Mitsui, Siemens, Unilever, Sumitomo, plus all the French giants – Elf-Aquitaine, Carrefour, Rhône-Poulenc. Along with a host of smaller firms: investment brokers, bioengineering outfits, design consultancies. I sound like a salesman, but when you get to know it you'll see what a remarkable place Eden-Olympia really is. In its way this is a huge experiment in how to hothouse the future.'

I turned to glimpse a vast car park concealed behind a screen of cypresses, vehicles nose to tail like a week's unsold output at a Renault plant. Somewhere in the office buildings the owners of these cars were staring at their screens, designing a new cathedral or cineplex, or watching the world's spot prices. The sense of focused brainpower was bracing, but subtly unsettling.

'I'm impressed,' I told Penrose. 'It beats waiting at tables or working as a checkout girl at a Monoprix. Where do you get the staff?'

'We train them. They're our biggest investment. It's not so much their craft skills as their attitude to an entirely new workplace culture. Eden-Olympia isn't just another business park. We're an ideas laboratory for the new millennium.'

'The "intelligent" city? I've read the brochure.'

'Good. I helped to write it. Every office, house and apartment cabled up to the world's major stockbrokers, the nearest Tiffany's and the emergency call-out units at the clinic.'

'Paul, are you listening?' Jane's elbow nudged me in the ribs. 'You can sell your British Aerospace shares, buy me a new diamond choker and have a heart attack at the same time . . .'

'Absolutely.' Penrose lay back, nostrils pressed to the worn seats, snuffling at the old leather smells. 'In fact, Paul, once you've settled in I strongly recommend a heart attack. Or a nervous breakdown. The paramedics will know everything about you – blood groups, clotting factors, attention-deficit disorders. If you're desperate, you could even have a plane crash – there's a small airport at Cannes-Mandelieu.'

'I'll think about it.' I searched for my cigarettes, tempted to fill the car with the throat-catching fumes of a Gitanes. Penrose's teasing was part camouflage, part initiation rite, and irritating on both counts. I thought of David Greenwood and wondered whether this aggressive humour had helped the desperate young Englishman. 'What about emergencies of a different kind?'

'Such as? We can cope with anything. This is the only place in the world where you can get insurance against acts of God.'

I felt Jane stiffen warningly against the steering wheel. The nearside front tyre scraped the kerb, but I pressed on.

'Psychological problems? You do have them?'

'Very few.' Penrose gripped the back of Jane's seat, deliberately exposing his bitten fingernails. At the same time his face had hardened, the heavy bones of his cheeks and jaw pushing through the conversational tics and grimaces, a curious display of aggression and self-doubt. 'But a few, yes. Enough to make my job interesting. On the whole, people are happy and content.'

'And you regret that?'

'Never. I'm here to help them fulfil themselves.' Penrose winked into Jane's rear-view mirror. 'You'd be surprised by how easy that is. First, make the office feel like a home – if anything, the real home.'

'And their flats and houses?' Jane pointed to a cluster of executive villas in the pueblo style. 'What does that make them?'

'Service stations, where people sleep and ablute. The human body as an obedient coolie, to be fed and hosed down, and given just enough sexual freedom to sedate itself. We've concentrated on the office as the key psychological zone. Middle managers have their own bathrooms. Even secretaries have a sofa in a private alcove, where they can lie back and dream about the lovers they'll never have the energy to meet.'

We were driving along the shore of a large ornamental lake, an ellipse of glassy water that reflected the nearby mountains and reminded me of Lake Geneva with its old League of Nations headquarters, another attempt to blueprint a kingdom of saints. Apartment houses lined the waterfront, synchronized brises-soleils shielding the balconies. Jane slowed the car, and searched the windows for a single off-duty resident.

'A fifth of the workforce live on-site,' Penrose told us. 'Middle and junior management in apartments and townhouses, senior people in the residential estate where you're going. The parkland buffers the impact of all the steel and concrete. People like the facilities – yachting and water-skiing, tennis and basketball, those body-building things that obsess the French.'

'And you?' Jane queried.

'Well . . .' Penrose pressed his large hands against the roof, and lazily flexed his shoulders. 'I prefer to exercise the mind. Jane, are you keen on sport?'

'Not me.'

'Squash, aerobics, roller-blading?'

'The wrong kind of sweat.'

'Bridge? There are keen amateurs here you could make an income off.'

'Sorry. Better things to do.'

'Interesting . . .' Penrose leaned forward, so close to Jane that he seemed to be sniffing her neck. 'Tell me more.'

'You know . . .' Straight-faced, Jane explained: 'Wife-swapping, the latest designer amphetamines, kiddy porn. What else do we like, Paul?'

Penrose slumped back, chuckling good-humouredly. I noticed that he was forever glancing at the empty seat beside him. There was a fourth passenger in the car, the shade of a doctor defeated by the mirror-walled office buildings and manicured running tracks. I assumed that Greenwood had suffered a catastrophic cerebral accident, but one which probably owed nothing to Eden-Olympia.

Beyond the apartments was a shopping mall, a roofed-in plaza of boutiques, patisseries and beauty salons. Lines of supermarket trollies waited in the sun for customers who only came out after dark. Undismayed, Penrose gestured at the deserted checkouts.

'Grasse and Le Cannet aren't far away, but you'll find all this handy. There's everything you need, Jane – sports equipment, video-rentals, the New York Review of Books . . .'

'No teleshopping?'

'There is. But people like to browse among the basil. Shopping is the last folkloric ritual that can help to build a community, along with traffic jams and airport queues. Eden-Olympia has its own TV station – local news, supermarket best buys . . .'

'Adult movies?'

Jane at last seemed interested, but Penrose was no longer

listening. He had noticed a trio of Senegalese trinket salesmen wandering through the deserted café tables, gaudy robes blanched by the sun. Their dark faces, among the blackest of black Africa, had a silvered polish, as if a local biotechnology firm had reworked their genes into the age of e-mail and the intelsat. By some mix of guile and luck they had slipped past the guards at the gate, only to find themselves rattling their bangles in an empty world.

When we stopped, pointlessly, at a traffic light Penrose took out his mobile phone and pretended to speak into it. He stared aggressively at the salesmen, but the leader of the trio, an affable, older man, ignored the psychiatrist and swung his bracelets at Jane, treating her to a patient smile.

I was tempted to buy something, if only to irritate Penrose, but the lights changed.

'What about crime?' I asked. 'It looks as if security might be a problem.'

'Security is first class. Or should be.' Penrose straightened the lapels of his jacket, ruffled by his involuntary show of temper. 'We have our own police force. Very discreet and effective, except when you need them. These gewgaw men get in anywhere. Somehow they've bypassed the idea of progress. Dig a hundred-foot moat around the Montparnasse tower and they'd be up on the top deck in three minutes.'

'Does it matter?'

'Not in the way you mean. Though it's irritating to be reminded of the contingent world.'

'A drifting leaf? A passing rain-shower? Bird shit on the sleeve?'

'That sort of thing.' Penrose smoothed himself down, hands pressing his burly chest. 'There's nothing racist, by the way. We're truly multinational – Americans, French, Japanese. Even Russians and east Europeans.'

'Black Africa?'

'At the senior level. We're a melting pot, as the Riviera always has been. The solvent now is talent, not wealth or glamour.

Forget about crime. The important thing is that the residents of Eden-Olympia think they're policing themselves.'

'They aren't, but the illusion pays off?'

'Exactly.' Penrose slapped my shoulder in a show of joviality. 'Paul, I can see you're going to be happy here.'

The road climbed the thickly wooded slopes to the north-east of the business park, cutting off our view of Cannes and the distant sea. We stopped at an unmanned security barrier, and Penrose tapped a three-digit number into the entry panel. The white metal trellis rose noiselessly, admitting us to an enclave of architect-designed houses, our home for the next six months. I peered through the wrought-iron gates at silent tennis courts and swimming pools waiting for their owners to return. Over the immaculate gardens hung the air of well-bred catatonia that only money can buy.

'The medical staff . . . ?' Jane lowered her head, a little daunted by the imposing avenues. 'They're all here?'

'Only you and Professor Walter, our cardiovascular chief. Call it enlightened self-interest. It's always reassuring to know that a good heart man and a paediatrician are nearby, in case your wife has an angina attack or your child chokes on a rusk.'

'And you?' I asked. 'Who copes with sudden depressions?'

'They can wait till morning. I'm in the annexe on the other side of the hill. North facing, a kind of shadow world for the less important.' Penrose beamed to himself, happy to speak frankly. 'The company barons who decide our pecking order feel they're beyond the need of psychiatric attention.'

'Are they?'

'For the time being. But I'm working on it.' Penrose sat up and pointed through the plane trees. 'Slow down, Jane. You're almost home. From now on you're living in a suburb of paradise . . .'

3

The Brainstorm

A GIANT CYCAD threw its yellow fronds across the tiled pathway to a lacquered front door, past a chromium statue of a leaping dolphin. Beyond the bougainvillaea that climbed the perimeter wall I could see the streamlined balconies and scalloped roof of a large art-deco villa, its powder-blue awnings like reefed sails. The ocean-liner windows and porthole skylights seemed to open onto the 1930s, a vanished world of Cole Porter and beach pyjamas, morphine lesbians and the swagger portraits of Tamara de Lempicka. The entire structure had recently been repainted, and a phosphor in the white pigment gave its surface an almost luminescent finish, as if this elegant villa was an astronomical instrument that set the secret time of Eden-Olympia.

Even Jane was impressed, smoothing the travel creases from her trousers when we stepped from the dusty Jaguar. The house was silent, but somewhere in the garden was a swimming pool filled with unsettled water. Reflections from its disturbed surface seemed to bruise the smooth walls of the house. The light drummed against Jane's sunglasses, giving her the edgy and vulnerable look of a studio visitor who had strayed into the wrong film set. Almost without thinking, Penrose stepped forward, took the glasses from Jane's face and placed them firmly in her hands.

A concrete apron sloped from the road to the aluminium shutters of a three-car garage. Parked on the ramp was an olive-green Range Rover of the Eden-Olympia security force. A uniformed guard leaned against the driver's door, a slim, light-skinned black with refined and almost east African features, a narrow nose and steep forehead. He picked the dust from the buttons of his mobile phone with a pocket knife, and watched without comment as we surveyed the house.

Penrose introduced us, his back to the guard, speaking over his shoulder like a district commissioner with a village headman.

'Jane, this is Frank Halder. He'll be within radio call whenever you need him. Frank, help Dr Sinclair with her luggage . . .'

The guard was about to step into his Range Rover. When he opened the door I noticed a copy of *Tender is the Night* on the passenger seat. He avoided my eyes, but his manner was cool and self-possessed as he turned to face the psychiatrist.

'Dr Penrose? I'm due in at the bureau. Mr Nagamatzu needs me to drive him to Nice airport.'

'Frank . . .' Penrose held his fingernails up to the sun and examined the ragged crescents. 'Mr Nagamatzu can wait for five minutes.'

'Five minutes?' Halder seemed baffled by the notion, as if Penrose had suggested that he wait for five hours, or five years. 'Security, doctor, it's like a Swiss watch. Everything's laid down in the machinery. It's high-class time, you can't just stop the system when you feel like it.'

'I know, Frank. And the human mind is like this wonderful old Jaguar, as I keep trying to explain. Mr Sinclair is still convalescing from a serious accident. And we can't have Dr Jane too tired to deal with her important patients.'

'Dr Penrose . . .' Jane was trying to unlock the Jaguar's boot, hiding her embarrassment over this trivial dispute. 'I'm strong enough to carry my own suitcases. And Paul's.'

'No. Frank is keen to help.' Penrose raised a hand to silence Jane. He sauntered over to Halder, flexing his shoulders inside his linen jacket and squaring up to the guard like a boxer at a weigh-in. 'Besides, Mr Sinclair is a pilot.'

'A pilot?' Halder ran his eyes over me, pinching his sharp nostrils as if tuning out the sweat of travel that clung to my stale shirt. 'Gliders?'

'Powered aircraft. I flew with the RAF. Back in England I have an old Harvard.'

'Well, a pilot . . .' Halder took the car keys from Jane and opened the boot. 'That could be another story.'

We left Halder to carry the suitcases and set off towards the house. Penrose unlocked a wrought-iron gate and we stepped into the silent garden, following a pathway that led to the sun lounge.

'Decent of him,' I commented to Penrose. 'Is humping luggage one of his duties?'

'Definitely not. He could report me if he wanted to.' Enjoying his small triumph, Penrose said to Jane: 'I like to stir things up, keep the adrenalin flowing. The more they hate you, the more they stay on their toes.'

Jane looked back at Halder, who was steering the suitcases past the gate. 'I don't think he does hate you. He seems rather intelligent.'

'You're right. Halder is far too superior to hate anyone. Don't let that mislead you.'

A spacious garden lay beside the house, furnished with a tennis court, rose pergola and swimming pool. A suite of beach chairs sat by the disturbed water, damp cushions steaming in the sun. I wondered if Halder, tired of waiting for us, had stripped off for a quick dip. Then I noticed a red beach ball on the diving board, the last water dripping from its plastic skin. Suddenly I imagined the moody young guard roaming like a baseline tennis player along the edge of the pool, hurling the ball at the surface and catching it as it rebounded from the far side, driving the water into a state of panic.

Penrose and Jane walked on ahead of me, and by the time I reached the sun lounge Halder had overtaken me. He moved aside as I climbed the steps.

'Thanks for the cases,' I told him. 'I couldn't have managed them.'

He paused to stare at me in his appraising way, neither sympathetic nor hostile. 'It's my job, Mr Sinclair.'

'It's not your job – but thanks. I had a small flying accident.'

'You broke your knees. That's tough.' He spoke with an American accent, but one learned in Europe, perhaps working as a security guard for a local subsidiary of Mobil or Exxon. 'You have a commercial licence?'

'Private. Or did have, until they took it away from me. I publish aviation books.'

'Now you'll have time to write one yourself. Some people might envy you.'

He stood with his back to the pool, the trembling light reflected in the beads of water on the holster of his pistol. He was strong but light-footed, with the lithe step of a professional dancer, a tango specialist who read Scott Fitzgerald and took out his frustrations on swimming pools. For a moment I saw a strange image of him washing his gun in the pool, rinsing away David Greenwood's blood.

'Keep flying speed . . .' He saluted and strode away. As he passed the pool he leaned over and spat into the water.

We sat on the terrace beneath the awning, listening to the gentle flap of canvas and the swish of lawn sprinklers from nearby gardens. Far below were the streets of Cannes, dominated by the twin domes of the Carlton Hotel, a nexus of noise and traffic that crowded the beach. The sun had moved beyond La Napoule and now lit the porphyry rocks of the Esterel, exposing valleys filled with lavender dust like the flats of a forgotten stage production. To the east, beyond Cap d'Antibes, the ziggurat apartment buildings of Marina Baie des Anges loomed larger than the Alpes-Maritimes, their immense curved facades glowing like a cauldron in the afternoon sun.

The swimming pool had calmed. Halder's glob of spit had almost dissolved, the sun-driven currents drawing it into a spiral like the milky arms of a nebula. An eager water spider straddled one of the whorls and was busy gorging itself.

Penrose's tour of the house had impressed Jane, who seemed stunned by the prospect of becoming the chatelaine of this imposing art-deco mansion. I hobbled after them as Penrose guided her around the kitchen, pointing out the ceramic hobs and the control panels with more dials than an airliner's cockpit. In the study, virtually a self-contained office, Penrose demonstrated the computerized library, the telemetric links to hospitals in Cannes and Nice, and the databanks of medical records.

Sitting at the terminal, Jane accessed the X-rays of my knees now held in the clinic's files, along with an unforgiving description of my accident and a photograph of the ground-looped Harvard. Tapping her teeth, Jane read the pathologist's analysis of the rogue infection that had kept me in my wheelchair for so many months.

'It's right up to date – practically tells us what we had for breakfast this morning. I could probably hack into David's files . . .'

I clasped her shoulders, proud of my spirited young wife. 'Jane, you'll tear the place apart. Thank God it doesn't say anything about my mind.'

'It will, dear, it will . . .'

Gazing at the garden, Jane finished her spritzer, eager to get back to the terminal.

'I'll give you a list of interesting restaurants,' Penrose told her. He sat by himself in the centre of the wicker sofa, arms outstretched in the pose of a Hindu holy man, surveying us in his amiable way. 'Tétou in Golfe-Juan does the best seafood. You can eat Graham Greene's favourite boudin at Chez Félix in Antibes. It's a shrine for men of action like you, Paul.'

'We'll go.' I lay back in the deep cushions, watching a light aircraft haul its advertising pennant along the Croisette. 'It's blissful here. Absolutely perfect. So what went wrong?'

Penrose stared at me without replying, his smile growing and then fading like a dying star. His eyes closed and he seemed to slip into a shallow fugue, the warning aura before a petit-mal seizure.

'Wilder . . .' Concerned for him, Jane raised her hand to hold his attention. 'Dr Penrose? Are you – ?'

'Paul?' Alert again, Penrose turned to me. 'The aircraft, they're such a nuisance, I didn't quite catch what you were saying.'

'Something happened here.' I gestured towards the office build-ings of the business park. 'Ten people were shot dead. Why did Greenwood do it?'

Penrose buttoned his linen jacket in an attempt to disguise his burly shoulders. He sat forward, speaking in a barely audible voice. 'To be honest, Paul, we've no idea. It's impossible to explain, and it damn near cost me my job. Those deaths have cast a huge shadow over Eden-Olympia. Seven very senior people were killed on May 28.'

'But why?'

'The big corporations would like to know.' Penrose raised his hands, warming them in the sun. 'Frankly, I can't tell them.'

'Was David unhappy?' Jane put down her glass. She watched Penrose as if he were a confused patient who had wandered into Casualty with a garbled tale of death and assassination. 'We worked together at Guy's. He was a little high-minded, but his feet were on the ground.'

'Completely.' Penrose spoke with conviction. 'He loved it here – his work at the clinic, the children's refuge at La Bocca. The kids adored him. Mostly orphans abandoned by their north African and pied-noir families. They'd never met anyone like David. He helped out at a methadone project in Mandelieu . . .'

Jane stared into her empty glass. The sticky bowl had trapped

26

a small insect. 'Did he ever relax? It sounds as if the poor man was overworked.'

'No.' Penrose closed his eyes again. He moved his head, searching the planetarium inside his skull for a glimmer of light. 'He was taking Arabic and Spanish classes so he could talk to the children at the refuge. I never saw him under any stress.'

'Too many antidepressants?'

'Not prescribed by me. The autopsy showed nothing. No LSD, none of the wilder amphetamines. The poor fellow's bloodstream was practically placental.'

'Was he married?' I asked. 'A wife would have known something was brewing.'

'I wish he had been married. He did have an affair with someone in the property-services division.'

'Man or woman?'

'Woman. It must have been.' Jane spoke almost too briskly. 'He certainly wasn't homosexual. Did she have anything to say?'

'Nothing. Their affair had been over for months. Sadly, some things are fated to remain mysteries for ever.'

Penrose scowled at the pool, and chewed on a thumbnail. The garden was now in shadow as the late-afternoon light left the valley of Eden-Olympia, and the top floors of the office buildings caught the sun, floating above the trees like airborne caravels. Our conversation had drained the colour from Penrose's face. Only his hands continued to move. Resting on the cushions beside him, they flinched and trembled with a life of their own.

'Was anyone else involved?' I pointed towards Cannes. 'Co-conspirators on the outside?'

'The investigating magistrate found nothing. He spent weeks here with his police teams, staging reconstructions of the murders. A strange kind of street theatre, you'd think Eden-Olympia was taking over from the Edinburgh Festival. Meanwhile, foreign governments were pressing hard for a result. Half the world's psychologists jammed the baggage carousels at Nice Airport.

There was even a televised debate in the conference room at the Noga Hilton. They came up with nothing.'

'He tried to kill you.' Jane pushed her glass away, distracted by the insect's angry buzzing. 'You were wounded. How did he look when he shot you?'

Penrose sighed, his heavy chest deflating at the memory. 'I didn't see him, thank heavens. I'm not sure that I was one of his targets. A glass door blew in while I was checking something in the pharmacy. David was firing from the outside corridor at Professor Berthoud. By the time I stopped bleeding he'd gone.'

'Grim . . .' I felt a sudden sympathy for Penrose. 'A nightmare for you.'

'Far more for David.' Penrose watched his restless hands and then nodded to me, grateful for this display of fellow-feeling. 'Paul, it's impossible to explain. Some deep psychosis must have been gathering for years, a profound crisis going back to his childhood.'

'Did David know any of the victims?'

'He knew them all. Several were patrons of the La Bocca refuge, like poor Dominique Serrou, the breast cancer specialist at the clinic. She gave a lot of her free time to the refuge. God only knows why David decided to kill her.'

'Was Eden-Olympia his real target?' Jane carried her glass to the open air and released the trapped insect. 'I love it here, but the place is disgustingly rich.'

'We thought of that.' Penrose watched the insect veer away, smiling at its angry swerves and dives. 'Eden-Olympia is a business park. This isn't Fritz Lang's *Metropolis*. Drive to Le Cannet or Grasse and you'll find a dozen old "zincs" where you can enjoy your pastis and bet on the horses at Longchamp.'

'Third-World politics?' I suggested. 'Multinational corporations make a perfect terrorist target.'

'IBM Europe? Nippon Telegraph?' Penrose reluctantly shook his head. 'Companies here aren't involved with the Third World.

None of them are sweating rubber or bauxite out of a coolie workforce. The raw material processed at Eden-Olympia is high-grade information. Besides, political terrorists don't rely on people like David Greenwood. Though you have to admire the way he carried it off. Once the alarm was raised he must have known all the doors would shut around him.'

'Which they did?'

'Tighter than a nun's knees. When he realized it was over, he came back here and killed his hostages, a couple of off-duty chauffeurs and a maintenance engineer. Why he seized them in the first place no one knows . . .'

'Wait a minute . . .' Jane stepped forward, pointing to Penrose. 'Are you saying . . . ?'

'Tragically, yes. He killed all three.'

'Here?' Jane seized my wrist, her sharp fingers almost separating the bones. 'You're saying this was David's villa?'

'Naturally.' Penrose seemed puzzled by Jane's question. 'The house is assigned to the clinic's paediatrician.'

'So the murders began . . .' Jane stared at the white walls of the sun lounge, as if expecting to see them smeared with bloody handprints. 'David lived in this house?'

Penrose ducked his head, embarrassed by his slip of the tongue. 'Jane, I didn't mean to alarm you. Everything happened in the garage. David shot the hostages there, and then killed himself. They found him inside his car.'

'Even so . . .' Jane searched the tiled floor at her feet. 'It feels strange. David living here, planning all those terrible deaths.'

'Jane . . .' I took her hands, but she pulled them away from me. 'Are you going to be happy? Penrose, can't we move to another house? We'll rent a villa in Grasse or Vallauris.'

'You could move, yes . . .' Penrose was watching us without expression. 'It will create problems. Houses here are at a premium – none of the others are vacant. It's a condition of Jane's contract that she stay within Eden-Olympia. We'd have to find you an

apartment near the shopping mall. They're pleasant enough, but
. . . Jane, I'm sorry you're upset.'

'I'm all right.' Jane took a clip from her purse. Staring hard at
Penrose, she smoothed her shoulder-length hair and secured it in
a defiant bunch. 'You're sure no one was killed here?'

'Absolutely. Everything happened in the garage. They say it
was over in seconds. A brief burst of shots. Heart-rending to
think about.'

'It is.' Jane spoke matter-of-factly. 'So the garage . . . ?'

'Virtually rebuilt. Scarcely a trace of the original structure. Talk
it over with Paul and let me know tomorrow.'

'Jane . . . ?' I touched her cheek, now as pale as the white
walls. Her face was pointed, like a worried child's, and the spurs
of her nasal bridge seemed sharp enough to cut the skin. 'How
do you feel?'

'Odd. Don't you?'

'We can move. I'll find a hotel in Cannes.'

Penrose took out his mobile phone. 'I'll get Halder to drive
you to the Martinez. We have several guest suites there.'

'No.' Jane brushed me aside, and took the phone from Penrose.
'I'm too tired. We've both had a long drive. We need time to
think it through.'

'Good. You're being very sensible.' Penrose bowed in an
almost obsequious way. Despite his concern, I was puzzled by
his behaviour. He had deliberately concealed from us the crucial
fact that David Greenwood had lived in this house and died within
its grounds. No doubt Penrose had feared, rightly, that Jane would
never have accepted the post at Eden-Olympia if she had known.

I examined the chairs and tables in the sun lounge, pieces of
department-store furniture in expensive but anonymous designs.
I realized that Jane was as much the hired help as Halder and the
security guards, the murdered chauffeurs and maintenance man,
and was expected to keep her sensitivities to herself. Ambitious
dentists did not complain about the poor oral hygiene of their

30

richer clients. I remembered Halder's sceptical gaze as he lounged by the Range Rover, making it clear that we were lucky to be admitted to this luxury enclave.

Penrose said his goodbyes to Jane and waited by the pool as I found my walking stick. He had replaced his sunglasses, hiding the sweat that leaked from his eye-sockets. In his creased linen suit, with its damp collar and lapels, he seemed both shifty and arrogant, aware that he had been needlessly provocative but not too concerned by our reactions.

Joining him, I said: 'Thanks for the tour. It's a superb house.'

'Good. You'll probably stay. Your wife likes it here.'

'I'm not sure.'

'Believe me.' His smile drifted across his face like a dismasted ship, detached from whatever he was thinking. 'You'll be very happy at Eden-Olympia.'

I walked Penrose down to the avenue, and waited while he called the nearest patrol car.

'One thing . . .' I said. 'Why did you tell Halder that I was a pilot?'

'Did I? I hope that wasn't indiscreet.'

'No. But you made a point of it.'

'Halder is a difficult man to impress. He has the special kind of snobbery that servants of the rich often show. As your security man it's important he take you seriously. I thought it might break the ice.'

'It clearly did. Is he an amateur pilot?'

'No. His father was in the US Air Force, stationed at a base near Mannheim. The mother was a German girl working in the PX. He abandoned her and the baby, and now runs a small airline in Alabama. He was one of the few black commissioned officers. Halder's never met him.'

'An airline? That's impressive.'

'I think it has two planes. For Halder, flying is confused with his wish to confront his father.'

'A little pat?'

Penrose playfully punched my shoulder, a hard blow that made me raise my stick to him. He stepped out of my way and signalled to an approaching patrol car. 'Pat? Yes. But I'm not speaking as a psychiatrist.'

'Are you ever?'

With a stage laugh, Penrose drummed his fist against the roller doors of the garage. He swung his large body into the passenger seat of the Range Rover, sprawling against the driver. The sound of his mocking cheer, good-humoured but derisory, was taken up by the vibrating metal slats, a memory of violence that seemed to echo from the sealed garage, eager to escape into the warm August air.

Jane had left the sun lounge and was sitting by the computer in the study, choosing a new screensaver. I limped towards her, already tired by the spaces of the large house. Jane raised a hand to me, her eyes still fixed on the screen. Alone in this white room, she seemed at her prettiest, a charming ingénue in a modern-dress version of a Coward play. I leaned against her, glad to be alone with my sane young wife.

'What was all that, Paul? You weren't hitting him?'

'As it happens, he punched me.'

'Vile man. Are you all right?' She took the walking stick and pulled up a chair for me. 'Speaking of punches, Dr Wilder Penrose was a bit below the belt.'

'Not telling us straight away about David? That's obviously his style – watch out.' I sat beside Jane, and stared at the complex patterns that revolved like a Paisley nightmare. 'What did you make of him?'

'He's an intellectual thug.' Jane massaged my knee. 'That set-to over our bags with Halder. And the nasty way he stared at the African salesmen. He's racist.'

'No. He was trying to provoke us. Visitors from liberal England, we're as naive as any maiden aunt, an unmissable target. Still, he's your colleague now. Remember that you have to get on with him.'

'I will. Don't worry, psychiatrists are never a threat. Surgeons are the real menace.'

'That sounds like hard-won experience.'

'It is. All psychiatrists secretly dream of killing themselves.'

'And surgeons?'

'They dream of killing their patients.' She rotated her seat, turning her back to the computer. 'Paul, that was a weird afternoon.'

'Very weird. I don't know whether you noticed, but a rather odd game is being played. Penrose is testing us. He wants to see if we're good enough for Eden-Olympia.'

'I am.' Jane's chin rose, exposing a childhood scar. 'Why not?'

'So you want to stay?'

'Yes, I do. There are possibilities here. We ought to explore them.'

'Good. I'll back you all the way.'

Jane waited as I embraced her, then held me at arm's length. 'One thing, Paul. It's important. We don't talk about David Greenwood.'

'Jane, I liked him.'

'Did you? I'm not so sure. Face it, we're never going to know what happened to him. He's not coming back, so stop worrying about him. Agreed? Let's go upstairs and unpack.'

Jane led the way, hefting her leather suitcase while I limped after her, stick in one hand and two of the soft bags in the other. Once we reached our bedroom Jane collapsed onto the ivory-white sofa. She ran her cheek along the silk cushions.

'Paul, isn't this a little lavish for a member of staff? Have you wondered why?'

'Are they trying to bribe us? I seriously doubt it. You're a consultant paediatrician, one of the new professional elite.'

'Come off it.' Jane unbuttoned her shirt. 'I'm a barefoot doctor with a short-service contract. Still, sitting in the sun will do you good. Before we leave, you'll be playing tennis again.'

'I might even beat you.'

'Losing to their favourite patients is part of a doctor's job. It happens every day in Bel Air and Holland Park.'

I wandered around the air-conditioned suite, with its dressing room and double bathroom. Despite Jane's comments, the furniture was more Noga Hilton than Versailles, and I guessed that the originals had been replaced. But there were faint ink-marks from a ballpoint pen on the fabric of an armchair by the window. I moved the chair to one side, then knelt down and felt the dents in the carpet, deep and smoothly polished by the castors. David Greenwood had probably slumped in this chair at the end of a long day, ticking off the latest bulletins from Médecins Sans Frontières. One May morning he sat with a rifle across his knees and a map of Eden-Olympia, working out a special itinerary.

Jane stood beside me, her dark hair falling to her bare shoulders. She had stepped from the dressing room and held her nightdress to her chin, admiring herself in the full-length mirror like a child trying on her mother's clothes.

'Paul, are you there?' Concerned, she took my hands, as if leading me out of a dream. 'You were asleep standing up. This house does odd things to people . . .'

She let the nightdress fall to the floor and drew me towards the bed. I lay beside her, resting my face against her small breasts, with their sweet scents of summer love. Once again I wondered how well she had known David Greenwood. It occurred to me that three of us would sleep together in this large and comfortable bed, until I could persuade David to step out of my mind and disappear for ever down the white staircase of this dreaming villa.

4

A Flying Accident

SUNLIGHT WAS INFILTRATING the misty lakes and forests of Eden-Olympia, probing the balconies of the residential enclave as if trying to rouse the company chairmen and managing directors, calling them out to play. I stood in the open doorway of the breakfast room, letting the warm air bathe my legs. An advertising plane was taking off from the Cannes-Mandelieu airfield, and I realized that my shadow was probably one of the few human silhouettes still visible from the sky over the business park.

It was 7.45, but my neighbours had already left for work. Long before the sun reached across the Baie des Anges the senior executives had finished their croissants and muesli, their mortadella and noodles, and set off to another long day at the office.

As I settled myself in a poolside chair the sun seemed to pause, surprised to find someone not already bent over a boardroom table or laboratory bench. Along the Croisette in Cannes the day would hardly have begun. The waiters at the Blue Bar would be pausing for a cigarette before they set out the table placements, and the water trucks would still be spraying the side roads off the Rue d'Antibes. But in Eden-Olympia the mainframes would be wide awake, the satellite dishes draining information stored in the sky. A busy electronic traffic was already sluicing through the cabled floors, bringing the Dow and Nikkei indexes, inventories of pharmaceutical warehouses in Düsseldorf and cod depositories in Trondheim.

Thinking of Jane, who had been up at six and off to the clinic before I woke, I eased myself onto the sun-lounger and lifted my right leg above the foam rubber cushion. After only three weeks at Eden-Olympia, as Jane had promised, I was free of the metal brace. Now I could drive the Jaguar and give Jane a rest from the heavy steering wheel. Above all, I was able to walk, and keep up with her as we strolled down the Croisette towards the seafood restaurants of the Vieux Port.

I counted the titanium claws that held the kneecap together. My wasted right calf was as thin as my forearm, and gave me a rolling, seadog gait. But exercise would strengthen the muscles. One day I would be able to work the heavy brake pedals of the Harvard and win back my private pilot's licence.

In the meantime I explored Eden-Olympia on foot, logging miles along the simulated nature trails that ended abruptly when they were no longer visible from the road. Ornamental pathways led to the electricity substations feeding power into the business park's grid. Surrounded by chain-link fences, they stood in the forest clearings like mysterious and impassive presences. I circled the artificial lakes, with their eerily calm surfaces, or roamed around the vast car parks. The lines of silent vehicles might have belonged to a race who had migrated to the stars.

By the early afternoon Charles's e-mails brought me final proof pages, cheery gossip about the latest office romances, and queries over the editorial copy of our aviation journals. I missed Jane, who never returned home before seven o'clock, but I was happy to doze on the sun-lounger and listen to the droning engines of light aircraft trailing their pennants across the cloudless sky, news from the sun of furniture sales, swimming pool discounts and the opening of a new aqua-park.

A lawnmower sounded from a nearby garden as the roving groundstaff trimmed the grass. Sprinklers hissed a gentle drizzle across the flowerbeds of the next-door villa, occupied by Professor Ito Yasuda, chairman of a Japanese finance house, his serious-faced wife and even more serious three-year-old son. On

Sundays they played tennis together, a process as stylized as a Kabuki drama, which involved endless ball retrieval and virtually no court action.

My other neighbours were a Belgian couple, the Delages, among the earliest colonists of the business park. Alain Delage was the chief financial officer of the Eden-Olympia holding company, a tall, preoccupied accountant lost somewhere behind the lenses of his rimless glasses. But he was kind enough to give Jane a lift to the clinic each morning. I had met the couple, Delage and his pale, watchful wife Simone, but our brief conversation across the roof of their Mercedes would have been more expressive if carried out by semaphore between distant peaks in the Alpes-Maritimes.

Intimacy and neighbourliness were not features of everyday life at Eden-Olympia. An invisible infrastructure took the place of traditional civic virtues. At Eden-Olympia there were no parking problems, no fears of burglars or purse-snatchers, no rapes or muggings. The top-drawer professionals no longer needed to devote a moment's thought to each other, and had dispensed with the checks and balances of community life. There were no town councils or magistrates' courts, no citizens' advice bureaux. Civility and polity were designed into Eden-Olympia, in the same way that mathematics, aesthetics and an entire geopolitical world-view were designed into the Parthenon and the Boeing 747. Representative democracy had been replaced by the surveillance camera and the private police force.

By the afternoon, all this tolerance and good behaviour left me feeling deeply bored. After a light lunch I would set off on foot around the business park. A few days earlier, while circling one of the largest lakes, I came across a curious human settlement in the woods. This was the lavish sports centre advertised in the brochure, a complex that contained two swimming pools, saunas, squash courts and a running track. It was fully staffed by helpful young instructors, but otherwise deserted. I assumed that the senior administrators at Eden-Olympia were too tired after a day's work to do more than eat supper from a tray and doze in front of the adult movie channel.

Jane had been swiftly drawn into this regime of fulfilment through work. She was stimulated by the new corporate ethos, so different from the shambles of a London teaching hospital. Guy's was a city under siege, filled with the sick, the lost and the confused, a shuffling host perpetually on the move in a vast internal migration.

At Eden-Olympia the medical staff were calm and unrushed, as I found when my knee was X-rayed. The lakeside reception area resembled the sun deck of a cruise liner. The cheerful young Frenchwoman who settled me on the X-ray table chatted to me about my flying days in the RAF and her own hang-gliding weekends at Roquebrune. I had the strong sense that we were friends who had known each other for years. Yet I had forgotten her face within seconds of leaving her.

Jane met me afterwards, barely recognizable in trim business suit and court shoes. I thought fondly of the hippie doctor I had met at Guy's, a chocolate bar next to her stethoscope in the frayed pocket of an off-white lab coat. She introduced me to the director of the clinic, Professor Kalman, a distracted but amiable man in his sixties who was a specialist in preventive medicine but had somehow failed to anticipate the outbreak of sudden death on his own premises. Jane accepted his generous compliments, and then proudly showed me round her comfortable suite with its bathroom and kitchen, almost as much a home as the villa we shared. Four months earlier it had been David Greenwood's office, and it surprised me that he had seen enough of his colleagues to dislike them, let alone set about killing them.

That evening, I drove Jane into Cannes. Holding her arm, I swung myself through the crowds on the Croisette. We drank too many Tom Collinses on the Carlton terrace, ate seafood from metal platters at a quayside restaurant, feeding each other titbits of petite friture, sea urchins and crayfish. We wandered tipsily around the Vieux Port, and I remade Jane's lipstick before showing her off to the Arabs lolling with their women on the white-leather after-decks of their rented yachts. I knew we were very happy, but at the same time I felt that we were extras in a tourist film.

A blind shivered behind a bedroom window on the first floor of the Delages' house. It rose and fell, manipulated by someone tired of the darkness but unimpressed by the possibilities of the day. The blinds settled themselves, and Simone Delage stepped onto the balcony, a dressing gown around her shoulders. She had slept late, and her cheeks seemed blanched by whatever exhausting dreams had drained away the night. Her handsome face, as grave as a cancer specialist's secretary, showed no expression when she noticed the Riviera coast, and her eyes scanned the contour lines of the Alpes-Maritimes in the way she might have glanced through a suspect biopsy. She had scarcely acknowledged my existence, and often sunbathed naked on the balcony, as if the anonymity of Eden Olympia made her invisible to her neighbours.

Was she aware of me watching her? I suspected that this private and moody woman – a trained mathematician, according to Jane, with a doctorate in statistics – took a perverse pleasure in exposing herself to the solitary man lying by the pool with his apparently withered leg. At night she and her accountant husband would wander naked around their bedroom, visible through the slatted blinds like figures on a television screen, unconcerned by their own bodies as they discussed sink funds and tax shelters.

She loosened her robe, then noticed a light aircraft that was circling Eden-Olympia, advertising a satellite-dish agency in Cagnes-sur-Mer. She retreated into her bedroom and stood by the window, smearing face cream onto her cheeks with an automatic hand.

I put aside the page proofs and watched the Cessna climb the hills above Grasse, its pennant shivering in the cooler air. The ligaments in my knee had begun to ache – more a response to stress, Jane told me, than a sign of recurring infection. I missed my old Harvard, now abandoned in its storage hangar at Elstree aerodrome, which I had bought by telephone at an aircraft auction in Toulouse. Once it had trained Nato pilots in Moose Jaw, Saskatchewan, and later posed as Zero and Focke-Wulf fighters in countless war movies. Traces of its film-studio livery, the rising-sun roundels and iron crosses, clung to its fuselage. I spent countless hours refitting the heavy-winged trainer, with its huge radial engine, pitch prop and retractable undercarriage, but I knew now that I might never take its controls again.

The Harvard had nearly killed me, on an autumn weekend a year earlier, when I set off to an aviation fair near St-Malo. Distracted by gossip of Charles's faltering marriage, and the financial settlement that would virtually break the firm, I had forgotten to file a flight plan. The tower recalled me, and I missed my take-off slot. Impatient to be airborne, I was heavy-handed with the throttle and pitch settings. As the powerful engine hurled me down the runway I lost control in a crosswind. I slewed into the deep grass, throttled up again to regain runway speed, tried to abort the take-off and ground-looped through the perimeter fence. The Harvard slid across an empty dual carriageway into the garden of a bungalow owned by a retired air-traffic controller. He had watched my botched take-off from his bedroom window, and his testimony sealed my fate. By the time the ambulance and fire trucks arrived my flying career was over.

But at least the crash had brought me to Jane, one of the teenage doctors, as I called them, who wandered around the surgical ward at Guy's. She was twenty-seven years old, but could have passed for seventeen, slumming through the ward in worn sandals with dirty toes and lank hair, lunching off a chocolate bar as she studied my temperature chart. Looking up from my pillow into her sceptical

41

gaze, I wondered why a beautiful young woman was disguising herself as a hippie.

She was gentle enough when she examined my knee. Her small hands with their chipped nails deftly removed the drainage tubes. She finished her chocolate, screwed up the wrapper and dropped it into my half-empty teacup.

'This knee needs to be flexed more – I'll get on to physio.' She studied my admission notes, tapping a pencil between her strong teeth. 'So you're the pilot here? You crash-landed your plane?'

'Not exactly. The plane never left the ground.'

'That must be quite an achievement. I like pilots – Beryl Markham is my hero.'

'A great flyer,' I agreed. 'Totally promiscuous.'

'Aren't all women, if they want to be? Men have such a hang-up about that.' She stuffed my file into its rack at the foot of the bed. 'They say flying and sex go together. I don't know about that side of your life, but it's going to be a while before you fly.'

'I'm set to lose my licence.'

'How sad.' She took a syringe from the kidney dish and eyed the meniscus. 'I'm sorry. Flying must be important to you.'

'It is. By the way, is that needle clean?'

'Clean? What an idea . . .' She eased the antibiotic into my arm. 'No one cleans hospitals these days – this isn't the 1930s. We spend the money on important things. Fancy wallpaper for the managers' dining room, new carpets for the senior consultants . . .'

Already I was staring at the high forehead she disguised behind a dark fringe, and the quick but oddly evasive eyes. I liked the bolshie cast of her mouth, and the lips forever searching for the choicest four-letter word. Her unlined face was pale from too many cigarettes, too many late nights with boring lovers who failed to appreciate her. Despite the name tag – 'Dr Jane Gomersall' – I almost believed that she was one of those impostors who masquerade so effortlessly as members of the medical profession, some renegade sixth-form schoolgirl who had borrowed a white coat and decided to try her hand at a little doctoring.

Keen to meet her again, I was soon out of bed, and spent hours in my wheelchair hunting the corridors. Sometimes I would see her loafing on a fire escape with the younger surgeons, laughing as they smoked their cigarettes together. Later, when we talked near the soft-drinks machine outside the lifts, I learned that she was not a hippie, but adopted her scruffy style to irritate the hospital administrators. She had specialized in paediatrics, but ward closures had reassigned her to general duties. Her clergyman father was the headmaster of a Church of England school in Cheltenham, and the role of rebel and classroom agitator had come early to her.

On my last day, a few minutes before Charles collected me, I heard the familiar flip-flop of worn sandals, and limped to the door as she sauntered past. She waited amiably for me to speak, but I could think of nothing to say. Then she raised her fringe, as if cooling her forehead, and suggested that I show her around Elstree Flying Club.

The next weekend she drove me from my house in Maida Vale to the airfield in north London. She was surprised by the aircraft in the hangars, by their rough, riveted skins and the harsh reek of engine coolant and lubricating oil. My Harvard, still stained by the traffic controller's rhododendrons, especially intrigued her. One of the watching mechanics helped her into the cockpit. Without a parachute to sit on, she was barely visible through the windscreen. She pushed back the canopy, stood on the metal seat-base and flung out an arm, in the posture of the winged woman screaming to her followers on the Arc de Triomphe. The sculpture had deeply impressed her during a school visit to Paris, and I only wished I could have supplied her with a sword.

Later she dressed in my white overalls and put on an old leather flying helmet, lounging around the Harvard like the women pilots in aviation's heroic days, smoking their Craven A's while they leaned against their biplanes and gazed at the stars.

We were married within three months. I was still on my crutches, but Jane wore an extravagantly ruched silk dress that seemed to inflate during the ceremony, filling the register office like the trumpet of a vast amaryllis. She smoked pot at the reception held at the Royal College of Surgeons in Regent's Park, sniffed a line of cocaine in front of her mother, a likeable suburban solicitor, and gave an impassioned speech describing how we had made love in the rear seat of the Harvard, a complete fiction that even her father cheered.

During our Maldives honeymoon she snorkelled on the outer, and dangerous, side of the reef, and befriended a female conger eel. More out of curiosity than lechery, she set my camcorder to film us having sex in our bamboo hut, watching me like a lab technician who had grown attached to an experimental animal. Sometimes I sensed that she might walk off into the sea and vanish for ever. At Maida Vale, a week after our return, a policeman called to question her, and she admitted to me that she supplied tincture of cannabis to psoriasis sufferers and had tried to grow hemp plants in a disused laboratory at the hospital. Already I guessed that the urge to work abroad was part of the same restlessness that had led her to marry me, a random throw of the dice.

'Paul, be honest,' she said when she learned of the Eden-Olympia vacancy. 'How do you feel? Dissatisfied?'

'No. Are you?'

'We all are. And we do nothing about it. You've stopped flying, and keep getting these knee infections. I'm a trained paediatrician and I practically carry bedpans. Think of something really perverse I could do.'

'Have a baby?'

'Yes! That's rather clever, Paul. But I can't. At least not now. There are problems.'

'Medical ones?'

'In a way . . .'

But I had seen Jane inserting her coil and could feel the drawstring emerging from her cervix.

Now, following David Greenwood, we had arrived in Eden-Olympia, among the most civilized places on the planet and one that promised to stifle the last vestiges of her hunger for freedom. The heroine of 'La Marseillaise' was about to sheathe her sword.

5

The English Girl

THE POOL LAY beside me, so calm that a film of dust lay on the surface. Through the cool depths I could see a small coin on the sloping floor, perhaps a one-franc piece that had slipped from the pocket of Greenwood's swimsuit. Burnished by the pool detergent, it gleamed like a node of silver distilled from the Riviera light, a class of pearl unique to the swimming pools of the rich.

I listened to the vacuum cleaners working in the bedroom, a relentless blare that had driven the echoes of the Harvard's engine from my mind. The two Italian maids arrived each morning at ten o'clock, part of the uniformed task force that moved from villa to villa. A gardener, Monsieur Anvers, appeared on alternate days, watered the grass and shrubs, and cleaned the pool. He was unobtrusive, an elderly Cannois whose daughter worked in the Eden-Olympia shopping mall.

One of the maids stared cheekily at me from a bathroom window, as if puzzled by my life of ease. Already the concept of leisure was dying in the business park, replaced by a grudging puritanism. Freedom was the right to paid work, while leisure was the mark of the shiftless and untalented.

Deciding to drive into Cannes, I gathered my proof pages and made my way back to the house. señora Morales, the Spanish housekeeper, moved busily around the kitchen, checking the cartons of groceries delivered from the supermarket. The ever-watchful but tolerant gaze of this middle-aged Spanish woman reminded me of my prep-school matron, translated from the gloom of West Hampstead to the sun terraces of the Mediterranean. She was helpful but garrulous, and I often heard her talking to herself in the kitchen, using a confused mix of Spanish and English.

She nodded approvingly as I took the soda-water siphon and a bottle of rosé Bandol from the refrigerator. Clearly she assumed that any Englishman of quality would be drunk by noon.

'My car,' I explained. 'It's very old. A few drinks make it go better.'

'Of course. You come to Valencia and open a garage.' She watched me raise my glass and toast the morning light. 'It's always good weather at Eden-Olympia.'

'That's true. Except for one very stormy day last May.' I felt the bubbles play against my nostrils and sipped the aerated wine. 'Señora, how long have you been at Eden-Olympia?'

'Two years. I was housekeeper for Mr and Mrs Narita.'

'The family next door, before the Yasudas? Dr Penrose told me – they were unhappy and moved back to Paris. It must have been a shock, like one of those comics the Japanese read.'

Señora Morales lowered her eyes to the figs and fennel. 'Before that I worked for Monsieur Bachelet.'

I put down my drink, remembering that Guy Bachelet, the head of security at Eden-Olympia, had been one of Greenwood's victims. 'I'm sorry, señora. How terrible for you.'

'Worse for him.'

'I was thinking of you. The pain you must have felt when you heard he'd been murdered in his own office.'

'No.' Señora Morales spoke firmly. 'Not in his office. He died at his house.'

'You weren't there, I hope?'

'I was coming from Grasse.' As if to justify her lucky escape, she said: 'I start at nine o'clock. Already the police were at the house.'

'That's right. It was very early. So Monsieur Bachelet was . . . ?'

'Dead, yes. And Dr Serrou.'

'Dominique Serrou?' Penrose had mentioned Greenwood's partner at the La Bocca refuge. 'She was shot at the clinic?'

'No.' Señora Morales inspected the fading bloom on a peach, as if tempted to return it to the supermarket. 'Also in the house.'

'I thought everyone was killed at Eden-Olympia? Dr Serrou lived in Le Cannet.'

'Not at *her* house.' Señora Morales pointed through the windows at the rooftops of the residential enclave. 'At Monsieur Bachelet's house. Four hundred metres from here.'

'They died there together? Dr Greenwood shot them both?'

'At the same time. Terrible . . .' Señora Morales crossed herself. 'Dr Serrou was very kind.'

'I'm sure. But what was she doing there? Was she treating him for something?'

'Something . . . ? Yes.'

I walked to the window and listened to the sprinklers refreshing the lawns and washing away the dust of the night. I assumed that Bachelet had fallen ill, perhaps with a sudden angina attack, and called an emergency number. Dominique Serrou had driven over, in what would be her last house call, just as another, deranged doctor was making his first of the day.

'Señora Morales, are you certain they died at Bachelet's house?'

'I saw the bodies. They took them out.'

'Perhaps they were taking them in? Bringing Bachelet home from his office? In the confusion you might easily –'

'No.' Señora Morales stared at me stonily. She spoke in a surprisingly strong voice, as if seizing her chance. 'I saw their blood. Everywhere . . . pieces of their bones on the bedroom wall.'

'Señora please . . .' I poured her a glass of water. 'I'm sorry I raised this. We knew Dr Greenwood. My wife worked with him in London.'

'They told me to go away . . .' Señora Morales stared over my shoulder, as if watching an old newsreel inside her head. 'But I went into the house. I saw the blood.'

'Señora Morales . . .' I poured my spritzer into the sink. 'Why did Dr Greenwood want to kill so many people? Most of them were friends of his.'

'He knew Monsieur Bachelet. Dr Greenwood visited him many times.'

'Was he treating him? Medically?'

Señora Morales shrugged her broad shoulders. 'He went in the morning. Monsieur Bachelet waited for him. Dr Greenwood lent him books, about an unhappy English girl. Always talking back to the queen.'

'An unhappy English girl? Princess Diana? Was he a royalist?'

Señora Morales raised her eyes to the ceiling. The vacuum cleaners had locked horns, expiring in a blare of noise that was followed by fierce shrieks. Excusing herself, she left the kitchen and strode towards the stairs. I paced the tiled floor, and listened to her raised voice as she berated the maids. Talking to me had released the tension of months.

Before leaving, she paused at the front door and treated me to a sincere, if well-rehearsed, smile.

'Mr Sinclair . . .'

'Señora?'

'Dr Greenwood – he was a good man. He helped many people . . .'

As I changed in the bathroom I could still hear the odd inflections in Señora Morales's voice. She had gone out of her way to raise my doubts, as if my louche and anomalous position at Eden-Olympia, my role as pool-lounger and morning drinker, made me the confidant she had been searching for since the day of the tragedy. Already I believed her account. If, as she hinted, Dr Serrou had spent the night with Bachelet, the inexplicable brainstorm

49

might have stemmed from a crime passionel. As Greenwood and Dominique Serrou gave their free time to the children's refuge at La Bocca, a warm affair could easily have sprung from their work. But perhaps Dr Serrou had tired of the earnest young doctor and found the security chief more to her taste. Once Greenwood had shot his rival and former lover he had rushed headlong into a last desperate rampage, murdering his colleagues in an attempt to erase every trace of a world he hated.

As for the book about the unhappy English girl, I guessed that this was a dossier on a child at the refuge, the abused daughter of some rentier Englishman, or the surviving victim of a car crash that had killed her parents.

At the same time, it surprised me that Penrose had confided nothing of this to Jane. But a sudden brainstorm was less threatening to future investors at Eden-Olympia than a tragedy of sexual obsession.

Satisfied that I had virtually solved the mystery, I took a rose from the vase on the hall table and slipped it through my buttonhole.

6

A Russian Intruder

THE SPRINKLERS HAD fallen silent. All over the residential enclave there was the sound of mist rising from the dense foliage, almost a reverse rain returning to the clouds, time itself rushing backwards to that morning in May. As I left the house and walked towards my car I thought of David Greenwood. The conversation with Señora Morales had brought his presence alive for the first time. During the weeks since our arrival, as I lay by the pool or strolled around the silent tennis court, the young English doctor had been a shadowy figure, receding with his victims into the pre-history of Eden-Olympia.

Now Greenwood had returned and walked straight up to me. I slept in his bed, soaped myself in his bath, drank my wine in the kitchen where he prepared his breakfasts. More than mere curiosity about the murders nagged at my mind. I thought again of his friendship with Jane. Had we come to Eden-Olympia because she was still fond of the deranged young doctor, and curious about his motives?

I walked past the garage, aware that I had never been tempted to raise the roller doors. Rebuilt or not, this macabre space was a shrine to the four men who had died inside it. One day, when my knee was stronger, I would use the remote control now resting in a bowl on the kitchen table.

The Jaguar waited for me in the sun, its twin carburettors ready to do their best or worst. Starting this high-strung thoroughbred was a race between hope and despair. By contrast, thirty feet from me, was the Delages' Mercedes, as black and impassive as the Stuttgart night, every silicon chip and hydraulic relay eager to serve the driver's smallest whim.

Simone Delage stood beside it, briefcase in hand, dressed for a business meeting in dark suit and white silk blouse. She stared at the damaged wing of the Mercedes like a relief administrator gazing at the aftermath of a small earthquake. A sideswipe had scored the metal, stripping the chromium trim from the headlights to the passenger door.

For once, this self-possessed woman seemed vulnerable and uncertain. Her manicured hand reached towards the door handle and then withdrew, reluctant to risk itself on this failure of a comfortable reality. The car was as much an accessory as her snakeskin handbag, and she could no more drive a damaged Mercedes to a business meeting than appear before her colleagues in laddered stockings.

'Madame Delage? Can I help?'

She turned, recognizing me with an effort. Usually we saw each other when we were both half-naked, she on her balcony and I beside the pool. Clothed, we became actors appearing in under-rehearsed roles. For some reason my tweed sports jacket and leather-thong sandals seemed to unnerve her.

'Mr Sinclair? The car, it's . . . not correct.'

'A shame. When did it happen?'

'Last night. Alain drove back from Cannes. Some taxi driver, a Maghrebian . . . he suddenly swerved. They smoke kief, you know.'

'On duty? I hope not. I've seen quite a few damaged cars here.' I pointed across the peaceful avenue. 'The Franklyns, opposite. Your neighbour, Dr Schmidt. Do you think they're targeted?'

'No. Why?' Uncomfortable in my presence, she hunted in her bag for a mobile phone. 'I need to call a taxi.'

'You can drive the car.' Trying to calm her, I took the phone from her surprisingly soft hand. 'The damage is superficial. Once you close the door you won't notice it.'

'I will, Mr Sinclair. I'm very conscious of these things. I have a meeting at the Merck building in fifteen minutes.'

'If you wait for a taxi you'll be late. I'm leaving now for Cannes. Why don't I give you a lift?'

Madame Delage surveyed me as if I had offered my services as the family butler. My exposed big toes unsettled her, flexing priapically among the unswept leaves. She relaxed a little as she slid into the leather and walnut interior of the Jaguar. Unable to disguise her thighs in the cramped front seat, she beamed at me pluckily.

'It's quite an adventure,' she told me. 'Like stepping into a Magritte . . .'

'He would have liked this car.'

'I'm sure. It's really a plane. Good, it goes.'

The carburettors had risen to the occasion. I reversed into the avenue, dominating the gearbox with a display of sheer will. 'It's kind of your husband to give Jane a lift to the clinic.'

'It's nothing. Already we're very fond of her.'

'I'm glad. She's talked about getting a small motorcycle.'

'Jane?' Madame Delage smiled at this. 'She's so sweet. We love to hear her talk. So many schoolgirl ideas. Look after her, Mr Sinclair.'

'I try to. So far, she's been very happy here. Almost too happy – she's totally involved with her work.'

'Work, yes. But pleasure, too? That's important, especially at Eden-Olympia.' For all her armoured glamour, Simone Delage became almost maternal when she spoke of Jane. Her eyes followed the road towards the Merck building, but she was clearly thinking of Jane. 'You must tell her to relax. Work at Eden-Olympia is the eighth deadly sin. It's essential to find amusements.'

'Sports? Swimming? Gym?'

Madame Delage shuddered discreetly, as if I had mentioned certain obscure bodily functions. 'Not for Jane. All that panting and sweat? Her body would become . . .'

'Too muscular? Would it matter?'

'For Jane? Of course. She must find something that fulfils her. Everything is here at Eden-Olympia.'

I stopped under the glass proscenium of the Merck building, an aluminium-sheathed basilica that housed the pharmaceutical company, an architect's offices and several merchant banks. Simone Delage waited until I walked around the car, as if opening the Jaguar's door was a craft skill lost to Mercedes owners.

Before releasing the catch I rested my hands on the window ledge. 'Simone, I meant to ask – did you know David Greenwood?'

'A little. Dr Penrose said that you were friends.'

'I met him a few times. Everyone agrees that he lived for other people. It's hard to imagine him wanting to kill anyone.'

'A terrible affair.' She appraised me with the same cool eyes that had gazed at the Alpes-Maritimes, but I sensed that she welcomed my interest in Greenwood. 'He worked too hard. It's a lesson to us . . .'

'In the days before the tragedy . . . Did you see him behave strangely? Was he agitated or – ?'

'We were away, Mr Sinclair. In Lausanne for a week. When we came back it was all over.' She touched my hand, making a conscious effort to be friendly. 'I can see you think a lot about David.'

'True. Living in the same house, it's hard not to be aware of what happened. Every day I'm literally moving in his footsteps.'

'Perhaps you should follow them. Who knows where they can lead?' She stepped from the car, a self-disciplined professional already merging into the corporate space that awaited her. She briefly turned her back to the building and shook my hand in a sudden show of warmth. 'As long as you don't buy a gun. You'll tell me, Mr Sinclair?'

I was still thinking about Simone Delage's words when I returned from Cannes with the London newspapers. I left my usual route across the business park and drove past the Merck building, on the off chance that she might have finished her meeting and be waiting for a lift home. In her oblique way she had urged me to pursue my interest in David Greenwood. Perhaps she had been more involved with David than I or her husband realized, and was waiting for a sympathetic outsider to expose the truth.

I parked the Jaguar outside the garage and let myself into the empty house, pausing involuntarily in the hall as I listened for the sounds of a young Englishman's footsteps. The Italian maids had gone, and Señora Morales had moved on to another family in the enclave.

As I changed into my swimsuit I heard a chair scrape across the terrace below the bedroom windows. Assuming that Jane had called in briefly from the clinic, I made my way down the stairs. Through the porthole window on the half-landing I caught a glimpse of a man in a leather jacket striding across the lawn to the swimming pool. When I reached the terrace he was crouching by the doors of the pumphouse. I assumed that he was a maintenance engineer inspecting the chlorination system, and set off towards him, my stick raised in greeting.

Seeing me over his shoulder, he kicked back the wooden doors and turned to face me. He was in his late thirties, with a slim Slavic face, high temples and receding hairline, and a pasty complexion unimproved by the Riviera sun. Beneath the leather jacket his silk shirt was damp with sweat.

'Bonjour . . . you're having a nice day.' He spoke with a strong Russian accent, and kept a wary eye on my walking stick. 'Doctor – ?'

'No. You're looking for my wife.'

'Natasha?'

'Dr Jane Sinclair. She works at the clinic.'

'Alexei . . . very good.'

He was staring over my shoulder, but held me in his visual field, the trick of a military policeman. His smile exposed a set of lavishly capped teeth that seemed eager to escape from his mouth. Despite his sallow skin, imprinted with years of poor nutrition, he wore gold cufflinks and handmade shoes. I assumed that he was a Russian emigré, one of the small-time hoodlums and ex-police agents who were already falling foul of the local French gangsters.

He raised his hand as if to shake mine. 'Dr Greenwood?'

'He's not here. Haven't you heard?'

'Heard nothing . . .' He stared cannily at me. 'Dr Greenwood live here? Alexei . . .'

'Alexei? Listen, who are you? Get out of here . . .'

'No . . .' He moved around me, pointing to the scars on my injured legs, confident that I was too handicapped to challenge him. Burrs covered the sleeves of his jacket, suggesting that he had not entered Eden-Olympia through the main gates.

'Look . . .' I moved towards the terrace and the extension phone in the sun lounge. The Russian stepped out of my way, and then lunged forward and struck me with his fist on the side of my head. His face was cold and drained of all blood, lips clamped over his expensive teeth. I felt my ringing ear, steadied myself and seized him by the lapels. The three months I had spent in a wheelchair had given me a set of power-ful arms and shoulders. My knees buckled, but as I fell to the grass I pulled him onto me, and punched him twice in the mouth.

He wrestled himself away from me, clambered to his feet and tried to kick my face. I gripped his right foot, wrenched his leg and threw him to the ground again. I began to punch his knees, but with a curse he picked himself up and limped away towards the avenue.

I lay winded on the grass, waiting for my head to clear. I fumbled for my walking stick, and found myself holding the Russian's calf-leather shoe. Tucked under the liner was a child's faded passport photograph.

'Taking on intruders is a dangerous game, Mr Sinclair.' Halder surveyed the diagram of scuff-marks on the lawn. 'You should have called us.'

'I didn't have time.' I sat in the wicker armchair, sipping the brandy that Halder had brought from the kitchen. 'He knew I was on to him and lashed out.'

'It would have been better to say nothing.' Halder spoke in the prim tones of a traffic policeman addressing a feckless woman driver. He examined the leather shoe, fingering the designer label of an expensive store in the Rue d'Antibes. Voices crackled from the radio of his Range Rover, parked in the drive next to the Jaguar. Two security vehicles idled in the avenue, and the drivers strode around in a purposeful way, chests out and peaked caps down, hands over their high-belted holsters.

But Halder seemed unhurried. Despite his intelligence, there was a strain of pedantry in the make-up of this black security guard that he seemed to enjoy. He switched on his mobile phone and listened sceptically to the message, like an astronomer hearing a meaningless burst of signals from outer space.

'Have they caught him yet?' I poured mineral water onto a towel and bathed my head, feeling the bubbles sparkle in my hair. Surprisingly, I seemed more alert than I had been since arriving at Eden-Olympia. 'He called himself Alexei. He shouldn't be too difficult to find. A man strolling around with one shoe on.'

Halder nodded approvingly at my deductive powers. 'He may have taken off the other shoe.'

57

'Even so. A man in his socks? Besides, it's an expensive shoe – welt-stitched. What about your surveillance cameras?'

'There are four hundred cameras at Eden-Olympia. Scanning the tapes for a one-shoed man, or even a man in his socks, will take a great many hours of overtime.'

'Then the system is useless.'

'It may be, Mr Sinclair. The cameras are there to deter criminals, not catch them. Have you seen this Alexei before?'

'Never. He's like a pickpocket, hard to spot but impossible to forget.'

'In Cannes? He may have followed you here.'

'Why should he?'

'Your Jaguar. Some people steal antique cars for a living.'

'It's not an antique. In a headwind it will outrun your Range Rover. Besides, he didn't come on like a car buff. Not the kind we're used to in England.'

'This isn't England. The Côte d'Azur is a tough place.' Concerned for me, Halder reached out to pluck some damp grass from my hair, and then examined the blades in his delicate fingers. 'Are you all right, Mr Sinclair? I can call an ambulance.'

'I'm fine. And don't worry Dr Jane. The man wasn't as strong as I expected. He's a small-time Russian hoodlum, some ex-informer or bookie's runner.'

'You put up a good fight. I'll have to take you on my patrols. All the same, you're still getting over your plane crash.'

'Halder, relax. I've wrestled with some very tough physiotherapy ladies.' I pointed to the faded passport-booth photo on the table. 'This child – it looks like a girl of twelve. Is that any help? He mentioned the name "Natasha".'

'Probably his daughter back in Moscow. Forget about him, Mr Sinclair. We'll find him.'

'Who do you think he is?'

Halder stroked his nostrils, smoothing down his refined features, ruffled by the effort of dealing with me. 'Anyone. He might even be a resident. You've been wandering around a lot. It makes people curious.'

'Wandering? Where?'

'All over Eden-Olympia. We thought you were getting bored. Or looking for company.'

'Wandering . . . ?' I gestured at the wooded parkland. 'I go for walks. What's the point of all this landscape if no one sets foot on it?'

'It's more for show. Like most things at Eden-Olympia.'

Halder stood with his back to me, searching the upstairs windows, and I could see his reflection in the glass doors of the sun lounge. He was smiling to himself, a strain of deviousness that was almost likeable. Behind the brave and paranoid new world of surveillance cameras and bulletproof Range Rovers there probably existed an old-fashioned realm of pecking orders and racist abuse. Except for Halder, all the security personnel were white, and many would be members of the Front National, especially active among the pieds-noirs in the South of France. Yet Halder was always treated with respect by his fellow guards. I had seen them open the Range Rover's door for him, an act of deference that he accepted as his due.

Curious about his motives, I asked: 'What made you come to Eden-Olympia?'

'The pay. It's better here than Nice Airport or the Palais des Festivals.'

'That's a good enough reason. But . . .'

'I don't look the type? Too many shadows under the eyes? The wrong kind of suntan?' Halder stared at me almost insolently. 'Or is it because I read Scott Fitzgerald?'

'Halder, I didn't say that.' I waited for him to reply, watching while he twisted the Russian's shoe in his hands, as if wringing the neck of a small mammal. When he nodded to me, accepting that he had tried to provoke me, I turned my bruised ear towards the intercom chatter. 'I meant that it might be too quiet here.

Your men have a job pretending to be busy. Apart from this man Alexei, there doesn't seem to be any crime at Eden-Olympia.'

'No crime?' Halder savoured the notion, smirking at its naivety. 'Some people would say that crime is what Eden-Olympia is about.'

'The multinational companies? All they do is turn money into more money.'

'Could be . . . so money is the ultimate adult toy?' Halder pretended to muse over this. He was intrigued by the stout defence I had put up against the intruder, but my excited sleuthing irritated him, and he was clearly relieved when the guards in the avenue walked up to the wrought-iron gate and signalled the all-clear.

'Right . . .' Halder glanced around the garden and prepared to leave. 'Mr Sinclair, we'll be stepping up patrols. No need for Dr Jane to worry. The Russian must have gone.'

'Why? He could be sitting by any one of a hundred pools here. He's looking for David Greenwood – he didn't even know the poor man was dead.'

'So he went back to Moscow for a few months. Or he doesn't watch television.'

'Why would he want to see Greenwood?'

'How can I say?' Wearily, Halder tried to disengage himself from me. 'Dr Greenwood worked at the methadone clinic in Mandelieu. Maybe he gave the Russian a shot of something he liked.'

'Did Greenwood do that kind of thing?'

'Don't all doctors?' Halder touched my shoulder in a show of sympathy. 'Ask your wife, Mr Sinclair.'

'I'll have to. How well did you know Greenwood?'

'I met him. A decent type.'

'A little highly strung?'

'I wouldn't say so.' Halder picked up the Russian's shoe. He stared at the blurred photograph of the girl, rubbing her face with his thumb. 'I liked him. He got me my job.'

'He killed ten people. Why, Halder? You look as if you know.'

'I don't. Dr Greenwood was a fine man, but he stayed too long at Eden-Olympia.'

I stood by the pool's edge, and searched the deep water. The strong sunlight had stirred up an atlas of currents that cast their shadows across the tiled floor, but I could see the wavering outline of the silver coin below the diving board. Behind me the sprinkler began to spray the lawn, soaking the pillows of the chairs that Halder had moved in his hunt for evidence. The grass still bore the marks of colliding heels, the diagram of a violent apache dance. The raw divots reminded me of the Russian's frightened body, the reek of his sweat and the sharp burrs on his leather jacket.

I left the pool and retraced the Russian's steps to the pump-house. The wooden doors had jumped their latch, exposing the electric motor, heater and timing mechanism. The cramped space was filled with sacks of pool-cleaner, the chlorine-based detergent that Monsieur Anvers poured into the loading port. Twice each day the soft powder diffused across the water, forming milky billows that dissolved the faint residues of human fat along the water-line.

I ran my hand over the nearest wax-paper sack. Its industrial seals were unbroken, but a stream of powder poured onto the floor from a narrow tear. Sitting down, my legs stretched out in front of me, I gripped the sack and pulled it onto the cement apron. A second vent, large enough to take a child's index finger, punctured the heavy wrapper, and the cool powder flowed across my knees.

I tore away the paper between the holes, and slid my hand into the sticky grains. They deliquesced as I exposed them to the sunlight, running between my fingers to reveal a bruised silver nugget like a twisted coin. I cleaned away the damp powder, and stared down at the deformed but unmistakable remains of a high-velocity rifle bullet.

I upended the sack and let the powder flow across the apron. A second bullet lay between my knees, apparently of the same calibre and rifling marks, crushed by its impact with a hard but uneven structure.

I laid the bullets on the ground and reached into the pump-house, running my hands over the remaining sacks. Their waxed wrappers were unbroken, and the pumping machinery bore no signs of bullet damage. I assumed that the stock of detergent had remained here when the pool motor was switched off after David Greenwood's death. Restarting the motor a few days before our arrival, Monsieur Anvers had decided to leave the punctured sack where it lay.

I turned to the wooden doors, feeling the smoothly painted panels, fresh from a builder's warehouse. The chromium hinges were bright and unscratched, recently reset in the surrounding frame. With my hand I brushed away the loose grains of powder and felt the apron beside the doors. The smooth cement had been faintly scored by a rotating abrader, and the steel bristles had left small whorls in the hard surface, as if carefully erasing a set of stains or scorch-marks.

I felt the bullets between my fingers, guessing that they had not been deformed by their impact with the pine doors or the detergent sack. A larger object, with a bony interior, had absorbed the full force of the bullets. Someone, security guard or hostage, had collapsed against the pumphouse doors, and had then been shot at close range, either by himself or others.

I listened to the cicadas in the Yasudas' garden, and watched the dragonflies flitting around the tennis court. According to Wilder Penrose, the three hostages had been killed inside the garage. I imagined the brief gun-battle that had taken place near the house, as David Greenwood made his final stand against the security guards and gendarmes. He had murdered the hostages in an act of despair, and then sat down against the pumphouse, ready to kill himself, staring for the last time at the skies of the Côte d'Azur as the police marksmen approached.

But no one, holding a rifle to his own chest, a thumb out-stretched to the trigger guard, could shoot himself twice. Whoever the victim, an execution had taken place beside the swimming pool of this quiet and elegant house.

A Range Rover of the security force cruised the avenue, and the driver saluted me as he passed. I stood outside the garage, the remote control unit in my hand. The doors rolled noiselessly, and light flooded the interior, a space for three cars with wooden shelves along the rear wall.

For all Penrose's assurance that the garage had been rebuilt, the original structure remained intact. The concrete floor had been laid at least three years earlier, and was slick with engine oil that had dripped from some of the most expensive cars on the Côte d'Azur. Cans of antifreeze stood on the shelves, along with bottles of windscreen fluid and an Opel Diplomat owner's manual.

I carefully searched the floor, and then examined the walls and ceiling for any traces of gunfire. I tried to imagine the hostages trussed together, squinting at the light as Greenwood entered the garage for the last time. But there were no bullet holes, no repairs to the concrete pillars, and no hint that the floor had been cleaned after an execution.

Almost certainly the three men, the luckless chauffeurs and maintenance engineer, had died elsewhere. At least one of them, I suspected, had been shot in the garden, sitting with his back to the doors of the pumphouse.

I closed the garage and rested against the warm roof of the Jaguar. It was a little after six o'clock, and the first traffic was leaving Cannes for the residential suburbs of Grasse and Le Cannet. But Eden-Olympia was silent, as the senior executives and their staffs remained at their workstations. Jane had asked me to collect her from the clinic at 7.30, when the last of her committee meetings would end.

A fine sweat covered my arms and chest as I walked back to the garden, a fear reaction to the garage. I had expected a chamber of horrors, but the ordinariness of the disused space had been more disturbing than any blood-stained execution pit.

I stripped off my shirt and stood by the diving board. Calming myself, I stared down at the dappled floor, a serene and sun-filled realm that existed only in the deeps of swimming pools. A water spider snatched at a drowning fly, and then skied away. As the surface cleared, I saw the bright node of the coin, a gleaming eye that waited for me.

I dived into the pool, broke through the foam and filled my lungs, then turned onto my side and dived again towards the silver pearl.

7

Incident in a Car Park

'THEY'RE RIFLE BULLETS, steel-capped,' I told Jane in her office at the clinic. 'Probably fired from a military weapon. Two of them were in the pumphouse. The third I fished out of the pool an hour ago.'

Jane watched me as I leaned across her desk and placed the three bullets in her empty ashtray. Stolen from a pub in Notting Hill, the ashtray was a reassuring presence, proof that a small part of Jane's rackety past still survived in this temple of efficiency.

Jane sat calmly in her white coat, dwarfed by a black leather chair contoured like an astronaut's couch. She touched the bullets with a pencil, and raised a hand before I could speak.

'Paul – take it easy.'

Already she was playing the wise daughter, more concerned about my adrenalin-fired nerviness than by the unsettling evidence I had brought. I remembered her under the roadside plane trees near Arles, calmly sucking a peach as the engine steamed and I rigged an emergency fan belt from a pair of her tights.

She prodded the bullets, moving them around the ashtray. 'Are you all right? You should have called me. This Russian – what's Halder playing at?'

'I told him not to worry you. Believe me, I've never felt better. I could easily have run here.'

'That's what bothers me. The Russian didn't hurt you?'

'He brushed my shoulder, and I slipped on the grass.'

'He spoke English?'

'Badly. He said his name was Alexei.'

'That's something.' Jane stood up and walked around the desk. Her small hands held my face, then smoothed my damp hair. She paused at the swollen bruise above my ear, but said nothing about the wound. 'Why do you think he was Russian?'

'It's a guess. He mentioned someone called Natasha. Do you remember those touts near the taxi ranks at Moscow Airport? They had everything for sale – drugs, whores, diamonds, oil leases, anything except a taxi. There was something seedy about him in a small-time way. Poor diet and flashy dentistry.'

'That doesn't sound like Eden-Olympia.' Jane pressed my head against her breast and began to explore my scalp. 'Awful man – I can see he upset you. He might have been lost.'

'He was looking for something. He thought I was David Greenwood.'

'Why? There's no resemblance. David was fifteen years younger . . .' She broke off. 'He can't have met David.'

I rotated my chair to face Jane. 'That's the point. Why would David have any contact with a small-time Russian crook?'

Jane leaned against the desk, watching me in a way I had never seen before, less the tired house-doctor of old and more the busy consultant with an eye on her watch. 'Who knows? Perhaps he was hoping to sell David a used car. Someone from the rehab clinic might have mentioned his name.'

'It's possible. Doctors doing charity work have to mix with a lot of riffraff.'

'Apart from their husbands? Paul, these bullets – don't get too involved with them.'

'I won't . . .'

I listened to the lift doors in the corridor as Jane's colleagues left the clinic after their day's work. Somewhere a dialysis machine moved through its cleaning cycle, emitting a series of soft grunts and rumbles, like a discreet indigestion. The clinic was a palace of calm, far away from the pumphouse and its bullet-riddled sack.

I gazed through the cruise-liner windows at the open expanse of the lake. A deep shift in the subsoil sent a brief tremor across the surface, as a pressure surge moved through a ring main.

Proud of Jane, I said: 'What an office – they obviously like you. Now I see why you want to spend your time here.'

'It was David's office.'

'Doesn't that feel . . . ?'

'Strange? I can cope with it. We sleep in his bed.'

'Almost grounds for divorce. They should have moved you. Living in the same villa is weird enough.' I gestured at the filing cabinets. 'You've been through his stuff? Any hints of what went wrong?'

'The files are empty, but some of his records are still on computer.' Jane tapped a screen with her pencil. 'The La Bocca case histories would make your hair curl. A lot of those Arab girls were fearfully abused.'

'Thanks, I'd rather not see them. What about the children here? Is there a lot of work for you?'

'Very little. There aren't many children at Eden-Olympia. I don't know why they needed a paediatrician. Still, it gives me a chance to work on something else. There's a new project using the modem links to all the villas and apartments. Professor Kalman is keen that I get involved.'

'Fine, as long as they don't exploit you. Is it interesting?'

'In an Eden-Olympia kind of way.' Jane played distractedly with the bullets, as if they were executive worry-beads supplied to all the offices. 'Every morning when they get up people will dial the clinic and log in their health data: pulse, blood-pressure, weight and so on. One prick of the finger on a small scanner and the computers here will analyse everything: liver enzymes, cholesterol, prostate markers, the lot.'

'Alcohol levels, recreational drugs . . . ?'

'Everything. It's so totalitarian only Eden-Olympia could even think about it and not realize what it means. But it might work.

Professor Kalman is very keen on faecal smears, but I suspect that's one test too far. He hates the idea of all that used toilet paper going to waste. The greatest diagnostic tool in the world is literally being flushed down the lavatory. How does it strike you?'

'Mad. Utterly bonkers.'

'You're right. But the basic idea is sound. We'll be able to see anything suspicious well in advance.'

'So no one will ever get ill?'

'Something like that.' She turned and stared at the lake. 'It's a pity about the paediatrics. At times I feel all the children in the world have grown up and left me behind.'

'Only at Eden-Olympia.' I reached out and held her waist. 'Jane, that's sad.'

'I know.' Jane looked down at the bullets in her palm, seeing them clearly for the first time. She pressed them against her heart, as if calculating the effect on her anatomy, and with a grimace dropped them into the ashtray. 'Nasty. Are you going to hand them in?'

'To the security people? Later, when I've had time to think. Say nothing to Penrose.'

'Why not? He ought to know.' Jane held my wrist as I reached for the bullets. 'Paul, stand back for a moment. You'd expect to find a few bullets in the garden. Seven people were killed. The guards must have been in a total panic, shooting at anything that moved. Stop putting yourself in David's shoes.'

'I'm trying not to. It's difficult, I don't know why. By the way, I'm sure David didn't shoot the hostages in the garage. I had a careful look inside.'

'But Penrose told us the garage had been rebuilt.'

'It wasn't. I'll show you around.'

'No thanks. I'll stay with Professor Kalman at the colorectal end of things. So where did David shoot the hostages?'

'In the garden. One probably died against the pumphouse doors. A second was shot in the pool.'

'Bizarre. What was the poor man doing – swimming for help?'
Tired of talking to me, Jane rested her face in her hands. She tapped
a computer keyboard, and a stream of numerals glimmered against
her pale skin.

'Jane . . .' I held her shoulders, watching the screen as it
threw up a list of anaesthetics. 'I'm badgering you. Let's forget
about David.'

Jane smiled at this. 'Dear Paul, you're so wired up. You're like
a gun dog waiting for the beaters.'

'There's nothing else to think about. Lying by a swimming
pool all day is a new kind of social deprivation. Let's drive down
to Cannes and have an evening on the town. Champagne cocktails
at the Blue Bar, then an aïoli at Mère Besson. Afterwards we'll go
to the Casino and watch the rich Arabs pick out their girls.'

'I like rich Arabs. They're extremely placid. All right – but I
have to go back and change.'

'No. Come as you are. White coat and stethoscope. They'll
think I'm a patient having an affair with his glamorous young
doctor.'

'You are.' Jane held my hands to her shoulders and rocked
against me. 'I need time to freshen up.'

'Fine. I'll get some air on the roof and bring the car round to
the entrance in twenty minutes.' I leaned across her and pointed
to the computer screen. 'What's all this? I saw David's initials.'

'Eerie, isn't it? You're not the only one finding traces of
the dead.'

'"May 22" . . .' I touched the screen. 'That was a week
before the murders. "Dr Pearlman, Professor Louit, Mr Richard
Lancaster . . . 2.30, 3, 4 o'clock." Who are these people?'

'Patients David was seeing. Pearlman is chief executive of Ciba-
Geigy. Lancaster is president of Motorola's local subsidiary. Don't
think about shooting them – they're watched over like royalty.'

'They are royalty. There's a second list here. But no times are
given. When was it typed in?'

'May 26. It's a list of appointments waiting to be scheduled.'

'But David was a paediatrician. Do all these people have children?'

'I doubt if any of them do. David spent most of his time on general duties. Paul, let's go. You've seen enough.'

'Hold on.' I worked the mouse, pushing the list up the page. '"Robert Fontaine . . . Guy Bachelet." They were two of the victims.'

'Poor bastards. I think Fontaine died in the main administration building. Alain Delage took over from him. Does it matter?'

'It slightly changes things. Only two days beforehand David was reminding himself to arrange their appointments. A strange thing to do if he planned to kill them. Jane . . . ?'

'Sorry, Paul.' Jane switched off the screen. 'So much for the conspiracy theory.'

I turned away and stared across the lake, expecting another seismic shudder. 'He was still booking them in for their check-ups. All that cholesterol to be tested, all those urinalyses. Instead, he gets up early in the morning, and decides to shoot them dead . . .'

Jane patted my cheek. 'Too bad, Paul. So the brainstorm theory is right after all. You'll have to go back to the sun-lounger, and all that deprivation . . .'

Waving to the night staff, I walked through the foyer of the clinic to the car-park entrance. As the lift carried me to the top floor I stared at my dishevelled reflection in the mirror, part amateur detective with scarred forehead and swollen ear – the price of too much keyhole work – and part eccentric rider of hobby-horses. As always, Jane was right. I had read too much into the three bullets and the intact garage. A nervy gendarme searching the garden might have fired into the pumphouse when the engine switched to detergent mode, startling him with its subterranean grumblings. The rifle round in the pool could have richocheted off the rose pergola and been kicked into the water by a passing combat boot. The hostages had probably died in the avenue, shot down by Greenwood as they made a run for it. Wilder Penrose's description of events, the official story released to the world by the press office at Eden-Olympia, was not to be taken literally.

The lift doors opened onto the roof, empty except for the Jaguar. The medical staff and visiting senior executives left their cars on the lower floors, but I always enjoyed the clear view over La Napoule Bay, and the gentle, lazy sea that lay like a docile lover against the curved arm of the Esterel.

I leaned on the parapet, inhaling the scent of pines and the medley of pharmaceutical odours that emerged from a ventilation shaft. I was thinking of Jane and her new office when I heard a shout from the floors below, a muffled cry of protest followed by the sound of a blow struck against human bone. A second voice bellowed abuse in a pidgin of Russian and Arabic.

I stepped to the inner balustrade and peered into the central well, ready to shout for help. Two Eden-Olympia limousines were making their way down the circular ramp. The chauffeurs stopped their vehicles on the third level, slipped from their driving seats and opened the rear doors, giving their passengers a ringside view of the ugly tableau being staged in an empty parking space.

A Senegalese trinket salesman knelt on the concrete floor in his flowered robes, beads and bangles scattered around him. Despite the dim light, I could see the streaming bruises on his face, and the blood dripping onto a plastic wallet filled with cheap watches and fountain pens. A dignified man with a small beard, he tried to gather together his modest wares, as if knowing that he would have little to show for the day's work. Patiently he retrieved a tasselled mask that lay between the booted heels of the security guards who were beating a thickset European in a cheap cream suit. The victim was still on his feet, protesting in Russian-accented French as he warded off the truncheon blows with his bloodied hands. Their blue shirts black with sweat, the three guards manoeuvred him into the corner and then released a flurry of blows that sank him to his knees.

I turned away, dazed by the violence, and then shouted to the executives watching from their cars. But they were too engrossed to notice me. Sitting by the open doors of the limousines, they were almost Roman in their steely-eyed calm, as if watching the punishment of a slacking gladiator. I recognized Alain Delage, the bespectacled accountant who gave Jane a lift to the clinic. He and the other executives were dressed in leather jackets zipped to the neck, like members of an Eden-Olympia bowling club.

The beatings ended. I listened to the Russian coughing as he leaned against the wall, trying to wipe the blood from his suit. Satisfied, the security men holstered their truncheons and stepped back into the darkness. Starter-motors churned and the limousines swung towards the exit, carrying away the audience from this impromptu piece of garage theatre.

I gripped the balustrade and limped down the ramp, searching the lift alcoves for a telephone that would put me through to the emergency medical team. The African was now on his feet, straightening his torn robes, but the Russian sat in his corner, head swaying as he gasped for air.

I circled the ramp above them, trying to attract their attention, but a uniformed figure stepped from behind a pillar and barred my way.

'Mr Sinclair . . . be careful. The floors are hard. You'll hurt yourself.'

'Halder?' I recognized his slate-pale face. 'Did you see all that . . . ?'

Halder's strong hand gripped my elbow and steadied me when I slipped on the oily deck. His aloof eyes took in my lumbering gait, assessing whether I was drunk or on drugs, but his face was without expression, any hint of judgement erased from its refined features.

'Halder – your men were there. What exactly is going on?'

'Nothing, Mr Sinclair.' Halder spoke soothingly. 'A small security matter.'

'Small? They were beating the balls off those men. They need medical help. Call Dr Jane on your radio.'

'Mr Sinclair . . .' Halder gave up his attempt to calm me. 'It was a disciplinary incident, nothing to concern you. I'll help you to your car.'

'Hold on . . .' I pushed him away from me. 'I know how to walk. You made a mistake – that wasn't the Russian I saw this morning.'

Halder nodded sagely, humouring me as he tapped the elevator button. 'One Russian, another Russian . . . examples have to be made. We can't be everywhere. This is the dark side of Eden-Olympia. We work hard so you and Dr Jane can enjoy the sun.'

'The dark side?' I propped the door open with my foot and waited for Halder to meet my eyes. 'Away from the tennis courts and the swimming pools you hate so much? I wouldn't want to spend too much time there.'

'You don't need to, Mr Sinclair. We do that for you.'

'Halder . . .' I lowered my voice, which I could hear echoing around the dark galleries. 'That was a hell of a beating your men handed out.'

'The Cannes police would be a lot harder on them. We were doing them a favour.'

'And the parked limousines? Alain Delage and the other bigwigs were watching the whole thing. Wasn't that just a little over the top? It looked as if it was staged for them.'

Halder nodded in his over-polite way, waiting patiently to send me and the lift towards the roof. 'Maybe it was. Some of your neighbours at Eden-Olympia have . . . advanced tastes.'

'So . . . it was arranged? Carefully set up so you could have your fun?'

'Not us, Mr Sinclair. And definitely not me.' He stepped away

73

from the lift, saluted and strode down the ramp, heels ringing on the concrete.

I settled myself in the Jaguar and inhaled the evening air. The scent of disinfectant and air-conditioning suddenly seemed more real than the sweet tang of pine trees. I felt angry but curiously elated, as if I had stepped unharmed from an aircraft accident that had injured my fellow-passengers. The sweat and stench of violence quickened the air and refocused the world.

Without starting the engine, I released the hand-brake and freewheeled the Jaguar along the ramp. I was tempted to run Halder down, but by the time I passed him the Russian and the Senegalese had gone, and the scattered beads lay blinking among the pools of blood.

8

The Alice Library

AS STOICAL AS the wife of a kamikaze pilot protecting the wreckage of his plane, Mrs Yasuda stood on the pavement outside the house and waited as her husband's damaged Porsche was hoisted onto the removal truck. The winch moaned and sighed, sharing all the pain inflicted on the car. An oblique front-end collision had torn the right fender from its frame, crushed the headlight and frosted the windscreen, through which Mr Yasuda had punched an observation space.

Staring at this hole, Mrs Yasuda's face was without emotion, her cheeks drained of colour, as if the accident to her husband's sports car had stopped the clocks of human response. When the removal driver asked for her signature she wrote her name in a large cursive script and closed the door before he could doff his cap.

Fortunately, Mr Yasuda had not been injured in the accident, as I had seen a few hours earlier. Still awake at three that morning, I left Jane asleep, face down like a teenager with a pillow over her head. Wandering naked from one room to the next, I was still trying to come to terms with the ugly incident in the clinic car park.

The display of brutality had unsettled me. I said nothing to Jane as we drove into Cannes for dinner, but a dormant part of my mind had been aroused – not by the cruelty, which I detested, but by the discovery that Eden-Olympia offered more to its residents than what met the visitor's gaze. Over the swimming pools and manicured lawns seemed to hover a dream of violence.

75

Slipping on my bathrobe, I kissed Jane's small hand, still faintly scented with some hospital reagent, and watched her fingers jump in a childlike reflex. I went downstairs, opened the sun-lounge door and strolled across the lawn, past the pool with its sealed surface like a black dance floor. I opened the wire gate into the tennis court and paced the marker lines that ran through the moonlight, thinking of the resigned eyes of the old Senegalese.

A car approached the Yasudas' house, its engine labouring. It limped along in low gear, metal scraping a tyre as it turned into the drive. A table lamp lit up Mrs Yasuda's first-floor study, where she had been sitting in the darkness, perhaps watching her English neighbour prowl the baselines of his mind. She moved to the window, and waved to her husband when he stepped from the damaged car.

A few minutes later I saw them through the slatted blinds of their bedroom. Still wearing his leather jacket, the stocky businessman strode around the room, gesticulating as his wife watched him from the bed. He seemed to be enacting scenes from a violent martial-arts film, perhaps shown that evening to the Japanese community in Cannes. He at last undressed, and sat at the foot of the bed, a portly would-be samurai. His wife stood between his knees, her hands on his shoulders, waiting until he slipped the straps of her nightdress.

They began to make love, and I left the tennis court and walked back to the house. Lying beside Jane, I listened to her breathy murmur as she dreamed her young wife's dreams. Somewhere a horn sounded in the residential enclave, followed by another in reply, as cars returned from the outposts of the night.

Señora Morales was giving the morning's instructions to the Italian maids. For an hour they would work downstairs, leaving me with ample time to shave, shower and muse over the possibilities of the day. The flow of faxes and e-mails from London had begun to fall away, and with my agreement Charles had taken over the editorship of the two aviation journals.

Faced with the imposed boredom of Eden-Olympia, I lay back on the bed, feeling the warm imprint of Jane's body beside me. We, too, had made love on returning from Cannes, a rare event after her long working days. Sex, at the business park, was something one watched on the adult film channels. But Jane had been excited by the illicit pleasure of leaving for Cannes on the spur of the moment. An impulsive decision ran counter to the entire ethos of Eden-Olympia. When she stepped from the car onto the Croisette she seemed almost light-headed. In a tabac near the Majestic she picked a *Paris-Match* from the racks and calmly walked out without paying. It lay on our table at Mère Besson beside the aïoli of cod and carrots, and Jane was well aware that she had stolen the magazine. But she shrugged and smiled cheerfully, accepting that a benign lightning strike had illuminated our excessively ordered world. The mental climate that presided over Eden-Olympia never varied, its moral thermostat set somewhere between duty and caution. The emotion had been draining from our lives, leaving a numbness that paled the sun. The stolen magazine quickened our lovemaking . . .

As the floor-polishers drummed away, I strolled through the empty bedrooms, searching for further traces of David Greenwood. I sat on the draped mattress in the children's room, surrounded by a frieze of cartoon figures – Donald Duck, Babar and Tintin – and thinking of the child that I hoped Jane would bear one day, and how it would sleep and play in a room as sunny as this one.

Next to the bathroom was a fitted cupboard, decorated with Tenniel's illustrations for the Alice books. I opened the doors, and found myself gazing at a modest library, the first real trace of Greenwood's tenancy. Some thirty copies of *Alice's Adventures in Wonderland* and *Through the Looking-Glass* sat on the shelves, translations into French, Spanish and even Serbo-Croat. Over drinks the previous weekend, Wilder Penrose had told me of David's enthusiasm for the Alice books, and the Lewis Carroll society he had formed at Eden-Olympia. The Paris surrealists embraced Carroll as one of their great precursors, but Eden-Olympia seemed an unlikely recruiting ground. Perhaps the multinational executives possessed a more whimsical sense of humour than I realized, and saw affinities between the business park and Alice's hyper-logical mind.

The copies were well thumbed, loaned to the youthful readership at the La Bocca children's refuge. The flyleaves were marked with names, in what I guessed was David's scrawl.

'*Fatima . . . Elisabeth . . . Véronique . . . Natasha . . .*'

'Curiouser and curiouser . . .' Jane ran a hand over the books in the cupboard. 'This Russian who mugged you turns out to be a devoted father, trying to borrow a library book for his daughter Natasha.'

'It does look like it.'

'Come on, Paul. You jumped into the deep end and went straight to the bottom. Not every Russian on the Côte d'Azur is a mafioso. The poor man was introducing Natasha´ to an English classic. You make fun of his teeth, steal one of his shoes, and launch a full-scale manhunt.'

'I know. I regret it now.'

'At least they didn't catch him. Halder looks as if he'd love to beat the hell out of someone.'

'I'm not so sure.' I straightened the row of books. 'For a library user, the Russian I saw was amazingly aggressive.'

'Of course he was.' Jane lay back on the bed, savouring her triumph. Still wearing her white hospital coat, she had come home to change before a conference in Nice. 'The Russians had to fight for the right to read . . . Mandelstam, Pasternak, Solzhenitsyn. Think of it, Paul. You were lining up with all those KGB types against this poor migrant worker and little Natasha.'

'You win.' I sat beside Jane and massaged her calves. 'It's a touching thought, all those Alice books in the refuge, pored over by Véronique and Fatima. Where are they now?'

'Working in some awful factory, I imagine, packing espadrilles for five francs an hour, while they wonder what happened to the kind English doctor. Don't think too badly of David. He did some good things here.'

'I accept that. How well did you really know him?'

'We worked together. Paul, what are you driving at?'

'Nothing. I've always been curious.'

'You know I don't like that. David isn't coming back, so forget about him.' Irritated by me, Jane rose from the bed and took off her white coat. She seemed older than I remembered, her hair neatly groomed, the scar from her nasal ring concealed with cosmetic filler. She raised a hand as if to slap me, then relented and took my arm. 'I keep telling you – I never had many lovers.'

'I thought you had an army of them.'

'I wonder why . . .' She stood by the window, looking across the business park towards the sea. 'You're still locked into the past. It's a huge phantom limb that aches and throbs. We're here, Paul. We breathe this air, and we see this light . . .'

I watched her chin lift as she spoke, and realized that she was staring, not at the handsome headland of Cap d'Antibes and the pewter glimmer of the sea, but at the office buildings of Eden-Olympia, at the satellite dishes and microwave aerials. The business park had adopted her.

'Jane, you like it here, don't you.'

'Eden-Olympia? Well, it has a lot going for it. It's open to talent and hard work. There's no ground already staked out, no title deeds going back to bloody Magna Carta. You feel anything could happen.'

'But nothing ever does. All you people do is work. It's wonderful here, but they left out reality. No one sits on the local council, or has a say about the fire service.'

'Good. Who wants to?'

'That's my point. The whole place is probably run by a management consultancy in Osaka.'

'Fine by me. It might be a lot fairer. At Guy's there are two sets of stairs. One at the front for the men that goes up to the roof, and the converted servant's staircase at the back that ends on the third floor. I don't need to tell you who that's reserved for.'

'Things are changing.'

'That old mantra – women have listened to it for too long. How many teaching professors are women? Even in gynae?' Lowering her voice, she said in an offhand way: 'Kalman tells me they haven't filled my post yet. He asked if I'd like to stay on for another six months.'

'Would you?'

'Yes, if I'm honest. Think about it. More time here would do you good. A mild winter, a couple of hours of tennis every day. We'll find someone to play with you – maybe Mrs Yasuda.'

'Jane . . .' I tried to embrace her, but she tensed herself, exposing the sharp bones of her shoulders. 'I have to get back to London. There's a business to run. Charles won't carry me for ever.'

'I know. Still, you could fly out at weekends. It's only an hour from London.'

'You work at weekends.'

She made no reply, and stared down at the swimming pool. Her eyes avoided mine, and she seemed to be mentally subdividing her new domain, unpacking her real baggage in the privacy of her mind.

'Paul, relax . . .' She spoke brightly, as if she remembered an exciting experience we had once shared. 'We stay together, whatever happens. You're my wounded pilot, I have to sew up your wings. Are you all right?'

'Just about.' For the first time the wifely baby-talk sounded unconvincing. I noticed the transfers of the Hatter, the Dormouse and the Red Queen that Greenwood had pasted to the wardrobe door. Jane was growing up, like the Alice of *Through the Looking-Glass*, and I sensed something of Carroll's regret when he realized that his little heroine was turning into a young woman and would soon be leaving him.

I closed the library door and said: 'You'd better change. Kalman's collecting you in an hour. Before you go, I'd like a printout of that appointments list.'

'David's? Why?' Jane picked up her white coat. 'I'm not sure.'

'No one will know. Can you access it on the terminal downstairs?'

'Yes, but . . . why do you want it?'

'Just a hunch. I need to track it down. Then I can lay David to rest.'

'Well . . . keep it to yourself. These senior people don't like their medical records floating around.'

'It's a list, Jane. I could have copied it out of the phone book.' I paused by the stairs. 'Have you been able to find out why they were seeing David? Was there anything wrong with them?'

'Just sports injuries. Nothing else. Skin lacerations, one or two broken bones. There's some very rough touch rugby being played at Eden-Olympia.'

The pressure of Jane's mouth still dented my lips as I walked to the car. I thought of her with the computer in the study, watching me warily as she searched through Greenwood's records. Had she been testing me, with her talk of extending the contract? After another six months she would be as institutionalized as any long-term convict, locked inside a virtual cell she called her office. Eden-Olympia demanded a special type of temperament, committed to work rather than to pleasure, to the balance sheet and the drawing board rather than to the brothels and gaming tables of the Old Riviera. Somehow I needed to remind Jane of her true self. In its way her theft of the magazine from the tabac was a small ray of hope.

I tucked the appointments list into my breast pocket and searched for the car keys. Parked behind the Jaguar on the sloping forecourt was Wilder Penrose's sports saloon, a low-slung Japanese confection with huge wing mirrors, grotesque spoiler and air intakes large enough for a ramjet. To my puritan eye the car was an anthology of marketing tricks, and I refused even to identify its manufacturer.

I assumed that Penrose was making a house call on Simone Delage, easing this highly-strung woman through the aftermath of some troubled dream or advising her about the impotence problems of over-promoted accountants. He had deliberately parked a few inches from the Jaguar, rather than on the Delages' forecourt, forcing me to make a tight turn that would show up the Jaguar's heavy steering.

I started the engine, listening with pleasure to the hungry gasp of the rival carburettors, for once ready to sink their differences against a common enemy. I edged forward and swung the steering wheel, but found my way blocked by the plinth of the dolphin sculpture. I reversed, careful not to touch the Japanese car, but at the last moment, giving way to a sudden impulse, I raised my foot from the brake pedal. I felt the Jaguar's heavy chrome bumper bite deep into soft fibreglass, almost buckling the passenger door of the sports saloon. It rocked under the impact, its hydraulics letting out a chorus of neurotic cries.

Trying to ignore what I had done, but admitting to a distinct lightness of heart, I rolled down the ramp towards the street.

9

Glass Floors and White Walls

'MR SINCLAIR, THERE'S no crime at Eden-Olympia. None at all.' Pascal Zander, the new head of security, sighed with more than a hint of disappointment. 'In fact, I can say that the whole concept of criminality is unknown here. Do I exaggerate?'

'You don't,' I told him. 'We've been here two months and I haven't seen a single cigarette stub or bubble-gum pat.'

'Bubble gum? The idea is unthinkable. There are no pine cones to trip you, no bird shit on your car. At Eden-Olympia even nature knows her place.'

Zander beamed at me, glad to welcome me to his den. An affable and fleshy Franco-Lebanese, he stood behind his desk, camel-hair coat over his shoulders, more public relations man than security chief. Crime might be absent from Eden-Olympia, but other pleasures were closer to hand. When his secretary, a handsome Swiss woman in her forties, brought in an urgent letter for signature, he stared at her like a child faced with a spoonful of cream.

'Good, good . . .' He watched her leave the office and then turned the same lecherous gaze towards me, letting it linger for a few moments without embarrassment. He sat down, still wearing his coat, and shifted his rump on the leather chair. As he flicked dismissively at the onyx pen-stand he made it clear that both the chair and the desk he had inherited from Guy Bachelet, his murdered predecessor, were too small for him. Already bored by my visit, he stared at the distant rooftops of Cannes, to an older

Côte d'Azur where the hallowed traditions of crime and social pathology still flourished.

For an unsavoury character, Pascal Zander was surprisingly likeable, one of the few openly venal individuals in Eden-Olympia, and I found myself warming to him. I had intended to report the brutal beatings in the clinic car park, but here was a police chief who sincerely believed that he had abolished crime. He was sympathetic when I described the Russian intruder who punched me, but plainly saw our brawl as little more than an outbreak of personal rivalry between expatriates, probably over the affections of my wife.

'At Eden-Olympia we are self-policing,' he explained. 'Honesty is a designed-in feature, along with free parking and clean air. Our guards are for show, like the guides at Euro-Disney.'

'Their uniforms are actually costumes?'

'In effect. If you want real crime, go to Nice or Cannes La Bocca. Robbery, prostitution, drug-dealing – to us they seem almost folkloric, subsidized by the municipality for the entertainment of tourists.'

'Unthinkable at Eden-Olympia,' I agreed. 'All the same, there was one tragic failure.'

'Dr Greenwood? Tragic, yes . . .' Zander pressed a scented hand to his heart. 'Every moment I spend in this chair I feel the tragedy. His behaviour was criminal, but of a kind beyond the reach of the law or police.'

'What happened to Greenwood? No one seems able to say.'

'Speak to Wilder Penrose. A bolt of lightning streaks through a deceased brain. Within minutes seven of my colleagues are dead. Men and women who gave everything to Eden-Olympia. Death stalked us all that morning, with a rifle in one hand and a box of dice in the other.'

'The killings were random?'

'There's no doubt. Nothing linked the victims to their murderer.'

'Except for one thing – they were his patients. Greenwood may have believed they had some fatal disease.'

'They did. But the disease was inside Greenwood's mind.' Zander leaned his plump chest across the desk, lowering his voice. 'We at security were heavily criticized. But how could we predict the behaviour of someone so deeply insane? You knew him, Mr Sinclair?'

'He was a colleague of my wife's in London. He seemed rather . . . idealistic.'

'The best disguise. There are many brilliant people at Eden-Olympia. For a few, their minds are lonely places, the cold heights where genius likes to walk. Now and then, a crevasse appears.'

'So it could happen again?'

'We hope not. Eden-Olympia would never survive. But sooner or later, who can say? We are too trusting, Mr Sinclair. So many glass floors and white walls. The possibilities for corruption are enormous. Power, money, opportunity. People can commit crimes and be unaware of it. In some ways it's better to be like Nice or La Bocca – the lines are drawn and we cross them knowing the cost. Here, it's a game without rules. One determined man could . . .' He seemed to stare into himself, then made an obscene gesture at the air and turned to me. 'You want my help, Mr Sinclair?'

'I'm interested in exactly what happened on May 28. The route Dr Greenwood took, the number of shots fired. They might give me a clue to his state of mind. As an Englishman I feel responsible.'

'I'm not sure . . .' Zander's hands fretted over his gaudy desk ornaments. 'Violent assassins renounce their nationality as they commit their crimes.'

'Could I talk to the next of kin?'

'The wives of the deceased? They returned to their home countries. Grief is all that's left to them.'

'The office staff? Secretaries, personal assistants?'

'They've suffered enough. What more can they tell you?

The colour of Greenwood's tie? Whether he wore brown or black shoes?'

'Fair enough. An overall report of the incident would help me. I take it you prepared one?'

'One? A hundred reports. For the investigating magistrate, for the Prefect of Police, for the Minister of the Interior, six foreign embassies, lawyers for the companies . . .'

'So you can lend me one?'

'They're still confidential. International corporations are involved. Claims of negligence may be brought against Eden-Olympia, which of course we deny.'

'Then —'

'I can't help you, Mr Sinclair.' For the first time Zander sounded like a policeman. He studied the scar on my forehead and my still-bruised ear. 'Does violence intrigue you, Mr Sinclair?'

'Not at all. I try to avoid it.'

'And your wife? For a few women . . .'

'She's a doctor. She's spent years in casualty wards.'

'Even so. Some people find violence is a useful marriage aid. A special kind of tickler. You're so involved with the Greenwood murders, but I'm sure your motives are sincere. Sadly, you are wasting your time. All conceivable evidence was tracked down.'

'Not all. . .' I took the three spent bullets from my pocket and rolled them across the desk. 'Rifle bullets — I found them in the garden at our villa. One was lying on the floor of the swimming pool. How it got there is hard to work out. For what it's worth, I don't think the hostages were shot in the garage.'

Zander took out a silk handkerchief and vented some unpleasing odour from his mouth. He stared at the bullets but made no attempt to examine them.

'Mr Sinclair, you did well to find them. My men told me they made a careful search.'

'You could match them to Dr Greenwood's rifle.'

'The weapon is held by the Cannes police. It's best if we don't involve them again. Other traces of Greenwood will appear. The greater a crime, the longer its effects poison the air. Have you found anything else?'

'Not at the villa. But there are one or two odd things going on at Eden-Olympia.'

'I'm glad to hear it.' Zander opened a window and let in the warm air, which he inhaled in short but hungry breaths. Recovering his poise, he turned to escort me to the door. '"Odd things" . . . I'd almost lost hope for our business park. Good news, Mr Sinclair. Keep your eyes open for me . . .'

'I will. Now, the hostages . . .'

'Mr Sinclair, please . . .' Zander put an arm around my shoulders, reminding me of the strength that an overweight body can hide. 'The dead no longer care where they were shot. Tell me about your young wife. Is she enjoying her stay with us?'

'Very much.' I stepped through a side door into the corridor, where a woman assistant was waiting. 'She works far too hard.'

'Everyone does. It's our secret vice. She needs to play a little more. You'll have to find some new activity that amuses her. There are so many interesting games at Eden-Olympia . . .'

His mouth began to purse again, showing the pink lining inside his black lips, but his eyes were fixed upon the three bullets that lay on his desk.

10

The Hit List

AN ALMOST DRUGGED air floated across the lake, a rogue cloud that had drifted down the hillside, carrying the scent of office-freshener from a factory in Grasse. I walked along the water's edge, attracting the attention of two security men in a Range Rover parked among the pines. One watched me through his binoculars, no doubt puzzled that anyone in Eden-Olympia should have the leisure to stroll through the midday sun.

Between the security building and the Elf-Maritime research labs was an open-air cafeteria, a facility intended to soften the public face of the business park and give it a passing resemblance to an Alpine resort. Tired after my meeting with Zander, I sat down and ordered a vin blanc from the young French waitress, who wore jeans and a white vest printed with a quotation from Baudrillard.

Zander had told me nothing, as I expected. Even his silences provided no useful clues. By now, nearly six months after the event, a relieved Eden-Olympia had erased David Greenwood from its collective memory, filing the tragedy in some administrative limbo assigned to earthquakes and regicides.

I thought of Zander: thuggish, bisexual and corrupt, qualities no doubt essential for any successful police chief. I could smell his aftershave on my right hand, and was tempted to walk to the water's edge and wash the scent away, but disturbing the surface would probably trigger a full-scale alert. Yet Zander was a potential collaborator, the only person I had met who saw the flaw at the heart of Eden-Olympia. Given the absence of an explicit moral order, where decisions about right and wrong were engineered into the social fabric along with the fire drills and parking regulations, Zander's job became impossible. Crime could flourish at Eden-Olympia without the residents ever being aware that they were its perpetrators or leaving any clues to their motives.

Zander, according to Jane, was the *acting* head of security, and was still waiting for his appointment to be confirmed. During the interregnum, as he fretted at his desk in his camel-hair coat, he might become a useful ally. I remembered the Alice images I had found in the children's room. Not for the first time it occurred to me that David Greenwood might never have committed the murders on May 28, and that the surveillance footage that showed him entering and leaving his victims' offices had been faked.

A blonde woman in her thirties, dressed in a dark business suit, sat down at a nearby table. She ordered a cappuccino and exchanged a few words of banter with the waitress, but her eyes were fixed on the top floor of the security building, where Pascal Zander had his office. She opened a laptop computer and tapped the keys, throwing up a sequence of property ads for expensive villas on the heights of Super-Cannes and Californie, all furnished with electric-blue lawns and emerald skies. She stared morosely at the overlit photographs and began a typed dialogue with herself, apparently setting out her day's schedule and answering her queries aloud in an ironic English voice. I imagined her stepping from her shower, towel twirled around her head, keying in the emotions she would feel that day, the memories to be cued, the daydreams to be assigned a few minutes of too-precious time, the whole programme laced with sardonic asides.

During a creative pause she gazed over the tables at me, revealing an attractive but moody face. I marked her down as a professional rebel, who resented the trappings of managerial success, club-class upgrades and company credit cards, the fool's gold that could buy an entire life and offer no discount for idealism or integrity, and I liked the sombre eye that she levelled at the business park. Her glance took in my open-necked shirt, tweed sports jacket and thong sandals, a garb never worn by anyone in Eden-Olympia at either work or play, but the off-duty dress at my Cyprus RAF base, circa 1978, and the guarantee, I was deluded enough to think, of a certain kind of honesty.

She watched me brush a leaf from my lapel, and a smile moved like a slow tic across her mouth. She sipped her coffee, then pressed a tissue to her lips, leaving the imprint of a crushed kiss on the table. She returned to the laptop, perhaps outlining a cost-benefit analysis of her next affair, the contingency funds to be assigned to minor cosmetic surgery, precautionary visits to the HIV clinic . . .

As if to encourage the fantasies of the stranger sitting nearby, she kicked off her high-heeled shoes and hitched up her skirt to scratch her stockinged insteps, exposing a satisfying glimpse of white thigh. Despite the smart suit, her blonde hair was a little too blown, giving her the look of a nervy and intellectual tart. Was she a call-girl, computerized like everyone else at Eden-Olympia? Her sceptical stare at the Elf building made it hard to believe that she worked as a contented member of anyone's team.

A security helicopter patrolled the lake, its soft engine barely audible across the impassive surface. For a few seconds I imagined that it was keeping watch on me after my collision with Wilder Penrose's car.

I had deliberately damaged the door, paying Penrose back for urging Jane to stay on at Eden-Olympia, but also for the sheer perversity of watching the fibreglass craze and splinter. It reminded me of an outburst of vandalism I had given way to as a boy of seven. My parents were on holiday in France, trying to jury-rig their becalmed marriage and aware that they were always happiest in a foreign country. I was staying with my mother's sister, a retired character actress with a churchy streak. She was devoted to me, but fiercely proscriptive about the television I was allowed to watch. Almost every programme that I liked seemed to remind her of her lapsed career. One afternoon, when she vetoed a science fiction series in which she appeared as a Martian psychiatrist, I managed to sneak out into the street with a can of spray-paint. In a few thrilling minutes I vandalized her car, aerosolling bizarre hieroglyphs over the doors and windscreen in what I imagined was an interplanetary language.

A traffic warden reported me to my aunt, but she managed to hush up the incident. We both knew that I was trying to punish my parents, but from then on she regarded me as a fallen angel. It no longer mattered what television I watched, a state of disgrace that heartened me for years. Damaging Penrose's car had been almost as satisfying. For a few seconds, despite myself, I felt like a boy again, with all the covert powers that a disturbed child wielded over the adult world.

The helicopter soared away, reflected in the mirror curtain-walling of the Crédit-Suisse building. The blonde woman with the laptop had gone. Her crushed tissue, still bearing the imprint of her lips, drifted across the floor to my feet. I held the waxy smear to my nostrils, inhaling the faint but potent scent.

A hand gripped my shoulder, almost forcing me to my knees.

'Paul, so this is where you hide . . . God, I envy you.'

Wilder Penrose beamed at me, unaware that he had knocked over my wine glass. He took the tissue from my fingers and dabbed at the stained cloth, leaving a vermilion smear. He wore another of his linen suits, a black silk tie fluttering like a miniature noose from his heavy throat. His eyes watched me in their unblinking way, detached from the rest of his face and from the broad smile that seemed to signal his genuine pleasure at finding me.

'Paul, I'm sorry – away from the clinic I'm unbelievably clumsy. Let's get you another drink.' Penrose signalled to the waitress, and gazed around him with unfeigned delight. 'It's lovely here. Luckily, I have a quiet day.'

'No patients? Isn't that a mark of success?'

'Sadly, there isn't a doctor in the world who would agree with you.'

When the waitress served his coffee Penrose broke open a sachet of sugar. His fingers were as awkward as a child's, and the loose grains clung to his knuckles when he sank his broad upper lip through the chocolate-speckled foam. Behind him, the waitress was clearing the blonde woman's table. She had left a mess of debris, tissues stained with coffee, cream spilt onto the paper cloth. Were bad table manners a quirk of Eden-Olympia's executive class, a safety valve for corporate tensions?

The Japanese sports saloon was parked near the lake, the dent in its door clearly visible. Penrose followed my gaze.

'Do you want a spin? It's an interesting car. Rather like your Harvard, I imagine.'

'Another time.' Calmly, I said: 'You've had a bump. Cutting corners too fast?'

'Only in my professional life. Those *clochards* in Cannes, mostly old soixante-huitards. They see a tribute to modern industrial genius and can't resist giving it a swift kick.'

Penrose watched me while he spoke, head lowered over his coffee as he licked up the foam, well aware that I had damaged the car. Surprisingly, I felt no guilt, almost as if I had acted with his approval.

'Now, what's the verdict on Eden-Olympia? You've settled in?'

'That took ten minutes. The villa is very comfortable – for a haunted house.'

'Good. And Señora Morales?'

'The body and soul of discretion. She wouldn't be shocked if I sneaked a fourteen-year-old up to the bedroom.'

'You should try it . . .' Penrose used his forefinger to clean the last drops from his cup. 'Of course, in her eyes you already have.'

'Jane? She's more mature than she looks.'

'I work with her, Paul. She's wiser than I'll ever be. As it happens, prepubertal betrothals are still common in rural Spain. It helps to advance the menarche and accelerate the supply of young farmhands. What about your neighbours?'

'We've met the Delages. Very new Europe, and extremely helpful. Mrs Yasuda bows to me, but I haven't got closer than thirty feet.'

'People at Eden-Olympia don't mix. It's a problem we're working on. By the time they get home they want to be alone, fix a martini, swim a few lengths. Their true social life is the office.'

'That sounds like a design error. Jane and I go into Cannes just to talk to the tourists at the next table.'

'I've tried that – odd, isn't it?' Penrose muffled his voice. 'Don't they seem a little strange?'

'Tourists in Cannes?'

'People outside Eden-Olympia. In some way a dimension is missing. There's a lack of self-corroboration. They stroll along the Croisette, talk about their flights to Düsseldorf and Cleveland, but it's all unreal. If you stand back for a moment, tourists are a very odd phenomenon. Millions of people crossing the world to wander around unfamiliar cities. Tourism must be the last surviving relic of the great Bronze Age migrations.'

'So they should stay at home?'

'Yes, but that won't help them. Go into Cannes and look around – the checkout girls at the Monoprix, the chauffeur walking a poodle, the dentist and his receptionist having their *cinq à sept* in a backstreet hotel. They're like actors improvising their roles, unaware that the production has moved on.'

'To Eden-Olympia? I haven't seen a copy of the script.'

'It's still being written. We'll all take part – the Delages, you and Jane and Mrs Yasuda. It's the only script that matters.'

'Let me guess.' I finished my wine and placed the empty glass in front of Penrose, wondering how long it would take him to knock it over. 'The characters never meet, except in the office.

There's no drama and no conflict. There are no clubs or evening classes . . .'

'We don't need them. They serve no role.'

'No charities or church fêtes. No fund-raising galas.'

'Everyone is rich. Or at least, very well off.'

'No police or legal system.'

'There's no crime, and no social problems.'

'No democratic accountability. No one votes. So who runs things?'

'We do. We run things.' Penrose spoke soothingly, exposing his badly bitten nails as if trying to present himself as vulnerable but sincere. 'Years ago people took for granted that the future meant more leisure. That's true for the less skilled and less able, those who aren't net contributors to society.'

'Such as?'

'Poets, traffic wardens, ecologists . . .' Penrose gestured dismissively, and struck my wine glass with his hand. He settled it on the table, embarrassed by his clumsiness, and continued: 'I'm being unfair, but I know you agree with me. For the talented and ambitious the future means work, not play.'

'Depressing. No recreation at all?'

'Only of a special kind. Talk to senior people at Eden-Olympia. They've gone beyond leisure. Playing around with balls of various shapes and sizes . . .' Penrose tripped over his tongue, and paused to flex his lips. 'That's something they left behind in childhood. Work is where they find their real fulfilment – running an investment bank, designing an airport, bringing on stream a new family of antibiotics. If their work is satisfying people don't need leisure in the old-fashioned sense. No one ever asks what Newton or Darwin did to relax, or how Bach spent his weekends. At Eden-Olympia work is the ultimate play, and play the ultimate work.'

'There's one thing missing. All I see are a lot of office buildings and car parks in a faked-up landscape. What happens to the law and the church? Where are the moral compass bearings that hold everything together?'

'They fall away. We shed them, like that brace you got rid of once you could stand on your own legs.'

'So Eden-Olympia has gone beyond morality?'

'In a sense, yes.' Controlling his clumsy hands, Penrose moved my wine glass to the next table. 'Remember, Paul, the old morality belonged to a cruder stage of human development. It had to cope with packs of hunter-scavengers who'd only just left the Serengeti plain. The first religions were forced to deal with barely socialized primates who'd tear each other's arms off given half a chance. Since they couldn't rely on self-control they needed ethical taboos to do it for them.'

'So, goodbye to the old morality. What then?'

'Freedom. A giant multinational like Fuji or General Motors sets its own morality. The company defines the rules that govern how you treat your spouse, where you educate your children, the sensible limits to stock-market investment. The bank decides how big a mortgage you can handle, the right amount of health insurance to buy. There are no more moral decisions than there are on a new superhighway. Unless you own a Ferrari, pressing the accelerator is not a moral decision. Ford and Fiat and Toyota have engineered in a sensible response curve. We can rely on their judgement, and that leaves us free to get on with the rest of our lives. We've achieved real freedom, the freedom from morality.'

Penrose sat back, hands raised to the air, part conjuror and part revivalist preacher. He was watching me to see how I reacted, less interested in converting me than in extracting a grudging concession that he might be right. At some point in his life, at his medical school or during his psychiatric training, someone had failed to take him seriously.

Unconvinced by his case, I said: 'It sounds like a ticket to 1984, this time by the scenic route. I thought organization man died out in the 1960s.'

'He did, our worried friend in the grey-flannel suit. He was an early office-dwelling hominid, a corporate version of Dawn Man who assumed a sedentary posture in order to survive. He was locked into a low-tech bureaucratic cave, little more than a human punch-card. Today's professional men and women are self-motivated. The corporate pyramid is a virtual hierarchy that endlessly reassembles itself around them. They enjoy enormous mobility. While you're mooning around here, Paul, they're patenting another gene, or designing the next generation of drugs that will cure cancer and double your life-span.'

'I'm impressed. Eden-Olympia is the new paradise. You should put up a sign.'

'We might, one day, but we don't want to boast.' Penrose beamed at me, broad smile lighting up his dead eyes. 'At long last, people are free to enjoy themselves, though most of them haven't realized it yet. In many ways I'm a kind of leisure coordinator. I run the adventure playground inside their heads. It's open to everyone here. You can explore your hidden dreams, the secret places of your heart. You can follow your imagination, wherever it leads.'

'Ennui, adultery and cocaine?'

'If you want to, but they're rather old-fashioned. You're a pilot, Paul, you've flown above the clouds. You owe it to yourself to be more inventive.'

'That sounds like a head-on collision with the law. Or a new kind of psychopathology.'

'Paul . . .' Pretending to be exasperated, Penrose leaned back with a deep sigh. 'The rich know how to cope with the psychopathic. The squirearchy have always enjoyed freedoms denied to the tenant farmers and peasantry. De Sade's behaviour was typical of his class. Aristocracies keep alive those endangered pleasures that repel the bourgeoisie. They may seem perverse, but they add to the possibilities of life.'

'That's a curious thing for a psychiatrist to say.'

'Not at all. Perverse behaviours were once potentially dangerous. Societies weren't strong enough to allow them to flourish.'

'But Eden-Olympia is strong enough?'

'Of course.' Penrose spoke soothingly, as if to a favourite
patient. 'You're free here, Paul. Perhaps for the first time in
your life.'

Penrose was watching me, curious to see my reactions, a forgotten smile lingering on his lips like a tide-mark. I wondered
why he was making this evangelical play for me, and whether he
had talked to Jane. Then I thought of another, more impressionable doctor.

'Free? It's hard to know how loose the handcuffs really are.
Did you discuss this with David Greenwood?'

'Probably. I'm something of a proselytizer. The middle classes
have run the world since the French Revolution, but they're
now the new proletariat. It's time for another elite to set the
agenda.'

'How did David take all this?'

'I think he agreed. By the way, he visited me professionally.'

'What was his problem? Too much sympathy for the poor and
orphaned?'

'I can't disclose that.' Penrose smoothed his silk tie. 'He was a
generous man, likeable in a boyish way. But . . . very repressed.'

'Sexually?'

'A little. I wanted David to be more robust, to strike out more
fearlessly.'

'Where?' I gestured at the lake and the sun-filled atria of
the office buildings. 'I don't see a rainforest waiting for its Dr
Livingstone. He shot ten people. Three of them in the back as
they ran away from him.'

'I know. Zander told me about the bullets. That's why I
dropped by. I can see you're unsettled.' Penrose chewed on a
thumbnail, pensively sniffing the eroded crescent. 'David could
be very naive, as he showed with his Lewis Carroll society. He

didn't realize that the French see the Alice books as a realistic picture of English life. Eden-Olympia failed David Greenwood, and we paid a heavy price. At least there were only ten deaths.'

'Only?'

'There's a rumour that he planned to kill more than ten people.' Penrose stared over my head into some private space, and rose heavily from the table. 'I must go. I'll tell Jane you're idling away here.'

'She won't mind. Work is all she thinks about.'

'Paul? That's close to self-pity.' Penrose raised a reproving finger. 'She's running a new computer model, tracing the spread of nasal viruses across Eden-Olympia. She has a hunch that if people moved their chairs a further eighteen inches apart they'd stop the infectious vectors in their tracks.'

'I thought people here were too far apart as it is.'

'Only in some ways. If the dance floor is less crowded you can really do your stuff.' Penrose pumped his arms in an energetic twist that knocked his chair to the floor. He stood behind me, large hands on my shoulders, as if reluctant to leave. 'The dance floor's empty, Paul. Make the most of it. If you want to, pick your tune . . .'

I listened to the fading burble of his exhaust, and then returned to my scrutiny of the lake. In front of me lay Penrose's debris, the swamped saucer, soaked tissues and coffee-stained sugar sachets. A passer-by would assume that he had been spoonfeeding a child.

A spoon of a notional kind had been pushed towards me, but what titbit lay inside it? I guessed that Penrose was using me to explore the Greenwood murders, to act as his proxy in an investigation he declined to share. Rather too casually, he had thrown in the 'rumour' that there had been other intended victims.

I took the appointments list from my wallet and spread it across the table. I scanned the names, with my scribbled comments identifying their posts at Eden–Olympia. Asterisks marked those who had died.

    Alain Delage. *CFO, Eden-Olympia holding company.*

   * Michel Charbonneau. *Chairman, Eden-Olympia holding company.*

   * Robert Fontaine. *Chief executive, E-O administration.*

   * Olga Carlotti. *Manager of personnel recruitment, E-O.*

   * Guy Bachelet. *Chief of security, E-O.*

   * Georges Vadim. *General manager, TV Centre, E-O.*

   * Dominique Serrou. *Physician.*

   * Professor Berthoud. *Chief Pharmacist.*

    Walter Beckman. *Chairman, Beckman Securities. Relocated New York City.*

    Henry Ogilvy. *Insurance broker. Ex-Lloyd's syndicate partner. Relocated Florida.*

    Shohei Narita. *President, investment bank. Former Greenwood neighbour.*

    F.D. ?

    Pascal Zander.

    Wilder Penrose.

Seven of the first eight had been killed by Greenwood, only forty-eight hours after he began to schedule their appointments. Two of the victims were fellow physicians at the clinic, and Jane had pointed out that doctors arranged to see their colleagues informally. Penrose, moreover, sat in the next office.

Alain Delage headed the list. I remembered that Simone had mentioned their trip to Lausanne. Had they stayed at Eden-Olympia, she told me, they would have witnessed the violent tragedy of the final shoot-out.

But perhaps more closely than she guessed. As I stared at the list I realized that I was looking at a schedule of appointments, but of a special kind. What I had taken from Jane's computer was a selection of targets.

A hit list?

11

Thoughts of Saint-Exupéry

'MONSIEUR DELAGE! COULD you wait? Alain . . . !'

I had left the Jaguar a hundred yards from the administration building, in the only free parking space I could find. As I limped between the lines of cars I shouted to the dark-suited figure who emerged from the revolving doors. Except at a distance, exchanging good mornings outside our garages, we had never spoken. Not recognizing my raised voice, Delage lowered his head and stepped behind a male aide. The chauffeur held open the door of his limousine, gloved fist raised warningly at me.

'Alain . . . I'm glad I caught you.' I stepped past the aide, who was handing a black valise through the open window. He barred my way, but I pushed him aside. The chauffeur's hands gripped my shoulders from behind, and he tried to wrestle me to the ground. I propped myself against the car, held his lapels and threw him against the boot. Then a far stronger pair of arms seized me around the waist, pinning my elbows to my chest. I could feel a security guard's hot breath on my neck. He swung me off balance, kicked my heels away and bundled me to the hard asphalt.

Delage looked down from the window, moustache bristling and pallid eyes alarmed behind his rimless spectacles. Then he recognized the dishevelled Englishman, cheeks grazed with gravel, trying breathlessly to call to him.

'Mr Sinclair? It's you?'

'Alain . . .' I forced the guard's hand from my chest and drew the appointments list from my pocket. 'Read this . . . you may be in danger.'

'Paul? Can you breathe? I wasn't expecting us to meet in quite this way.'

Delage stood by the car, blinking at me with concern as he dusted the grit from my jacket. I rested on the passenger seat, leaning against the open door with my feet on the ground.

'I'm fine. Give me a moment.' I tested my knee, relieved that the pins still held. 'Sorry to ambush you like that. There may be a threat to your life.'

'Let's think about *your* life, Paul. I can call the clinic. Jane will come with the medical team.'

'Don't bother her.' I saluted the security man, still watching me warily, radio at the ready. The chauffeur was limping across the drive to retrieve his peaked cap, which the aide had located under a nearby car. 'I'm glad security is up to scratch. He was quick off the mark.'

'Naturally.' Delage seemed glad. 'After all that happened last May. If you want to kill someone at Eden-Olympia it's best to make an appointment. Now, you spoke of danger?'

'Right . . .' I opened the crushed printout. 'I took this from a computer in Greenwood's office. Jane came across it by chance. She doesn't know that I have it.'

'I understand. Go on, Paul.'

'It's a list of names, drawn up by Greenwood two days before the murders. Seven of the people listed he shot dead.'

'Tragic, for them and the families. Every day I thank God we were away.'

'Your name is top of the list.'

Delage took the sheet from me and stared hard at the list with his accountant's eye. He ducked his head in an oddly uneasy way, as if he had just overheard some unpleasant corridor gossip about himself.

'I'm here, yes. Why, I can't imagine.' He folded the sheet, punctiliously using the original creases. 'You have a copy of this?'

'Keep it. It's only a guess, but it may be a target list. If Greenwood had collaborators you could still be in danger.'

'You were right to show it to me. I'll pass it to Mr Zander.' He spoke quickly to his aide, a slim young man who still seemed shaken by our brief confrontation. He took the printout and headed towards the building. Delage watched him disappear through the revolving doors and then turned to me, his manicured hand brushing the last dust from my jacket. He was clearly weighing the seriousness of my message against my scruffy appearance.

'Paul, you've put your spare time to good use. I'm off to Nice Airport, but we can speak en route to the heli-shuttle in Cannes. Afterwards the car will bring you back. It's not often that you see your name on a death list . . .'

The limousine moved swiftly through the outskirts of Le Cannet, a target safely ahead of any possible attacker. Through the window divider I watched the chauffeur speaking on the carphone, eyes meeting mine in the rear-view mirror. No doubt the security apparatus at Eden-Olympia was at full alert, with a Range Rover parked outside the Delages' house.

But Alain had recovered his poise. The tentative hands that had straightened my shirt and jacket emerged from crisp cuffs that concealed the strong tendons of his wrists. I guessed that he had been a dedicated athlete in his earlier days, handicapped by poor sight and the seriousness of a born accountant. Behind the expensive suiting a masculine tension was waiting to be released. I could see him ranging along the baseline, playing his methodical returns as he watched for his opponent's weaknesses, now and then attempting a lob or backhand pass that never quite found its mark. I remembered that he had been present at the brutal beating in the clinic car park, one of the executives who had stopped their cars to watch a display of summary justice at its most unpleasant. The beatings had probably helped to draw some of the tension from him, but he was a man who would never completely relax, except in the company of his passive and ever-watchful wife.

I assumed that he had already amortised the threat to himself. In an effort to distract me, he pointed to a heritage sign at the junction with the Mougins road.

'If you're interested in painting, Bonnard's house is here in Le Cannet. Picasso worked at Antibes, Matisse further down the coast at Nice. In many ways modern art was a culture of the beach. They say it's the light, the special quality of quartz in the Permian rock.'

He spoke in the fluent, uninflected English of the international executive, with the kind of arts connoisseurship picked up in the antique shops that lined the lobbies of luxury hotels. I gazed at the roadside, lined with speedboat dealerships, video warehouses and swimming-pool showrooms. Together they crowded the few spaces between the autoroute access ramps.

'The light? Or were people more cheerful then? Picasso and Matisse have gone, and the business parks have taken their place.'

'But that's good. It's the turn of the sciences. Everything is possible again – organisms with radial tyres, dreams equipped with airbags. What do you think of our new silicon valley? You've had the leisure to look around.'

'I'm impressed, though leisure is in short supply. The new Côte d'Azur doesn't have time for fun.'

'That will change.' Delage gripped his briefcase, as if about to offer me a position paper. 'People realize they can work too hard, even if work is more enjoyable than play. Your countryman, David Greenwood, was a sad example.'

'You knew him well?'

'We were neighbours, of course, but he was always busy with

the refuge at La Bocca. We never met socially – my wife found him far too earnest. She likes to sunbathe, and it made him uncomfortable, he would even lower the blinds.' Delage stared at his thighs, and then hid them behind his briefcase. 'Now, this list. I'm grateful for your concern, but I doubt if these names are what you think. Perhaps Greenwood was drawing up a group of volunteers for a medical experiment.'

'It's possible. Though he did shoot seven of them. Is there any reason why he might have wanted to kill you?'

'None. It's inconceivable. Believe me, find a different approach. I hear you have new evidence.'

'Three spent bullets. I handed them in to Zander this afternoon. I'm surprised you know.'

'Monsieur Zander and I speak all the time. Tell me, Paul, how good is our security?'

'First class. There's no doubt about it.'

'Even so, you were able to get within a few feet of me. Suppose you had been carrying a gun? Who told you I was leaving for Nice?'

'No one. I wanted to see you at your office. It was pure chance.'

'Chance can work for terrorists. Pursue your enquiries, but keep Zander informed. You may come up with something important.'

'Unlikely. Apart from this list there's nothing to go on. I need to know the exact sequence of deaths that morning. It might explain Greenwood's state of mind.'

'Ten people were killed – what does the sequence matter?' Delage pushed his glasses against his eyes, scanning the small print of my quibbles and queries. 'Your friend wasn't designing a ballet.'

'All the same, the pattern of deaths may say something. Who was the first to die?'

'I've no idea. Try *Nice-Matin*, they have an office in Cannes. The municipal library has back copies of important newspapers.'

'And the police?'

'If you want to waste your time. They're happy to have an Englishman who went mad without cause. That's your historical role.'

'We're the village idiot of the new Europe?'

'The misfit, the holy fool. Think of David Greenwood, this poor poetic doctor with his children's shelter . . .' Delage spoke with pleasant but cruel humour, part of the sadistic strain in this repressed accountant that I had already noticed. He moved into the corner of the leather seating and observed me in his steely way. 'You're very concerned with Greenwood – it may be that you need a mystery. Did you know him well?'

'Hardly at all.'

'And Jane? Slightly better, perhaps?'

'No husband can ever say.' Moving on from his veiled suggestion, I spoke briskly: 'I'm impressed by Eden-Olympia, but there are things that seem deliberately out of focus. Putting us in Greenwood's house. Giving Jane the same office. It's as if someone is flashing a torch in the dark, sending a message we should try to decode. Half the victims were senior managers at Eden-Olympia. Suppose there are rival groups locked in a power struggle? You say Greenwood was your holy fool, but a better term might be fall guy. I haven't seen any evidence yet that he fired a single shot.'

Delage flicked at a loose thread on his cuff. I had taken a gamble, rattling my stick in an apparently empty kennel, in the hope that a drowsing beast might emerge.

'The evidence is there, Paul . . .' Delage had withdrawn behind his watery lenses. 'I'll speak to Zander: we need to be less secretive. Eden-Olympia is home to the greatest corporations in the world. Their chief executives are too valuable to risk in a small local feud. Greenwood killed his victims, stalking them one by one. Secretaries saw him walk through their offices and open fire. As they knelt behind their desks they were showered with their employers' blood.'

'Even so . . .'

But Delage was speaking to the chauffeur as we rolled down the Boulevard de la République, past the elegant apartment houses that lay below the heights of Super-Cannes. I sat forward when we reached the Croisette, for once needing to get my bearings in the maze of afternoon traffic. Crowds strolled under the palms, enjoying the warm autumn day, like citizens of another world who had come ashore for a few hours. Wilder Penrose had been right to say that there was something unreal about them.

Delage beckoned to me. 'Paul, the Noga Hilton. There are nice shops in the lobby. Buy Jane a present.'

'I will.'

'Simone and I are very fond of her. She has an ingénue's charm and directness. Why keep her to yourself? You should join more in our social life.'

'Is there such a thing?'

'It's private, but very active. Work is so enjoyable, while play is demanding. It requires special qualities and offers special rewards.' He opened the nearside door for me and stared at the sea. 'I envy you, Paul, but be careful. You're a pilot, like Saint-Exupéry – and he ended there, lying in the deep water . . .'

As he held out his hand I noticed the livid bruises above his wrist, the blue and yellow clouds of damaged skin hidden by his shirt cuffs. I imagined him involved in a masochistic game with his bored wife, probably involving more than a brisk rap on the knuckles. Behind the rimless glasses I could see an almost Calvinist repression at work. At the same time he seemed to be smiling at some unexpected good fortune, like a suburban bank manager discovering a book of intriguing phone numbers left by his predecessor.

'*Nice-Matin* – check them out, Paul.'

'I will. Don't worry, I'll get a present for Jane.'

'Good.' He waved from the window as the limousine slid away. 'And think about Saint-Exupéry . . .'

12

A Fast Drive to Nice Airport

A PUBLICITY PLANE flew along the Croisette, its pennant fluttering like the trace of a fibrillating heart, unnoticed by the sunbathers stretched on their loungers in the hotel concessions. The pilot banked steeply when he was level with the Martinez and soared towards Juan-les-Pins and the Antibes peninsula, his propeller shredding the air and throwing shards of sunlight across the vivid sea.

I watched until it disappeared, wishing that I sat in the cockpit of my old Harvard, deafened by the roar of the engine and gagging on the stench of lubricating oil, flight plan clipped to my knee, three bottles of iced beer in a cool-bag hanging from the throttle mount, cigar smouldering in the ashtray sellotaped to the instrument panel. I needed the rush of icy air over the canopy, and the flood of light that irrigated every cell in the retina, every waiting space in the soul.

At the public beach near the Palais des Festivals the speedboats of the water-ski school rocked beside the landing stage as their customers buckled on the safety harnesses. Tourists crowded the Croisette, amiable Americans on short-stay package deals, Germans of technical mind studying the microlight seaplanes moored to the wooden piers, restless Arabs on the terrace of the Carlton, bored with sex and drugs, and waiting for the gaming rooms to open.

There was a whiff of crepes and frites from the lunch stalls, but Wilder Penrose's strictures had begun to bite. The crowds drifted in slow motion, gathering in clumps around the tabacs and the bureaux de change like platelets blocking an artery. With their camcorders and light meters, body bags packed with spare lenses, they resembled a huge film crew without a script.

I was frustrated, and knew it. My irritation was magnified by Alain Delage's veiled threat. He had flattered me by referring to Saint-Exupéry, but the great pilot's bones lay on the seabed in the remains of his Lightning, somewhere near the Baie des Anges. I could take the hint. But why had Delage bothered to give me a lift into Cannes, unless my plumb-line was at last touching bottom?

As he suggested, I visited the offices of *Nice-Matin*. The back issues told me nothing about David Greenwood and his day of death, and how this amateur marksman had managed to seize his hostages and then kill his victims, despite the substantial distances involved and the elaborate security. There were photographs of Greenwood posing with his orphans at the La Bocca refuge, but no conceivable bridge between the smiling, dark-eyed girls and the harsh news pictures of bullet-starred doors and bloody elevators.

The microfiche copies of the *Herald Tribune* in the American Library were no more use. A helpful assistant suggested a local newspaper for English-speaking residents, but after a taxi ride to La Napoule I found only the back-street office of a free-sheet listing properties for sale, swimming-pool constructors and dealers in used Mercedes.

Drained by the sun, I walked past the car-park entrance to the Palais des Festivals. The heat rose from the ornamental tiles like a headache. Behind me, ten yards to my left, a blonde woman in a dark suit followed me across the terrace. Face shielded from the sun by a copy of *Vogue*, she tottered along on high-heels, as if trying to sidestep her own shadow. Then it occurred to me that she might be drunk, and I thought of the air-conditioned bars hidden away in the Palais des Festivals.

Here, in the much-derided pink bunker, where the competing entries in the film festival were screened each May, a congress of orthopaedic surgery was taking place. The American and German tourists I had so looked down on were probably distinguished surgeons from Topeka and Düsseldorf, far closer in spirit to Eden-Olympia than I assumed.

I stepped from the sun into the cool of the foyer, where an accreditation desk was issuing passes to the delegates. Without exception, the surgeons wore trainers and sportswear, and for once my trousers and thong sandals allowed me to merge seamlessly into the crowd. The attendants checking the delegates' badges waved me through. Leaving the others to attend a lecture on tuberculosis of the hip joint, I strolled towards a trade fair on the ground floor. Sales staff patrolled their stands, filled with displays of surgical armatures and corrective body-appliances.

Remembering my modest knee-brace, I stopped by a glass cabinet that displayed two lifesize mannequins in full orthopaedic rig. Replicas of a man and a woman, they each wore a cuirass of pink plastic around the torso, and their jaws were supported by moulded collars that encased them from the lower lip to the nape of the neck. Elaborately sculptured corslets and cuisses, like the fantasies of an obsessive armourer, surrounded their hips and thighs, discreet apertures provided for whatever natural functions were still left to these hybrid creatures.

'Dear God . . .' an English voice murmured over my shoulder. 'Now we know. Love in Eden-Olympia . . .'

I turned to find the tipsy woman in the business suit who had followed me across the terrace. Her make-up was still in place, but the sunlight had drawn a film of perspiration through her lipstick and eye shadow. As she swayed on her high-heels I assumed that she was the raunchy wife of a British surgeon attending the congress, an afternoon vamp on the Croisette prowl.

'Marriage à la mode . . .' She pressed her hands against the display case and peered challengingly at the models. 'But do they love each other? What do you say, Mr Sinclair?'

She steered the blonde hair from her forehead, and I recognized the woman with the laptop who had sat near me in the open-air café near the Elf building. She was sober but ill at ease, her fingers fretting at the copy of *Vogue* she carried. A male sales assistant moved past us, and she handed him the magazine, waving him away before he could speak. I noticed the dust on her shoes, and assumed that she had been following me for longer than the brief walk across the terrace of the Palais des Festivals.

Irritated that Eden-Olympia was keeping its cyclops eye on me, I tried to step around her, tripped over an uncovered cable and pulled my knee. Wincing at the sudden pain, I leaned against the display case.

'Mr Sinclair?' Her hands steadied me. 'Are you . . . ?'

'Don't tell me, I know . . .' I pointed to the orthopaedic models. 'I've come to the right place.'

'You need to sit down. There's a bar upstairs.'

'Thanks, but I have to go.'

'I'll buy you a drink.'

'I don't need a drink.' Annoyed by the clinging edginess, I spoke sharply. 'You work at Eden-Olympia. For Pascal Zander?'

'Who could? I'm in the property services department – Frances Baring.' She frowned into the mirror of her compact, stung by the rebuff and irritated with herself for having to approach me so clumsily. 'Please, Mr Sinclair. I need to talk to you about an old friend of ours.'

As the waiter took our order she tore a sachet of salt and poured the grains into the ashtray. She twisted the paper square into an arrow and pointed it at me.

Still unsure why this attractive but prickly woman had approached me, I said: 'We're neighbours – I saw you this afternoon at Eden-Olympia.'

'Alcatraz-sur-Mer.'

'Where?'

'Catch up. It's my nickname for Eden-Olympia.'

'Not bad. But is it a prison?'

'Of course. It pretends to be a space station. People like Pascal Zander are really living on Mars.'

I stopped her mutilating a second sachet. 'Frances, relax. Our drinks are coming.'

'Sorry.' She flashed a quick smile. 'I hate this kind of thing. I'd never have made a good whore. I could cope with the sex, but all those smoky glances across crowded lobbies . . . . I wanted to talk to you, away from Eden-Olympia. I'm due to see your wife soon, I believe.'

'Jane?'

'Yes. One of the endless check-ups Eden-Olympia arranges. When they find nothing wrong you love them all the more. I look forward to meeting her.'

'She helps out with colonoscopies.'

'You mean she'll put a camera up my bottom? I've always wanted to be on television. What about you?'

'I'm on holiday. It's lasted a little longer than I planned.'

'We've all noticed. You're the Ben Gunn of our treasure island. I thought you were writing a social history of the car park.'

'I should. It's like Los Angeles, the car parks tend to find you, wherever you are. My legs need the exercise – they're getting over a flying accident.'

'Yes, you're a pilot . . .' She lit a cigarette, briefly setting fire to the ashtray. 'Does that mean you have an interesting sex life?'

'I hope so – I'm a devoted husband. That must strike you as totally deviant.'

'No. Just a little against nature. Rather romantic, though.'

Tired of this forced banter, I waved away the cigarette smoke and tried to meet her eyes. Was she holding me here until Zander's men arrived? A team could have followed Delage's limousine to Cannes, tipped off by the aide, then lost me as I zigzagged on my abortive errands. Frances Baring had picked up the trail as I wandered along the Croisette.

But if she was a femme fatale she was a surprisingly inept one, working on her own with only the roughest idea of how to pursue her agenda. I was struck by how much she differed from Jane. My teenage doctor was girlish but supremely confident, while Frances was sophisticated but unsure of herself, probably climbing the upper slopes of the corporate pyramid with little more than her scatty humour to protect her. I looked over the balcony at the orthopaedic mannequins wearing their fetishist armour. Jane would break down in guffaws if I suggested that she wore one of the cuirasses as an erotic aid, but I could imagine Frances harnessing up without comment.

Seeing me smile at her, she sipped her drink and then held the glass between us, exposing the waxy imprint of her lips like the forensic trace of a kiss, the second I had seen that day.

'Right, Paul,' she announced. 'I'm relaxed.'

'Good. Now, who is the friend we share? Friendship isn't that common at Eden-Olympia.'

'This friend isn't there any more.' Her fingers moved towards a salt sachet, stopped and calmed themselves by eviscerating the stub of her cigarette. 'He died a few months ago. Last May, in fact . . .'

'David Greenwood?' When she nodded, her face clouding, I said: 'How long have you been at Eden-Olympia?'

'Three years. It feels longer since David died.'

'You were close?'

'On and off. He was very busy.'

'The children's refuge, the methadone clinic. And the Alice library.'

'Alice, yes. "Never seen by waking eyes . . ."' She stared at the imprint on her glass, unaware that her lips were moving, a sub-vocal message across the void.

Concerned for her, I reached out and steadied her hands. 'Were you there on May 28?'

'In my office at the Siemens building. I was there all day.'

'You saw the police arrive and heard the shooting?'

'Absolutely. Helicopters, ambulances, film crews . . . the whole nightmare played itself out like an insane video game. I haven't really woken up.'

'I understand.' I held her empty glass, hot from the fever of her hands. 'All those deaths. They hardly seem possible.'

'Why?' She frowned at me, assuming that I was making some abstruse point. 'Everything's possible at Eden-Olympia. That's its *raison d'être*.'

'But the murders don't chime with Greenwood's character. He was a builder, a creator of projects, not a destroyer. Jane says he was an old-style idealist.'

'Maybe that explains it all – idealists can be dangerous.'

'You're saying he shot all those people from some higher motive?'

'What other reason is there? A sudden "brainstorm"?'

'It seems likely.'

'Eden-Olympia is a brainstorm.' She spoke with soft disgust. 'Wilder Penrose is storming the brains . . .'

'I take it you don't like the place?'

'I love it.' She signalled to the waiter, ordering another round of drinks. 'I make three times the salary I did in London, there are perks galore, a gorgeous flat at Marina Baie des Anges. And all the games I want to play.'

'Are there any games? The sports clubs are empty.'

'Not that sort of game.' She watched me with the first real curiosity, her eyes running over my tweed sports jacket. 'These are games of a different night.'

'They sound like quite an effort.'

'They are. Games at Eden-Olympia are always the serious kind.'

'The man who gave me a lift to Cannes seemed to be saying that.'

'Alain Delage? Be careful with him. He looks like a mousy accountant but he's a textbook anal-sadist.'

'You must know him well. Were you lovers?'

'I don't think so. His wife is more my type but she plays hard to get. That's the trouble with Eden-Olympia – you can't remember if you once had sex with someone. Like Marbella or . . . Maida Vale.'

She had tossed in my London address, a friendly warning that she knew more about me than I assumed. But I was sure now that Frances Baring was not working for Zander or anyone else at Eden-Olympia. For reasons of her own she had set up our accidental encounter, and was now pretending to flirt with me, unsure whether I was worth the effort. In her edgy way, nervous of being rebuffed, she was reaching out to me. I sensed that she needed my help, but would take her time in coming to the point. Already I had warmed to her, to the tart tongue and wary eyes, to the full figure she casually used to keep the waiters in their place. At last I had met someone who was a direct link to David Greenwood and not afraid to speak her mind.

'You wanted to talk about Greenwood,' I reminded her. 'How well did you know him?'

'We met at official functions, topping-out ceremonies. He was lonely and didn't realize it. But you understand how that feels.'

'Am I lonely?'

'Limping around all day?' She brushed her cigarette ash from my sleeve, and seemed almost concerned for me. 'Poor man, I've watched you.'

'Frances . . . could someone else have carried out the killings? Suppose David was framed. A young English doctor . . .'

'No.' Her eyes roamed around the bar, in search of another drink, but she spoke distinctly. 'David killed them – seven of them, anyway.'

'And the hostages?'

'I doubt it. Not much point.'

'The Cannes police say they were shot in the garage. Everyone accepts that, like the brainstorm explanation.'

'It's the perfect alibi.' She lowered her voice as two elderly American surgeons in tracksuits sat at the next table. 'But it only just worked. David Greenwood nearly destroyed Eden-Olympia. Huge amounts of corporate funding were pulled out. We had to renegotiate leases, cut rents and offer rebates that were practically bribes. Who cares about a couple of dead chauffeurs?'

'All the same, there's something going on. It's not a conspiracy, or even a cover-up. David may have killed those people, but no one will say why.' I took a spare copy of the appointments list from my breast pocket and placed it in front of Frances. 'Recognize the names?'

'All of them.' She ran a varnished finger down the column, stabbing at those who had died. 'Mostly the great and the good.'

'I took it from David's computer. I think it's a hit list.'

'That makes sense. It even includes Wilder Penrose. Good for David – let's kill all the psychiatrists.'

'You don't like Penrose?'

'He's charming, in that brutal way of his. Eden-Olympia is a huge experiment for him. All that brochure-speak about the first intelligent city, the ideas laboratory for the future. He takes it seriously.'

'Don't you?'

'Sure. We're the vanguard of a new world-aristocracy. Penrose would get a shock if he knew that one of his prize pupils set out after breakfast to kill him.'

'I don't think he'd mind.'

'Of course not. He'd be flattered.' She scanned the names. 'Robert Fontaine – he was rather charming. Very Walloon, loved Clovis Trouille and all those nuns being buggered. Olga Carlotti, head of personnel. Tough luck, she was Eden-Olympia's uncrowned queen. A cool, glamorous dyke.'

'Are you sure?'

'You sound shocked. She had the pick of the office juniors. Guy Bachelet, head of security. Superbly lecherous, a great loss. He often needed a safehouse for the private detectives he brought in from Marseilles. Spent his time gazing at my legs.' Frances returned the list to me. 'Sad, isn't it? One moment you're propositioning the hired help, and the next you're looking down at your own brains spattered across the desk . . .'

'You heard the shots?'

'Not really. Alarms started ringing, all the elevators stopped. I was amazed at the number of doors that automatically locked. David got onto the roof of the car park next to our building.'

'And then?'

'The security people pulled their fingers out.'

'So David knew it was all over and went back to the villa?'

'I suppose so.' Frances stared hard at her knuckles. 'David was very sweet. It's sad that Eden-Olympia changed him.'

'How, exactly?'

'The way it changes everyone. People float free of themselves . . .' She frowned at the flushed cheeks in her compact mirror, and picked up the bill. Suddenly keen to leave, she said: 'There's an English-language radio station in Antibes – Riviera News. Last July they broadcast a special feature. The reporter followed the death route. Give them a call.'

We left the mezzanine and walked down to the floor below. As Frances swayed against the display cases I realized that we were slightly drunk, though not from the two glasses of wine.

Frances stopped by the mannequins in their orthopaedic cell. 'All that armour – can you see yourself wearing it to make love?'

'Can you?'

'It might be worth a try. Why not?'

'I wore a knee-brace after my accident. It did nothing for my sex life.'

'How sad . . .' Frances took my arm, as if I were a near-senile cripple who had renounced all earthly pleasures. 'That's the saddest thing I've heard all day . . .'

On the steps of the Palais des Festivals the orthopaedic surgeons were emerging from their lecture. I followed Frances into the narrow streets to the west of the Gray d'Albion Hotel, happy to be in the company of this distracted but glamorous woman. As we passed the American Express office she slipped on the crowded pavement and steadied herself against an open-topped BMW parked by the kerb. She peered into her compact, and examined her teeth.

'My mouth smells like a bar. I'm seeing my dentist in ten minutes. Remember Riviera News.'

'I will.' I touched her cheek, removing a loose eyelash. 'You've helped me a lot over David Greenwood. We could meet here again. I may have more questions you can answer.'

'I'm sure you will.' She stared at me over her sunglasses. 'That's very forward of you, Mr Sinclair.'

'I mean well.'

'I know what you mean.' Her hips pressed against the BMW, and the curvature of its door deflected the lines of her thigh, as if the car was a huge orthopaedic device that expressed a voluptuous mix of geometry and desire. She rooted in her handbag. 'Tell me, how's your car?'

'The Jaguar? Ageing gracefully.'

'I was worried about it. I hear it was involved in a small collision with a Japanese sports saloon.'

'Did Penrose tell you that?'

'Who knows? He's very forgiving. But I'm interested in why you damaged his car.'

'The light was bad.'

'It wasn't.' She waited as three French sailors stepped past, each carefully inspecting her deep cleavage. 'You don't dislike Penrose. So why?'

'It's hard to explain. I was . . . corrupting myself. Eden-Olympia encourages that.'

'Very true. The first sensible thing you've said. We desperately need new vices. Yes, we might well meet . . .'

Before I could reply she waved and strode away, losing herself in the afternoon tourists. I stood in the sunlight, savouring the scented air she had left behind her. I realized that she had never explained what she wanted to talk about, but it no longer mattered.

A group of schoolchildren emerged from a nearby travel agency, and forced me against the BMW. I leaned back, supporting myself on the windscreen. A clutch of holiday brochures lay on the open passenger seat. Tucked beneath them was a set of keys, linked to a medallion that bore the BMW logo, forgotten by the car's owner when he left for a nearby appointment.

The schoolchildren returned in a noisy posse, shouting at a missing friend. As they shielded me from the travel agency windows I unlatched the door of the BMW and slipped into the driver's seat. Traffic blocked the street as I started the engine. When it cleared I pulled out in front of a municipal water cart. Careful not to attract the interest of the policemen on duty outside the Palais des Festivals, I turned onto the eastbound carriageway of the Croisette.

I passed the Majestic, the Carlton and the Martinez, my eyes watching the rear-view mirror, and followed the Croisette towards the Palm Beach casino. Rounding the point, I set off along the free beach where off-duty waiters lounged in their skimpy briefs, watching the young women play volleyball on the chocolate sand.

As I joined the fast corniche road to Golfe-Juan a publicity aircraft was towing its pennant above the lighthouse at La Garoupe. Powerboats cut through the waters around the Îles de Lérins. The cool air moved over the windscreen, carrying away the sweat of fear from my face, urging everything to flow faster through an afternoon of eroticism and possibility.

Relaxing on the coast highway, I changed down to third gear. For the next thirty minutes I drove like a Frenchman, overtaking on the inside lanes, straddling the central marker lines on the most dangerous bends, tailgating any woman driver doing less than seventy, my headlamps flashing, slipping the clutch at traffic lights as the exhaust roared through the muffler and the engine wound itself to a screaming 7000 revs, swerving across double yellows and forcing any oncoming drivers to dig their wheels in the refuse-filled verges.

Only once, surprisingly, did I have a minor accident. Reversing from a cul-de-sac at Cagnes-sur-Mer, I cracked a rear brake light against a badly sited lamp standard. But the highway police who haunted the RN7 had taken off for the day, leaving me alone with the wind and the slipstream.

Three hours later I parked the Jaguar outside our villa. Dusk lay over the lakes and forest trails, and the upper floors of the office buildings seemed to drift above the autumn mist that filled the valley. I switched off the engine, and listened to the sounds of Jane showering in the bathroom. I had left the BMW near the main entrance of Eden-Olympia, and then walked across the business park to the administration building, where earlier that afternoon I had caught up with Alain Delage. Routine security checks the next morning would log the BMW's licence number into the Cannes police computer, and soon reunite the owner with his vehicle. I regretted the irritation and anxiety I had caused him, but stealing the car had satisfied an urgent need, in some way triggered by Frances Baring and the orthopaedic mannequins at the Palais des Festivals.

I crossed the shadow-filled garden, glad that I would soon see Jane again. The water in the swimming pool was still choppy, and a pair of tights lay across a sun-lounger. After returning from her conference in Nice, Jane had stripped off and swum in the nude.

I thought of her diving through the dusty surface, her pale figure bringing light to the sombre water.

I climbed the stairs, my legs exhausted after pumping the brake and clutch pedals of the BMW. I stood on the half-landing, the tights in my hand. Jane was drying herself in the bedroom, holding the bath towel behind her shoulders, her small breasts and childlike nipples flushed from the power jet, her quiff a barely visible thread. She played the towel to and fro as she pivoted on her bare feet, a matador at a naturist corrida. As I walked into the bedroom she greeted me with a flourish, and tossed the towel high into the air.

I embraced Jane, surprised by her cold skin. Over her shoulder I noticed Simone Delage standing on her balcony, face lit by the violet light of the Esterel, her eyes staring openly at Jane's naked body.

13

A Decision to Stay

'PAUL, CAN WE talk this through? I don't want to upset you.'

'Fire away.' Croissant in hand, I looked up from the breakfast tray. 'Do you mean last night?'

'When?' Buttoning her silk blouse, Jane stared at me as if I were one of her dimmer patients. 'Where, exactly?'

'Nothing.' I gestured with the croissant and dripped strawberry jam over the sheet. 'Forget it.'

'Jesus . . .' Jane pushed me aside and scraped the jam with a teaspoon. 'Señora Morales will think you've deflowered me. I have a hunch she suspects we're father and daughter.'

'Interesting.'

'Really? Now you tell me.' Jane ran a hand over my scarred knee. 'It's inflamed a little, you'll have to look after it. This thing last night. I thought we smoked a little pot, watched a blue movie and had a damn fine fuck.'

'We did.'

'Good. I waited a long time for that. Something perked you up yesterday.' Catching sight of the Delages' balcony, where a maid was wiping the table, she turned to me. 'Last night? I get it . . . when you came in I was having a shower. I assume Simone was watching?'

'You know she was. The only thing missing was the Toreador theme from Carmen. I hope Simone enjoyed the show.'

Jane took the croissant from me and dropped it into my coffee. 'Who are you – Nanook of the North? I'm not some eskimo squaw covered in whale oil, handed to any Inuit who drops by for the night.'

'I love whale oil . . .' I raised my hands when Jane threatened to punch me. 'Dr Sinclair, I'll report you to Professor Kalman. Physical abuse of the patient.'

'Don't bother. He thinks you need a lobotomy. He told me you're obsessed by car parks.' Honour satisfied, Jane smoothed her black skirt in the mirror. 'Anyway, you're right. Who cares? Sex isn't about anatomy any more. It's where it always belonged – inside the head.'

I sat on the side of the bed and held her waist. 'What is it you wanted to talk through?'

Jane stood between my scarred knees, hands on my shoulders, the scents of oestrogen and shower gel competing for my attention. 'Yesterday I spoke to Kalman about my contract. They still haven't found a permanent replacement. They're prepared to offer a relocation bonus.'

'For a further three months?'

'Six, probably. I know you want to get back to London. It's mad trying to run a publishing firm by fax and e-mail. You need to see the reps, and so on. But I've nothing to go back to. The work here is so interesting. We may be on to something with these self-diagnostic kits. The first hint of liver disease and diabetes, prostate cancer . . . You don't realize what a single drop of blood can say about you.'

'You sound like Adolf Hitler.' I lay back on the bed. 'Okay, then.'

'Okay, what?'

'We'll stay. Three months, six if you want to. I know how much it means. I'll sort things out with Charles.'

'Paul?' Jane sounded almost disappointed. 'You're a very sweet man. Nothing's decided yet, there are endless committees . . .'

'That makes sense. They don't want another English doctor running amok.'

'We'll take turns flying in and out. Say, every three weekends. That way we won't lose touch.'

'Jane . . .' I held her wrist when she tried to move away from me. 'I'll stay.'

'Here? At Eden-Olympia?'

'Yes. I'm still your husband.'

'As far as I know. That's wonderful, Paul.' Pleased but puzzled, Jane dipped a finger in the jam dish. She sucked it pensively, my teenage doctor again.

We walked arm in arm to Jane's new rented Peugeot, as the sprinklers circled and the scents of autumn lilac bathed the garden. A white detergent cloud billowed across the swimming pool, watched by Simone Delage as she prowled her balcony, sun oil in hand.

'Mysterious soul,' I commented as Jane waved to her. 'Too many white Nordic nights. She's very fond of you.'

'I talked to her yesterday. She suggested we all do something together.'

'That's a breakthrough. She knows you're married?'

'I did mention it. What do you suppose she has in mind? Something deeply corrupt?'

'I hope so.'

'She thinks my striptease is a cry for help.'

I opened Jane's door and helped to stow her briefcase, guilty that I had another day of leisure to look forward to. 'Don't let them work you too hard. I hope Wilder Penrose helps out with the routine stuff.'

'He's far too busy. He sees a constant stream of high-level people. All the CEOs and company chairmen. He has them working in therapy groups.'

'Do they need therapy?'

'I wouldn't think so. They're middle-aged men with sports

injuries. Your friend Zander was in yesterday. Nasty cuts over his back and shoulders.'

'S/M? Some of these powerful men like their chauffeurs to give them six of the best.'

'Not Zander. He said he'd been playing touch rugby on the beach at Golfe-Juan.' Jane closed her door and in an offhand way said: 'You might like to know that David was treating some of the girls at the La Bocca refuge for VD.'

'Well, it was a refuge. All the same, it does give a new slant to Alice Liddell. Sitting primly in her Victorian lace, arguing with the Red Queen, while the chancres erupt and the spirochaete burrows . . .'

'Paul, you're sick. Talk to Penrose.'

She was gone with a wave, tooting the horn as she sped down the avenue, my doctor, wife and lover again.

The last residents of the enclave had left for their offices, and only the sprinklers played over the gardens, whispering as they moved to and fro. A brief interregnum reigned before the maids arrived, during which my mind took on an almost amphetamine clarity. I lay on the jam-smeared sheet, my head in Jane's pillow, and felt the mould of her hips and shoulders, the faint tang of her vulva still on my hands.

Looking at the sunlight, I felt as elated as the rainbows conjured into the air by the lawn sprinklers. The insane, tearaway drive along the coast in the stolen BMW, Jane's teasing strip for Simone Delage, and my encounter with Frances Baring had rearranged the perspectives of that virtual city called Eden-Olympia.

I sat at the dressing table and ran my fingers over Jane's hair-brush, breathing the sweet scent of her scalp that clung to the bristles. I opened the centre drawer, a clutter of rouge-smudged cotton-wool balls, forgotten lipsticks and a Dutch cap, now home to a foil packet of cannabis resin. I loved to sift through this familiar debris of a young wife too distracted to discard anything. The contents of a woman's dressing table were as close as a husband could ever get to her unconscious mind.

In the right-hand drawer was a leather medical valise and a copy of the Peugeot garage's rental agreement. I scanned the debit columns, checking its arithmetic, and noted that the agreement ran for a year, with the option of a further six months' extension.

So Jane, as I guessed, had already decided to stay on at Eden-Olympia. She had assumed that I would return to London with the Jaguar and had rented the little Peugeot, the first unilateral decision of our marriage.

Trying not to face the implications of this minor betrayal, I opened the valise, a gift from Jane's mother. Inside was a clutter of prescription pads and a carton containing a collection of diamorphine syrettes and a dozen ampoules of pethidine. A hypodermic syringe lay inside a leather wallet, part of a cache of sedative drugs that Jane had probably found in Greenwood's desk at the clinic and brought back to the villa for safekeeping.

Holding one of the ampoules to the light, I remembered my early career as a drug dealer during the first unsettled term at my prep school. Left alone at home with a bored au pair, I searched my mother's bedside table. There I found a selection of slimming pills, and without thinking I swallowed several of the drinamyl tablets. Ten minutes later I was soaring around the house like a bird, my mind a window filled with light. I raced into the garden, pursued by the au pair, my feet scarcely touching the ground. Years later, when I took up gliding, I realized what had spurred me on.

The stolen tablets established my authority at school, and my mother's repeated attempts to diet provided an unlimited supply. The older, teenage boys were experienced users of alcohol and pot, but I was the youngest dealer in the school. When my mother took herself off the contraceptive pill, in a desperate throw of the sexual dice, I at last came to grief. I squeezed the tabs from their

foil wrapper and passed them off to my seven-year-old classmates
as a new psychedelic. Panic followed when a senior boy explained
the true role of the contraceptive pill. With a straight face he told
us that the pill's effects were reversed by the male endocrine system
and we would all become pregnant . . .

I put away the pethidine ampoule and closed the valise. Jane's
pocket radio lay at the bottom of the waste basket. Retrieving
it, I reset the batteries, and searched the waveband for Riviera
News. I listened to the stream of pop music and plugs for
video-rental shops and pool cleaners. Snatches of international
news broke the flow, references to civil war in the Cameroons
and an assassination attempt on the Israeli prime minister, but they
seemed inconsequential compared with the graphic accounts of a
yacht fire in the Golfe-Juan marina, or a landslip at Théoule that
had cracked a swimming pool. On the new Riviera, only the
trivial had any importance.

    Yet David Greenwood had sat at this dressing table, perhaps
with a high-powered rifle across his knees, looking out at the
office buildings of Eden-Olympia. I switched off the radio and
threw it back into the waste basket. I still approached the murders
as if they were a momentary aberration, a paroxysm of anger in
the executive washroom. To understand Greenwood I needed to
think of other assassins, those deranged men who stared through
the telescopic sights of their sniper's rifles, ready to grace with
their own madness the last moments of a president or a passing
pedestrian. I needed to trap the ghost of the young doctor in whose
bed I slept. Above all, I needed to dream the psychotic's dream.

14

Riviera News

THE CHILDREN'S CAROUSEL rotated in the Place des Martyrs, a gilded roundabout untouched by time. A small boy sat solemnly in a miniature aeroplane, circling to the same music I had first heard thirty years earlier. Antibes never changed, perhaps the reason why Greene, who spent his life seeking change, had settled there so contentedly.

I left the Jaguar in the underground car park near the Post Office and walked through the streets of the Old Town to the Place Nationale, where the restaurant tables were laid out under the plane trees. My parents and I had eaten lunch here during a sudden cloudburst, as raindrops danced in our soup.

I found the offices of Riviera News above an outboard-motor dealers in a side street off the Avenue de Verdun. The manager, Don Meldrum, was an affable Australian with a drinker's puffy face disguised by a tennis tan. A Fleet Street veteran of the hot-metal days, he had moved to the Mediterranean and spotted an anglophone niche among the marinas and yacht brokers.

He beckoned me into his cupboard of an office, where I sat with my back to a partition wall and my knees against his desk.

'If you're in pain, let out a shout. You need to be a contortionist here, and I'm not talking about the programmes.' He pressed his head to the wall and listened to the commercial break from the adjacent studio, advertising a gourmet caterer eager to perform his magic in the smallest yacht-galley. 'So, Mr Sinclair . . . you're reporting in from the battle-front?'

'Is there a war on?'

'Bet on it. Eden-Olympia versus the rest of the Côte.'

'Who's winning?'

'Need you ask? Whatever the physicists say, time here runs one way, head-first into the future. There's no looking back, and almost everyone knows it.'

'Almost?'

'A few old-fashioned folk still think people come to the Côte d'Azur to have a good time. You and I know they come here to work. This is Europe's California. High-tech industries, an army of people programming the future, billions surfing on a silicon chip.'

'And once a year you have the movies?'

'Exactly.' Meldrum tapped his veined nose. 'But forget about Hollywood and the Palme d'Or. I'm talking about one-man-and-a-dog operations from the Philippines. If I wanted to be accurate I'd say one-woman-and-a-dog. Now, I hear you're a close friend of David Greenwood. Or were.'

'To be honest, I hardly knew him. I was trying to impress your secretary.'

'You did. She has more news sense than I do. She tells me your wife took over from Greenwood at the Eden-Olympia clinic. A nifty berth. Some say the best hospital on the coast. When Jacques Chirac sprained his thumb opening an oyster at the Colombe d'Or that's where they took him. I hope they gave you a luxury flat.'

'Greenwood's old villa. Nothing else was available.'

'Makes sense – just about. A cold lot of fish, but that's corporate life. At least someone in the family can look after you if things go wrong.'

'I hope nothing does.' I waited until a timeshare commercial came to an end. 'I'm keen to know what happened on May 28. That's one day when something did go wrong.'

'For Greenwood, and ten other poor sods.' Meldrum fiddled

with a transcript on his desk. 'So you're having a quiet rake through the ashes. Can I ask why?'

'He was a fellow Brit. My wife knew him. I sleep in the man's bed, eat at his breakfast table, shit in his toilet. I'd like to know the truth.'

'Sounds like a personal crusade. Worst reason for getting involved. I take it you've come up with something? A diary? Confessional tapes?'

'Sorry. But there are things that don't add up.'

'Such as?'

'Motive. There isn't one.'

'Or one you understand. If I were you, I'd stay close to the nearest piña colada.'

Ignoring this, I said: 'I've talked to people who knew Greenwood, doctors who worked with him. No one has any idea why he went berserk. They're not covering up, but . . .'

'There's nothing to cover up.' Tiring of me, Meldrum stared at the Arab yachts in the harbour. 'For once, you can believe the official story. This young English doctor, practically the Albert Schweitzer of the Côte d'Azur, was working too hard for his own good. One day a fuse blew and the lights went out.'

'Or another set of lights came on. Brighter and harder lights that made everything seem very clear. Especially inside his own head.'

Meldrum laughed ruefully at this. 'Mr Sinclair, you should be working for one of those concierge rags in Paris. My reporter spent a lot of time at Eden-Olympia. It was a big case. CNN, the London tabloids, all the news agencies. They found nothing.'

'They were looking for a crime passionel among the roulette wheels. Drugs and decadent film stars. Handsome chauffeurs sleeping with the film producer's wife . . . Someone at Eden-Olympia said she'd heard a report on Riviera News that mapped out Greenwood's route. I mentioned it to your secretary.'

'I looked it out for you.' Meldrum pushed the transcript across the desk. 'One of our stringers did a round-up piece. He added a few contact numbers you might find useful.'

'It's a big help.' I searched the faded photocopy. 'What's the reporter's name?'

'Roger Leland. That was his last effort. He took off and moved down to the Algarve.'

I started to read the transcript, no more than three paragraphs. '"One minute, fifty-two seconds . . ."? A little on the short side?'

'Here that's practically Marcel Proust. Keep it to yourself. The people who run Eden-Olympia have a lot of power.'

'I understand.' I noticed the date of transmission. 'July 25? Nearly two months afterwards?'

'We had some late info.'

'A tip-off? Someone at Eden-Olympia?'

'Who can say? Leland kept his sources to himself. Take it easy, Mr Sinclair.'

I shook his hand and eased myself around the door. 'Do you ever get out to Eden-Olympia?'

'Not if I can help it. People there keep to themselves.'

'Are they popular along the coast?'

'Some are. Some definitely aren't. A bunch of them were making trouble in Mandelieu last weekend. They set up a late-night brawl with the local Arabs in the fruit market.'

He watched me make my way down the stairs. As he waved, I called up to him: 'These brawlers from Eden-Olympia – were they wearing black leather jackets?'

'You know, I believe they were. It looked like they were part of a bowling team . . .'

I returned to the Place Nationale and sat under the plane trees outside the Oasis restaurant, where the rain had once danced in my soup. Cooling my hands around a vin blanc, I studied the transcript. The transmission times on July 25 were listed: 2.34 p.m., 3.04, 3.34, presumably following the half-hour news breaks. The abrupt end hinted that pressure had been brought to bear from Eden-Olympia, which wanted nothing to rekindle the anxieties of staff and corporate clients.

Roger Leland, speaking from Eden-Olympia, site of the greatest tragedy to hit the Côte d'Azur in recent years. Two months have passed since the horrific day when a young English doctor, thirty-two-years-old David Greenwood, ran amok with an automatic rifle, killing ten victims before turning the weapon on himself. Investigating judge Michel Terneau is still no nearer finding a motive, but has repeatedly stated that Greenwood acted alone and chose his victims at random.

Riviera News has now uncovered new facts that suggest the killings were carefully planned and involved at least one co-conspirator. Video film from the business park's surveillance cameras reportedly revealed Greenwood and an unidentified white male in the TV centre car park, transferring weapons from an unmarked van into Dr Greenwood's Renault Espace. Sadly, this film was accidentally destroyed. Mystery also surrounds Greenwood's movements in the last minutes of his life. Driven back by gunfire as he attempted to enter the Siemens building, Greenwood returned to his villa and immediately murdered his three hostages. Logs of police radio traffic suggest that Greenwood made the 2.8 kilometre journey on foot, taking just over three minutes, a feat even Olympic athletes would find impossible. There were no reports of stolen or hijacked vehicles.

Was there an accomplice who helped Greenwood make his escape? The possibility that a second assassin is still at large, perhaps planning his revenge, has sent alarm bells ringing throughout the business park, still struggling to regain its calm after the tragic events of May 28. Roger Leland, for Riviera News, reporting from Eden-Olympia.

I read the transcript again, disappointed that it provided no details of Greenwood's murder route. The references to a co-conspirator were speculation, and I turned to the contact list at the foot of the page.

Among the worthies named were Professor Kalman, director of the clinic; Pascal Zander, acting chief of security; Claudine Galante, manager, press bureau.

Scribbled in longhand at the bottom of the page were four more names, each with its telephone number.

Mlle Isabel Duval. Secretary of Dr Greenwood.
Mme Cordier and Madame Ménard. Wives of dead hostages.
Philippe Bourget. Brother of dead hostage.

All, surprisingly, as their phone numbers indicated, were still resident in the greater Cannes area, as if the magnitude of the crime still held them in its grip, part of the business park's baleful gravity that would never release those who came within its orbit.

15

A Residential Prison

THE ELDERLY BOULES players in the Place Delaunay stood in their Zen poses, waiting for the click of a metal ball to alter the geometry of their game. Admiring their self-control, I left the Jaguar in the Rue Lauvert. Across the RN7 were the Antibes-Les-Pins apartments, a huge residential complex that covered thirty acres between the Place Delaunay and the sea, another of the security-obsessed compounds that were reshaping the geography and character of the Côte d'Azur.

Surveillance cameras hung like gargoyles from the cornices, following me as I approached the barbican and identified myself to the guard at the reception desk. Once my appointment was confirmed, I followed his directions towards the Résidence de la Plage, the group of seven-storey apartments nearest to the sea. Decorative gardens in the formal French style surrounded the pathway, refreshed by an irrigation system that left the brickwork perpetually damp. But the shrubs and flowering plants seemed pallid and defeated, the ground beneath them so crammed with electronic ducting that no roots could prosper. Together they awaited their deaths, ready to be replaced by the month's end.

High above me, fluted columns carried the pitched roofs, an attempt at a vernacular architecture that failed to disguise this executive-class prison. Taking their cue from Eden-Olympia and Antibes-les-Pins, the totalitarian systems of the future would be subservient and ingratiating, but the locks would be just as strong.

If this modern-day utopia demanded a new kind of urban survivalist, Isabel Duval personified her, from pale-grey make-up to hand-knitted wool suit. She was a handsome woman in her late thirties with a pleasant but toneless face from which all emotion had long been drained. As she welcomed me into her apartment she reminded me of the deputy principal of a private girls' school who had been passed over for the headship too many times. Any resentment had been carefully defused, wrapped in sterile gauze and placed on a secure back shelf of her mind.

'Monsieur Sinclair . . . ?' Her smile was as quick as a camera shutter, the same flicker of the lips that had beckoned the senior executives of Eden-Olympia towards their cholesterol tests and prostate examinations. I had introduced myself over the phone, explaining that Jane had taken over from Greenwood, whom I posthumously promoted to close family friend.

But Isabel Duval seemed not entirely convinced. Her nostrils trembled, perhaps picking up some intrusive scent from my clothes, the stale cigar smoke from Meldrum's office. She stepped back, giving a wide berth to my rogue gait, unused to the presence of a strange man in her apartment.

'Madame Duval, it's good of you to see me. I must seem like a ghost from the past.'

'Not at all. An old friend of David Greenwood, how could I refuse?'

She guided me to a chair in the sitting room. The balcony windows looked out, not at the sea and beach, but into an inner courtyard, providing a superb view of the cameras beneath the eaves.

'So many cameras,' I commented. 'You're taking part in an extraordinary film that no one will ever see.'

'I hope not. That would be a sign of failure by the security system. Regrettably, there are many thieves on the Côte d'Azur. They say we are safer here than in the vaults of the Bank of France.'

'I'm glad. Is the security keeping the thieves out, or you in?'

I had hoped to relax her with this modest quip, but she stared at me as if I had recited a verse of the Kamasutra. I knew that she would not be keen to talk about Greenwood. At the same time she seemed intrigued by my motives, her eyes noting every wayward crease in my trousers and the chipped toenails in my open sandals.

'It was all so tragic,' she said. 'When did you last see David?'

'About a year ago, in London. It's hard to believe what happened.'

'It was a shock to us, too. In many cases, fatal. May I ask how you found my telephone number?'

'I asked someone at the clinic. Penrose's secretary, I'm not sure . . .'

'Dr Penrose? That doesn't surprise me.' She glanced at the nearest security camera, as if warning it that the burly psychiatrist was prowling nearby. 'Dr Penrose has made a career out of being indiscreet.'

I leaned forward, trying to hold her attention, which seemed to wander into the side corridors of her mind. 'Madame Duval, I'm trying to understand what happened on May 28. In London, David seemed so clear-headed.'

'He was. As his secretary, I knew him well. Of course, I wasn't involved in his charity work at La Bocca.' She spoke sharply, as if she disapproved of the refuge. 'It's too late now, but I criticize myself.'

'You were with him for many hours each day. What do you think drove him over the edge?'

She stared at her immaculate carpet, where a stray grey hair caught the light. 'I can't say. He never confided his doubts to me.'

'He had doubts?'

'Like all of us. Sadly, I wasn't with him during the last days. I might have been able to help him.'

'You were away?'

'He asked me to take a week's leave. This was in April, a month earlier. He said he was going to a medical conference in Geneva.'

'Presumably you saw the tickets?'

'And the hotel reservations. But Professor Kalman told me that David was at the clinic throughout the time of the conference. For some reason, he decided not to go to Geneva.'

She spoke as if Greenwood had let her down, and I wondered if she saw the murders as a kind of unfaithfulness.

'A month . . .' I repeated. 'He was planning well ahead. Madame Duval, he was trying to protect you. Everything you say suggests it wasn't a brainstorm. He didn't suddenly go mad.'

'He was never mad.'

She spoke in a calm but firm voice. I imagined her lying awake at night, in this electrified but nerveless world, thinking that if only she had forgone her holiday she might have reached out to Greenwood and calmed his dream of death.

'Was he working too hard?' I asked.

'It wasn't a matter of hard work. David committed himself too much to other people and their special needs. He was very distracted, it explained his . . . carelessness.'

'Over what?'

Madame Duval glanced around the sitting room, carrying out a quick inventory of the table lamps, desk and chairs, reestablishing her tenancy of this segment of space-time.

'His mind was on his patients and their medical needs. Sometimes he took things from the shops in the Rue d'Antibes and forgot to pay. Once the Gray d'Albion stopped him at the door. They called the police, but Professor Kalman explained the misunderstanding.'

'The police didn't charge him?'

'It was too trivial. An atomizer of scent – we exchanged gifts on our birthdays. His thoughts were elsewhere.'

'The orphanage at La Bocca? If your mind is on higher things, it's easy to –'

'Higher things?' She laughed at my naivety. 'Those girls used him. Arab street children are completely ruthless. He had money and they thought he was a fool. Another time he borrowed a car without permission.'

'Is that wrong? There's an emergency car pool for doctors at the clinic.'

'This was in Cannes, outside the railway station. A man stepped out to kiss his wife. He left the engine running.'

'And David drove it away?'

'The police caught him on the Croisette. He said it was a medical emergency.'

'Perhaps it was. But Professor Kalman hushed it up again?'

'He set out the situation with the commissaire. Eden-Olympia is very important to the police. They benefit from off-duty payments, special fees and so on.' Madame Duval stood up and stepped to the window, as if hoping to catch a glimpse of Eden-Olympia and the happier hours she had spent in Greenwood's office. 'I knew David. He would never steal. He cared nothing for money, and gave away half his salary.'

'But he was distracted?'

'He tried to help so many people – poor Maghrebians looking for work, students, old women. He would take drugs from the pharmacy to help the addicts at the free clinic in Mandelieu. When he was mugged it created problems with the police.'

'Mugged? Are you sure?'

'He had many bruises. Cannes La Bocca is not like the Croisette. He tried to stabilize the addicts before he could treat them. They were selling their drugs on the street outside the clinic. David didn't realize it, but he became a kind of dealer.'

'Doctor Serrou worked with him. Everyone speaks well of her. Why did David shoot her?'

'Who can say?' Madame Duval turned her face in profile,

trying to hide the flush in her cheeks. 'She was not a good influence.'

I waited for her to continue, but she had finished with me. As we stood up, I said: 'You've helped me greatly. Did you mention any of this to the investigating judge?'

'No.' She pursed her lips, frowning from an imaginary witness box. She spoke scathingly of herself. 'It was the time to speak out, but I let David down. I wanted to defend his name. Believe me, there are others to blame here.'

'Madame Duval . . . did David actually kill the victims?'

'Kill them? Of course.'

Surprised by my obtuse question, she opened the front door. The colour drained from her throat as she waited for me to leave.

'It's very pleasant here,' I told her. 'But why did you resign from the clinic?'

'They offered me a special retirement plan. Eden-Olympia is very generous. They understood how shocked I was. At the time many people feared another attack.'

'So you wanted to retire?'

'I accepted that a reassignment of personnel was necessary. My presence was . . .'

'An embarrassment? I'm sorry you left, my wife would have enjoyed working with you. It might be best not to speak about this conversation. Are you in touch with Professor Kalman?'

'No. But someone from the finance department comes every month, to see if I have special needs. There are accumulated cash benefits paid to founder-employees like myself.'

'As long as the business park prospers?'

'Exactly.' Isabel Duval smiled her first smile, a slow grimace of the lips that revealed a dry knowingness. 'Eden-Olympia is very civilized, and very corrupt. Once you are there, they look after you for ever . . .'

16

Widows and Memories

'FOR EVER' WAS a difficult concept to grasp along this ever-changing coastline. Port-la-Galère, where the chauffeurs' widows now lived, lay between Théoule and Miramar, five miles to the west of Cannes. I set out along the beach road from the Vieux Port towards La Napoule. A midnight storm had covered the sand with driftwood carried across the water from the Îles de Lérins, where legend had imprisoned the man in the iron mask for ten years in the grim Ste-Marguerite fortress.

By contrast with its gloomy cells and triple bars, Antibes-les-Pins was a most civilized detention centre. Isabel Duval was, after all, free to leave at any time. I imagined this rather proud and strained woman moving among the holiday-makers in the streets of Juan-les-Pins, staring into the windows of the boutiques as she held tight to her memories of David Greenwood. Her apartment at Antibes-les-Pins was a decompression chamber, where the explosive forces set off on May 28 were allowed to leak away.

If anything, Isabel Duval was still suffering from rapture of the deep. Her picture of the shoplifting and car-stealing doctor, exploited by orphans and drug addicts, was the reverse of the haloed image that bereaved spouses usually created. Her desperate listing of Greenwood's petty failings was an attempt to fix his reality in her mind before it faded for good. The shoplifting at the Gray d'Albion was probably part of the same recklessness that Jane had shown in the tabac near the Majestic Hotel. The commandeering of the car, unlike my own light-headed prank, might well have been the reflex of an exhausted doctor alerted by his mobile phone to yet another medical emergency.

At La Napoule I crossed the motor bridge over the marina complex and drove into the hills of the Esterel. A few cork trees and umbrella pines had survived the forest fires, but most of the hillsides were bare, exposing the red porphyry to the sunlight, the ancient rocks so porous that they resembled immense rust-spills, the waste tips of past time.

Port-la-Galère would be more modest, I assumed, a survival of the old Côte d'Azur, an unspoilt fishing port with cobbled quays and net-strewn jetties. Here the chauffeurs' widows would eke out a modest living gutting dorade and boiling crayfish, close-mouthed about their husbands' years at Eden-Olympia.

My problem was to persuade them to speak freely to me. I remembered the ampoule of pethidine in my jacket pocket, which I had taken from Jane's valise, intending to show it to Wilder Penrose, a possible clue to Greenwood's state of mind. The widows might appreciate the sedative drug, ready to try anything that would free them from the stench of the quayside.

Théoule was so discreet that I almost failed to notice the resort, an enclave of luxury houses rented by fashion designers and media academics. I passed a tracked excavator digging a trench along the kerb of the corniche road, laying the land lines for a cable-television contractor. Rather than sit on their balconies with an evening drink, enjoying one of the world's most striking views, the owners of these exclusive villas preferred to slump in the dark of their rumpus rooms, watching Hitchcock films and English league football.

I overtook the excavator, and turned left at a sign that advertised 'Port-la-Galère' in rustic lettering. Beyond the guardhouse an asphalt road curved around the hillside towards another gated community. The villas and apartment houses had been designed by a latter-day Gaudi, the walls and balconies moulded into biomorphic forms that would have pleased the creator of the

Sagrada Familia. Not a dorade was being gutted, nor a crayfish simmered. The marina was filled with yachts and powerboats, sleek multihulls fitted with the latest satellite-navigation gear that would steer the owners painlessly towards similar luxury berths at Portofino and Bandol. I edged the Jaguar between the parked Porsches and Land-Cruisers. At the waterside cafés a Parisian smart set in weekend yachting rig chattered against a backdrop of chandlers furnished like boutiques and boutiques furnished like chandlers.

Madame Cordier and Madame Ménard, the chauffeurs' widows, were cut from plainer cloth. We met as arranged in Madame Cordier's second-floor apartment, shielded from the sea by the coiled extrusions of yellow plaster that formed the balcony railings. The widows were in their mid-forties, watchful and circumspect women with faintly north African features, the daughters, I guessed, of pied-noir parents who had left Algeria in the 1960s.

They were dressed in black, almost certainly for my visit. On the telephone Madame Cordier had spoken in a halting English, no doubt learned from her dead husband, strong on traffic and parking tips, and assumed that I was a member of the Eden-Olympia inspectorate. Seeing my casual sportswear, she warily shook my hand, suspecting that the finance department at Eden-Olympia had made an unwise lunge into informality.

Fortunately, Philippe Bourget, the brother of the third murdered hostage, was also present. A slim young man with the pensive air of a doctoral student, he taught at a lycée in Mandelieu and was a fluent English speaker. He had driven to Port-la-Galère on the Mobylette cooling itself in the downstairs hallway.

Trying to ignore the Parisian chatter below the balcony, I expressed my deep regret over the tragedy. Then, deciding to jump in with both feet, I said to Bourget: 'Please explain that my wife is a doctor at Eden-Olympia. We were close friends of David Greenwood.'

The women's chins rose, and I expected a show of hostility.

But they nodded without emotion. Madame Cordier, a tall and strong-faced woman, beckoned me to a chair, and then slipped away to prepare tea. Madame Ménard, a more placid and reserved figure, watched me with a slowly waking smile, her hands quietly gesturing to each other.

'I'm glad,' I said to Bourget. 'I was afraid they might not want to see me.'

'They know you weren't involved.' Bourget studied me, as if estimating my likely sympathies and intelligence. 'You and your wife were in England at the time?'

'Thankfully. We arrived in August. The longer we're here the stranger everything seems. It's impossible to believe that Dr Greenwood shot your brother.'

'I agree.' Bourget spoke matter-of-factly. 'Does that surprise you?'

'It does. Coming from you, it counts for something. Are you saying Greenwood may not have killed his victims?'

'Not exactly. He killed the first seven who died. Sadly, there's no doubt about that.'

Madame Cordier arrived with her tea tray. The widows turned to gaze at me, their faint smiles floating above the scent of camomile.

'What about the hostages?' I asked Bourget. 'Your brother and the two husbands? Did he . . . ?'

'Kill them?' Bourget hesitated, one hand touching the air as if searching for a blackboard. 'It's hard to decide. Perhaps not.'

'What makes you doubt it?'

'It's a question of character.'

'You don't think Greenwood could have shot three men in cold blood?'

'It's unlikely. Still, we have to accept the court's decision.' He shrugged forbearingly, and stared at a framed photograph of Monsieur Cordier on the mantelpiece.

'Did you meet Greenwood?' I asked him.

'No. But my brother often spoke of him. He was an engineer at the TV centre. Greenwood sometimes made health-and-safety broadcasts.'

'He knew Greenwood?' Without thinking, I handed my tea-cup back to Madame Cordier. 'I thought Greenwood seized the hostages at random. What about the husbands? Had they met him?'

'Yes.' Sitting forward, Madame Ménard spoke up strongly. 'Pierre met him many times. Five, six, more times . . .'

'And Georges.' Madame Cordier nodded vigorously. 'They saw him together.'

'At the clinic?' I asked. 'Dr Greenwood was examining them?'

'No.' Madame Ménard spoke in precise tones. 'Not the clinic. At the Capitol.'

'The Capitol? Is that an office building?'

'It's a bar in Le Cannet.' Bourget stared hard at the two women, showing his disapproval of these unnecessary confidences. Before they could speak again, he added: 'He advised them in a dispute with the personnel department.'

'With the employment law,' Madame Ménard explained. 'He helped them at Eden-Olympia.'

Bourget pretended to search for his cycle clips. 'There was a disagreement over evening work. They were expected to drive for too many hours.'

'Pressure was put on them? They were threatened – ?'

'With dismissal.' Bourget's voice expressed his distaste. 'Dr Greenwood intervened, and the hours were reduced. They no longer had to drive in the evening.'

'Evening . . .' Madame Cordier mimicked the violent move-ments of a steering wheel. 'Bad time in La Bocca.'

'And Pierre,' Madame Ménard agreed. She clapped her hands above the teacups, trying to picture a blur of colliding cars. 'Not a good time . . .'

The women broke off into French, voices raised as they

shared their indignation. Bourget beckoned me to the mantel-piece.

'It was generous of Greenwood to intervene. In many ways he was a decent man. But we musn't alarm them.'

'I'm sorry.' I watched the animated widows in their bombazine dresses, capping each other's memories. 'They don't seem too alarmed. Did the husbands have any idea what Greenwood was planning?'

'How could they?'

'It would explain why he took them hostage.' Before Bourget could stop me, I turned to the women. 'Madame Cordier, it's a very sad time for you and Madame Ménard. I don't want to upset you. Do you remember everything that happened on May 28?'

'Of course.' Madame Cordier composed herself like a witness in court. 'Please speak, Monsieur Sinclair.'

'Did your husband say anything about Dr Greenwood on the day before? Had he found something suspicious?'

'Nothing. Georges said nothing about Dr Greenwood.'

'Pierre told me he had many clients that day,' Madame Ménard interjected. 'He left very early for work.'

'Right. What time did he usually report to the transport office?'

'Before eight o'clock.'

'So it took an hour or so to get there?'

'No.' Madame Ménard covered her watch. 'We lived in Le Cannet.'

'A ten-minute drive? And when did he leave on May 28?'

'Six o'clock.'

'He gave himself nearly two hours? Madame Cordier – can you remember when your husband left home?'

'The same time. We lived in Grasse. A few minutes before six.'

I was about to question the women further, but Bourget took my arm. Patiently but firmly, he drew me to the balcony.

144

'They know nothing, Mr Sinclair.' He spoke with school-masterly disapproval. 'They have no idea why Dr Greenwood seized their husbands. All these questions make it difficult for them to forget.'

'Are they trying to forget? It seems to me that . . .'

But I paid my respects to the widows, who came to the door to see me off. For a moment, as they smiled at me, they seemed sorry to see me go.

I followed Bourget down to the entrance hall. He released the lock on his Mobylette and wheeled it into the road. Despite my challenge to his supervisory role over the widows, I sensed that he was glad to hear my questions aired. Once away from the women, his manner became more friendly.

As we walked towards the Jaguar, I said: 'They weren't too upset?'

'They needed to talk. Were you surprised by how warmly they spoke of Greenwood?'

'Very surprised. How did your brother feel about him?'

'Jacques admired him. They were due to testify together as wit-nesses to a traffic accident. Now the case will never be heard.'

'Who was involved?'

'A junior manager in the personnel department at Eden-Olympia. A car forced him off the road. Greenwood helped him in the minutes before he died.'

'Greenwood was in the car?'

'No. He was passing in another vehicle. Along the coast road to Juan-les-Pins. Joyriders accelerate to dangerous speeds.'

'And your brother?

'He was in the manager's car. They were friends, and often went hiking together. It's lucky that Greenwood was driving by.'

'And quite a coincidence – though not the first.' I was aware that Bourget was watching me, like a teacher with a promising pupil. Deciding to be frank with him, I said: 'On May 28, Greenwood seized three hostages. Ten thousand people work at Eden-Olympia, but he picks the two chauffeurs, knowing he may have to kill them. These are men he's helped, with wives dependent on them. He needs a third hostage, and somehow chose your brother, even though they are going to testify in court together . . .'

'He picked people he knew,' Bourget pointed out. 'Perhaps it was easier to approach them, rather than complete strangers. He was very disturbed, Mr Sinclair.'

'Even so.' I looked back at Madame Cordier's apartment, where the widows watched from the balcony. 'The husbands lived within ten minutes of Eden-Olympia, but left almost two hours before they needed to check in for work. Why?'

'Impossible to say. People behave in unexpected ways. My brother was an active member of the Green movement. One day he took up sport shooting. He had a game licence to hunt deer. We were amazed.'

'When was this?'

'In April, about a month before he died. He often went to the military range at Castellane. I still have his weapons and ammunition. How do you explain that?'

'I can't.' We had reached the Jaguar, in the crowded car park beside the quay. 'I'm trying to start the clock on May 28. What was your brother doing so early in the car park of the TV centre? The station doesn't transmit programmes until six in the evening.'

'Does it matter, Mr Sinclair?' Bourget put a hand on my shoulder, noticing my limp and anxious that I was overtaxing myself. 'Can I ask why you're so involved? You didn't really know Greenwood.'

'Why do you say that?'

'You're very concerned, but for a different man. David Greenwood was not a victim.'

'No . . . I'm not sure what he was.' I looked at the crowded quayside, with its chic young yachtsmen and their girlfriends. 'Port-la-Galère . . . it's charming, in its way. A curious retirement home for two chauffeurs' widows.'

'Eden-Olympia supplied the apartments. And the pensions.'

'I hope they're generous. Port-la-Galère looks rather fashionable.'

'With a certain class of Parisian.' Bourget helped me into the driver's seat, clearly relieved that I was about to start the engine. 'People come here to take cocaine and sleep with each other's wives.'

'Hardly a place for grieving widows? At the same time, there's not much danger of them talking to the wrong people. Did Eden-Olympia offer you compensation?'

'Naturally. It was substantial.'

'And you accepted?'

'Mr Sinclair . . .' Bourget smiled to himself and patted the roof of the car, as if urging the Jaguar to take me back to the corniche road. With his cycle clips and Mobylette he looked like a French trainspotter, but I sensed that he had thought through Eden-Olympia's involvement in his brother's death and had a larger grasp than I did of the tragedy that surrounded David Greenwood. 'The compensation . . . ? I handed it to my brother's former wife. It waits in trust for their son. Eden-Olympia looks after everything, Mr Sinclair.'

17

Refuge at La Bocca

PORT-LA-GALÈRE AND ITS secrets fell behind me as I climbed the steep incline to the coastal road. The guards at the rustic checkpoint logged the car's numberplate into their mobile radios, waiting patiently as I fought the transmission system for possession of second gear. They were dressed in the chocolate-coloured uniforms favoured by supermarket security men. When they saluted, it struck me that this would be the chosen costume of any future army ordered to pacify a civilian population, reminding it of happier days spent in the confectionery aisles.

As I drove towards Cannes a light aircraft was taking off from the Cannes-Mandelieu airport near La Bocca. I pulled onto the verge, earning a rebuke from two elderly Frenchmen whose espadrilles I almost crushed. They slapped the Jaguar's roof, but I let this pass, and watched the aircraft climb across La Napoule Bay. Layers of dust and humidity formed strata in the soft air, through which the hotels of the Croisette trembled like uneasy spectres, a dream about to collapse into itself.

I turned off the Cannes highway and followed the access roads that led to the small airport. Single-engined aircraft were parked in their green collapsible hangars, like the canopies of giant perambulators, and executive jets waited for their corporate fares by the passenger terminal. The dead chauffeurs, Cordier and Ménard, would have sat here in their limousines on countless days, staring through the wire fence and breathing the heady tang of aviation fuel. Already I was certain that they had not been David Greenwood's hostages.

I circled the car park and stopped outside a small single-storey building like a general store in a mock-up of a Wild West frontier town. These were the offices of Nostalgic Aviation. The nose and cockpit section of a 1970s jet bomber was mounted on blocks beside the entrance, the equivalent of a cigar-store indian or a rusting cigarette machine. The showroom was filled with aviation memorabilia – helmets, parachutes and radio gear from the Cold War period, piston heads and propellers, several ejector seats and a radial engine.

The store had closed for the afternoon, and an almost tangible melancholy hung over everything, gathering the same dust as the model aircraft strung from the ceiling, the same sediment of past time that fell from the memories of old pilots and cloaked this miniature museum. The gyrocompasses and Strategic Air Command fuselage art – 'SAC Time', with naked blonde and priapic nuclear bomb – were fossils embedded in the past, like my old Harvard in the hangar at Elstree, as distant from the executives boarding the Nice shuttle as trilobites encased in prehistoric shale.

I stepped into the Jaguar, another rolling museum of itself, left the airport and drove into the industrial suburb of La Bocca. As the wheels struck the disused railway lines embedded in the road I remembered another dream that had died here, within earshot of the aircraft that patrolled the beaches of Cannes and Juan-les-Pins, advertising the discount furniture sales and speedboat auctions that helped to define the future of the new Côte d'Azur.

The children's refuge at La Bocca, to which David Greenwood had devoted so much time, lay between the freight depot of the SNCF and a cluster of run-down tenements that offered temporary housing to Maghrebian workers. The two-storey building had gothic windows and a steeply pitched roof, and was the schoolhouse of a teaching order of African nuns. The dozen nuns, black sisters from former French colonies, had welcomed Greenwood's offer to provide medical care for the girls in their charge. After May 28 the municipal authorities had closed the refuge, and the twenty girls were now in foster homes.

'It was unsuitable for them to stay,' Sister Émilie, a middle-aged nun from Dahomey, explained as she unlocked the doors and led me into the schoolhouse. 'Journalists came every day, television cameras, even tourists . . .'

'I understand. It would be dangerous for them.'

'Not for the girls. You never had daughters, Mr Sinclair? You can control one thirteen-year-old. Two girls control each other. But twenty? Impossible. No man would be safe.'

The girls, she explained, were orphaned or abandoned daughters of migrant workers, and keenly interested in the bright lights of the Croisette. The dayroom on the ground floor was furnished with lumpy sofas and chairs, armrests scorched by cigarette burns. A crucifix hung from the wall, along with a Raphaelesque reproduction of the Saviour's undernourished face and uplifted eyes, the image of a tubercular sexual fanatic that must have appealed to the girls who lay around gossiping and smoking their cigarettes.

Greenwood and Dominique Serrou had paid the salaries of two helpers and a cook. Only the generous funds donated by Eden-Olympia allowed the impoverished teaching order to educate the girls and provide them with books and a computer.

'Such kind people. They gave everything and took nothing. In the end . . .' Sister Émilie clapped her hands, as if the multiple killings had been an inexplicable accident.

'Did Dr Greenwood get on with Dr Serrou?'

'Were they . . . intimate?' Sister Émilie paused on the creaking stairs. 'No. Anyway, not here. They didn't ask for my permission. Dr Greenwood was very young, and very tired.'

'There were no disagreements? Over running the refuge?'

'Never. Busy people have no time to disagree. They were committed to their work.'

The dormitory on the second floor had been divided into barrack-style cubicles, each with three beds. The mattresses were bare, strewn with old scent bottles, broken mobile phones and music CDs.

Sister Émilie stared patiently at the debris, clearly eager to sweep everything into the nearest rubbish bin.

'The police told me to touch nothing. So . . .'

'Maybe the girls will come back one day?'

'It's possible.' The prospect seemed to cheer her. 'Your wife is a doctor, Mr Sinclair?'

'A paediatrician, like Dr Greenwood.' Embarrassed by the nun's hopeful gaze, I could only say: 'She has many responsibilities . . .'

I opened the wooden lockers behind the beds, filled with a clutter of shoes and spent cosmetics. From a peg hung a miniskirted cocktail dress with zebra stripes, an electric eyesore that could only have been worn within the lurid imagination of a twelve-year-old. On the shelf below was a pair of fishnet tights.

'Those girls . . .' Sister Émilie averted her gaze. 'They had so many clothes.'

'Dr Greenwood was generous with pocket money?'

'Too much. He was sorry for the girls. Dr Serrou gave them one hundred francs, then another hundred francs . . .' She shuffled to the door. 'You stay and look, Mr Sinclair. Maybe you can find something about your friend. Poor Dr Greenwood . . .'

When she had gone I stood among the cubicles, inhaling the still potent scent of young women's bodies. Supervising the troubled teenagers would have required heroic patience. By day Greenwood could check their health, prescribe vitamin supplements and hand out his Alice books, but at nightfall the girls would dress up in their finery and dial the immigrant bars in La Bocca, shrieking as they teased the mystified construction workers.

I imagined the high jinks in this shabby dormitory, like the tricks that Jane and the women doctors at Guy's played on the unwary housemen. Remembering how Jane had scuffed through the wards, fingers stained with nicotine, I picked up the zebra frock and the dusty tights. I felt a curious affection for the unknown teenager who had worn them. She would soon forget the earnest English doctor, smiling through his fatigue, who had tried to introduce her to the White Rabbit and the Red Queen.

I left the dormitory and crossed the landing into a high-ceilinged room that had been Greenwood's office. The bare desk was flanked by empty medicine cabinets and Arabic posters warning against the dangers of alcohol and tobacco. Jane had told me that Greenwood was treating some of the girls for venereal complaints, and I tried not to think of the childhoods from which he had rescued them.

I sat behind the desk, and imagined myself dispensing medicines and affection to the girls, until the day when tiredness and despair suddenly fused, and tore up all scripts and scenarios. La Bocca was a long way from Cannes, but separated by a universe from Eden-Olympia.

I opened the desk drawer and took out a mounted photograph that I assumed had hung from a nearby wall. David Greenwood stood in the centre of a group portrait, his blond hair and pale English face lit like a flag among the suntanned Cannoises. He seemed slightly drunk, not from alcohol but exhaustion, his broad grin failing to mask his unfocused gaze.

Beside him was a handsome woman with a quirky and defensive smile, fair hair hiding one cheek, whom I had last seen outside the American Express offices in Cannes. Frances Baring leaned against Greenwood's shoulder, clearly trying to support him. Her eyes were fixed on his face with an expression of concern, less like a lover about to bestow a kiss than a mother helping a child to swallow a difficult morsel.

Around them stood a confident group of Eden-Olympia

executives, familiar to me from the press cuttings Charles had sent. I recognized Michel Charbonneau, chairman of the Eden-Olympia holding company; Robert Fontaine, chief executive of the administration; and Guy Bachelet, the security head. Danger seemed far from their minds as they raised their glasses to Greenwood. They posed for the camera in a large, gilt-ceilinged room furnished with formal Empire chairs, like the antechamber to a presidential suite. Together they seemed to be celebrating a notable achievement, perhaps a large and unexpected donation to the refuge. Yet, apart from Frances Baring, no one was aware that David Greenwood was at the end of his tether.

'Mr Sinclair? Enough of the girls now . . .'

Sister Émilie called from below. I put away the photograph and closed the office door behind me. As I walked down the stairs I noticed that I was still carrying the zebra dress and fishnet tights. Rather than hand them to the nun, I stuffed them into my jacket.

After making my thanks and a cash donation to Sister Émilie, who silently bowed to me, I returned to the Jaguar. I drove through the shabby streets of La Bocca, with their melancholy Arab men haunting the doorways. I was glad to be within a twenty-minute drive of the Croisette and its kingdom of light. A smell of cheap perfume filled the car, rising from the zebra bundle on the passenger seat. I stopped by a dustbin outside a supermarket, stepped from the car and slid the garments under the lid.

The teenager's scent, rancid but curiously stirring, still clung to my hands. But I was thinking of the photograph I had seen in Greenwood's office at the refuge. Frances Baring was dressed in a business suit, but all the others in the group, including Greenwood himself, were wearing their leather bowling jackets.

18

The Street of Darkest Night

DUSK CAME QUICKLY to Cannes, in the few moments that distracted me as I ordered another Tom Collins from the waiter at the Rialto Bar. The sky seemed to tilt, tipping the sun like a slew of glowing ash behind the heights of the Esterel, taking with it the hang-gliders who sailed the evening airs. The hotels along the Croisette retreated into themselves, withdrawing behind their formal facades. The lights had moved offshore. Electric snowflakes marked the Christmas-tree rigging of the yachts moored near the beach, and a blaze of candlepower bathed the two cruise liners anchored in the Napoule Channel.

Shore parties of passengers strolled under the palm trees, too unsteady after their days at sea to risk crossing the Croisette. They stared at the hundreds of Volvo salesmen emerging from a conference at the Noga Hilton, like travellers glimpsing an unknown tribe about to perform its rites of passage with its sacred regalia, the marketing brochure and the promotional video.

Prostitutes came out at dusk, usherettes in the theatre of the night, shining their miniature torches at any kerb that threatened their high-heels. Two of them entered the Rialto and sat at the next table, muscular brunettes with the hips and thighs of professional athletes. They ordered drinks they never touched, killing time before they set off to trawl the hotels.

I, too, was waiting for the clock to move on, but with rather less hope. Jane was chairing another late-evening committee at the clinic, mapping out a further stage in the scheme that would bring, if not immortality, then perpetually monitored health to

Eden-Olympia. Our brains, I often told her, would soon need a false ceiling to make room for the ducting demanded by our 'intelligent' lifestyle. Before breakfast we would set ourselves a psychological test, tapping yes-or-no answers to alternative-choice questions, while a standby alarm offered an emergency package entitled 'What to do till the psychiatrist comes'.

As the prostitutes talked to each other in a creole of French and Arabic, their scent drifted over my table, a dream of houris borne by the night-world of the Croisette, the untaxed contraband of the senses in this lazy entrepôt of chance and desire. I needed to escape from Eden-Olympia, with its ceaseless work and its ethic of corporate responsibility. The business park was the outpost of an advanced kind of puritanism, and a virtually sex-free zone.

Jane and I rarely made love. The flair she had shown during my days as a virtual cripple had been smothered by a sleep of eye-masks and sedatives, followed by cold showers and snatched breakfasts. She moved naked around our bedroom, in full view of Simone Delage and her husband, flaunting not her sex but her indifference to it.

Cannes offered an antidote to this spartan regime. My parents had been unfaithful, but in the old, unhappy way. My father's affairs complicated his busy life, giving him the harassed existence of a secret agent, forever one step ahead of being unmasked, a fraying conspiracy of rented cars and silent phone calls. He communicated with one lover, the wife of an architect in the same street, by adjusting the roller-blinds, a prearranged code that my mother discovered in a flash of insight worthy of the Bletchley Enigma team. As soon as my father left the house she ran from room to room, raising and lowering the blinds at random. I remembered the lover's bemused gaze as she drove past, trying to make sense of the baffling signals, and my mother's smile of triumph. Less happily, I once found her ironing a half-burned credit-card receipt she had fished from a lavatory bowl.

*   *   *

The streetwalkers stood up, testing their stilettos before stepping into the night. The younger of the two, a twenty-year-old with eyes wiser than any grandmother's, glanced at me for a microsecond too long, as if ready to fit a car-park quickie into her busy evening schedule.

But sex with prostitutes required a special knack, as I had learned during my RAF days in Germany. My girlfriends in England on the whole seemed to like me, at least on even days of the month, from the sixteen-year-old ballet student who dragged me into the family-planning clinic to the adjutant's secretary who listened good-naturedly as I worried on about my parents' postponed divorce. The Polish whores in the bars outside RAF Mülheim were a different breed, scarcely women at all but furies from Aeschylus who intensely loathed their clients. They were obsessed with the Turkish pimps and their children boarded with reluctant sisters, and any show of feeling disgusted them. Warmth and emotion were the true depravity. They wanted to be used like appliances rented out for the hour, offering any part of themselves to the crudest fantasies of the men who paid them.

But at least they were real, in a way that eluded Eden-Olympia. I finished my drink, left a 500-franc note on the saucer and stood up to explore the night. I felt surprisingly light-headed, like a dreamer who had strayed onto a film set of tropical palms and cruise liners. At any moment an orchestra would strike up and the crowds on the Croisette, the Volvo dealers and Arab playboys and orthopaedic surgeons, would form themselves into a disciplined, arm-swinging chorus, belting out a big-band hit.

I followed the two prostitutes past the Noga Hilton, curious to see how far I could go before the puritan conscience pulled the plug. Uninspired by the car-dealers, the women locked arms and strode down the Rue Amouretti to the Place Dubois. They paused to scream abuse at a passing motorist, and veered away into the darkness.

Unable to keep up with them, I rested my knee outside Mère

Besson. After scanning the evening's menu I set off towards the multistorey garage near the railway station, where I had parked the Jaguar. A darker Cannes gathered itself around me once I crossed the Rue d'Antibes. Off-duty chauffeurs, Arab pushers and out-of-work waiters filled the narrow bars. They played the fruit machines, their thighs rocking the pintables until the tilt-signs flashed, an eye on the new arrivals who stepped from the Marseilles train, would-be construction workers and pairs of sharp-tempered young women who shouldered their way to the head of the taxi queue. Pimps ambled around the tunnel entrance to the underpass, a cloaca that drained away the festival city's dreams of lust and fortune.

Inhaling the heady air of north African tobacco, and the cheap aftershave of nerve-gas potency, I crossed the Rue Jaurès to the garage. I fed my ticket into the pay-machine as two men and a young girl walked down the concrete ramp towards the street. With their leather jackets and hard shoulders, the men looked like plainclothes police, and I guessed that they had caught an absconding eleven-year-old trying to board the Paris express. Neither of the men spoke to the girl, who trotted obediently after them, eyes lowered to the ground.

They paused in the entrance, the men searching the street. The girl heard the clatter of coins from the pay-machine, and turned to smile at me, as if pleased that I had won a jackpot. She was dressed in a French schoolgirl's blue skirt and white blouse, dark hair bunched behind her head. With her rouged cheeks, silver lipcoat and mascara she might have been any girl after an hour at her mother's dressing table. But there was nothing childlike about her gaze, and I knew that she was not on her way to the police station. She took in the passing traffic and the lights of the railway station, and then nodded to the men that she was ready to move on.

Forgetting the Jaguar, I walked down the ramp and followed the trio as they set off for the underpass. The Paris express was leaving the station, passengers standing at the windows of the couchettes, their cars stacked on the transporter wagons at the rear of the train. I entered the tunnel as the wheels bit into the steel rails over my head, a noise like pain through which the silver-lipped child walked and skipped.

In the nexus of narrow streets beyond the Boulevard d'Alsace congregated another constituency of the night: Maltese whores and their pimps, transvestites from Recife and Niteroi, runners for the dealers waiting in their cars off the Avenue St-Nicolas, smartly dressed matrons who seemed never to find a client but returned evening after evening, teenage boys waiting for the limousines that would ferry them to the villas of Super-Cannes, the mansions of light that rose above the night.

After dinner in the Vieux Port, Jane and I would sometimes detour through these shabby streets, amazed by the cool professionalism of the working children and the indifference of the local vice squad who made no attempt to rescue them. Thinking of the refuge at La Bocca, I remembered the zebra-striped dress and fishnet tights, and the Alice library that David Greenwood had so touchingly collected. Here in the Rue Valentin the Red Queen was a brothel-keeper and the only looking-glasses were the smudged mirrors in the whores' compacts.

A blond transvestite with the body of a rugby forward stepped into a streetlight, huge feet in a pair of stiletto boots, thighs exposed by minuscule satin shorts. His eyes swept the street, and followed a cruising car driven by a middle-aged man with the face of a depressed bank manager. The car paused and a door opened, and the transvestite dived into the passenger seat, filling the car like a gaudy circus horse.

A party of Volvo dealers, one with his conference name-tag on his breast pocket, watched the Arab factory workers bargain-hunting among the bored whores. I followed the minders and their schoolgirl to the end of the Rue Valentin, where three unmarked vans were parked in a side street. A door slid back and a driver stepped onto the cobbled road. He spoke to the minders and then beckoned to the girl, who dutifully climbed into the passenger seat.

From the darkness around me mobile phones bleeped against the static of two-way radios. I glanced into the second van, where a fair-haired youth in a tracksuit sat behind the wheel. He steered his cigarette smoke away from his passenger, a girl of twelve who wore a Marie-Antoinette gown and silk shoes. She stared through the smeary windscreen, fingers playing aimlessly with a tasselled umbrella.

The schoolgirl I had followed from the garage was listening to the dashboard radio. Her chin bobbed to the disco rhythm, and she seemed cheerful and confident, adjusting the driver's mirror to check her lipstick, a vision of a child-woman as confusing as the doctor's daughter with whom I had first made love so many decades ago. That fumbling sex, the miracle of an attic mattress and a sharp-kneed thirteen-year-old biting my shoulder, had been beyond anything my boyish mind could imagine, promises of wonder that only returned when I saw Jane slumming around my hospital bed.

I opened my wallet and took out the photo-booth picture I had found in the Russian's shoe after our struggle beside the swimming pool. Even in the garish light of the Rue Valentin I could see the resemblance between the smudged image of a demure and placid child, photographed in a Moscow flat, and the mature schoolgirl rebunching her hair, raised arms pressing her small nipples against her cotton blouse.

'Natasha . . .'

I put away the photograph, trying to decide if she would still be here when I brought the Jaguar from the garage. With luck I could pay off her bodyguards, give them the slip and deliver the child to Sister Émilie at La Bocca.

A black estate car turned off the Rue Valentin and stopped behind the vans. A well-groomed woman in her forties, dressed like a hostess working for a private airline, stepped from behind the wheel. She walked to the nearest van and spoke to the blond driver. He helped Marie-Antoinette from her seat, lifting her by the waist of her embroidered dress, and carried her umbrella as she ran in her silk shoes to the estate car. They left together, the child in the rear seat behind the woman driver, the van following with its headlights dimmed.

'*Monsieur . . . ? Ça va . . . ?*'

One of the leather-clad minders strolled towards me, as if ready to discuss the next day's football matches. He lit a cigarette, cupping his hands over a brass lighter and revealing a high Polish forehead.

The schoolgirl noticed me, her head nodding at the music. There was a brief smile as she remembered my jackpot win at the garage pay-station. Then she launched into a sales demonstration of herself, raising her chin and rocking her shoulders. Her eyes watched my hands, waiting for me to open my wallet.

I gestured towards the minder. 'Okay? You wait here with her. I'll bring my car.'

'*Sept mille francs.*'

'*Sept mille?* That's steep. She must be very young.'

'Seven thousand francs . . .' The minder was about twenty years old, with the same pointed nose and chin, and it struck me that he might be the girl's brother.

'It's a deal.' I opened my wallet. 'Natasha?'

'Whatever you like. Natasha, Nina, Ninotchka, it's still seven thousand frances. No Mastercard, no platinum Amex.'

I took all the banknotes from my wallet. Once the girl was in the Jaguar I knew that I could outrun the rusting van. I offered him the loose wad of francs. 'Three thousand now, the rest later.'

'Later? When you come back from heaven?' The Pole turned away, dismissing me to the darkness. 'Later . . .'

'Wait!' I took the ampoule of pethidine from my pocket and

handed it to him. 'Take a close look – you'll find it interesting . . .'

He squinted at the label in the darkness, tapped on the windscreen of the van and pointed to the headlamps. Still bobbing to
the music, the girl switched on the sidelights. The Pole read the
label, and shouted to two men standing in an alleyway next to
the shuttered warehouse of a building merchant.

They stepped from the alley, leather coats greasy in the yellow
glare of the sodium lights. The slimmer of the two drew a cigarette
from a gold case.

'Greenwood?'

'*Da.* Eden-Olympia Polyclinic.'

Cheap teeth gleamed like marked dice. I recognized the Russian
who had grappled with me on the lawn. Holding the ampoule in
his open palm, he walked towards me with almost soundless steps.
I noticed that he wore another pair of expensive shoes from the
Rue d'Antibes. Seeing me, he stepped back, aware that my eyes
were on his feet.

'Mr Sinclair?'

'Alexei – we've met before. At Eden-Olympia.'

'I know. You have my shoe.' He raised the ampoule to the
streetlight. 'Dr Greenwood? You take over?'

'That's it.' Seizing my chance, I said: 'The free clinic – I have
access to the old stock. Methadone, diamorphine, pethidine . . .
as much as you want. I'll get my car and go with Natasha.'

'Good . . .' He watched the girl playing with the radio. Then,
with a flick of his cigarette, he signalled to the Pole, who seized
my shoulders in his heavy hands. 'First, we take your shoes, Mr
Sinclair . . .'

He was staring, unbelievingly, at my thonged sandals when
lights flooded the narrow street, as if a master switch had
illuminated a darkened stage. Three Range Rovers swerved
into the Rue Valentin and swept past us, tyres thudding across
the cobbles, headlamps flashing along the doorways and side

alleys. The streetwalkers and matronly whores, the pimps and Volvo dealers were frozen among the veering shadows.

Then the headlamps dimmed and everyone was running towards the Avenue St-Nicolas. Burly men in black helmets, like the members of a police parachute brigade, leapt from the Range Rovers. All wore the tight-waisted bowling jackets I had first seen in the clinic car park. Clubs in hand, they set upon the fleeing crowd. Two of them chopped a Volvo dealer to the ground, raining blows on his head and back. The streetwalkers I had followed from the Rialto Bar emerged from the scrum, tight skirts rucked around their waists. As they fell to the ground, huge limbs uncoupling from their torsos, legs spread under the whipping truncheons, I saw that both of them were men.

I knelt on the cobbled road, my hands cut by shards of glass from the broken ampoule. The posse moved past, and a flurry of truncheons shattered the windscreen of the van. The schoolgirl had taken shelter behind the steering wheel. Ignoring the violence around her, she fumbled with the radio and picked fragments of windscreen glass from her blouse. She had chewed away part of her silver lipcoat, and the raw flesh showed through the shiny lacquer, as if a too eager lover had taken a bite from her mouth.

'Natasha . . . !' Trying to reassure her, I tapped the passenger window. Then a hand gripped my shoulder.

'Mr Sinclair . . . it's time to leave.'

'Halder?' I turned to face the dark-skinned security guard. He had appeared suddenly from the shadows, stepping from the alley behind me, but I sensed from his nervous feet and fixed eyes that he had been only a few steps from me since my arrival in the Rue Valentin. He was dressed in black trousers, sneakers and sweater, as if he had spent the day among the yachting fraternity at Port-la-Galère. He was unarmed, and ducked when a confused Arab searching for his glasses ten feet from us was clubbed to the ground.

'Halder!' I pulled at his sweater. 'Are you with the police? What's happening here?'

'Let's go, Mr Sinclair . . . we can talk later.' Halder seized my elbow and steered me into the alley behind the builder's warehouse. He grimaced at my cut hands, but pointed to the helmeted men at the end of the Rue Valentin. Having cleared the street, they were striding back to the Range Rovers. One of the drivers sat at his open door, filming the scene with a small camcorder. I assumed they were all members of an auxiliary police unit, a group of volunteer constables recruited to the vice squad.

'They're coming back. It's best if we wait here.' Halder pressed me against a shuttered doorway. He silenced me with a hard hand over my mouth. 'Not now, Mr Sinclair . . .'

Headlamps flared from the Range Rovers, again illuminating the cobbled street, littered with stiletto heels, sequinned purses, pieces of underwear and cigarette lighters. Alexei had held on to his expensive brogues, but the white nodes of broken teeth lay among the fragments of the pethidine ampoule.

The leader of the posse led his squad back to the cars. When he pulled off his helmet I recognized Pascal Zander, panting hard as he stuffed his truncheon into his belt. His fleshy face seemed even coarser in the heat and sweat of violence, his engorged tongue too large for his mouth. He shouted at the camcorder operator, then spat onto the bloody cobbles at his feet.

Around him were three others I knew by sight: Dr Neumunster, chief executive of a German investment bank, who lived on the same avenue in the enclave; Professor Walter, head of cardiology at the clinic; and an American architect named Richard Maxted, a bridge partner of Wilder Penrose. They lounged against the Range Rovers, joking with each other like hunters returning from a boar shoot, happily charged by adrenalin and the camaraderie of the chase.

Within seconds they had gone, the heavy vehicles reversing in a flurry of slamming doors, headlamps hunting for the Avenue St-Nicolas, heading towards Super-Cannes and the presiding powers of the night.

'Mr Sinclair? We can move now.'

I felt Halder's trapped breath leave his lungs, a coarse reek of garlic, spice and fear. He calmed himself, trying to steady his pulse, relieved that I had made no attempt to provoke the posse.

'What about the girl?' I pointed to the damaged van. 'We can't leave her here.'

Natasha sat behind the steering wheel, bobbing to herself in the silence. Flecks of glass gleamed like jewels on her blouse. She seemed unaware of the violence that had erupted around her, as if nothing in her life could ever be a surprise.

'Halder, we need to get her to the police.'

Wearily, Halder held my arm. 'She's best here. Her friends will be back for her.'

'Friends? Halder, she's a child . . .'

'It's been a long day, Mr Sinclair. I'll take you to the garage.'

As we left, the police sirens wailed down the Rue Jaurès, and the first of the barefooted streetwalkers were making their way towards their shoes.

'Are you all right to drive? You look shaky, Mr Sinclair.' Halder helped me into the Jaguar. 'I'll call a taxi. You can collect the car tomorrow.'

'I'm fine.' I felt a painful weal across my right shoulder, realizing for the first time that one of the posse had struck me with his truncheon. 'Those clubs are hard.'

'They were having fun.' Halder pointed to the blood dripping onto the passenger seat. 'You cut your hands. When you get back, see a doctor.'

'I'm married to one.' I took an engine rag from the glove compartment. 'Thanks for helping me. It's a good thing you were there. They wanted heads to crack.'

'Someone needs to keep an eye on you, Mr Sinclair.' Halder nodded at this sage advice, his eyes scanning the cars in the garage. His nostrils flickered at the scent of exhaust fumes, but he still breathed through his mouth. I knew from his huge pupils how frightened he had been, and the special danger in which his darker skin had placed him.

'This Russian, Alexei, and the young Pole — they'll go back for the girl?'

'Of course. She's valuable to them.'

Trying to explain myself, I said: 'I saw them take her to the Rue Valentin. I tried to buy her . . . you know, for an hour. I wanted to get her into the refuge at La Bocca.'

'I understand.' Halder's expression was deliberately neutral, the gaze of a security man who had glanced into too many bedrooms ever to be shocked. 'You were worried for her.'

'They asked for seven thousand francs. Who carries that kind of cash around? What does the girl have to do to earn it?'

'Nothing much. Being eleven is enough.'

'She was lucky the Range Rovers arrived on time. Who were they? Zander was leading the whole thing.'

'That's right. It's a special action group.'

'Volunteer police? Very public-spirited.'

'Not exactly. Think of it as . . . therapeutic.'

'And the Rue Valentin is the disease? That makes sense. Were you with them?'

'No. Let's say I was passing by.' Halder took the car keys from my bloody hand and slid them into the ignition. He wrenched the gear lever into neutral and turned on the engine, using the manual choke to set a fast idling speed. Above the clatter of unaligned carburettors he shouted: 'Go back to Eden-Olympia. See Dr Jane about those hands.'

'Frank . . .' I wanted to thank him, but he had already withdrawn from me, annoyed with himself for having shown his fear. 'I'm glad you were there. I don't know how you managed it.'

'Easy, Mr Sinclair. I followed you all day.' Halder stared at me in his distant way, then relented and slapped the roof above my head as I reversed out of the parking space. 'Tomorrow I'll come round and collect you. We'll go on a special tour.'

'Where exactly?'

'Eden-Olympia. You've never really been there . . .'

19

Elopement

PAIN AU CHOCOLAT IN hand, I watched from the breakfast terrace as Jane climbed from the pool and walked dripping to the diving board. She blew her nose into her fingers, and strutted down the board with the clipped steps of a dressage horse. She sprang into the air and jack-knifed into a clumsy pike before following her hands into the water.

She surfaced with a scowl, and swam to the poolside. Unable to lift herself onto the verge, she waded through the seething foam to the ladder.

'Paul, towel . . . did I make a splash?'

'Dear, you always make a splash.'

'Here. In the pool.'

'A small one. You can dive through a keyhole.'

'Not any longer.' She frowned at the unsettled water. 'That was a lousy dive. I'm out of practice.'

'You work too hard.'

She let me swathe her in the towel. Her hair was flattened to her scalp, exposing a scratch-mark from her broken nails, her eyebrows sleeked back and blanched lips set in a chalky face. She panted as I embraced her shoulders, her skin as cold as a shark's.

'Jane, you're freezing. The pool heater must be on the blink.'

'I switched it off last night. Need to be awake today. Very awake.'

'More committees? Try seeing a patient or two. It might relax you.'

'I'm off to Sophia-Antipolis. We may share medical databanks.'

'So their computers will snuggle up with ours?'

'That's the way the future's going.'

She kissed me with her cold lips, tongue teasing a flake of chocolate from my mouth. She stepped back when I winced at the pressure of her hands on my back.

'Paul? What's happened?'

'Nothing. I caught myself on the car door.'

'Poor man. That's fifties design for you. Time to forget about the Harvard, Paul . . .'

I sat on the terrace, sharing the last of the pastry with a sparrow that had followed me across the garden. Señora Morales was moving around the lounge, discreetly clearing the ash from the settee cushions before the maids arrived.

I had reached home at midnight to find the front door ajar. In the lounge the cannabis and cigarette smoke hung in layers, a microclimate like a volcano's crater. Ash lay on the carpet and coffee tables, marked with curious doodles. Through the blanket of pot I could smell Simone Delage's pallid scent, a pheromone emitted by an ice queen.

Jane was asleep, a Sabena face-mask over her forehead. Careful not to wake her, I soaked my hands in the bathroom, hunting with her eyebrow pincers for any shards of glass. Through the mirror I noticed her lying on her side, staring at my bruised back. She was barely awake, drifting in a dull, narcotic stupor, eyes focusing with an effort as I bandaged my right hand.

'Paul . . . ? What are you doing here?'

'Going to bed. Did I wake you?'

'Can't sleep. Too tired . . .'

'I'll get something for you.'

'Already did. Helps me relax. Your back . . . ?'

She drifted away, sinking her face into the airline mask. I sat beside her, waiting until she breathed steadily, unsure whether to call the night staff at the clinic. As I tried to take her pulse I saw the fresh puncture mark in the crook of her left arm.

By morning she had recovered, refreshed by the deep diamorphine night. Making coffee for her before Señora Morales arrived, I listened to Riviera News for a bulletin on the incident in the Rue Valentin. As I expected, no one had reported the vigilante raid to the Cannes police.

Feeling the bruise on my back, I remembered the truncheons fracturing the windscreen of the van. The violence had been deeply satisfying for Pascal Zander and his senior executives. Entombed all day in their glass palaces, they relished the chance to break the heads of a few pimps and transvestites and impose the rule of the new corporate puritanism.

Yet no one had been concerned about the child-whore sitting alone in the ransacked van. For that matter, I was still unsure about my own motives, and why I had followed little Natasha from the car park. I thought of her stepping confidently into the lurid night, but still childish enough to be pleased by the sound of tumbling coins. Sitting at the kitchen table, I looked through the change in my pocket, the nickel and brass that had bought her smile. Eden-Olympia was an engine of self-deception.

'Paul, is Penrose here?'

'Not yet.'

'It's 9.30. He's supposed to be driving me to Sophia-Antipolis. God, I've been stood up by a psychiatrist.'

'That's professional disgrace. I'll report him to the GMC for ungallantry.'

'Wilder would love that. He's dying to be struck off.'

Jane strode around in her crispest underwear, gazing at the suits and skirts laid out on the bed. Her gestures seemed coarser, but she had recovered her pep and bounce, as if lit by a powerful stimulant.

Admiring her, I found it easy to forget the drugged young woman slumped across the pillows. Physicians, Jane assured me, often prescribed themselves a sedative or booster, no more threatening to health than a double gin or a pan of Turkish coffee.

When she stumbled on the carpet I caught her arm. 'Jane, are you well enough to go?'

'Sure. Why not?'

'I was late last night – problems with the car. Who was here?'

'Alain Delage and Simone. We had fun, watching some screwy sex film. I couldn't sleep, so I gave myself a toot.'

'Bad for you? Your diving is really off.'

'Fuck the diving. I'm the doctor here.' Jane gripped my hands, her numbed fingers missing the bandage on my right palm. 'How did yesterday go?'

'More detective work. I went over to Port-la-Galère and met the widows of the hostages.'

'That must have been awkward. Were they very hostile?'

'Not at all. They knew David and liked him a lot. They still do.'

'Isn't that a little odd? He's supposed to have killed their husbands.' Jane shuddered, and then reached up to smooth my eyebrows, still flaring after the evening's violence. 'It's time you gave up this whole David business.'

'Why? I've found almost nothing.'

'That's what I mean. You're much too involved. All these theories. You're setting up some kind of strange crime rather than trying to solve one. Still, it sounds like quite a day. Then what?'

'I ran into Halder on the Croisette. We had a few drinks together.'

'Halder?' Jane sniffed the crutch of her trouser suit. 'He's rather sweet. He helps me park my car, and hangs around the clinic with those calm eyes. He's waiting for something to happen.'

'He probably fancies you.'

'All men fancy me. It means zilch. The real question is . . . ?'

'Do you fancy him?'

'A little. He's so heroically above it all. He offered me his copy of *Tender is the Night*. Don't sneer, Paul – how many men have tried to improve my mind?' She broke off when a horn sounded from the avenue. 'Wilder . . . Tell him to let me drive. I refuse to die in a car crash with a psychiatrist . . .'

The Japanese sports saloon was parked across the drive, again blocking the Jaguar, its damaged door provocatively close to the chromium bumper whose contours it so closely matched. But Wilder Penrose seemed delighted to see me. He beamed at me as he rolled his large body from the driver's seat. The grimace of pleasure seemed to migrate around his face, colonizing new areas of amiability. With his silk suit and heavy shoulders he resembled a retired boxer who, to his own surprise, had transformed his reserves of aggression into universal goodwill. He kept his fists near his waist, but his upper arms feinted at me as he approached.

'Paul, you're still in one piece? I'm told you were caught up in a bit of unpleasantness last night. Some kind of police action in the Rue Valentin.'

'Vigilantes. Zander and his bully boys from Eden-Olympia.'

'They do help out the local gendarmerie.' Penrose showed me his teeth, as if advertising a dentifrice. 'I'm sorry you were involved. It sounded rather nasty.'

'It was. Zander and his pals had a thoroughly good time.'

'Pascal can be a little heavy-handed. There's a streak of cruelty there, but at least it's channelled into something socially useful. You've come out of it looking well. There's nothing like a little violence to tone up the system.' He glanced at the upstairs window as Jane shouted to Señora Morales. 'Is Jane calling for help? We ought to be off.'

'Give her five minutes. I kept her awake last night.' I added: 'She finds it hard to sleep – it's a little worrying.'

'Too many sleeping pills?'

'Stronger than that.'

Penrose's face arranged itself into a reflective cast. He put an arm around my shoulders. 'You're concerned, Paul, like any husband. But Jane's too intelligent, she won't come to any harm. Besides, she's exploring herself. If you're worried, come to me.'

'I will. By the way, say nothing about the Rue Valentin.'

'Of course not.' Still gripping my shoulders in his bear-like paw, Penrose gazed contentedly at the Jaguar. 'Halder tells me he's taking you on a tour of Eden-Olympia.'

'Later this afternoon. I assume he'll follow the murder route. I want to stage a reconstruction.'

'Not with live ammunition?' Laughing at his own joke, Penrose slapped my back. I guessed that Halder had told him of my bruised skin. 'Forget that, Paul. You deserve to be encouraged. You're our village historian. Eden-Olympia has its corporate past, stored away in all those disks and annual reports, but it has no vernacular history. May 28 was our Dealey Plaza. Like it or not, it's all the history we have.'

'I'll do my best.'

'Good.' Penrose lowered his voice. 'By the way, what exactly were you doing in the Rue Valentin? It's not your kind of beat.'

'It isn't. I saw this child outside the railway station with a couple of local thugs. Something didn't seem right.'

'That makes sense. So you followed her?'

'Into the Rue Valentin. Then I realized why she was there.'

'Sordid. What can one say? Tragic for the child, but sexual pathology is such an energizing force. People know that, and will stoop to any depravity that excites them.'

'The Russian who attacked me here was some sort of minder. He wanted seven thousand francs.'

'That's a lot. Seven hundred pounds? She must be very pretty.'

'She is. There's a kind of sweetness about her. Along with more or less total corruption.'

'Sad . . .' Penrose was at his most sympathetic. 'Someone saw you offering money for her. Not true, I take it?'

'I did. I wanted to get her away from there, take her to the nuns at La Bocca. At least, I think that's what I wanted to do.'

'You're not sure?'

'Not entirely. It's hard to admit.'

'Paul, I understand.' Penrose spoke in a conspiratorial murmur. 'It's brave of you to face up to it. These impulses exist in all of us. They're the combustible fuel the psyche runs on.'

'Much too combustible. I could have burned more than my fingers.'

'No . . .' Penrose pressed a hand to my cheek, speaking in a barely audible voice that seemed to come from the air around us. 'We're talking about thoughts, not deeds. We don't give in to every passing whim or impulse. But it's a mistake to ignore them.'

'And what if . . . ?'

'You feel drawn from thought to deed?' Penrose bunched his huge fists in front of my nose. 'Seize the hour. Pay the price. Be true to your real self, embrace all the possibilities of your life. Eden-Olympia will help you, Paul . . .'

I waved to Jane as the car accelerated away, but she was already brandishing a position paper in Penrose's face. I assumed that the psychiatrist was watching me in his rear-view mirror. In his playful way he was egging me on, urging me to board the escalator of possibility that had begun to unroll itself at my feet.

Yet his words had been reassuring, and I felt less concerned that I had tried to buy the Russian girl from her minders. Had the vigilante group not burst upon the Rue Valentin I would have taken the child with me, and the journey to La Bocca would have had the character of an unconscious elopement . . .

20

The Grand Tour

HALDER'S MOTIVES WERE more difficult to read. He arrived soon after three o'clock, when I was working on the latest batch of proofs sent to me by Charles, an act of charity that allowed me to maintain the illusion of my editorship. While I changed, Halder glanced sceptically at the pages, his curiosity roused by the aircraft illustrations. He wandered out to the swimming pool, where he bounced the beach ball across the water in his usual morose way.

'Ready, Mr Sinclair?'

'I hope so. Why not?'

'No reason. This is your day.'

Halder led the way to his Range Rover. Once again I was struck by how detached he seemed from Eden-Olympia. His slender fingers, as sensitive as a neurosurgeon's, touched the controls on the instrument panel, as if retuning the image of the business park in his mind. He reminded me of an experienced embassy official in a foreign capital, always exploring the terrain of possibilities open to him, the concealed entrances to exclusive hotels, the after-hours drinking clubs where the important contacts were made.

In turn, I suspected that he saw me as the naive spouse of a middle-ranking employee, trapped in a self-created maze of two-way mirrors and sexual impulses I scarcely understood. I wondered how the Reverend Dodgson's Alice would have coped with Eden-Olympia. She would have grown up quickly and married an elderly German banker, then become a recluse in a mansion high above Super-Cannes, with a fading facelift and a phobia about reflective surfaces. Halder might have been her chauffeur but never her lover. He was too fastidious, his sensitive nostrils forever flickering at some passing mood, and too suspicious of other people's dreams. I knew that he was using me for purposes of his own, but I guessed that, despite himself, he almost liked me.

'Mr Sinclair – are you sure? This could be stressful for you.' Halder hesitated over the ignition keys. 'You were very close to Greenwood.'

'I hardly knew him.'

'You know him a lot better now.'

'You're right. By the way, thanks for stepping in last night.'

'Glad to be there.' Halder nodded at my bandaged hand. 'What you ran into was a "ratissage". A bowling-club speciality.'

'They enjoyed themselves. There's nothing more satisfying than a fit of old-fashioned morality.'

'That was nothing to do with morality.' Halder flashed his headlamps at a passing security vehicle. 'Just an evening workout for one of our self-help groups.'

'There are others? What do the Cannes police feel about them?'

'They keep out of the way. Zander and Delage are important people. Be careful, Mr Sinclair.'

'Am I in danger?'

'Not yet. I'll warn you when the time comes.'

'Thanks. Am I asking too many questions?'

'About Greenwood's death? Who could object to the truth?'

'A lot of people. Especially if Greenwood didn't carry out all the killings.'

'You think he didn't?'

'I'm not sure.' I watched Halder start the engine, and waited for him to drive off, but he seemed in no hurry to move. 'I think Greenwood probably killed Bachelet and Dominique Serrou –

an old-fashioned crime of passion. But the others? There are corporate rivalries here fuelled by billions of dollars. One faction decided to seize its chance and settle a few scores. Charbonneau, the chairman of the holding company, was the real target, along with Robert Fontaine. The others were window-dressing – Professor Berthoud, the chief pharmacist, and Vadim, the manager of the TV centre . . . they're too unimportant, but killing them creates the impression of a series of random murders. A distraught English doctor has just shot his lover and her boyfriend. He's been burning with jealousy for months, practising his marksmanship for the moment he catches them in bed together. Now he's wandering around with a smoking gun, his mind in a daze of death. It's the perfect opportunity to rearrange the chessboard. More shots ring out, and the real killers step back into the looking-glass.'

'So Greenwood was a patsy – like Lee Harvey Oswald?'

'It's just about feasible. Why did it take the security system here so long to react? Because a secret group of very senior people were talking on their mobile phones. The clocks stopped while they decided on their targets.'

'And Greenwood? What is he doing while all this goes on?'

'Sitting in his office, staring at the blood on his hands. Or he never left Bachelet's house. He lay down next to his dead lover and blew his brains out. That must have been a huge bonus to the conspirators. For an hour or so they could kill anyone they liked and blame it on Greenwood. Halder, the jigsaw fits.'

'It doesn't. It doesn't fit at all.' Halder pressed his slim hands to his face, massaging his drawn cheeks. 'You think too much about Greenwood. I liked him, he helped me get my job, but . . . Let's assume Greenwood did carry out the killings, and see where that leads us.'

'Fine by me.' I took the Riviera News transcript from my pocket. I paused while Halder reversed into the avenue, realizing from his clumsy gear change that he was as much under strain as

I was. 'Everything starts at the TV centre, where Greenwood is supposed to have seized his hostages.'

'Right.' Halder stopped by the kerb and stared at the wind-screen, his eyes fixed on a dead fly embedded in a pool of its own amber. When he spoke, his voice was flat and well rehearsed. 'A camera in the car park picked him up at 6.58 a.m. The film is lost, but the security people on duty say he was talking to an unknown man, maybe one of the chauffeurs. We assume Green-wood ordered him into the car at gunpoint. When he drove off it's likely he had all three hostages with him. Agreed, Mr Sinclair?'

'If you believe the story of this "lost" film. I don't think they were hostages, and he certainly didn't kill them. They were there to help him in some way. Bachelet might have suspected that something was brewing up, and kept Greenwood under surveillance. The chauffeurs probably smuggled in the rifle and planned to drive Greenwood over the border into Italy. Nothing else makes sense. Why would he need hostages at all? Why not go straight into the first killing?'

'Who can say? Maybe he was lonely.' Halder raised a hand to calm me. 'I mean it. He has a long day ahead of him. He's been up for three or four hours, assuming he had any sleep at all. He's been cleaning his weapon, checking his ammunition packs. For the first time he realizes what the next hour is going to involve. He's passing the TV centre and sees the chauffeurs and the engineer in the car park. He knows them slightly and feels they'll understand what he's doing.'

'It's possible. Just . . .'

'Either way, with three hostages he has a fall-back position. He can negotiate a deal if things go wrong. So he bundles them into his car.'

'Quite an achievement,' I commented. 'He can drive a car and keep his weapon fixed on three prisoners.'

'Suppose one of the chauffeurs drove? They knew Greenwood, and could see he was very disturbed. They decided not to excite

177

him.' Halder pointed to the raised garage door. 'Greenwood brings them here and ties them up. It's about 7.20, and he has five minutes to reach the Bachelet house. It's four hundred yards from here, and target number one. Now he's on the move, ready to kill his first victims . . .'

Halder steadied his breathing, and let the Range Rover roll down the avenue. We cruised under the plane trees and passed a group of Portuguese cleaning girls climbing into their bus. They spent the days polishing the mirror-like parquet floors, wiping the last white crystals from the smeary table-tops, throwing out the condoms stuck in the toilet traps, probing everything except the dreams of their coporate employers.

Were assassins aware of the contingent world? I tried to imagine Lee Harvey Oswald on his way to the book depository in Dealey Plaza on the morning he shot Kennedy. Did he notice a line of overnight washing in his neighbour's yard, a fresh dent in the next-door Buick, a newspaper boy with a bandaged knee? The contingent world must have pressed against his temples, clamouring to be let in. But Oswald had kept the shutters bolted against the storm, opening them for a few seconds as the President's Lincoln moved across the lens of the Zapruder camera and on into history.

Had Greenwood felt the same clamour of the contingent? Had he seen the satellite dishes on the Merck building as they locked onto the sky, downloading Tokyo stock prices and Chicago pig-meat futures? The gun-metal office buildings and unwalked forest paths must have seemed like a film set waiting for the opening credits.

'Three minutes, twenty seconds left . . .' Halder checked his watch. 'Not much time to change his mind.'

We climbed a small hill, then freewheeled to a halt behind a pick-up loaded with pool maintenance equipment.

'Where are we?' I asked. 'Wilder Penrose lives somewhere here.'

'This is the Bachelet house.' Halder pointed to a three-storey villa with a boxy mansard roof and arsenic-green roof-tiles. High wrought-iron gates were topped by a pair of entry cameras. 'Dr and Mrs Oshima of the Fuji Corporation live here now.'

'Very discreet. It's quite a fortress.' I thought of Greenwood parking his car and drawing the rifle onto his lap as he stared at this house of death. 'I'm surprised he could get in. The windows weren't forced?'

'No sign anywhere. But people get careless, they leave doors unlocked, forget to set the alarm system.'

'Bachelet was head of security. Still, Greenwood might have walked up to the front door and rung the bell. Where were they shot?'

'In Bachelet's bedroom, on the second floor.'

I looked at the immaculate gravel, and almost heard the crunch of Greenwood's steps as he approached the house, rifle in his hands. I folded the Riviera News transcript, aware that the typewritten text no longer matched the reality of the killing ground. An upstairs window opened, revealing the geisha-like face of a middle-aged Japanese woman wearing a mask of white cream. With the windows closed to seal in the air-conditioning, the brief sounds of gunfire would have been barely audible.

'Mrs Oshima . . . I don't suppose a well-bred Japanese woman would show us round her bedroom.'

'I doubt it.' Halder pulled a large manila envelope from the instrument panel shelf. He slid out three black-and-white photographs. 'These might give you a feel for the atmosphere.'

I lowered the sun visor to shield my eyes from the afternoon light. Taken by a police cameraman, the first photograph showed a forty-year-old man lying across a double bed, his back to the pillows. An overnight growth of beard stained his chin, and his handsome face was disfigured by the blood that flushed his nose and mouth. This was Guy Bachelet, the former security chief at Eden-Olympia, whose picture I had last seen in the framed group portrait at the La Bocca refuge.

Two bullet holes marked his barrel chest, one in his breastbone and the other below his left nipple. Neither had led to heavy bleeding, but a third bullet wound to his right thigh had leaked a pool of blood that covered his legs in a black mantle.

I assumed that Greenwood had shot Bachelet from the bedroom doorway, first hitting him in the thigh. As blood pumped from his victim's femoral artery Greenwood had taken more careful aim, then shot him twice through the chest.

The second photograph showed an almost naked woman sprawled on the tiled floor beside the bed. She lay face up, one hand pressed against the carved oak footboard, the other raised to her face, as if trying to ward away any further bullets. Her mouth was open, exposing a gap in her upper teeth, where a partial dental plate had fallen onto the floor. Her pale skin was speckled with black dots, but her face was clearly that of an intelligent Frenchwoman of the professional class.

She had been shot once through the heart at close range, and burns from the explosive charge had seared the white skin around the wound. She wore a cupless black brassiere that exposed her small breasts, one of them licked by the tongue of blood that flowed from the entry wound. I guessed that she and Bachelet had been playing some erotic game the previous evening, and that she had been too sleepy or too drugged to remove the garment.

The third photograph was a close-up of the bedside table. Behind the digital clock, a corporate gift from Monsanto, were a crack pipe and a plastic bag holding half a dozen cocaine pellets. Matches, paper spills and twists of silver foil filled an ashtray, and a video remote control rested on two cassettes with handwritten labels. Below, lying in the open drawer, was a collection of jewellery, triple-stranded pearl necklaces, diamond chokers and emerald pendants, all with their sales stickers still attached.

'Sweet dreams . . . .' With a shudder, I held the photographs at arm's length. 'What films were they watching?'

'Does it matter?' Halder frowned at my morbid question. 'If you want, I can find out.'

'Forget it – I think we know. Where did you get hold of the prints?'

'The security files. There are other sets. No one knows I borrowed them.'

'These scene-of-the-crime photos freeze the blood. We're looking into Greenwood's head.'

'Greenwood's?'

'More than the victims'.' I ran my finger over the background details, the deco lamp on the bedside table, the marks on the wall where the headboard had chafed the plaster, perhaps during bouts of cocaine-driven sex between the security chief and his mistress. The spectacle of their intimate clutter, the crack pipe and cassettes, must have burned themselves into Greenwood's mind. Only this blood-stained tableau was left, the postures of death and the peek-a-boo bra of a middle-aged doctor.

'Dr Serrou . . .' I commented. 'The selfless lady of the refuge.'

'She was. People have private lives, Mr Sinclair. Even you. It's possible he didn't mean to kill her. She just picked the wrong bedroom to wake up in.'

'I don't think so.' I pointed to the floor around the bed. Bloody footprints marked the tiles, so clear that even Dr Serrou's quirky toes, hooked by a lifetime of ward rounds and constricting shoes, were clearly visible. 'Imagine what happened. The first shot wakes her up. Bachelet's blood is pumping all over the bed, her legs are covered with the stuff. Then Greenwood steps forward and shoots Bachelet through the chest. There's a roar of noise, a red spray in her face. Greenwood turns the rifle on her, but perhaps he hesitates – after all, they were colleagues, they'd started the refuge together. She looks pleadingly at this English doctor she knows so well, now obviously out of his mind. She gets off the bed and walks towards him, leaving footprints in her lover's blood. Somehow she hopes to calm him.'

'And then?'

'He shoots her dead. At the last moment she realizes that friendship counts for nothing and that she's about to fade into Greenwood's dream of death.'

'So . . .' Halder pinched his nose, and calmed his fluttering nostrils. 'Was it a crime passionnel?'

'No, it wasn't. I was wrong there. Completely wrong.'

'He would have shot her first?'

'Not necessarily. But she and Bachelet weren't having a secret affair. This was a long-standing relationship – the crack pipe, the porno-cassettes, the underwear. These were two people who'd spent a lot of time exploring each other. She owed nothing to David Greenwood.'

'Then why did he kill her?'

'That I can't say. But it looks as if . . .'

'He killed some of the others? Maybe all of them? And there wasn't a conspiracy?'

'It's possible.' I stared at the photograph of the bedside table. 'There are too many question marks and no answers. These necklaces and chokers – they still have their price tags on.'

'They come from a jewellery heist in Nice. About three weeks before the murders.'

'Why are they here?'

'Maybe Bachelet was holding them for a French undercover team.'

'And you believe that?'

'I don't have to.' Halder moved restlessly in his seat, as if we had spent too long at this first murder site. 'I don't know why any of this happened. Greenwood didn't leave a suicide note.'

'He thought he'd get away with it.'

'Never. Greenwood was no fool. At the end he didn't have

enough time. That's always the trouble with mass-killers. They run out of time.'

'He hated something about Eden-Olympia. I think you know what it was.'

'He never told me.'

I handed the photographs back to Halder. 'Any others I can see?'

'A few. We'll wait till we get there.' Halder started the engine with a flourish, and waved to Mrs Oshima, watching us suspiciously from her bedroom window. 'We need fresh air, Mr Sinclair. Fresh air and fresh minds . . .'

21

Drugs and Deaths

THE EARLY DAY shift was leaving the clinic, nurses and technicians driving from the exits in their identical small cars. A young houseman wearing his white coat and name-tag walked past us towards the apartment houses beside the lake. He was barely an arm's length from the Range Rover, but so self-engrossed that he failed to notice when Halder saluted him.

'That says a lot about Eden-Olympia . . .' I watched the distracted medico stride away, oblivious to the lake and parkland, his head responding only to the flicker of a lizard beside the path. 'People are so immersed in their work they wouldn't recognize the end of the world. It explains why no one saw anything unusual about Greenwood. There's no civic sense here.'

'There is.' Halder pointed to a nearby surveillance camera. 'Think of it as a new kind of togetherness.'

Halder had recovered from his nervousness outside the Bachelet house, and was ready to humour me and resume his role as tour guide to an obsession. He opened his envelope of photographs, waiting for me to calm myself. By abandoning the conspiracy theory I had returned to earth, a hard landing that had wrecked my hopes of finding a larger explanation for David Greenwood's psychotic behaviour. But the authority of the murder photographs was overwhelming. A violent rage had written itself across the blood-stained walls, a death warrant signed in fragments of bone and gristle.

'All set, Mr Sinclair? Good . . . I'll take it slowly.' Halder spoke in a low, unemotional voice, as if describing a minor traffic incident. 'The third person to die was Professor Berthoud, chief pharmacist at the clinic. An inside security camera caught Greenwood entering the lobby at 7.52. No weapon was visible, but we assume he carried the rifle under his white coat.'

'The metal detectors didn't pick it up?'

'None are installed. This is a hospital. Metal objects are everywhere – emergency trolleys, hip replacement pins, oxygen cylinders . . .'

'Fair enough. Go on.'

'Berthoud was in his private office in the pharmacy on the sixth floor, next to the strongroom where all the drugs at Eden-Olympia are held. He was sitting at his desk when Greenwood fired at him through the outer glass door.'

'Why didn't he go straight in?'

'The door was electronically locked from Berthoud's desk. It gave access to the office and a side corridor to the drugs room.'

'Berthoud would have buzzed him in.'

'Greenwood needed surprise. He must have known how shaky he was starting to feel. Berthoud might have guessed something was wrong and alerted security.'

'And Wilder Penrose?' I asked. 'Greenwood wounded him.'

'He was in the corridor, coming back from the drugs room. He probably caught a look at the rifle barrel, stepped back and was cut by the flying glass.'

'But Greenwood didn't see him, or he would have finished him off. Why didn't Greenwood look for Penrose in his office?'

'Maybe he did. But he had to move fast. Security would start closing around him at any moment. From now on he was after targets of opportunity.'

'That makes sense.' I stared at the surveillance camera near the Range Rover, realizing that Halder and I were being watched in the security building. Our battlefield tour had almost certainly been authorized by Pascal Zander. 'Anyway, imagine Greenwood's state of mind. He's just killed three people. He can't think coherently, but he knows he has to make it to the next target. One thing bothers me – why didn't Penrose raise the alarm?'

'Greenwood locked the outer doors when he left, trapping Penrose in the corridor. The security people found him an hour later, practically unconscious, trying to tourniquet his arm with his coat sleeves. He only just made it.' Halder shook his head in genuine admiration. 'You need to be a psychiatrist to cope with something like that.'

'But no one heard anything? Isn't that a little strange?'

'This is a hospital,' Halder again reminded me. 'The walls are well insulated. So the patients don't hear machinery or . . .'

'. . . other patients in pain. Are there any photos?'

'Just one.' Halder's hands were on the steering wheel, and he made an effort to control his fretting fingers. He wiped the thin film of sweat from his face, and then opened the manila envelope. 'I don't know if it says much.'

I held the photograph against the instrument panel. The pharmacist's office was a windowless room filled with metal cabinets and bookshelves stacked with pharmaceutical directories, drug manuals and updated regulations of the French Ministry of Health.

Professor Berthoud sat at his desk, face and torso turned to the camera, as if noticing someone at the glass door. He was a plump, suave-looking man in his late forties, with a neat moustache and even neater desk, in the centre of which lay a metal suitcase. Berthoud had removed the jacket of his dove-grey suit, and wore a striped shirt and paisley tie. He had yet to put on his lab coat, suggesting that he was about to carry out a private task before taking up his official duties.

Whatever the task, he had not been able to see it through. His head and shoulders rested against the ventilation shaft behind his desk. His mouth was open, as if he had been trying to call to someone in the next room. His tie hung vertically from his tight collar, with the small knot of a punctilious and pedantic man.

I could see the bullet hole that punctured one of the whorls of the paisley pattern. Blood ran onto his lap, flowing down one leg to form a pool between his feet, but the neatness of this trimly professional man was preserved in death. His cheeks had slipped down his face, losing their hold on the underlying muscles, yet his hands remained calmly on the desk, protecting a plastic sachet filled with a chalk-like powder. A dozen or so sachets lay inside the suitcase.

I pointed to a set of electronic scales on the desk. 'He was weighing something. What exactly was in the sachets?'

Halder pinched his nostrils, and shrugged with studied vagueness. 'I guess . . . pharmaceuticals?'

'But what kind? It looks as if Greenwood walked in on a drug-running operation.'

'Mr Sinclair . . . a lot of white powders are moving around. Some have Max Factor printed on them. Industrial chemicals, detergents used to clean out dialysis machines . . .'

'And all in special packs with the manufacturer's brand-name and seal. Why would Berthoud be using the scales?'

Halder leaned against his headrest and turned to watch me. 'You think the powder was cocaine or heroin?'

'It looks like it. Something illicit was going on. And Penrose must have known about it.'

'You ought to talk to him, Mr Sinclair.'

'I will, when the time is right. I'm surprised the investigating judge wasn't more interested. But why would a man as senior as Berthoud risk everything on a small consignment of illegal cocaine, when he could legitimately order the stuff by the hundredweight? This suitcase and the scales are amateurish. It's as if he was playing a game out of sheer bravado.'

Halder nodded approvingly, pleased by my progress through the obstacle course. 'Go on, Mr Sinclair . . .'

'How is it that Greenwood arrived just as Berthoud is getting his shipment ready? That's quite a coincidence. And what was Penrose doing in the drug store?' I handed the photograph back to Halder. 'Where did these photos come from?'

'The Cannes police. Their eyes aren't as sharp as yours.' He started the engine of the Range Rover. 'We ought to move on. Ghosts are walking around Eden-Olympia . . .'

The TV centre's car park was full, and Halder paused in an access lane fifty yards from the mirror-clad building. The international soccer results and the digests of German, Japanese and French news bulletins were broadcast from the basement, a maze of airless recording studios and edit suites. Here I had once lost myself after being interviewed about my first impressions of Eden-Olympia. Wandering through the wrong doors, I found myself an involuntary guest on a wine-tasting programme run by two strong-minded Swiss women.

'The TV centre, Mr Sinclair,' Halder told me. 'It's where I came in . . .'

I waited for him to drive towards the entrance, but he was staring in an oddly fixed way at the revolving doors. The muscles of his face had tightened, pulled by a set of interior strings he could barely control.

'Halder, can we park in the shade?' I pointed to the awning over the entrance. 'It's getting hot out here, in all senses . . .'

'Not yet.' Halder opened his door and touched the tarmac with his foot. 'This is where I parked on May 28. Right here. A kind of personal ground zero, Mr Sinclair.'

'Halder, relax . . .' Concerned for him, I held his wrist as he drummed his foot against the ground. 'You were waiting here when Georges Vadim was shot?'

'We arrived ten minutes later. Vadim was already dead, and Greenwood had gone.'

'What time was this?'

'About 8.35 a.m.' Halder closed the driver's door and composed himself, his hands gripping the steering wheel. When he spoke he seemed to be addressing himself rather than me. 'I checked into the security office at eight. At 8.30 a sound engineer contacted a guard on duty outside the TV centre. He reported a rifle shot in one of the studios. The guard assumed he'd heard gunfire coming from a movie soundtrack. But Captain Kellerman sent three of us over to check things out.'

'You went into the building?'

'I was the rookie – I'd been at Eden-Olympia only two weeks. The other two, Henri Gille and a Spaniard called Menocal, left me sitting in the car. Seconds later, they rushed out in a panic. They said the general manager had shot himself. They'd found Vadim in an edit suite with a Remington pistol. It was his personal weapon, registered with security. I radioed through to Captain Kellerman, and he tried to contact Bachelet.'

'And Bachelet wasn't answering his phone?'

'We thought he was in the pool or having a shower.'

'But why no general alert?'

'Vadim's death looked like suicide. We had orders to act normally and hush everything up. Captain Kellerman came over. He checked the Remington and knew it hadn't been fired. Then Menocal found a rifle cartridge behind the door. It looks as if Greenwood spoke to Vadim long enough for him to get out the pistol.'

'So Greenwood shot him dead.' I gazed at the revolving door, and imagined the white-coated doctor with the rifle under his arm, blinking at the bright May sunlight as he emerged from the building. 'I've always thought he was mad, but he must have been very controlled.'

'Greenwood was unlucky.' Halder spoke in a neutral tone, as if describing a conflict between strangers. 'The sound engineer was walking down the corridor, or no one would have heard about the shooting.'

'How did Greenwood know Vadim would be in that particular

edit suite? I've been down there – the place is a maze of cubicles and double doors.'

'Vadim's secretary said he always used that suite to check out new videos. Stuff made by amateur film groups at Eden-Olympia.'

'So Greenwood knew he'd be there. Any photos?'

'None. Someone held them back.' Halder shrugged tolerantly. 'I heard they showed certain "forbidden" things, the kind that would be bad for Eden-Olympia's image. Gille told me he switched on the edit machine. It played some very interesting material.'

'Films for the evening's adult channel?'

'More interesting than that.' Halder spoke without irony. His face was toneless, a hollowed black stone. All emotion had withdrawn from his features, hiding behind the sharp bones of his nose and cheeks. He seemed to have aged in the brief time we had toured the murder sites of Eden-Olympia.

Making a guess, I asked: 'Something to do with children?'

'I think so. Keep it to yourself.'

'No wonder the photos are missing.'

A security guard emerged from the TV centre and scanned the parked cars. He noticed the Range Rover and strolled towards us, then saluted when Halder waved to him.

'Time to leave,' Halder said. 'After May 28 they have . . . expectations of violence. It's the perfect set-up for another David Greenwood. Even the guards don't trust each other.'

'You'll be able to take over. I imagine Captain Kellerman is no longer working for us.'

'He left in June. How did you know?'

'I assumed the pension package was too generous to turn down.'

'You're right. He's running a bar in Martinique. Eden-Olympia helped with the finance.' Halder started the engine and drove between the lines of parked cars towards the exit. '"Take over . . ." That's a fascinating idea, Mr Sinclair.'

'Thank you. The most interesting one I've had? I dare say you've given it a lot of thought . . .'

22

The Roof Deck

WE CIRCLED THE perimeter road, taking a last look at the TV centre, and then drove down the main avenue, past the office blocks set so securely in their plots of parkland. Halder stopped outside a seven-storey building sheathed in pale travertine marble. The imposing structure overlooked a landscaped roundabout that marked the western limit of the avenue. The administrative headquarters of Eden-Olympia displayed an almost imperial grandeur, with its classical pilasters rising to a stylized post-modern pediment. This was the first office building to be constructed at the business park, but after a bombastic overture the architecture that followed was late modernist in the most minimal and self-effacing way, a machine above all for thinking in.

As a nerve jumped in his cheek, Halder left the engine running and scanned the satellite dishes hiding behind a Grecian colonnade. I suspected that he had volunteered his services to Pascal Zander, offering to take me around the murder route, but now regretted the decision. The blood-steeped circuit had become an unwelcome tour of the memories inside his own head.

'The main administration building,' I commented. 'The brain centre of Eden-Olympia. This is where Charbonneau and Fontaine died?'

'Impressive, isn't it? Don't believe what you see. The place looks as tight as Fort Knox but it's as easy to step into as a Vegas hotel.'

'Even so, how did Greenwood get in? These were the two

most senior people in the business park. A full-scale alert must have been under way.'

'Not yet. Greenwood was fifteen minutes ahead of us.' For once, Halder sounded almost defensive. 'Remember, we still hadn't found Bachelet or Professor Berthoud. We didn't know who Vadim's killer was or whether he had any more targets. Greenwood was a doctor at the clinic, with top-level clearance, wearing a name-tag and a white coat, carrying an electronic pass-key that could get him through any door.'

'So no one tried to stop him when he walked in.' I thought of Greenwood, parking here only a few months earlier. He had moved around Eden-Olympia like a messenger from the dark gods, leaving little parcels of death. 'Where did he shoot Charbonneau – in his office?'

'In the private suite next door. A six-room apartment fitted with gym, massage table, Jacuzzi. Greenwood told the secretary he'd brought a new prescription. He took Charbonneau into the bathroom, made him strip and shot him dead in the Jacuzzi. The suite was soundproofed.'

'Why was that?'

'For private reasons. The secretary didn't know what had happened until the security alert ten minutes later. Then she had a nervous breakdown.'

'Grim.' I stared up at the roof. 'She was having a nightmare and no one told her she was awake. Any photos?'

'Not available. Charbonneau was naked. I hear the photos are . . . indelicate.'

'Unpleasant wounds?'

'Not the kind caused by gunshots.'

'What other kind are there?'

'Let's say, recreational.'

'He was into S/M?'

'That kind of thing. Not a good advertisement for Eden-Olympia.'

'That explains the soundproofing.' I reached across Halder and switched off the engine, glad to have a moment's silence. 'Then Greenwood moved off to find Robert Fontaine?'

'He didn't have far to go. Fontaine had a penthouse on the seventh floor.'

'And he let Greenwood in?'

'Greenwood was treating him for prostate problems. Bear in mind it's only 9.05. Captain Kellerman was still trying to contact Bachelet.'

'So Greenwood shot Fontaine dead. In bed?'

'In his political office. Fontaine was planning to run as a deputy in the local elections.'

'Not as a communist, I take it?'

'More right-wing. In fact, so right-wing it's off the scale.'

'National Front?'

'Closely linked.' Halder smiled thinly. 'Fontaine's group targeted "social" opponents. Their identity photos covered the walls where he was shot. His blood was all over them. Greenwood had a nice sense of humour.'

'"Social" opponents.' I echoed Halder's ironic stress. 'Not rival candidates?'

'More the people who might vote for them. People with faces they didn't like.'

'Darker faces? Maghrebians?'

'Blacks, yellows, browns. Anything except pinko-grey. Faces like mine. People of the "other" side.'

'Who might canvass and vote for left-wing candidates. How did Fontaine and his people target them? I take it they used market-research firms?'

'Why bother? They saw them walking down the back streets in La Bocca and Mandelieu.'

'But they had their photos? It sounds very professional.'

'Mr Sinclair . . .' Halder surveyed me patiently. 'We're talking about coolie labour – factory hands, van drivers, building-site workers. The photos in Fontaine's office were taken after they were dead.'

'After . . . ? How did they die?'

'All kinds of sudden ways. Traffic accidents, mostly. The back streets in La Bocca get very dark at night. It's easy for a truck to swerve. There's a squeal of tyres, and then the photoflash . . .'

'Halder — you've seen this?'

But Halder made no reply. He waved me away when I reached for the envelope of photographs. Since our arrival at the Bachelet house he had been trying to provoke me, but had succeeded only in provoking himself. He drummed at the gear lever, irritated that he had trapped himself within the loop of his own anger.

'Last one . . .' Halder turned off the avenue, so sharply that my head struck the window pillar. Without apology, he drove three hundred yards into the park, and stopped outside a dome-shaped building that housed the personnel department of Eden-Olympia. The ground-floor picture windows were filled with dioramas of lakeside apartments, and illuminated displays adver-tised vacancies for office juniors, cleaners and gardeners, the invisibles of Eden-Olympia, a population who left no shadows in the sun.

A party of hopefuls, mostly Spanish women in their best formal wear, dismounted from a bus, awed by the silent perfection of this lake and forest world. Halder watched them file into the building, shaking his head with the weary tolerance of a veteran eyeing a squad of callow recruits.

'Olga Carlotti . . . ?' I took the photograph from Halder. 'She was director of personnel for the whole of Eden-Olympia. I assume Greenwood had no problems getting in to see her?'

'A doctor in a white coat isn't most people's idea of a serial killer. The security men saw him cross the lobby and said he looked normal. The place was filled with ushers, applicants coming out of interview booths, clerks checking social-security references. He showed his pass and went straight up to her.'

Death at Eden-Olympia seemed to come by flashlight, in the lens of a police photographer. Olga Carlotti lay across her desk, arms hanging loosely, ringed fingers almost touching the floor. She had been shot while inspecting a selection of passport-booth snaps. Blood from the bullet wound in the back of her head formed a mask of black lace across the features of a well-groomed Italian woman in her forties.

A canted interior window looked down into the concourse below. The interview booths were empty, but a crowd of security guards, French police and office personnel stared up at the Carlotti office, watching the forensic team at work.

'I've seen enough.' Chilled by this last death, I handed the print back to Halder. 'Let's call it a day. Counting up all these murders is a nasty kind of arithmetic. Where were you at this time?'

'9.45? Driving with Captain Kellerman to the Siemens building. An armed man had tried to slip through the entrance on the garage roof. Someone parking a car said he saw a doctor with a rifle.'

'Greenwood? Did he enter the building?'

'Briefly. He reached the lobby but ran off when the security men challenged him. By now the general alert had gone out.'

Halder cruised along the central avenue, holding the Range Rover to the pace of a running man. For all his self-control, a fine sweat covered his amber skin, as if he were watching the murders inside his head and was even more disturbed by the replay.

He turned onto an access road that led to the multistorey garage behind the Siemens building. He raised the sun visor and pointed to the roof.

'There's a footbridge from the top deck to the senior executive offices. Security is light – it's a clever way to get in.'

'Who was the target?'

'No one knows – other companies share the building. Some president or CEO. We'll go up.'

'Halder, let's give it a rest. I know what a garage roof looks like.'

'This one is interesting . . .'

Ignoring me, Halder entered the garage and accelerated sharply. He swung the heavy vehicle past the parked cars, like a mountaineer making his final assault on the summit. Sweat drenched his uniform shirt as he pumped the brake pedal and forced the engine to labour in low gear. I sensed that he needed the Range Rover's howling supercharger to distract him from the private drama that had dogged him all afternoon.

We emerged onto the roof and swerved around an electrician's van that sat alone in the sun. Shielding my eyes, I thought of the white concrete searing Greenwood's retinas as he stepped breathless from the staircase. Thirty feet away was the pedestrian bridge to the top three floors of the building.

Halder switched off the engine and lay back in his seat. I stepped out, and waited for him to join me, but he was staring at the parapet to our right. I walked around the car and leaned against his windowsill.

'So this is where it ended? Greenwood had killed seven people, and now he knew it was all over.' I pointed to the digital security panel beside the entrance. 'If the alert was on, his electronic pass-key wouldn't have worked. How did he get into the lobby?'

'He called someone he knew – a woman in one of the offices. She came down and let him through.'

'Isn't that strange? There was a killer on the loose.'

'She didn't know it was Greenwood. His name had only gone out to the security teams. Some people say she tried to calm him down.'

'Brave woman. What was her name?'

'Madame Delmas. Very brave – and lucky. Greenwood had problems with his rifle.'

'He tried to shoot her?'

'That's what the security men said.' Halder noticed a face

watching us from a window and lowered his visor. 'Greenwood was inside the lobby, trying to eject the empty magazine. When he put in a new clip the guards challenged him.'

A uniformed security man appeared at the glass doors, reluctant to test the heat of the open roof. He raised a hand in a deferential salute, as if Halder were a minor celebrity.

'You have an admirer,' I commented. 'In fact, you're quite a star.'

'I wouldn't say so. The guards here panicked a little.'

'But not you. So Greenwood backed away and disappeared into the garage, then somehow made his way to the villa?'

'That's it. End of story.'

'Almost.' I remembered the Riviera News transcript. 'He had less than five minutes to reach the villa and start killing the hostages. How did he manage it?'

Halder gestured evasively, trying to wipe the flood of sweat from his face and neck. 'Who knows? Maybe he stole a car – the garage is full of them. People forget their keys in the ignition.'

I waited for Halder to start the engine, but he seemed curiously reluctant to leave the roof. He stepped out and stared stonily at the glass curtain-walling, then walked towards the waist-high parapet. His fists were clenched at his sides, his shoulders braced so tightly that the sweat-drenched fabric of his shirt seemed about to split.

He leaned against the parapet, dislodging flakes of white cement into the rain gutter. A few inches from his knee a hole had been crudely drilled into the parapet. A second puncture, like a crater on a lunar map, marked the cement a foot away.

'Bullet holes . . .' I joined Halder and pointed to the puncture points. A third aperture was filled with a plug of Ciment Fondu. I looked back at the entrance and imagined the disoriented guards opening fire at Greenwood as he ran to the stairs.

'Halder, there was shooting here.'

'That's right.' Halder watched me examine the bullet holes. 'There was quite a firefight.'

'Greenwood shot back?'

'He got off a few rounds.'

'Was he wounded?'

'Wounded?' Halder frowned at the sun, pondering the exact meaning of the term. 'No, you couldn't say he was wounded.'

I knelt down, and with my fingers explored the rain gutter. The shallow gulley ran to a drainage vent six feet away. The zinc surface of the down-pipe gleamed in the sunlight among the debris of leaves and book matches.

I felt the polished metal with my hand. The surface was covered by a hatchwork of lines incised by an abrading power tool. I remembered the concrete floor near the pumphouse of the swimming pool, marked by the same fine abrasions. The drainage vent had been carefully scoured, as if to erase the shadow of the desperate man who had paused here.

'Mr Sinclair . . .' Halder was standing close to me, a hand reaching for the parapet. 'It's getting hot out here . . .'

The sweat streamed from his face and arms, as if his body was releasing all its fluids in an attempt to wash away a virulent toxin. He swayed from the parapet and searched for the Range Rover, ringing the ignition keys like a blind man with a bell.

'Halder . . . ?'

'I'm ready. We'll go now. Where's the car?'

'It's there. In front of you.'

I started to follow him, but his head was lolling on his shoulders. I could sense the roof deck tilting in his eyes while the paintwork of the Range Rover reached its melting point. Halder leaned against the car, his hands pressed to the hot surface as if sinking into soft tar.

I opened the passenger door and stepped behind him, then caught his shoulders when he fainted into my arms.

23

The Confession

'FRANK . . . ? HEAD BETWEEN your knees . . . you're fine now.'

I drove the Range Rover onto the floor below, and stopped in the cool shadows among the parked cars. I steadied Halder against the seat, and let the icy breeze from the air-conditioning system play across his face.

'Mr Sinclair . . . ?' With an effort he focused his eyes. 'I blacked out for a few seconds. Was it hot up there?'

'Like a furnace.' I searched for a radiophone. 'I'll call for a paramedic.'

'No.' Halder took the phone from me. 'I need a minute to cool off. I guess too much light on anything isn't a good idea.'

He grimaced to himself, accepting the embarrassment he had caused. The roof had been hot, but repressed emotions had played a stronger role. I waited as Halder recovered his poise, and thought of the bullet holes in the parapet.

David Greenwood's murder spree had ended on the exposed deck above our heads, when a faulty magazine had saved the Frenchwoman from becoming his last, unintended victim. The clocks in Eden-Olympia had stopped for two hours as the deranged doctor moved on, rifle in hand, the silence of death around him. When he killed his victims he had probably heard nothing, not even the shots from his rifle. But on the roof of the car park a nervous guard had returned fire, and then Greenwood was back in real time, the sounds of police sirens and helicopters filling his head.

Halder adjusted the air-conditioning fan, and watched the sweat evaporate from his shirt. Trying to recover his self-possession, he removed the keys from the ignition lock. He waited for me to leave the driving seat, but I sat back, my hands gripping the wheel.

'Frank, you've been a huge help. Showing me the route in detail, and the scene-of-the-crime photos. It was good of you, but why do it?'

'I liked Greenwood. It's as simple as that. I wanted you to see it all from his point of view. Something happened on May 28, something that wasn't right.'

'And affected you badly. That's what our tour has really been about – you, not Greenwood.'

'Not exactly.'

'Zander knows you're here. He authorized the photographs.'

'Zander and Dr Penrose.'

'Why Penrose?'

'He was interested to see how you'd react. Looking the truth in the face, not some fantasy garbled together from rumours and maids' gossip.'

'So they assigned you to keep an eye on me. When did this start?'

'After you went to Riviera News. The manager's secretary called us. I was to pick you up there.'

'So that's why Meldrum kept me talking. You followed me to Antibes-les-Pins and Port-la-Galère. I'm surprised I didn't see you.'

'Among all those chic suntans? Not so chic as mine.' Halder patted his cheeks, trying to force the blood into his face. 'I parked on the corniche road. A security man tipped me off when you were leaving. He used to work at Eden-Olympia.'

'And now he's keeping an eye on the widows. Making sure they don't talk too much to amateur detectives. But why trail me to the Rue Valentin? Zander didn't know I'd be there.'

'I was working in my own time, Mr Sinclair. I heard from the other guards that a special action was booked for last night. I was concerned for you. When you took off after the girl I thought you might get into trouble.'

'I did. I can still feel the truncheons . . .' I felt my bruised shoulder, wondering how to explain to Halder the confusions of middle-aged sexual nostalgia. 'What were Zander and his posse doing in the Rue Valentin? Anything involved with David Greenwood?'

'Nothing. The Rue Valentin is one of their favourite workouts. They can beat the shit out of a few whores and transvestites and feel good about it. I guess that's better than raping the Third World.'

'That sounds a little harsh. You don't much like Eden-Olympia. Why not make things up with your father and go home?'

'Home?' Halder turned to stare at me, as if I had announced that the earth was flat. 'America isn't my home. My mother comes from Stuttgart. I'm German. Do you know Germany, Mr Sinclair?'

'I was stationed at Mülheim for three months. A great country. The future is going to be like a suburb of Stuttgart.'

'Don't knock it. I had a great time there. My mother worked at the base PX. The Air Force looked after her when my old man left for the States. He denied paternity and resigned his commission. I was friends with all the American kids and went to the base school until some of the parents complained. My mother really scared hell out of the general's wife.'

'She sounds a character.'

'One tough German Frau. The last of the old-style hippies. She taught me to masturbate when I was twelve, and how to roll a joint. I want her to come out here as soon as I get promotion.'

'I'm sure you will. They treat you with a lot of respect.'

'I want more. Places like Eden-Olympia have very high estimates of people. That means something when you're at the bottom of the ladder.'

'Remember that when you reach the top. All that rarefied air. There must be a temptation to feel like God.'

'God?' Halder smiled into his elegant hands. 'The people here have gone beyond God. Way beyond. God had to rest on the seventh day.'

'So how do they keep sane?'

'Not so easy. They have one thing to fall back on.'

'And that is?'

'Haven't you guessed, Mr Sinclair?' Halder spoke softly but with genuine concern, as if all our time together, the extended seminar he had been conducting with full visual aids, had been wasted on this obtuse Englishman. 'Madness – that's all they have, after working sixteen hours a day, seven days a week. Going mad is their only way of staying sane.'

'And Eden-Olympia is happy with that?'

'As long as they stay well outside the business park. In fact, it does everything it can to help . . .'

After exchanging seats, we left the garage. I told Halder that I would walk back across the park, half-hoping that I might find some clue to Greenwood's return route. Halder drove at a cautious pace down the spiral ramp, but I hesitated before stepping from the car.

'Halder – you're safe to drive? Think of that promotion.'

'It was hot on the roof, Mr Sinclair. I humiliated myself a little. That's all. I can give you a lift.'

'I'll walk. There's a lot to think about, most of it grim.' I gazed at the lines of office buildings rising from the park like megaliths of the future. 'Corbusier's Cité Radieuse – I'm sorry David Greenwood wasn't happy here.'

'He was pretty confused. At the end all his shadows ran up to greet him.'

'Even so.' Reluctant to leave Halder, I pointed to the manila envelope. 'I don't think he was confused. Those pictures show the murders were very carefully planned. Greenwood must have guessed that the victims would be photographed. Each murder scene is a kind of tableau. Bachelet with his crack pipe and stolen jewellery. Berthoud with his suitcase of heroin. Vadim and the kiddie porn. Each photograph isn't Greenwood's crime scene – it's theirs.'

'Kiddie porn, drugs, fascist ideas . . . not exactly serious crimes these days.'

'But serious enough. And only the tip visible above the water. These bowling clubs, and the road accidents . . . something deeply criminal has taken root here. The senior people at Eden-Olympia think they're lords of the chateau, free to ride out and trample down the peasantry for their own amusement.'

'You're wrong, Mr Sinclair.'

'I can't believe Greenwood killed himself.' Ignoring Halder, I pressed on. 'I'm sure he gave himself up. He'd killed seven people and he needed to explain why. He wanted to go to trial.'

'That's a dangerous theory. Keep it to yourself.'

'He knew the police photographs would prove his case. Other witnesses would come forward and confirm what he'd seen. But he hadn't counted on the enormous power that Eden-Olympia controls, or the total ruthlessness. Somewhere near here, probably only a few hundred yards away, he surrendered to the security people chasing him. Almost certainly, they took him back to the villa and executed him there.'

'No.'

'Frank?'

'They didn't.' Halder spoke so quietly that I could scarcely hear him above the engine. He composed himself, waiting for the muscles of his face to calm themselves. 'Take it from me, he wasn't executed.'

'No? Then why are there no photos of Greenwood's body? *Paris Match*, *Der Spiegel*, the London tabloids – they've never printed a single one. I suspect they'd show a few bullets in the back.'

'They don't.' Halder spoke tersely, swaying against the steering wheel as if about to faint again. 'Believe me, Mr Sinclair.'

'Have you seen the photos?'

'I don't need to. I was there when Greenwood died.'

'Frank? You were with the security unit who tracked him down?'

Halder waved me away, reciting his words like a familiar private mantra. 'Greenwood went down fighting . . . he'd taught himself to handle a firearm. He wasn't afraid at the end, and he didn't care if it all came out. Something went wrong for him at Eden-Olympia, and he tried to put it right. He wasn't interested in what anyone thought about him . . .'

'Frank . . . wait. Who shot him?'

I tried to climb back into the car, but Halder closed the passenger door. He thrust the envelope of photographs through the open window, his face fully calm for the first time that day.

'I shot him, Mr Sinclair. I was the rookie here and they told me what to do. I was so scared I couldn't think. David Greenwood was the only man I liked in the whole of Eden-Olympia. And I shot him dead.'

24

Blood Endures

FANNING MYSELF WITH the manila envelope, I watched the Range Rover roll away beneath the plane trees. Its dark paintwork moved from light to shade, at times becoming almost invisible, a conjuring trick with the eye that seemed part of the huge illusion created by Eden-Olympia. I admired Halder for making his confession, and felt concerned for him, but his motives were just as checkered. Zander and Wilder Penrose were using this moody young black to keep me primed with fresh information, steering me from one loose paving stone to the next, confident that I would peer into every murky space.

But Halder had an agenda of his own. He had used the murder tour to provoke himself, preparing the emotional ground for his confession, but his anger had been addressed to Eden-Olympia. I could well imagine the sly pleasure that Penrose had taken in assigning the killer of Jane's former colleague and possible lover to our security detail. I remembered Halder bouncing the beach ball across the pool and then spitting into the water, not far from the pumphouse where Greenwood had probably collapsed after making his way back to the villa from the Siemens building. Halder would have walked towards him, the novice in his crisp new uniform, thinking of his salary cheque and pension plan, and then hearing the command to shoot and kill. Eden-Olympia had used him, but Greenwood's death had given him a celebrity that he in turn had begun to exploit.

Yet Greenwood, according to Halder, had fired back in the

seconds before he died. No doubt Halder had flinched, but his nerve had held, and he had done as he was told. I looked up at the roof of the car park, where the security guard leaned on the parapet, a hand cupped over his eyes as he followed Halder's Range Rover across the park. He saluted smartly, without a hint of irony, displaying the same deference towards Halder shown by all the security men. Only the killing of David Greenwood would have earned the respect of these crude and racist men.

I stepped from the car-park lift onto the overheated roof, a cockpit of sun and death. In the mirror curtain-walling of the office building I could see myself reflected like an unwary tourist who had strayed through the wrong door into the danger-filled silences of a bullring. The guard had withdrawn across the bridge into the cool shadows of the lobby. I waved to him, and strolled to the parapet, pretending to gaze across the green heights of the business park.

I counted three more bullet holes in the parapet, each reamed out and filled with a plug of Ciment Fondu, then covered with a finish of coarse sand. Six bullets had been fired, the full load of a large-calibre revolver discharged at close range.

Leaving the roof, I made my way down the stairs to the welcome shade of the deck below. I moved through the parked cars to the south-east corner, where the drainage pipe emerged from the roof.

A metal clamp locked the plastic tube to the vent above my head, its funnel polished by the abrading tool. The junction was six feet away, well beyond my reach even if I stood on a car roof, but a second clamp was a few inches from the floor, securing the down-pipe to the vertical segment below it. I took out my car keys and searched for a flat edge, then began to turn the metal bolt, loosening the joint between the sections of piping.

Steps sounded from the staircase, the rapid heels of a young man in a hurry. A Japanese executive in a blue suit, chrome-trimmed briefcase in hand, strode across the concrete deck. I crouched behind the rear wing of a nearby Saab, and waited while the Japanese stepped into his sports car. After checking his teeth and tongue in the rear-view mirror, he started the engine and reversed from the parking space, emitting a roar of confidence-building exhaust.

His noisy gear changes masked the sound of tearing plastic as I wrenched the drainage pipe from its roof mount. I laid the tubular section on the floor and pressed my hand into the upper end, then scraped the inside surface with my keys.

Clumps of black organic matter, like the residues of a partly digested meal, covered my fingers with a faint ruddiness. I raised the fragments to my nose, and caught the acrid tang of animal remains.

Already I assumed that I could smell David Greenwood's blood. He had never returned to the villa, but had died here on the roof of the Siemens Building, in this place of death and the sun.

'You . . . look at me! What are you doing here?'

I turned from the drainage pipe to find a fair-haired woman in a black business suit calling from the central aisle. She backed away from me, startled to see an intruder kneeling among the parked cars. With one hand she clasped her purse, either protecting her credit cards or reaching for a tear-gas spray.

When I stood up she brushed the blonde hair from her eyes and lowered her head like a pointer.

'Frances?' I asked, unsure of the light. 'Frances Baring?'

'Sinclair? Jesus, that frightened me. You bloody near ruined a new pair of tights. Are you stealing a car?'

'No . . . checking something. I didn't hear you coming. The sound travels in a peculiar way.'

'Mostly inside your head. Why are you playing with that pipe?'

She stepped towards me and frowned at the hole in the ceiling. 'Did you do this? I work in the property office here. I could have you arrested.'

'Don't bother. I'll put it back.' I took the handkerchief from my pocket and wiped the blood-stains from my fingers. I lifted the drainage pipe and forced it into place, then kicked the loose floor bracket under the Saab. 'Good as new . . .'

'You're really a very strange man. This garage isn't a Meccano set.' She strolled around me, and then turned towards the parapet. Trying to manoeuvre me into the light, she exposed her nervy beauty to the open air, the lack of confidence and untrusting mouth. Aware of my admiring stare, she donned a large pair of sunglasses, evidently the most potent weapon in her purse. But she stepped forward to steady me when I stumbled against the Saab. 'Paul – are you all right? You look shaky.'

'A little. Pulling that pipe down was an effort. Still, the Chinese boxes are starting to unpack themselves.'

'At last. I saw you on the roof with one of the guards.'

'Halder, yes. He took me on the grand tour.'

'Of what? Security systems?'

'Death. Seven deaths. Or eight, to be exact. We started at the villa and followed Greenwood's route on May 28.'

'Dear God . . .' Frances raised a hand to her mouth. 'It sounds gruesome.'

'It was. An extremely graphic reconstruction, with a well-informed commentary, so packed with gory details I nearly missed the subtext. There was even a surprise ending. I feel a lot clearer about everything.'

'What was the surprise?'

'Halder told me who killed Greenwood.'

'So . . .' Her eyes briefly emptied. 'Who did?'

'Halder claimed he did.'

'And you believe him?'

'Halder's the sort of man who takes a special pride in being honest, especially when it serves his own interests.'

'And where did this happen?'

'He didn't say. But I think I know.'

She picked a spur of plastic from my lapel, trying to delay her question. 'In the garage with the hostages?'

'No. Right here, in this car park. A few feet above where you're standing.'

'No . . .' She shook her head and backed away from me, as if I had opened one trap-door too many in the floor around her. 'Why here?'

'Frances, I'm sorry . . .' I hesitated before pressing on. 'My guess is that Greenwood was shot on the roof. He was probably lying wounded against the parapet. I'm surprised you didn't see what happened.'

'No one saw anything. The sun shields were closed. Security moved everyone to the north side of the building.'

'How long did that take?'

'Ten minutes or so. Then we heard some shots. That was the end.'

'It was for Greenwood . . .' Matter-of-factly, I said: 'There's a cluster of bullet holes in the parapet. Someone filled them in, but forgot to clean the drain pipe.'

'Why bother? It almost never rains here.'

'This time it rained blood. A short deadly shower.' I unfolded my handkerchief and showed Frances the haemoglobin stains.

'Blood?' She picked at the stains with a varnished forefinger, nostrils flicking as they caught some long-lost scent. She stared at a drying smear that my thumb had left on the cuff of her white silk blouse, and smiled brightly. 'I'll get it DNA-tested. If you're right it's part of David. What does it matter where he died?'

'It matters a lot. If Greenwood died here he couldn't have shot the hostages. Someone else ordered them killed. That broadens out the whole picture.'

'Maybe they weren't hostages?'

I followed her eyes as they drifted around the parked cars. Despite the recent tears, her face was resolute. Once again she had made a course correction, steering me back onto the road she had chosen.

I said: 'They were Greenwood's partners, not his hostages. None of them ever went near the garage – at least, not until they were dead. They were waiting for David in the TV centre car park.'

'Too many car parks – always a sign of a troubled mind. But why the TV centre? People will kill to get on television, but weren't they going a little far?'

'They wanted to seize the station and expose a scandal at Eden-Olympia. I'm not sure what.'

'Financial swindles?'

'Unlikely. Chauffeurs don't get outraged over corporate skulduggery – it's part of the air they breathe. Have you heard any talk of "ratissages"?'

'Cullings? It's an old French Army term from the Algerian war – thinning out the fedayeen. Not much in use along the Côte d'Azur.'

'I'm not so sure. I was in the Rue Valentin last night . . .' I gestured at the air, unsure how to explain my interest in an eleven-year-old girl. I leaned against the Saab, my legs aching after the effort of sitting in the Range Rover with the highly strung Halder. 'Frances . . .'

'What is it? You look worn out. Rest in my car for a minute.'

'I'm fine.'

'Don't talk. I'll give Halder hell for this.' She took the manila envelope from the roof of the Saab and slipped her arm around my shoulders. 'Your wife's a doctor – she ought to look after you more.'

'Patients . . . they're completely passé.' Glad to feel her strong body against mine, I let her help me through the parked vehicles. She paused to search the shadows, and approached an open-topped BMW, a similar model to the car I had stolen near the American Express office in Cannes.

Then I recognized the broken brake light, and the heap of estate agents' brochures. Before walking away to her dental appointment Frances had leaned against the car, confident that the world at large would happily submit to the pressure of a handsome thigh. It had never occurred to me that the car was hers, or that the driving keys had slipped from her bag as she checked her teeth.

'A neat little car,' I commented, lying back in the passenger seat. 'Fun to drive?'

'Too much. A joyrider pinched it in Cannes a few days ago. Really thrashed the engine. The garage said he must have been high. Or very repressed.'

'It might have been a woman.'

'No. You can always tell when a man's driven your car. Brakes, accelerator, even the windscreen wipers – they're all keyed up in a peculiar male way.'

I raised the sun visor, and in the vanity mirror noticed a smear of Greenwood's blood on my cheek. Had Frances dropped the keys deliberately, testing me to see if I could be trained to act impulsively? Already I sensed that I was being auditioned for a role that was about to be assigned to me. I assumed that she had long known the truth about Greenwood's last moments, that his life had ended on the roof above us. But her grief had been genuine, a touching mix of anger and regret that was impossible to fake.

She reversed from the space and set off down the ramp, missing the parked cars by inches. In the entrance she braked hard before we reached the sunlight, throwing me against the seat belt like a crash-test dummy.

'You look better already,' she told me. 'There's nothing like a woman's driving to revive a man. What about a trip along the coast? I have to look at a house in Miramar.'

'Are you kidnapping me?'

'If you want me to. You need to get away from Eden-Olympia. It's setting up a branch office inside your head.'

'Right, I'm game.'

'Good. First, let's get rid of the war paint.'

She licked a tissue and began to work at the smudge of blood on my cheek. The soft scent of her neck and breasts, the faint bitter-sweetness of her tongue, were belied by her surprisingly rough hands, as if she resented the stain on my skin, and my lack of title to this last signature trace of the dead doctor.

'David's blood . . .' She spoke to herself. 'All gone. It's rather sad . . .'

She stared at the ruddy tissue. The stain seemed to glow more brightly in the fading afternoon light, as if revived by the breath between her lips and her memories of Greenwood.

25

The Cardin Foundation

ACROSS LA NAPOULE BAY the evening mist veiled the Croisette, and the black breasts of La Belle Otero seemed to float above the Carlton Hotel, like gifts from one pasha to another borne on a cushion of vaporizing silk. The sea was smooth enough to xerox, a vast marbled endpaper. But three hundred yards below me the waves were channelled into the cove that separated Port-la-Galère from the Miramar headland, and spears of foam leapt through the dark air like berserk acrobats.

The vacant house we were visiting was virtually a small chateau, built into the rocks of the Pointe de l'Esquillon, with its round-the-compass views of the sea. The presence of the orienteering platform helped to straighten my own perspectives, after days of unsettling truths and evasions. Now Frances Baring had dealt herself back into the game, playing with her marked cards and her rigged shoe. Already I suspected that I would do anything to lose to her.

Unsure why she had taken me on her house-call, I suggested that we stop at a café in Théoule. She sat over her citron pressé, watching as I poured a cognac into my espresso coffee, and then ordered another for me before I could ask for the bill. Her moods flared and darkened in a few seconds, a shift of internal weather almost tropical in its sudden turns. She reminded me of the women pilots at the flying club, with their wind-blown glamour and vulnerable promiscuities. She still played with the blood-stained tissue, and I took for granted that she had been Greenwood's lover.

★ ★ ★

'Paul, what do you think? Is it worth renting?'

Her heels clicked across the parquet of the high-ceilinged drawing room. As she stepped onto the terrace the wind rushed to greet her, filling out her skirt and jacket. Frogs honked at her from the half-filled fountain, but nothing else had disturbed the garden for months. The flowerbeds had run to seed, and globes of unpicked fruit rotted around the lemon and grapefruit trees.

I pointed to the swimming pool, filled with an opaque white fluid. 'I hope that's mare's milk. Ninety thousand francs a month? Are you planning to move here?'

'No fear. Some snobby little yachting resort? I rent villas for corporate visitors and high-powered academics.' She leaned on the balcony and slipped her arm through mine. 'Feeling better?'

'By the second. I'm glad I came.' I held her wrist when she tried to move away. 'Frances, I take it we didn't meet by chance at the Palais des Festivals?'

'Not exactly. I saw you looking a little lost, as usual, and thought you might be interesting.'

'Was I?'

'More than you realize.' She turned her back to the sea. 'You're a political prisoner. You wander round all day, searching for the escape tunnel, while getting more and more involved with the guards.'

'I could drive back to London tonight.'

'Rubbish. And it isn't just Jane who keeps you here. Why do you think you're so obsessed with David? You're in a trance.'

She smoothed my lapel, as if suddenly concerned for me. Her hands were forever brushing away imaginary flecks in a kind of submissive grooming. At the same time she eyed me in an openly calculated way.

'A trance? More than likely. I was the joyrider who stole your car.'

'You took it?'

'Frances . . . don't be so arch. You invited me to steal it.'

'Did I? I think I was slightly drunk.'

'You left the keys on the passenger seat. Why?'

'I was curious about you. It was a sort of test.'

'To see if I had what it takes to steal? I might have killed myself.'

'Never. You're too cautious.'

'So I failed the test?'

'Six out of ten. I want you to understand Eden-Olympia. Then you might be able to help me.'

'But first I have to change?'

'A little. Admit it, you enjoyed stealing the car. I watched you drive down the Croisette. You had wings again.'

'You're right.' The lights had come on at Port-la-Galère, and I thought of the chauffeurs' widows sitting in their honeycomb apartments. 'Flying, yes . . . the first take-off after having sex. What's the next test?'

'You decide that. Tell me about the ratissage. The Rue Valentin may be more your street than you realize . . .'

She took a lighter and cigarette case from her purse. Cupping one hand, she lit the cigarette, but the wind blew a shred of burning tobacco over her shoulder. It landed on the parquet floor of the drawing room and glowed brightly in the air, a fire-creature breathing the wind. Intrigued by it, and tiring of me for the moment, Frances left the terrace. Her feet scattered the embers, which danced around her heels as she crossed the floor.

She began a circuit of the dining room, peering at the baronial fireplace with its andirons the size of torture racks, and heavy oak carvers like gnarled thrones. She jotted a comment in her notebook, but I knew she was covering up her embarrassment. I had been too slow to respond to her, and she faulted herself for not playing the femme fatale more skilfully. I was attracted to her sexually, but she needed my complete submission if I was to join the secret game she controlled.

A brochure she had left on the terrace table began to flutter in the evening air. I turned it face down, and then read the printed name on the addressee label. 'Mme Frances Delmas, Marina Baie des Anges, Villeneuve-Loubet.'

I remembered the cryptic initials on Greenwood's target list. 'F.D.'

Carrying the brochure, I followed Frances into the kitchen, where she stood on the small balcony overlooking the hillside. A hundred yards away was a large building that easily eclipsed the oddities of Port-la-Galère. Like a segmented flying saucer, it resembled a spacecraft that had landed by error in the steep hills of the Esterel and then reconfigured itself among the pine trees. A series of interlocking domes were pierced by porthole windows a dozen feet in diameter. Together they sprawled towards a terrace wide enough to stage a football tournament.

Lights flared through the portholes, as if a computer in the control room was waking from its slumbers and testing its own sentience. Teams of athletic young men and women stepped onto the terrace, setting up film lights, cameras and reflector screens. They wore jeans and trainers, money pouches slung from their waists, baseball caps over their Asian faces. To one side, waited on by a retinue of attendants, stood a favoured group of fashion models, dressed for the night in lustrous fur coats, stoles and bolero jackets. The platinum and auburn pelts seemed to drain the last light from the evening air, distilling the lees of the sun in their exquisite filaments. But the models stared expressionlessly at the film cameras, like the chorus in an avant-garde version of *Madam Butterfly*.

'They're Japanese,' I said to Frances. 'Where exactly are we?'

'The Pierre Cardin Foundation. One day all his paintings and sculpture will be on show here. It's rented out for big functions – a Tokyo advertising agency is making a fur commercial.'

'Bizarre. The whole place looks like a film set.'

'It is – it just happens to be real. David loved it. Last year we

216

went to an Eden-Olympia reception there and got wonderfully drunk with two Nobel Prize winners. They were great sports.'

Smiling to herself, she stared through the fading light at the terrace. Teams of technicians steered their reflectors into position, like players pushing their pieces in a monster game of illuminated chess.

'You knew Greenwood well,' I said. 'He must have been a lot of fun.'

'He was. He worked hard, but he knew how to relax.'

'How long did your affair go on?'

'Affair? Sordid word.' She grimaced at an unpleasant after-taste. 'It sounds like some dodgy business with the petty cash. We were happy, and then . . . we weren't happy. Let's say I didn't like the way he was changing. Some of the things he got involved with were . . .'

'Too sophisticated for him?'

'Just a little.' She raised a resigned hand to the darkness, as if waving the night away. 'Idealists can be quite a problem when they get disgusted with themselves. He didn't like what Eden-Olympia had done to him.'

'And the murder plan? He told you – ?'

'Absolutely nothing. Believe me, Paul.'

'I do. You were one of his targets.'

'Why do you say that?'

'"Mme Frances Delmas."' I showed her the property brochure. 'You, I take it?'

She stared at the label, then let her arms fall to her sides as the last cigarette smoke left her lungs. 'That was my married name. My husband was an accountant with Elf-Maritime. We separated two years ago, but it takes the computers a long time to catch up.'

'So you're "F.D."? The woman Greenwood called from the car-park roof? He was going to kill you.'

'No!' Her fist drummed on the balcony rail. 'For God's sake, he was standing in front of me with a rifle in his hands. If he wanted to kill me he'd have done it there and then.'

'He hesitated. The guards say he was trying to reload, but I think he wavered when he saw you. For a few seconds, long enough for Halder and Kellerman to reach the roof. He loved you, Frances.'

'I know.' She crushed her cigarette on the rail. 'I helped to get him killed. At least I didn't see what happened – the guards bundled me away. If I'd let him in . . .'

'He'd have shot you. Why? It could be the clue to everything.'

'It is.' She spoke calmly, her face only a few inches from mine, and I could smell the sweet Turkish tobacco on her breath. 'Why did he want to kill me? Because I was too much like him.'

'In what way?'

'How we relaxed, the games we played. Sooner or later, though, all games become serious.'

'And serious games are more serious than anything else. What did these games involve?'

Before she could answer, the lights on the terrace of the Cardin Foundation flooded the hillside. An intense electrical whiteness sent huge beams through the porthole windows. The technicians and assistants froze in their places, like figures in a clay burial army. The make-up specialists applied their last touches to the fur-clad models and then shrank back into the watching throng.

Without thinking, I held my breath, but the filming ended after four or five seconds. The lights dimmed, and everyone began to move around, waiting as the models changed into a new set of furs. Armed security men stood beside a wheeled pantechnicon, checking each garment on their clipboards before returning the silky pelts to their air-conditioned racks.

'Television commercials and mink coats rented by the hour . . .' Frances sighed audibly. 'That's glamour for you on the new Côte d'Azur. Garbo and Crawford would be amazed.'

'Why stay?' I sat on the balcony rail, catching the waxy stench of insects burned to a crisp by the film lights. I watched Frances tapping the rail, but she seemed in no hurry to return to her car. 'And why come to Eden-Olympia in the first place?'

'Why? In those days my head was filled with . . . passionate dreams.'

'I like that.' I took her hands, surprised by how cold they were. 'What exactly?'

'The usual deluded rubbish. Interesting work, a few close friends, a warm relationship with someone who needs me. My foster parents are sure I'll meet him.'

'Good for them. You're an orphan?'

'My mother's still alive. She had a small stroke when my father died and couldn't cope with me. My foster parents are schoolteachers in Cambridge. They pushed me in a really loving way. After the LSE I worked at Lloyd's, and then got headhunted out here.'

'I bet you had a very good time?'

'I loved it. All that alienation. Those huge men shaving after lunch in their private bathrooms. It didn't take long before I felt utterly depraved. A very handsome Elf accountant was on loan to us one day a week, and I let him use my bathroom. I loved the smell of male urine and the reek of his groin on my bath towels after he'd had a shower. He was very sexy. We had a great honeymoon at Aspen, and he taught me to ski. That was about the last I saw of him.'

'Hard to believe.' I massaged her unsettled hands, thinking of all the bedrooms in the darkened house. 'He walked out on you?'

'No. We moved into an apartment at Marina Baie des Anges. But he worked till nine every night. He was always flying to Oman and Dubai. One day I found this mysterious wardrobe full of men's suits and shirts. There were drawers of socks and underpants that didn't seem familiar. I remember thinking: there must be a man attached to these.'

'They were your husband's? So you got divorced?'

'In a friendly way. I kept the apartment, and he moved to Paris . . .' She stared at her shoes, as if wondering where they would next lead her, and turned to follow my raised hand. 'Paul, what is it?'

'I'm not sure.' Shielding my eyes from the glare, I scanned the Cardin terrace. 'There's some sort of brawl. The Japanese are fighting each other.'

'Makes sense. TV commercials are life-or-death affairs.'

'Wait . . .'

A huge mêlée had engulfed the terrace. Groups of technicians and make-up assistants cowered against the balustrade, watching as vicious fist-fights erupted among the camera crew and the guards near the pantechnicon. A second group of security men had appeared from within the museum, and lashed out with their clubs like warriors in a battle scene from a Kurasawa epic.

A spotlight teetered on its stand, sweeping the terrace with its harsh light before falling on its face. I recognized the leather jackets that I had seen in the Rue Valentin. Three of the assailants were unloading furs from the pantechnicon, while others in the gang stood over the guards they had beaten to the floor. A helmeted man with a raised shotgun threatened the cowed technicians, who crouched on the tiled floor among the light meters and make-up cases. On the steps into the museum a man with a face I almost remembered was filming the assault with a camcorder. The squealing falsettos of the Japanese women rose across the hillside, and lights flared from the balconies of villas above the coast road.

'Frances . . .' Without thinking, I drew her from the balcony. 'It's the bowling club . . .'

'Who?'

'It's another ratissage. A special action.'

'I can't see anything.' She pulled at my arm. 'There's a telescope in the library.'

'Forget it.' I tried to calm her. 'They've gone.'

The snatch squad had left with their booty. Behind them, the terrace resembled the scene after a terrorist bomb attack. Technicians sat on the floor, clutching at each other among the overturned lights and cameras. Many of the women assistants were still shrieking, as the stunned director and his crew shouted into their mobile phones.

From the road above the museum came the sound of accelerating engines. A black Range Rover swept down the hill, its lights off and almost invisible in the darkness. It swerved across the car park of the Tour de l'Esquillon Hotel, and headed at speed towards Théoule.

'God, they're like commandos . . .' Frances pushed herself from the balcony, as if the slipstream of violence might suck her over the edge. 'Paul, who were they? You recognized them.'

'I can't really say. It might have been . . .'

Two more Range Rovers swept below us, nose-to-tail as they moved at speed. Their tyres struck the loose gravel in the car park like breakers hitting a shingle beach. Headlamps flared, and they pulled into a sharp right turn, taking the coast road towards St-Raphaël.

At the Cardin Foundation the film crew and their assistants had fled indoors. A confused technician turned on the sound system, and a burst of amplified music drummed into the night, huge fragments of sound that rolled down the hillside like boulders.

Frances stepped into the kitchen and seized the telephone beside the refrigerator. She raised the receiver and pumped the cradle, hunting for a dialling tone. 'I'll call the police. Come on, god dammit . . . *vite, vite!*'

'Frances, wait. I need to think.'

'Why? There's nothing to think about . . .'

'There's everything.'

I took the receiver from her, opened a drawer of the kitchen table and placed the phone next to an old Gault-Millau guide.

When Frances reached into the drawer I closed it with my knee, catching her hand.

'Frances, take it easy. They've gone.'

'Paul . . . ?' Frances rubbed her bruised wrist. 'What are you playing at? You recognized some of them.'

'I might have done.'

'Who were they? Did they come from Eden-Olympia?'

'It's possible.'

'Then let's stop them. Either way, they're trapped on the coast road.'

'Not now. This isn't the time.'

'You're in a trance again.'

She stood in front of me, small fists raised pugnaciously. She had been frightened by the attack, and perspiration soaked her white blouse, exposing the dark roses of her breasts. But my mind was with the leather-clad men racing through the darkness in the Range Rovers. The speed and aggression of the robbers, their brutal efficiency, had almost winded me. I forced myself to breathe, gasping the night air with its reek of burnt insects, fear and Japanese scent. I felt the hair prickling on the nape of my neck, and a stream of sweat cooling between my shoulder blades. A potent odour lifted from my crutch, a deep hormonal call to violence. My penis thickened, and my scrotum gripped my testicles like a fist. I remembered my erection after my first solo landing at the RAF flying school, as all the tension of the unaccompanied take-off released itself.

'Paul . . . we ought to leave.'

Frances stood close to me, the beam from an upended film light shining on the damp silk of her breasts. With her wary eyes and half-open mouth she resembled a conspirator who had snatched too quickly at a new cover story, and was giving everything away in a flood of anxious sweat. Even now I held only part of her attention. She was waiting for the police sirens, her eyes searching the headlights on the coast road. Had she known of the ratissage in advance? Already I had enfolded her into a fantasy of my own, a dream of speed and violence that had hovered against the ceiling of my mind since I followed little Natasha to the Rue Valentin.

She leaned against me, listening to the cries of the Japanese women.

'Paul, the police will be here.'

'Forget them. We'll lock the doors and they'll think the house is empty.'

'My car's in the drive. The engine's still warm. Come back to Marina Baie des Anges. There are one or two things you ought to see . . .'

26

Flying Again

'FRANCES, I'M FLYING again . . .'

I stood on the terrace of her apartment, and let the wind play on the silk dressing gown, searching through its frayed seams like an affable pickpocket. As the sleeves filled with the night air I felt myself soar between the apartment towers of Marina Baie des Anges. The curving facades with their step-pyramid profiles seemed detached from the ground, floating above the swimming pools and marinas that lay between the causeways like sections of a stolen sea.

Three miles to the south-west was the Garoupe lighthouse on Cap d'Antibes, its beam tirelessly sweeping the shore. On the beach nearby, Scott and Zelda Fitzgerald had drunk their whisky sours at the Château of La Garoupe, but that had been another Riviera, as remote from this futuristic apartment complex as the casino at Monte Carlo was from the temple of Karnak.

Frances joined me on the terrace, setting the drinks tray on a table. 'Paul, view good enough for you?'

'All this curved space? We're coming in to land at Babylon airport. One day the whole Côte d'Azur will be like this.'

'On the drawing board it already is. Everything five minutes old is waiting for the clearance sale.'

'Everything? That's sad.' I slipped my arm around her waist and held her against the night. 'Memories, dreams . . . ?'

'Yesterday's software. Lots of heavy discounts and knock-down prices. Sorry, Paul.'

She held the white-wine spritzer to her face, letting the wind carry the cool effervescence into her eyes. Tiny points of moisture glittered on the tips of her lashes. On the drive from Théoule she had been too distracted to talk, watching the rear-view mirror like a car thief. But when we left Antibes and reached the apartment complex at Villeneuve-Loubet she recovered herself and returned to the real business on her mind.

As we rode the lift to the fifteenth floor she leaned against my shoulder and pressed a hand to my diaphragm. Without turning on the lights, she stepped into the hall and led me straight to her bedroom. Still excited by the violence at the Cardin Foundation and the plaintive cries of the Japanese make-up girls, I quickly undressed her. But I was a poor lover, aware of Jane watching me from the back of my mind, and barely able to maintain the erection that had sprung to life so eagerly during the robbery. When I came at last, an orgasm as faked as a bored housewife's, Frances had smiled the microsecond smile of an escort agency whore. She smoothed the damp hair from my forehead, already working out the next move in the game she was playing with me, like an older sister with a docile small brother who would end up trussed and gagged in the toy cupboard.

But the playrooms of the new Riviera were as large as the Cardin Foundation. The speed and thuggish efficiency of the fur thieves had impressed me. Standing at the rail as I sipped my drink, I thought of the swinging clubs, and felt again the blow across my shoulders in the Rue Valentin. In a reflex of anger I raised my right fist, ready to hit back.

'Paul . . .' Alarmed, Frances held my wrist. 'Calm down. You're safe here.'

'Frances . . . I was miles away.'

'You were going to hit me. Go on, if you need to . . .'

'It's the last thing I want to do. Frances, I like you . . . strange baggage and all. That robbery pulled a set of triggers I'd forgotten about.' I sat next to her on the wicker settee. 'I remember the hazings we used to dish out to new recruits at my RAF flying school.'

'Horseplay?'

'Hardly. They were brutal beatings. It took me years to admit I thoroughly enjoyed them.'

'So that's your special scene? I'll buy a riding crop.'

'Please . . . there's nothing special and it's not my scene. Memories jump the rails and speed off down the wrong track. All the same, why didn't I let you call the police?'

'I'd like to know.' She pointed to the extension phone on the table, sitting next to the manila envelope of Halder's photographs. 'I could call them now.'

She waited, cool as night. I liked her for the way she was still pushing her amateur conspiracy along, the big sister with baby brother in the pram, searching for a secret entrance to the park.

'It's too late.' I waved the phone away. 'Three hours after the crime — what do we say to the police?'

'Easy — we were so excited we had to go home first and have great sex. They must hear that all the time.'

'I bet. They don't need us — they have dozens of Japanese witnesses.' I took her hand, and tried to ease the blue shadows from her bruised wrist. 'It wasn't great sex — I'm sorry.'

'We'll try again. A different tack . . .' She leaned against my shoulder, but her face had darkened, as if I were tacitly blaming her for my failure. 'You think the gang came from Eden-Olympia? They looked awfully fit.'

'Off-duty security guards do the stick-work. Several vigilante groups are involved. The powers-that-be at Eden-Olympia aren't satisfied with the Cannes police, so they take action on their own.'

'Against a Japanese advertising agency? Why? For making a fur-coat commercial?'

'It could be racist, or some mad animal rights thing. Fanatical

Greens always veer off-course, and end up trying to save the smallpox virus. On the other hand –'

'Paul, not now . . .'

Frances placed my hand on her left breast, setting my fingers over her nipple. Despite my lacklustre performance, she was trying to rouse me again. I looked down at her face, with its lips that were almost white in the darkness, reflecting the light from the opposite apartments. Her wet hair seemed darker, and for a moment she resembled Jane. As a lover she had worked hard, careful not to hurt my scarred knees, sitting astride me like a determined first-aid worker trying to revive a comatose patient.

'Frances, did David ever come out here?'

'Of course. That's his dressing gown.' She stroked the lapels with the back of her hand. 'Along with an old tuxedo, it's all he left me.'

'I'm sorry.' Concerned for her, I said: 'I still can't grasp why he put you on . . .'

'The target list? Does it matter? Don't always look for motives – they don't explain everything.'

'Even so.' I lifted Halder's envelope from the table. 'While you were in the shower I glanced through the photos again. There's one you ought to see.'

'No thanks. They're a new kind of pornography.' She shivered in the night air, and stared at the photograph of Olga Carlotti, the business park's personnel manager, slumped across her desk. 'Nasty . . . poor woman. Did David –?'

'Shoot her? I'm afraid so. But have a look at the applicants' snaps on her desk. She must have been checking through them when she died.'

Frances covered her exposed breast. 'They're amiable girls from small-town lycées. I hope they got the office jobs they wanted.'

'Some of the jobs weren't in anyone's office. More like the couch in the next-door sitting room.' I pointed to a row of polaroids set against the inkstand. In one of the prints a stout blonde in a low-cut cocktail gown leaned towards the camera, lips parted in a parody of vampdom. In the next a dark-haired teenager sat naked on the verge of a swimming pool, her small breasts in silhouette.

'Pretty, isn't she?' Frances stared at the miniature image. 'The office junior?'

'I hope so. It's a strange photo to send to a personnel manager.'

'That depends on the kind of personnel Olga was recruiting.' Frances moved my hand over her nipple. 'Do you find her attractive?'

'Olga Carlotti? She's lying face down with her brains across her knuckles.'

'The office junior.'

'Attractive? Yes, but a little young. Fourteen, fifteen . . . ?'

'Who's counting? She reminds me of Jane.'

'Come on . . .' I gazed into the block of night air between the apartment buildings. Logic and reality curved at Marina Baie des Anges, warped by a relativity that applied to more than time and space. 'Jane is twenty-eight.'

'With the body of a teenager. I almost fancy her myself.'

'Simone Delage got there first. Jane's found the head girl she always needed to look up to.'

'But you still have sex?'

'We live in a company house. I don't think it's allowed.'

'That's why I moved here. Is she faithful?'

'As far as I know. A month before we married she had a fling with a surgeon at Guy's. That shook me, but Jane coped with it very well. Unfinished business, she told me, very common among brides . . .'

'Let's not talk about Jane.' Frances traced the scars on my knees with a finger, as if rethinking the incisions. 'Will she be awake when I drive you back?'

'I doubt it. She sleeps soundly.'

'The sort of sleep that leaves puncture marks?' Frances took the glass from my hand and sat up. 'Let's go back to bed. We have unfinished business of our own . . .'

I followed her into the bedroom, and wandered over to the bookshelf as she slipped into the bathroom. There was a row of textbooks on French property law, and a single copy of *Through the Looking-Glass.* As I turned the well-thumbed pages, smiling at the Tenniel illustrations, I realized that this was the first copy in Greenwood's Alice library that anyone had read.

I lay beside Frances, admiring her sprawled figure in the over-head mirror. She seemed to fly across a darkened sky, a nymph from a baroque ceiling asleep on a passing cloud. As she gazed at her reflection, hands behind her head, I ran my fingers over the hollows of her armpits, eddies in the smooth skin that flowed to her hips. Her body was still unpacking itself for me. The small scars below her chin, the erect right nipple that seemed to have a life of its own, the strong ribcage and blonde pubic pelt were a raid on my senses.

She turned to face me, tactics decided. She cupped a hand around my penis, fingers feeling for its root, and weighed my testicles like a stockwoman with an elderly breeding bull.

'You're still tense, Paul. Think about the robbery. If the mirror bothers you I can turn off the light.'

'Leave it on – I've got two of you to look at.'

'David liked doing that. Which was the real me, he used to ask . . . philosophy in the boudoir. The mirror was his idea.'

'David's?' My fingers paused as they grazed in the damp water-meadow between her thighs. 'I'm impressed.'

'At times he surprised himself. That's what I want you to do, Paul. I want you to shock yourself.'

'And what about you, Frances? What shocks you?'

'Nothing about sex ever shocks women. At least, men's kind of sex. We clean up after you, like those charladies with brooms who follow the coronation coach.' She kissed my mouth, curious about the taste of my lips, and then tested my still-flaccid penis, nodding like a serious-minded child with some difficult homework. 'Let's concentrate on you. We'll open a few doors. That robbery excited you. What else is there?'

'Try me. Turn a key.'

'I will . . . do you want to beat me?' She lay on her stomach, looking over her shoulder at her image in the mirror, and smacked her plump bottom. 'I've got a nice rump – deliciously spankable, David used to say. There's a dressing-gown cord in the bedside table.'

'Frances . . .' I caressed the white skin, glad to find no trace of weals. 'The last thing I'm going to do is hurt you.'

'Do you want to tie me up? We'll go into the bathroom, you can rope my wrists to the bidet taps and bugger me. Some people like fucking in bathrooms. All that baptism and absolution. Paul?'

'Not for me. No religious streak. Frances, I'm sorry – it'll come back.'

'It hasn't gone away.' She lay beside me, the moisture from my lips glistening on her breasts, talking in a low but firm voice. 'We're relaxing, Paul, so you don't need to worry. What about stealing? That was something you did as a boy. And those hazings in the RAF that got you going? Think about flying your first solo, and the big erection in the cockpit. Do you want to see me fucked by another man? Maybe it's too soon for that. We'll wait till you need me more. Do you want to watch Jane being fucked? It's every husband's dream. Yes, Paul, you're waking up . . . think about Jane being fucked by Halder or Alain Delage. Fucking someone else makes her a stranger again, stranger and more interesting. There are things between them you'll never know. Not the old bathroom smells and the sheets stained with your cock. Someone else's semen lying between you . . . yes, you like that. Paul, do you want me to pee or shit on you? A little warm sprinkle?'

'Frances, dear . . .' I held her breasts as she squatted across me, and felt the warm urine on my thighs, hotter than I expected from her cold hands. A quick scent, sweet and ammoniacal, rose from her pubis. 'Frances, give up . . .'

'No, we don't give up.' She blew the damp hair from her eyes. 'Let your mind drift . . . you're on the taboo coast, there are dark harbours here. We'll find the door, the special one . . .'

She stopped, and stared with a look of frustration at my limp penis, then sprang from the bed towards the bathroom.

'Don't move. I'll be back.'

'Frances, please – no shit.'

'No shit, don't worry.'

When the door closed I heard her rooting through the laundry basket. I moved from the urine-damp patch. Beyond the terrace the apartment buildings of Marina Baie des Anges made their curved passage through the night. I had disappointed Frances, though she was taking my failure in good part. Jane still hovered somewhere within my mind, but she had begun to fade from me. My visceral response to the Cardin robbery seemed to justify infidelity. The contingent world, as always, rewrote the rules and sanctioned everything.

I heard Frances switch off the bathroom light. The door opened, and her hand reached to the wall switch, dimming the bedside lamp.

'Right . . .' Frances stood beside the bed, swaying to the faint North African music that came from an apartment above us. 'Don't tell me you're asleep.'

'I've never been more awake.'

I sat up and leaned against the quilted headboard, feeling its buttons in my back. Frances raised her arms to the ceiling mirror, as if about to join her second self among the clouds. She wore a zebra-striped cocktail dress that exposed her crutch, a parody of a gun-moll's gown in a gangster musical. The cheap fabric clasped her hips and waist, and the plunge neckline almost bared her breasts. Her legs were sheathed in a tattered pair of fishnet tights, holes as large as my hand around patches of pale skin. A slash of two-tone lipstick, scarlet and mauve, turned her mouth into a lurid grimace, a tough-teen fad I had seen in the bars of La Bocca, a convent girl's notion of a streetwalker's smile, alienating and alluring.

'Paul? Still here?'

I placed my feet on the tiled floor. Clasping her hips, I drew her towards me. The acrylic fabric slid like oiled rubber in my hands. I felt the torn mesh of her tights, searching for the pools of smooth skin among the nail-catching threads.

I pressed my lips to the gusset, inhaling the odour of adolescent hormones and cheap perfume that clung to the fabric, the heady, derailing reek of pubescent girls that had filled the refuge, the smells of dust and the ancestral dirt of dormitories, the jarring clash of unwashed underwear discarded by the Alice-reading girls.

'Paul . . .' Frances stopped me when I searched behind her back for the zip. Holding my now erect penis, she waited as I pressed my face to her pubis, breathing the stale scents on the stained fabric. 'I'll leave the dress on – it took a miracle to get into . . . How are you?'

'Young again . . .'

27

Darkness Curves

DARKNESS CURVED AROUND the apartment towers of Marina Baie des Anges, one night enclosing another as the realms of physics and the dreamtime merged into each other. The last trains of balcony lights bent into themselves as the people of the cliff face lowered their blinds for bed. A jazz piano sounded faintly from a roof terrace, overlaid by the siren of a cruise liner avoiding a flotilla of fishing craft, carbide lamps over their sterns.

Still wearing the zebra dress, Frances had slept beside me. Her smudged make-up, the streaks of mascara and lipstick on her chin turned her face into an amiable kabuki clown's. She brushed the hair from her eyes and stared at herself in the ceiling mirror.

'Paul? I'll drive you home.'

'I'll find a cab – the concierge can call one.'

'It's better if I take you. Anyway, I need to look in somewhere first.' She ran a hand across my chest, then kissed my nipple in a show of affection. 'You really woke up. I hope it wasn't just this nasty little frock.'

She sat up and let me lower the zip, then eased the tight sheath over her shoulders. She tossed it onto a chair, where it settled into itself, desire deflating.

'Yuck – I'll throw it away.'

'Don't. I like it.'

'Why? I'll get it dry-cleaned. No? Isn't that going a little far?'

Curious to know everything about me, she examined my face in the pale light, her finger tracing the contours of my cheeks and chin. She had moved me a few squares across the board inside her head, at the cost of enormous effort, but her confidence in herself had returned.

'Where did you get the dress?' I asked, certain that I had thrown it away after leaving the refuge. 'And the tights?'

'Not in the Rue d'Antibes. They were in a rubbish bin near La Bocca.'

'You were following me?'

'No. But a lot of people are.'

'Why?'

'They think you may find something.'

'About Greenwood?'

'Maybe. Or something about you.' She sighed and scratched an ear, concerned for my naivety. On the way to the bathroom she collected the zebra dress, and briefly posed with it. 'Your friend Halder saw you stuff it into the bin. He was a bit shocked, so he passed it to me. Of course, I knew exactly what it meant. Does it suit me?'

'After midnight? Absolutely.'

'It makes me look twelve.'

'Thirteen. There's a difference.'

'I suppose there is. Have you ever had sex with a thirteen-year-old?'

'As it happens, I have.'

'Really? I'm impressed. You don't look the type.'

'I was twelve at the time. She was my girlfriend. I always did exactly what she told me.'

'Sensible little chap,' Frances commented. 'No wonder I like you.'

'One day she said we were going to have sex. So we did.'

'Thirteen years old. Any others since then?'

'Of course not.'

'Why "of course"? Let your imagination go out to play. You're not a paedophile.'

'Does that make it all right?'

'In a way, I think it does.'

We sped along the RN7 towards Antibes, past the Casino hyper-market at Villeneuve-Loubet and the Fort Carré. The ceramics shops sat in the darkness, their terracotta urns facing each other across the road like chesspieces. I lay back in the passenger seat of the BMW and let the night air rush into my face, thinking affectionately of Frances. She made love in the same single-minded way that she drove her car, firmly gripping the controls and scanning the road ahead for unexpected potholes. She was still using me, for reasons I was too tired to fathom, but my head felt clearer than it had for months.

We left Golfe-Juan and its marina, a white city asleep on the water. Near the old Ali Khan mansion, where the prince had first noticed Rita Hayworth's fading mind, Frances turned off the RN7. We began to climb the steep road that led towards the billionaire heights of Super-Cannes. Luxury villas as lavish as palaces stood in their groomed parks. On the wrought-iron gates, surveillance cameras crouched like hawks.

Frances fumbled over the repeated gear changes as we struggled towards the high corniche. She stalled the engine beneath a sallow array of sodium lights at the junction with the Vallauris road.

'Frances, do we need to come this way? It's like Everest without the charm.'

She started the engine again, and tapped a folder filled with property brochures that lay on my lap. 'I promised to leave these with Zander. He's at the Villa Grimaldi – the bigwigs at Eden-Olympia do their entertaining there.'

'They'll all be asleep. It's 3.30. Four hours from now they'll be at their desks.'

'Not tomorrow. They're holding some kind of reunion dinner. Look around the place – you won't have to talk to them.'

We turned off the corniche road and stopped on a gravel fore-court like a moonlit beach. Two security men in Eden-Olympia uniforms checked Frances's pass and waved us forward as the gates opened. Screened by tall cypresses, the Villa Grimaldi stood above its sloping lawns, a former palace hotel of the *belle époque*. We passed the car park, where chauffeurs dozed over their steering wheels, and followed the drive towards a side entrance. A black Range Rover clumsily straddled a flowerbed, its tyres flattening the rose bushes. Isolated figures patrolled the lawns, like shadows free to play among themselves for a few hours each night. Behind the shrubbery sounded the low-pitched murmur of radio traffic, a soft anatomy of the night.

'Give me five minutes.' Frances switched off the engine and took the brochures from me. 'Use the men's restroom – there's some expensive aftershave. Jane might spot that La Bocca pong . . .'

We stepped through the conservatory entrance of the former hotel. The glass-ceilinged lounge was lit by the moon, and uphol-stered chairs were drawn around a concert platform where dust covers concealed a grand piano. A single standard lamp shone in the central hallway. Statues of condottieri stood in their airless niches, darkness flaring in their eye sockets and nostrils.

A steward carrying a tray of glasses and a bottle of Armagnac greeted Frances and gestured towards an interior courtyard, where a dinner party was still in progress. The four remaining guests sat in shirtsleeves around a table loaded with the debris of a lavish midnight breakfast. Spent champagne bottles lay on their sides among a clutter of silver cutlery and lobster claws.

The guests were senior executives at Eden-Olympia. Besides Pascal Zander, I recognized the chairman of a German mer-chant bank and the chief executive of a French cable company. The fourth man was Robert Fontaine's successor, an affable American named George Agassi, to whom I had briefly spoken in Jane's office. They were pleasantly high, but in an almost self-conscious way, as if they were members of a tontine blessed by the unexpected death of two or three of its members. An aggressive male banter crossed the night air, watched at a distance by the stewards. Only Zander was drunk, barking at a steward to light his cigar, white shirt open to the waist, its silk facings smeared with shellfish. He raised his glass to Frances when she handed the brochures to him, and opened a folder at random. As he questioned her about the property his left hand began to feel her thighs.

Leaving them to it, I walked back to the conservatory. Searching for the men's room, I followed a sign that pointed down an oak-lined corridor to the library. The purple carpet, trodden perhaps by Lloyd George and Clemenceau, muffled my steps, and I could hear a curious wailing, like the bleating of sheep, coming from the smoking room.

I paused by a pair of glass swing doors fitted with ornate brass bars. A television set played in a corner of the smoking room, watched by two more of the dinner guests, sitting in their leather armchairs. The only light came from the screen, its reflection trembling in the glass eyes of the dead moose whose stuffed heads hung from the walls. A stack of video-cassettes lay on a table between the two men, who scanned the clips like film producers seeing their studio's daily rushes. They sat with their backs to me, nodding their appreciation of the finer points of the action. One of the men had cut away his shirtsleeve at the elbow, and a lint bandage covered his forearm, but he seemed untroubled by the injury.

I recognized the scene they were watching, filmed from the terrace steps at the Cardin Foundation, which I had witnessed only a few hours earlier. This time the robbery appeared in close-up, taking place within yards of the cameraman's lens, but there were the same swerving lights, raised truncheons and panic, the same stunned technicians and reeling make-up girls.

I listened to the screaming of the Japanese women. The noise ended when the man with the bandage operated the remote control, and replaced the Cardin cassette with another. The two men sat back to watch a scene filmed in an underground car park, where an elderly Arab in a grey suit lay on the concrete floor beside a car with a broken windscreen.

Some shift of light in the smoking room made both men turn, perhaps sensing my presence. I drew back into the corridor. Beyond the smoking room was the library, its leather-padded doors slightly ajar.

I stepped into the high-ceilinged room, its stale air heavy with the immemorial odour of unread books, pierced by a sharper and more exotic scent that I had caught earlier that night. Glass-fronted mahogany cases lined the walls, filled with leather-bound volumes that no one had opened for a century. A faint light shone from the gilt-ribbed spines, but a far greater lustre glowed from the booty in the centre of the room.

Fur coats were heaped high on the billiard table, the rich pelts of lynx, sable and silver fox. There were more than a dozen coats, some full-length, others with puffed sleeves and exaggerated shoulders. Two mink stoles and an ocean-blue sheared-mink poncho lay on the floor, their resilient pile still recovering from the booted feet that had stepped across them.

I looked down at this hillock of hair, savouring the curious perfume that had drifted across the night air from the Cardin Foundation. In their terror, the Japanese models had shed the powder from their skin, and the ice-like talc now lay on the dusty linings.

'Paul . . . ?' A voice spoke behind me. 'I didn't know you were here. My dear man, you should have joined us at dinner.'

I turned to find Alain Delage standing in his shirtsleeves by the doors. He greeted me affably, unconcerned by his slurred speech and flushed face. He swayed in the dim light, trying to find his feet, and I noticed the bruises on his chest and arms, as if he had been involved in a violent street-brawl.

In one hand he held a cassette, and he seemed about to present me with a record of our shared evening. Did he know that I had seen the robbery take place? His eyes wandered around my face, searching for a sign of my approval, as if he were a moderate tennis player who had managed to beat the club professional.

'Magnificent, aren't they?' He pointed to the fur coats. 'The finest graded pelts. We should give one to Jane.'

'Alain, that's kind of you. But her generation . . . they have a thing about fur. What about Simone?'

'Yes, well, she'd love one. Think of the two women in mink together. Jane likes to do what Simone says . . .'

'Where did the furs come from?'

'I'm not sure.' Delage gazed around the shelves of books, hoping for an answer in their sealed pages. 'We borrowed them from an advertising company. We're using them in a film for Wilder Penrose.'

'They're props, then?'

'That's it.' Alain smiled at me, happy to display a freshly chipped tooth. He blinked behind his lenses, an earnest accountant who was proud to have acquitted himself well in this dangerous action. I sensed that he wanted to confide in me, and assumed that I was about to become one of his intimate circle.

Frances was waiting for me in the conservatory, brochures under her arm. I already guessed why she had made the detour to the Villa Grimaldi, another stage of my education into the realities of Eden-Olympia.

'Paul, are you all right? You look as if you've seen something.'

'I have.' I opened the passenger door of her car, realizing the role played by the brochures. I glanced at the Range Rover parked across the rose bushes. In his escape from the Cardin Foundation, the driver had torn a deep rent in the wing. 'Frances, for the first time I understand what's going on.'

'Tell me. I've been trying to find out for years.'

'These robberies, the amateur drug-dealing, all this playground violence – the people running Eden-Olympia are pretending to be mad. Frank Halder was right . . .'

28

Strains of Violence

'PAUL . . . ? THIS IS very hush-hush. Slip in before anyone sees you.'

A smiling conspirator, Wilder Penrose opened his front door and drew me into the hall. He pretended to glance up and down the quiet avenue, taking in the plane trees freighted with Sunday morning light.

'Safe to breathe?' Penrose closed the door and leaned against it. 'It looks as if only you and the sun are up.'

I let Penrose enjoy his joke and followed him into the living room. 'Sorry for the short notice – we could meet at the clinic, but it's too exposed.'

'It's a hive of gossip.' Penrose beckoned me to a chrome and black leather chair. 'I'm happy to see you here at any time. And Jane. It's not a medical emergency?'

'In a way, it is . . .'

'Really? Yes, I can see you're under some strain.'

Penrose's heavy mouth parted in a grimace of concern, revealing his strong, unbrushed teeth. He was barefoot, and wore a collarless white shirt that exposed the thuggish build of his shoulders. He was glad to see me, though I had woken him when I telephoned at seven o'clock. He hovered around my chair, so close that I could smell the sleep odours on his unshowered body.

'Paul, rest here while I make coffee.' He snatched at a beam of sunlight, as if swatting a fly. 'There's a dream I can't get rid of . . .'

When he had gone I strolled around the room, empty except for the two chairs and a glass table, and so cool and white that I imagined it suffused by a residual glow long after nightfall. Looking around this minimalist space, with its implicit evasions, I thought of Freud's study in his Hampstead house, which I had visited with Jane soon after our wedding. The entire room was filled with figurines and statuettes of pagan deities, like a hoard of fossilized taboos. I often wondered why Jane had taken me to the great analyst's house, and whether she suspected that my leg injuries, which had lasted so many months, were not entirely physical.

By contrast, Penrose's living room was devoid of bric-à-brac, a white cube whose most real surface was the large Victorian mirror in a crumbling frame that leaned against one wall. Its faded silver-screen resembled a secret pool clouded by time.

'Mysterious, isn't it . . . ?' Penrose steered a coffee tray through the double doors. 'I bought it from an antique shop in Oxford. It's just possible the young Alice Liddell stared into it.'

'Perhaps one day she'll step out . . . ?'

'I hope so.'

I moved along the mantelpiece, dominated by a silver portrait frame enclosing a photograph of a strongly built man in his fifties. He wore khaki fatigues and smiled at the camera like a tourist, but in the background was the burnt-out hulk of a battle-tank.

'My father . . .' Penrose took the frame from me and repositioned it. 'He was killed by a stray mortar shell in 1980, working for Médecins Sans Frontières in Beirut. One of those pointless deaths that make the rest of life seem a complete mystery. I read medicine out of a need to be like him, and then became a psychiatrist to understand why.'

Next to the father's portrait was a photograph of a young man with the same heavy brows and aggressive build, standing in a boxing ring with his seconds. He wore gloves, high-waisted shorts and a sweaty singlet, and was being presented with a championship shield. He smiled attractively through his bruises, and I assumed he was the younger Wilder Penrose, taken years earlier after a testing bout.

'So you boxed, Wilder? You look almost professional.'

'That's my father again, back in the fifties.' Wilder nodded to the photograph, springing lightly on his bare feet. 'He was a keen amateur, a heavyweight with really fast hands. He boxed for his college, then for the army during his national service. He loved it – he was still climbing into the ring twenty years later.'

'When he was a doctor? Isn't that a strange sport to take up? Head injuries . . .'

'No one worried about brain damage then.' Penrose's fists clenched and unclenched. Across his face moved emotions of envy and admiration he had long come to terms with, but had no wish to share. 'Boxing released something in him – he was a gentle man out of the ring, a very good husband and father, but vicious inside the ropes. One of those genuinely violent people who never realize it.'

'And you?'

'Am I genuinely violent?' Grinning, Penrose lightly punched my left kidney. 'Paul, what a suggestion!'

'I meant, did you take up boxing?'

'I did, for a while, but . . .'

'The ring triggered the wrong emotions?'

'A good guess, Paul. That's perceptive of you. Still, it gave me an important idea – my father's boxing career, in particular . . .' Penrose sat down in the chair facing mine and poured the coffee. His lips parted in a generous smile that exposed a small scar on his lip. 'Never mind about me. We'll talk about your problems. This medical emergency – it's not venereal, by any chance?'

'Not as far as I know.'

'Good. People are coy about sexual ailments, for sound Darwinian reasons. In your case, sharing the marriage bed with a physician . . .'

'Wilder, the emergency doesn't concern me. Not yet.'

'That's a relief. So it concerns –?'

'Eden-Olympia. More exactly, the senior management.'

'Go on.' Penrose set down his cup and lay comfortably in the chair. His arms hung loosely from his shoulders, knuckles touching the floor, making him as unthreatening as possible. 'Have you spoken to Jane?'

'She's too busy with her work.' Collecting myself, I said: 'I want to go to the French authorities – serious matters have to be brought to their attention. Powerful people at Eden-Olympia and the Cannes police are involved, and I need someone to back me up, a person with a certain amount of clout. Otherwise I'll get nowhere.'

Penrose examined his deeply bitten fingernails. 'You mean me?'

'You're the chief psychiatrist here. It might be a mental health problem. You're one of the few senior people who isn't involved.'

'I'm glad to hear it. Is this anything to do with David Green-wood?'

'It's possible. He knew what was going on, and might have been killed because he planned to take action. But it goes far beyond Greenwood.'

'Right . . . Now, what exactly do you want to report? A crime of some kind?'

'Of all kinds.' I lowered my voice, suddenly aware of the mirror behind me. 'Everything you can think of – armed rob-beries, murders, drive-by killings, drug-dealing, racist attacks, paedophile sex. There's a well-financed criminal syndicate, prob-ably involved with the Cannes police.'

Penrose raised his hands to silence me. 'Whoa . . . these are huge charges. Who actually is involved in these crimes?'

'Senior management at Eden-Olympia. Pascal Zander, Alain Delage, Agassi and any number of company chairmen and managing directors. Plus most of those killed by Greenwood – Charbonneau, Robert Fontaine, Olga Carlotti. I realize it's a serious accusation to make.'

'It is.' Penrose sank lower into his chair, shoulders straining through his cotton shirt. 'Tell me, Paul – why are you the only one aware of this crime wave?'

'I'm not. People know more than they let on – most of the security guards, Greenwood's secretary, the widows of the dead chauffeurs. Talk to them.'

'I will. The armed robberies and racist attacks – you're sure they're taking place?'

'I've seen them.'

'Where? On film? The surveillance cameras are hopelessly unreliable. Someone tries to unlock his car with the wrong key and you're convinced you've seen the Great Train Robbery. Who showed you the tapes? Halder?'

'I haven't watched any tapes. The crimes I've seen I witnessed myself.'

'Where? In some theatre of the mind?'

I ignored this and pressed on. 'Three nights ago there was an armed robbery at the Cardin Foundation. A gang stole a collection of furs being filmed in a Japanese commercial.'

'Right. I read about it in *Nice-Matin*. Economic terrorism, or some local turf war. You saw that take place?'

'Very clearly. It started at about 8.30 and was over sixty seconds later. The gang were highly professional.'

'Latvian KGB, probably. They have a lot of experience with valuable furs. And you were actually there? At the Foundation?'

'I was in a house nearby. Frances Baring was looking at a property. We had a clear view of the whole thing.'

'Frances Baring? She's rather attractive in her intense way. An old flame of Greenwood's . . .' Momentarily lost, Penrose searched the ceiling. 'Frightening for you. But why do you assume the gang were involved with Eden-Olympia?'

'Frances drove me home. She dropped off some brochures for Zander. Do you know the Villa Grimaldi?'

'In Super-Cannes? It's owned by Eden-Olympia. We hold receptions and conferences there. It has a superb view – on a clear day you can practically see Africa, the next best thing to for ever . . .'

'I wandered into the library, and had quite a surprise. The billiard table was piled three feet high with stolen furs.'

'Why stolen?' Penrose massaged his face, as if trying to unify its separate components. 'There was a party going on – I was hoping to be there myself. The furs belonged to the wives. It was a cool night, perfect for a little power-dressing.'

'It was a stag party. No women were there. The furs carried Japanese designer labels. They were covered with talc and body paint – the models must have been naked.'

'Naked? Not quite what senior wives get up to at Eden-Olympia. More's the pity. But the furs . . .'

'Wilder, I saw them.'

'You thought you saw them. It's dark inside the Villa Grimaldi, you might have seen a *trompe-l'oeil* painting, some second-rate Meissonier.' He raised a hand to silence me. 'Paul, you've had a lot of spare time to cope with. Too much, perhaps. If you don't keep busy it's easy to find yourself in a state close to sensory deprivation. All kinds of chimeras float free, reality becomes a Rorschach test where butterflies turn into elephants.'

'No . . .' Doggedly, I said: 'The furs were there. I touched them with my hands. I saw the robbery take place. Alain Delage and another guest were watching a video taken at the scene.'

Penrose leaned back in his chair, bare left foot almost touching my knee in a curiously intimate gesture. 'They filmed their own crime? Isn't that a little strange?'

'I thought so. But the Cardin robbery was really a kind of

sporting event. The film was a record of a successful hunting party. In fact, all the crimes are somehow . . . recreational.'

'That's rather good news.' Penrose chuckled over this. 'I didn't know there were any recreations at Eden-Olympia. And the racial crimes?'

'Raiding parties, usually against Arabs and blacks – ratissages, Halder calls them. Action groups drive into La Bocca and Mandelieu. They like to run Maghrebians off the road. Several victims have died, but the Cannes police hush it up.'

'Paul . . .' Penrose tried to calm me. 'Think about it a little. People drive more aggressively through immigrant areas. They're frightened of being stopped and robbed. Genuine accidents happen, though hating the Arabs doesn't help. Still, you've put together quite a dossier. Have you talked to anyone else?'

'No one. Not even Jane.'

'And Halder? I hear he fainted on the roof of the Siemens car park.'

'He claims he shot Greenwood. He probably did – there are bullet holes in the parapet and a drainpipe caked with blood. Halder can't cope with the idea that he killed Greenwood.'

'So he wants revenge – it's a way of shifting the blame.' Penrose roused himself, his powerful arms straining the leather straps of his chair. 'All this crime – why do you think it's happened?'

'I can't say. It amazes me that people here have the time and energy. They work all hours of the day, and must be exhausted when they get home. Somehow they pull themselves together and organize an armed robbery or beat up some Arabs.'

'Just for kicks?'

'No. That's the curious thing. None of them look as if they're having any fun. There's only one explanation.'

'And that is?'

'They're temporarily insane. Something about Eden-Olympia is driving them into brief fits of madness. You're the psychiatrist. You must know what's going on.'

'I do.' Penrose stood up, speaking briskly as he tightened his snakeskin belt. 'As it happens, I understand exactly.'

'Then come with me to the French authorities. We'll ask to see the Prefect.'

'I don't think so.'

'Why not? There'll be other violent crimes – you'll find a murder on your hands.'

'Very likely. But I have to think of the people here. Most of them are my patients.'

'Then why protect them?'

'That's not the point, Paul.'

'What is the point? Wilder, you can tell me.'

'It's been under your nose for months.' Penrose walked around my chair and placed his hands on my shoulders, like a headmaster with a promising but earnest pupil. 'You've come a long way. We're all very impressed.'

'Wilder . . . !' I shrugged off his hands. 'If I have to, I'll see the Prefect alone.'

'That wouldn't be wise.' He moved towards the door on his bare feet. 'I'll explain everything in a moment. There's an advanced therapy programme you'll find interesting. You might even want to join us . . .'

'Wilder, I mean it.'

'It's all right. I don't want you to worry.' He stood by the Alice mirror, smiling with genuine warmth, as if he had just emerged from Carroll's paradoxical world. 'The people at Eden-Olympia aren't mad. Their problem is that they're too sane . . .'

29

The Therapy Programme

ELABORATELY WRAPPED IN rice paper, the parcel lay across my lap, emitting the softest breath of rustling fur.

'Is it alive?' I touched the chrysanthemum-patterned paper. 'Wilder . . . ?'

'It's a present for Jane. A token of our thanks to you both. Open it, Paul. It won't bite.'

I unfolded the envelope and exposed a lustrous pelt, the fur of some drowsing creature in a Dutch genre painting, every hair as vibrant as an electron track in a cloud chamber.

'It's a stole, Paul. The best ranch mink, so they say. We thought Jane would like it.'

A faint scent rose from the fur, the body odours of Japanese models chilled by the Riviera night. I laid the parcel on the coffee table. 'Thanks, but it's the last thing she'd wear. Still, you've made your point.'

'Paul?'

'The raid at the Cardin Foundation – the stole was part of the booty. It's your sly way of telling me you knew about the robbery.'

Penrose sat facing me, elbows on his heavy knees. He raised his hands, as if to ward off a blow. 'Paul? You're trembling. Not with rage, I hope?'

'Just for a moment. I'm tempted to punch you in the face.'

'I understand. I'm not sure how I'd react. You must feel you've been . . .'

'Used? A little.' The parcel lay against my knee, and I kicked it onto the floor. 'You knew the Cardin robbery was going to take place.'

'I suppose I did.'

'And the other robberies and special actions I've spent months tracking down – they're not exactly a surprise to you?'

'That's true.'

'The ratissage in the Rue Valentin? The road-rage attacks in La Bocca? The drug-dealing business run by Professor Berthoud and Olga Carlotti's teenage vice ring? You knew all about them?'

'Paul, it's my job. I have to know everything about the people here. How else can I care for them?'

'Does that include David Greenwood? As a matter of interest, why did he go berserk?'

'No . . .' Penrose reached out and gripped my shaking hands, releasing them when I sat back. 'That I can't explain. We hoped you might tell us.'

'You've known everything about Eden-Olympia and done nothing?' I gestured at the antique mirror. 'It's another Alice world – corporate profits are higher than anywhere else in Europe and the people earning them are going mad together.'

'Only in a way . . .' Penrose raised his voice, placing a professional distance between us. For the first time I knew that he had always seen me as a patient. 'Mad, no. Though one or two of them are a little odd.'

'Odd? Their idea of fun is beating some Arab pimp half to death.'

'But there's nothing vicious in it. You have to understand that these attacks are set tasks, assigned to them as part of a continuing programme of psychotherapy.'

'Assigned by whom?'

'Their case officer. As it happens, myself.'

'You planned the Cardin robbery? The road-rage attacks, the ratissages – they're all your idea?'

'I plan nothing. I'm merely the doctor in charge.' Penrose's eyes had almost closed as he contemplated his responsibilities. 'The patients decide what form their therapy projects will take. Luckily, they show a high degree of creative flair. It's a sign we're on the right course. You don't realize it, Paul, but the health of Eden-Olympia is under constant threat.'

'And you prescribe the treatment?'

'Exactly. So far it's been remarkably effective.'

'What is the treatment?'

'In a word? Psychopathy.'

'You're a psychiatrist, and you're prescribing madness as a form of therapy?'

'Not in the sense you mean.' Penrose studied his reflection in the mirror. 'I mean a controlled and supervised madness. Psychopathy is its own most potent cure, and has been throughout history. At times it grips entire nations in a vast therapeutic spasm. No drug has ever been more potent.'

'In homoeopathic doses? How can they help what's going on here?'

'Paul, you miss the point. At Eden-Olympia, madness is the cure, not the cause of the malaise. Our problem is not that too many people are insane, but too few.'

'And you fill the gap – with robberies, rapes and child sex?'

'To a limited extent. The cure sounds drastic, but the malaise is far more crippling. An inability to rest the mind, to find time for reflection and recreation. Small doses of insanity are the only solution. Their own psychopathy is all that can rescue these people.'

I listened to Penrose's dreamy voice, addressed as much to the mirror as to myself. Controlling myself, I said: 'There's a problem, though. It's wholly criminal. Who else knows about this?'

'No one. It's not the sort of breakthrough you can write about in the psychiatric journals. It may seem a rather extreme form of therapy, but it does work. Levels of overall health, resistance to infections . . . all have markedly improved, at the cost of a few abrasions and the odd case of VD.'

'I can't believe it . . .' I watched Penrose smiling his most benign smile, clearly glad to lay out the truth for me. He ran his fingertips across his teeth, tasting his nail-quicks, a mix of arrogance and insecurity. I thought of David Greenwood, the idealist with the children's refuge, and at last understood why he wanted to kill Penrose. I asked: 'Did Greenwood know about this?'

'In general terms. He often sat in that chair while I held forth over our chess games.'

'And he approved?'

'I hope so. Poor man, he had problems of his own.' Penrose leaned forward and touched my hand, trying to steady my resolve. 'Paul? You've made a decision?'

'Of course. I'll see the British consul in Nice and take his advice. The French authorities need to be told about this.'

'I understand . . .' Penrose seemed disappointed in me. 'But let me fill in the background. If that doesn't change your mind I won't stand in your way. Fair enough?'

'Go on.'

'First, I'm sorry you were so close to the exercise at the Cardin Foundation. Frances Baring has always been a law unto herself.' Penrose spoke soothingly, and the warring elements in his face, the lax mouth and alert eyes, at last seemed to be synchronized. 'These robberies and outbreaks of violence – you might think the senior managers at Eden-Olympia are in a state of deep mental deterioration.'

'I do. There's no doubt about it.'

'In fact, that isn't the case. By any objective yardsticks, compared with the health of executives in Manhattan, Zurich and Tokyo, the physical and mental well-being of the five hundred most senior people at Eden-Olympia is extremely high. Visit the clinic – it's virtually empty. Almost no one ever falls ill, though they spend hundreds of hours a year in under-ventilated passenger jets, exposed to God only knows what infections. It's a great tribute to the architects of Eden-Olympia.'

'I've read the brochures.'

'Everything they say is true. However, it wasn't always so. When I came to Eden-Olympia four years ago it was approaching a crisis. On the surface, all looked well. These huge companies had successfully relocated themselves, and everyone was delighted with the housing and leisure facilities. But below the surface there were some very serious problems. Almost all the senior people were constantly ill with respiratory complaints. They were plagued by bladder infections and abscessed gums. A healthy executive would fly to New York and back, and spend the next week in bed with some opportunist fever. We carried out careful tests of resistance levels and were amazed by how low they were. Yet everyone said they liked Eden-Olympia and enjoyed living here.'

'Were they sincere?'

'Absolutely. There was no malingering, no secret disaffection. Yet chief executives and main-board directors stumbled into work with persistent viral complaints. Worse than that, they all reported a loss of mental energy. Decision-making took longer, and they felt distracted by anxieties they couldn't identify. Chronic fatigue syndrome haunted the place. We checked the ventilation systems and water supply, we looked into radon emissions from the deep-site work. Nothing.'

'The malaise wasn't physical – it was all in their minds?'

'Yes . . . though to be exact, the two had fused.'

Penrose lay back, his large body relaxed in its leather sling. I could see that he was keen to be frank with me, and confident that he could convert me to his cause. For the first time, a strain of idealism lit his unwavering eyes, a commitment to his patients that went far beyond professional concern. Watching his little smirks and ingratiating grimaces, I knew that nothing would be gained by challenging him. The more freely he spoke, the more he would incriminate himself.

He smiled at the sun, talking in an almost rueful tone. 'When I came here, Paul, I thought Eden-Olympia was the anteroom to paradise. A beautiful garden city, everything town-planners have been working towards for centuries. All the old urban nightmares had been dispelled at a stroke.'

'Street crime, traffic congestion . . . ?'

'Minor irritations. The real problems had simply been left out of the blueprint. And that's a little worrying. Whether we like it or not, Eden-Olympia is the face of the future. Already there are hundreds of business and science parks around the world. Most of us – or at least, most professional people – are going to spend our entire working lives in them. But they all suffer from the same defect.'

'Too much leisure?'

'No. Too much work.' Penrose flexed his arms, and then allowed them to settle themselves. 'Work dominates life in Eden-Olympia, and drives out everything else. The dream of a leisure society was the great twentieth-century delusion. Work is the new leisure. Talented and ambitious people work harder than they have ever done, and for longer hours. They find their only fulfilment through work. The men and women running successful companies need to focus their energies on the task in front of them, and for every minute of the day. The last thing they want is recreation.'

'The active mind never needs to rest? That's hard to accept.'

'It needn't be. Creative work is its own recreation. If you're drafting the patent on a new gene or designing a cathedral in São Paulo, why waste time hitting a rubber ball over a net?'

'Your children can do that for you . . . ?'

'Assuming you have any children. Alas, today's corporate city is superbly talented, adult and virtually childless. Look around you at Eden-Olympia. No leisure activities, no community life or social gatherings. How many parties have you been invited to in the last four months?'

'Hard to remember. Very few.'

'Practically none, if you think back. People at Eden-Olympia have no time for getting drunk together, for infidelities or rows with the girlfriend, no time for adulterous affairs or coveting their neighbours' wives, no time even for friends. There are no energies to spare for anger, jealousy, racial prejudice and the more mature reflections that follow. There are none of the social tensions that force us to recognize other people's strengths and weaknesses, our obligations to them or feelings of dependence. At Eden-Olympia there's no interplay of any kind, none of the emotional trade-offs that give us our sense of who we are.'

'But you like it here.' I tried to speak jokingly. 'After all, it *is* the new paradise. Does it matter?'

'I hope it does.' Accepting my raillery, Penrose bared his teeth. 'The social order must hold, especially where elites are involved. Eden-Olympia's great defect is that there's no need for personal morality. Thousands of people live and work here without making a single decision about right and wrong. The moral order is engineered into their lives along with the speed limits and the security systems.'

'You sound like Pascal Zander. That's a police chief's lament.'

'Paul . . .' Penrose raised his hands towards the ceiling, trying to defuse his impatience with me. 'I take the point – a sense of morality *can* be a convenient escape route. If the worst comes to the worst, we tell ourselves how guilty we feel and that excuses everything. The more civilized we are, the fewer moral choices we have to make.'

'Exactly. The airline pilot doesn't wrestle with his conscience over the right landing speed. He follows the manufacturer's instructions.'

'But part of the mind atrophies. A moral calculus that took thousands of years to develop starts to wither from neglect. Once you dispense with morality the important decisions become a matter of aesthetics. You've entered an adolescent world where

255

you define yourself by the kind of trainers you wear. Societies that dispense with the challenged conscience are more vulnerable than they realize. They have no defences against the psychotic who gets into the system and starts working away like a virus, using the sluggish moral machinery against itself.'

'You're thinking of David Greenwood?'

'He's a good example.' Penrose sat up and rubbed at a coffee stain on his white shirt, irritated by the dark smudge. 'The security people here won't admit it, but on May 28 they took at least an hour to react coherently, even when they actually heard gunshots. They couldn't believe that a madman with a rifle was walking into offices and shooting people dead. Their moral perception of evil was so eroded that it failed to warn them of danger. Places like Eden-Olympia are fertile ground for any messiah with a grudge. The Adolf Hitlers and Pol Pots of the future won't walk out of the desert. They'll emerge from shopping malls and corporate business parks.'

'Aren't they the same thing? Eden-Olympia as an air-conditioned Sinai . . . ?'

'Absolutely.' Penrose pointed approvingly at me, the alert student in the front row of the lecture hall. 'We're on the same side, Paul. I want people to come together, not divide themselves into separate enclaves. The ultimate gated community is a human being with a closed mind. We're breeding a new race of deracinated people, internal exiles without human ties but with enormous power. It's this new class that runs our planet. To be successful enough to work at Eden-Olympia calls for rare qualities of self-restraint and intelligence. These are people who won't admit to any weakness and won't allow themselves to fail. When they arrive their health is at a peak, they rarely touch drugs and the glass of wine they have with dinner is a social fossil, like the christening mug and the family silver.'

'But things go wrong?'

'Nothing too obvious at first. But by the end of the first year their energy levels begin to fall. Even a twelve-hour day, six days a week, isn't long enough to get everything done. At the clinic we've watched it happen dozens of times. People complain about the recirculated air and pathogens breeding in the filter fans. Of course, none of the air at Eden-Olympia is recirculated.'

'And the filters? They screen something out.'

'Bird droppings and toilet wastes from aircraft using Nice Airport. Then people worry about security inside their office buildings. That's always a key indicator of internal stress, the obsession with the invisible intruder in the fortress – the other self, the silent brother who clones himself off from the unconscious. The neural networks are starting to uncouple themselves. Committee meetings are rescheduled for Sundays, holidays abandoned after twenty-four hours. Finally they make their way to the clinic. Insomnia, fungal infections, respiratory complaints, inexplicable migraines and attacks of hives . . .'

'Old-fashioned burnout?'

'That's what we thought with the first cases. Presidents of multinational companies and their CEOs. These people weren't anywhere near burnout.' Penrose sounded almost disappointed as his eyes strayed across the white walls, searching for a blemish. 'But the creative edge was blunted, and they knew it. We urged them to take up skiing or yachting, book a suite at the Martinez and spend the weekend with a crate of champagne and a pretty woman.'

'The perfect prescription,' I commented. 'Did it work?'

'No. There was no response at all. But the health checks threw up a curious fact. There was a very low level of venereal complaints, surprising when you think of these attractive men and women at the height of their powers, and all the business trips around the world.'

'They weren't having much sex?'

'Worse. They weren't having sex at all. We set up a bogus lonely-hearts club, hinting that there were any number of bored secretaries eager for a fling. No takers. The adult film channel, hours of explicit hardcore, did no better. People watched, but in a nostalgic way, as if they were seeing a documentary about morris dancing or roof-thatching, an old craft skill popular with a previous generation. We were desperate. We held corporate parties with a chorus line of kiss-me-quick beauties, but all they did was look at their watches and keep an eye on their briefcases in reception.'

'They'd forgotten they were living in paradise?'

'This was an Eden without a snake. Short of making sexual intercourse a corporate requirement, there was nothing we could do. Meanwhile, immune levels across a hundred boardrooms continued to fall. Faced with all this insomnia and depression, I went back to old-fashioned depth psychology.'

'The leather couch and the lowered blinds?'

'More the armchair and the sun-filled room – psychiatry has moved on.' Penrose stared at me, aware that I was waiting for him to trip himself. For all his jovial asides, his manner was relentlessly aggressive. As he flexed his legs and openly displayed his heavy thigh muscles it occurred to me that psychiatry might be the last refuge of the bully.

'Of course, Wilder,' I apologized. 'I'm behind the times. Jane showed me round Freud's house in Hampstead . . . dark and very strange. All those figurines and ancient idols.'

'The antechamber to a pharaoh's tomb. The great man was preparing for death, and surrounded himself with a retinue of lesser gods paying tribute to him.' Forgiving me with a raised hand, Penrose went on: 'Classical psychoanalysis starts with the dream, and that was my first breakthrough. I realized that these highly disciplined professionals had very strange dreams. Fantasies filled with suppressed yearnings for violence, and ugly narratives of anger and revenge, like the starvation dreams of death-camp prisoners. Despair was screaming through the bars of the corporate cage, the hunger of men and women exiled from their deeper selves.'

'They wanted more violence in their lives?'

'More violence and cruelty, more drama and rage.' Penrose clenched his huge fists and drummed them on the table, sending the coffee cups into a frenzy. 'But how to satisfy them? Today we shun the psychopathic, the dark side of the sun and those shadows that burn the ground. Sadism, cruelty and the dream of pain belong to our primate ancestors. When they surface in a damaged adolescent with a taste for strangling cats we lock him away for good. The run-down chief executives with their hives and depression were sane and civilized men. Maroon them on a desert island after a plane crash and they'd be the first to perish. Any perverse elements in their lives would have to be applied externally, like a vitamin shot or an antibiotic.'

'Or a small dose of madness?'

'Let's say, a carefully metered measure of psychopathy. Nothing too criminal or deranged. More like an adventure-training course, or a game of touch rugby.'

'Shins will be barked, eyes blacked . . .'

'But no bones broken.' Penrose nodded approvingly. 'I wish you'd been with me, Paul. You obviously have a feel for this sort of thing. Still, I needed to test the theory, and start rolling this very odd-shaped ball. I could hardly sit at my desk in the clinic and tell some depressed CEO that he'd cure his insomnia by vandalizing a few Mercs in the Palais des Festivals car park. Then a senior manager with Hoechst showed me the way. He'd been out of sorts for months and suffered from attacks of dermatitis, even thought of transferring back to the head office in Düsseldorf.'

'And what saved him? I think I can guess.'

'Good. He saw a woman tourist in Cannes being mugged by an Arab youth, and went to her rescue. While she called the police he gave the fellow a good beating, kicked him so hard that he broke two bones in his right foot. He came in a week later to have the cast removed, and I asked him about the dermatitis. It had gone. He felt buoyant and confident again. Not a trace of depression.'

'He knew why?'

'Absolutely. Whenever he felt the blues coming on he would take one of the security men into La Bocca and provoke an incident with a passing immigrant. It worked a treat. He coopted a couple of close colleagues and they too cheered up. I asked if I could keep a professional eye on the exercise. Soon we had an active therapy group with a dozen senior executives. At weekends they'd start brawls in Maghrebian bars, trash any Arab cars that looked unroadworthy, rough up a Russian pimp or two. The health benefits were remarkable. Bandaged fists and plastered shins on Monday mornings, but clear, confident heads.'

'Tough on the Arabs, though.'

'True. But on the whole the immigrant community benefits. Eden-Olympia is a scrupulous equal-opportunities employer, with no racial bias. We hire a disproportionate number of north Africans as gardeners and road sweepers. The immigrant population gains from the clearer heads of the people who do the hiring.'

'A tricky balance to weigh. I assume the therapeutic system began to expand.'

'I was surprised by how quickly. Vigilante actions, incidents of deliberate road rage, thefts from immigrant markets, tangles with the Russian mafiosi. Other therapy groups spread out into the fringes of drug-dealing and prostitution, burglaries and ware-house robberies. A picked group of security men were paid foot soldiers, earning generous bonuses we deducted from the arts and recreations budget. The benefits were astounding. Immune levels rose through the ceiling, within three months there wasn't a trace of insomnia or depression, not a hint of respiratory infections. Corporate profits and equity values began to climb again. The treatment worked.'

'No side effects?'

'A few.' Penrose watched me as he spoke, curious to see how I reacted, and clearly pleased that I had not leapt from my chair in outrage. He spoke matter-of-factly, like an architect setting out the pros and cons of an experimental sewerage system. 'There's a risk element, but it's acceptable. Eden-Olympia has a lot of clout with the local authorities. In many ways we're carrying out tasks the police would do anyway, and we free them for other duties. The sex side can be troubling. A few prostitutes have needed remedial surgery. Your friend Alain Delage is a little too free with his fists. There's a remarkable need for punitive violence hidden away in the senior executive mind.'

'And sex tends to release it?'

'It's meant to, for sound biological reasons. Sex is such a quick route to the psychopathic, the shortest of short cuts to the perverse. We aren't running an adventure playground, but a forcing house designed to expand the psychopathic possibilities of the executive imagination. It needs to be carefully monitored. Sadomasochism, excretory sex-play, body-piercing and wife-pandering can easily veer off into something nasty. It's surprising how many prostitutes object to rape, even of the most stylized kind.'

'Unimaginative of them.'

'Who knows?' Penrose shrugged generously at the world and its curious ways. 'A few times I've had to step in and redirect the therapy. On the whole, though, it's worked well. Almost every senior executive at Eden-Olympia is now involved in the programme, even if only at the margins.'

'And David Greenwood was aware of all this?'

'To a large extent. He and I discussed it with Professor Kalman. The department heads at the clinic are in the know. They can see the benefits, and on the whole David approved. The drug rehab centre in Mandelieu was plagued by smalltime gangsters trying to muscle in on the methadone supply. It was a big help to him when the therapy groups came down from Eden-Olympia and drove them out. The more aggressive road attacks bothered him, but he knew that the violence against the local prostitutes was a special kind of rehabilitation, a form of shock treatment that would send them back to their factory jobs.'

Penrose turned from me, a hand raised to catch a ray of sunlight over his head. He glanced at the opaque mirror behind him, as if waiting for an audience's response. His exposition had been almost playful, testing me with his callous asides. But he was clearly proud of his dubious achievement and its insane logic, a therapeutic breakthrough that would never be awarded the gold medals of the leading medical societies. This lonely commitment to his radical vision gave him an almost bearlike dignity.

'The murders on May 28,' I said. 'Were they part of David's therapy programme?'

'Paul . . . that's the great mystery of Eden-Olympia. In his deranged way, David was a minor prophet, guiding us into the future. Meaningless violence may be the true poetry of the new millennium. Perhaps only gratuitous madness can define who we are.'

'At the cost of breaking the law? Your senior executives at Eden-Olympia are committing enough crimes to get themselves locked away for the rest of their lives.'

'That's true, on a literal level. Remember that these criminal activities have helped them to rediscover themselves. An atrophied moral sensibility is alive again. Some of my patients even feel guilty, a revelation to them . . .'

I listened to a car alarm sounding in the avenue, and imagined the French police bursting in to arrest us. 'Guilt? Isn't that a design error? It only needs one CEO to go to the authorities and your therapy programme will be over. Curing a few cases of insomnia will count for nothing.'

'Not just a few. But I agree with you.' Penrose stared over my head, weighing the objection in his mind. 'So far people have been intelligent enough to see the point. They grasp the value of . . .'

'Beating up an out-of-work Arab? Some labourer with a wife and four children living in a tin shack at a *bidonville*?'

'Paul . . .' Pained by my crude questions, Penrose reached out a hand to settle me, like a minister with a restive congregation. 'Sit back and think things through. The twentieth century was an heroic enterprise, but it left us in the dark, feeling our way towards a locked door. Here at Eden-Olympia there's a chink of light, a thin and fierce glow . . .'

'Our own psychopathy?'

'Whether we like it or not. The twentieth century ended with its dreams in ruins. The notion of the community as a voluntary association of enlightened citizens has died for ever. We realize how suffocatingly humane we've become, dedicated to moderation and the middle way. The suburbanization of the soul has overrun our planet like the plague.'

'Sanity and reason are unworthy of us?'

'No. But a vast illusion, built from mirrors that lie. Today we scarcely know our neighbours, shun most forms of civic involvement and happily leave the running of society to a caste of political technicians. People find all the togetherness they need in the airport boarding lounge and the department-store lift. They pay lip service to community values but prefer to be alone.'

'Isn't that odd, for a social animal?'

'Only in some ways. Homo sapiens is a reformed hunter-killer of depraved appetites, which once helped him to survive. He was partly rehabilitated in an open prison called the first agricultural societies, and now finds himself on parole in the polite suburbs of the city state. The deviant impulses coded into his central nervous system have been switched off. He can no longer harm himself or anyone else. But nature sensibly endowed him with a taste for cruelty and an intense curiosity about pain and death. Without them, he's trapped in the afternoon shopping malls of a limitless mediocrity. We need to revive him, give him back the killing eye and the dreams of death. Together they helped him to dominate this planet.'

'So psychopathy is freedom, psychopathy is fun?'

'A natty slogan, Paul, but it does contain a certain fiery truth.'

Penrose beamed at me, openly pleased with my progress. 'We're creatures of the treadmill: monotony and convention rule every-thing. In a totally sane society, madness is the only freedom. Our latent psychopathy is the last nature reserve, a place of refuge for the endangered mind. Of course, I'm talking about a carefully metered violence, microdoses of madness like the minute traces of strychnine in a nerve tonic. In effect, a voluntary and elective psychopathy, as you can see in any boxing ring or ice-hockey rink. You've served in the armed forces, Paul. You know that recruits are deliberately brutalized – the drill sergeant's boot and the punishment run give back to young men a taste for pain that generations of socialized behaviour have bred out of them.'

'The toy poodle becomes a wolf again?'

'But only when it wants to. Remember your childhood – like all of us you stole from the local supermarket. It was deeply exciting, and enlarged your moral sense of yourself. But you were sensible, and kept it down to one or two afternoons a week. The same rules apply to society at large. I'm not advocating an insane free-for-all. A voluntary and sensible psychopathy is the only way we can impose a shared moral order.'

'And if we do nothing?'

'Danger will rush up to us and put a knife to our throat. Look at the century that lies ahead – an upholstered desert, but a wasteland all the same. An absence of faith, except for a vague belief in an unknown deity, like the sponsor of a public-service broadcast. Wherever there's a vacuum, the wrong kind of politics creep in. Fascism was a virtual psychopathology that served deep unconscious needs. Years of bourgeois conditioning had produced a Europe suffocating in work, commerce and conformity. Its people needed to break out, to invent the hatreds that could liberate them, and they found an Austrian misfit only too happy to do the job. Here at Eden-Olympia we're setting out the blue-print for an infinitely more enlightened community. A controlled psychopathy is a way of resocializing people and tribalizing them into mutually supportive groups.'

'Like divisions of the Waffen-SS? At the Cardin Foundation there was real violence. People might have been killed.'

'It was more choreographed than you think. Violence is spectacular and exciting, but sex has always been the main hunting ground of psychopathy. A perverse sexual act can liberate the visionary self in even the dullest soul. The consumer society hungers for the deviant and unexpected. What else can drive the bizarre shifts in the entertainment landscape that will keep us "buying"? Psychopathy is the only engine powerful enough to light our imaginations, to drive the arts, sciences and industries of the world. Your passing infatuation with that child in the Rue Valentin might spark off some vital new development in aviation . . .'

Penrose stood up, kicked the fur stole out of his way and began to stroll around the room, almost dismissing me with a flourish. Scenting the sunlight, he opened a window and filled his lungs. He had been saving little Natasha to the last, warning me from any rush to judgement. After inspecting himself in the mirror, he turned to stare down at me. The warring elements in his face, the ready smile and steely eyes, gave me the sense that several personalities were jostling for space in his large skull.

'Paul, you can tell me – are you going to the police?'

'Probably. I need to think about it.'

'I've been completely frank. I've held back nothing.'

'The Cannes police wouldn't understand a word. If they did, they'd probably agree with you.'

Penrose chuckled over this. 'Still . . . the Cardin Foundation robbery. Are you going to report it?'

'Not for a day or two. I'll tell you when I do.'

'Good. I need to know. There are large issues here.'

'Involving a great many powerful people. Don't worry, it would be easy to arrange a ratissage for an Englishman who's overstayed his welcome. An old Jaguar with fading brakes, the high corniche road, an empty bottle of cognac in the wreckage . . . at least I'd have cured some chief executive's migraine.'

'Paul . . .' Penrose seemed disappointed in me. 'This isn't a regime of gangsters.'

'Gangsters and psychopaths? Surely that's the prospectus you've been setting out? What I still can't grasp is where David Greenwood fits into all this.'

I waited for Penrose to reply, but he stood with his back to the sun, arms limply at his sides, his large chest deflating. As I watched his uneasy grimaces, the heavy knuckles that cuffed his nose, I realized that he was hoping for my approval. He needed me to understand him, and the brave gamble he had taken for the sake of Eden-Olympia. In some way he had failed David Greenwood, and he was now doing his best to avoid failing me.

Then he noticed me standing by the coffee table and rallied himself. Smiling affably, he strolled up to me and held my shoulders. He steered me towards the Alice mirror, as if we were about to step together into its glassy deeps. He swerved away at the last moment and pushed me to the door, laughing soundlessly to himself.

'Paul, sit by the pool and give it some thought.' Before propelling me into the avenue, he whispered fiercely: 'Think, Paul. Think like a psychopath . . .'

30

Nietzsche on the Beach

AFTER LEAVING PENROSE, I needed breakfast, and the strongest coffee I could make. Dust lay over the swimming pool, an overnight veil disturbed by the feeble movements of a waterlogged fruit fly, struggling against the meniscus that gripped its wings in a mirror harder than glass. Sympathizing with the creature, whose predicament matched my own, I searched for the damp footprints that usually marked Jane's race back to the house and a long bath, earphones over her soapy head as the Walkman played Debussy.

But the tiled verge was dry in the late November sun. I walked to the terrace and stepped into the hall, where I bruised my shins against two of my leather suitcases. I gripped the handles, and guessed from their weight that they held my entire wardrobe.

Upstairs, drawers slammed as Jane roamed the cupboards. The punitive jolts of Carmina Burana sounded from the bedroom, a call to marital strife. Without thinking, I knew that Jane was throwing me out, and felt a deep regret that we would never drive the RN7 back to Paris together. Our marriage had ended, like those of my friends, in a mess of trivial infidelities and questions with no conceivable answers.

I had reached the villa at midnight, after an evening in Antibes with Frances Baring. From the clinic Jane had earlier called me to say she would be late, and suggested that I see a film in Cannes. But as I tiptoed past the darkened lounge the faint moonlight revealed that she had recruited other company to amuse her. The carpet was marked by almost lunar ridges, left by heel marks that belonged to neither Jane nor myself.

Aware of Frances's scent on my hands, I moved to the children's room, and slept soundly among Tenniel's amiable menagerie. I woke at seven and telephoned Wilder Penrose from the bathroom, determined to confront him with the criminal reality of Eden-Olympia.

Jane was still asleep when I left to see Penrose. She lay facedown, an infected puncture point on the inside of her thigh oozing a faint lymph. I eased back the drawer of the dressing table and counted the used syrettes, hoping that my arithmetic was at fault.

Jane breathed quietly, an ageing Alice in an expurgated chapter of her own book. Careful not to wake her, I kissed her open lower lip, still marked by the paste of another woman's lipstick.

I met her on the landing, dragging a suitcase from the bedroom. As always, she had recovered quickly from the dose of diamorphine. She wore jeans and white vest, a garb she had abandoned soon after arriving at Eden-Olympia. But her skin was pale and puttycoloured, and her face seemed toneless. She had cut her left hand on one of the suitcase locks, but had yet to notice the blood.

She saw me watching from the door, reached into a wardrobe and pulled out a heavy rucksack.

'Paul? You can help me. Stick that on the bed.'

'Sure. Tell me what's happening.'

'Nothing to worry about. You're leaving half an hour from now.'

'I'm leaving? Why?'

'We're both leaving. We're saying goodbye to Eden. I've told personnel to post an angel with a flaming sword by the gate.'

'Jane . . . .' I stepped through the clutter of unpaired shoes that she was rooting from the cupboard, placed my hands under her arms and lifted her to her feet, surprised by how much weight she had lost. 'Calm down. Now when exactly are we leaving?'

'Now. Today. As soon as I'm packed.'

'And where are we going?'

Jane shrugged, staring at the chaos of half-filled suitcases. 'England, London, Paris, anywhere. Away from here.'

I reached out to the radio on the bedside table and switched off the French concert commentator. 'Why? You have another six-month contract to run.'

'I'll take a week's compassionate leave. We'll simply not come back.'

'Professor Kalman won't like that. It could damage your career.'

'Staying here will finish it. Believe me, the last thing they want is another English doctor going insane.'

'Jane . . .' I tried to take her shoulders, but she sidestepped me, marking the pattern of her bare feet in the talc like an evasive dance step. 'Are you all right?'

'Completely *compos mentis*.' She stared at herself in the dressing-table mirror, jaw thrust forward. 'No, I'm not all right. And nor are you. Where's the getaway car? I don't want to drive to Calais in the little Peugeot.'

'The Jag's outside. Tell me why you want to leave. Is it anything I've done?'

'Have you done anything? I'm amazed.' Jane rolled her eyes in mock alarm. She placed her hands on my chest. 'Dear husband, you're a decent and kindly man – more or less – and I want to keep you that way. I don't know where you stay out all night and I won't ask. I hope she's sweet and appreciates you. But I'm sure of one thing – remain here any longer and you'll end up like the rest of us.'

'Jane, why now? Has something worried you – the business at the Cardin Foundation?'

'Cardin? Not my favourite schmutter. You mean the robbery at Miramar?'

'You've heard about it?'

'Simone and I saw it on the news. Alain was driving through Théoule as the gang sped off and tried to stop them. Poor man, he was covered with bruises. I had to patch him up.' She rubbed the infected needle mark on her thigh. 'Alain said he saw you later at the Villa Grimaldi.'

'A stag night, laid on by Pascal Zander.'

'Ghastly man. I'm glad I wasn't there. He invents imaginary venereal symptoms so he can roll out his big cannon. It's quite a spectacle. He's perpetually tumescent in a nasty way.'

'A good reason for leaving. So it isn't me that you want to get away from?'

'I want to get away from myself.' She sat on the bed, hands over her small breasts as if feeling her tender nipples. 'There are too many mirrors in this house and I don't like what I see in them. Outside the clinic I hardly exist. I'm tired all the time and I keep picking up small infections. For the last two months I've had swollen tonsils – if you tried to kiss me you'd never get your tongue in my mouth.'

'Have you talked to Penrose?'

'Wilder Penrose . . . for a clever man he has some odd ideas. He thinks we need to freshen up our sex life. How, he didn't quite say – something about prepubertal girls. I told him that wasn't your scene, you liked them a good bit older. That's why you married me. Isn't it?'

'You know it is.'

'Good . . .' She stared at my hands as I sat beside her, her eyes slightly out of focus. She raised my fingers to her lips, and caught a strange scent clinging to the nails. Her eyes sharpened, and she glanced at me without comment. 'Paul . . . you know I'm going to bed with Simone?'

'No. But I guessed.'

'I was so sleepy, it happened before I realized it. I thought we were playing girls in the dorm, but she had other ideas. You're not upset?'

'A little. We talked it through long ago. Have you . . . ?'

'Since school? Once. Heterosexuality is hard work – men make it into a big effort. When I get back from the clinic I'm too tired for all those emotions. With Simone I can switch off.'

'What about Alain?'

'He likes to watch. Sorry, Paul . . . you're too sane. If we stay here any longer I'll go to bed with Alain. I don't want that to happen.'

She sniffled into a corner of the sheet. Searching for a tissue, I pulled back the dressing-table drawers, and exposed the clutch of ampoules in her valise. 'Jane . . . all this pethidine. How much can you take?'

'They're nothing. Better for me than too many double scotches.'

'The diamorphine? It's pure heroin.'

'I'm all right!' She closed the drawer, and then stared at me curiously. 'You never tried to stop me. Not seriously. That's a little surprising.'

'You're the doctor, you know how to handle the stuff.'

'No.' Jane took my chin, forcing me to look her in the face. 'You're keeping an eye on me, Paul. I'm your guinea pig. You want to know what happens to people in Eden-Olympia.'

'That may be true. I'm sorry, I hadn't realized it.'

'It's part of your search for David Greenwood. You're totally obsessed with him. Why? Because we were lovers once? It was a long time ago.'

'Never long enough.' I felt myself sink slightly. 'David was making a stand against Eden-Olympia. It's the proving ground for a new kind of world, and he couldn't cope with that.'

'You've been listening to Wilder. Nietzsche on the beach – Philip Glass could set it to music.'

'He's serious, but he's starting to give himself away. I need

271

more time, Jane. That's why I'd like to stay on for a while. Let me explain it to you, and then you can decide if we leave.'

'All right . . .' She leaned against me, her breathing shallow, her putty skin giving off a stale odour that I had never noticed. As I listened to her slow heartbeat I knew how deeply exhausted she was.

I cleared a space among the suitcases and laid her on the bed, straightening the pillow under her head. I sat beside her, holding her hands between mine, and thought about her affair with Greenwood, and their quick sex probably snatched at Guy's in darkened laundry rooms. Jane was fond of me, but our marriage had been the last of her hippie gestures, the belief that impulsive acts alone gave meaning to life. Sex and drugs had to be casually dispensed, as a way of defusing the myths around them.

'Paul . . . I'm going to sleep for a little.' Jane smiled at me as I stroked her damp forehead. Together we listened to an approaching publicity plane that climbed the valley from the coast, bringing to the business park its tidings of another marina complex or discount furniture sale. A few hundred yards from us Wilder Penrose would be standing at his kitchen window, watching the wavering pennant as he laid his own very different plans for the new Riviera.

PART II

31

The Film Festival

ON THE ROOF of the Noga Hilton the samurai warrior had lowered his sword, as if unable to decide how many of the thousands of heads in the Croisette he would strike from their shoulders. His black helmet, the size of a small car, tilted towards the sea, moving jerkily as the Japanese technicians swarmed over his back, their arms deep in his electromechanical heart.

But the crowd's attention had turned to a trio of stretch limousines emerging from the drive of the Martinez. The onlookers surged against the railings, angry cries sounding a clear threat above the excitement. Hands patted the sleek roofs of the vehicles, fingers pressed at the tinted windows and left their smeared prints on the glass. A middle-aged woman in a baseball cap fired a canister of liquid confetti over the last Cadillac, entrails of iridescent air-weed that clung to the radio masts. Glamour moved through Cannes at five miles an hour, too fast to satisfy their curiosity, too slow to slake their dreams.

I sat at my table in the Blue Bar, waiting for Frances Baring to join me. After avoiding me for a week, hiding behind the answerphone at Marina Baie des Anges, she had called my mobile, a wilfully cryptic edge to her voice. She suggested that we have an early-evening drink in Cannes, though the Croisette was the last place for a secret rendezvous.

Ten feet from my kerbside table the limousines moved on towards the Palais des Festivals between the lines of police and security men. Helicopters circled the Palm Beach headland, waiting to land at the heliport, like paramilitary gunships about to strafe the beachside crowds. Their white-suited passengers, faces masked by huge shades, stared down with the gaze of gangster generals in a Central American republic surveying a popular uprising. An armada of yachts and motor cruisers strained at their anchors two hundred yards from the beach, so heavily freighted with bodyguards and television equipment that they seemed to raise the sea.

Yet a short walk from the Croisette, as I had seen while driving down the Rue d'Antibes, the Cannes Film Festival might not have existed. Elderly ladies in silk suits and pearls strolled in their unhurried way past the patisseries or exchanged gossip in the *salons de thé*. Toy poodles soiled their favourite pavements, and tourists scanned the estate agents' displays of new apartment complexes, ready to invest their savings in a prefabricated dream of the sun.

The film festival measured a mile in length, from the Martinez to the Vieux Port, where sales executives tucked into their platters of *fruits de mer*, but was only fifty yards deep. For a fortnight the Croisette and its grand hotels willingly became a facade, the largest stage set in the world. Without realizing it, the crowds under the palm trees were extras recruited to play their traditional roles. As they cheered and hooted, they were far more confident than the film actors on display, who seemed ill at ease when they stepped from their limos, like celebrity criminals ferried to a mass trial by jury at the Palais, a full-scale cultural Nuremberg furnished with film clips of the atrocities they had helped to commit.

A limousine with Eden-Olympia pennants paused in the stalled traffic outside the Blue Bar. Hoping to catch sight of Jane, I stood up at my table. With Simone and Alain Delage, she was attending a seven-o'clock reception for a Franco-German film financed by one of the business park's merchant banks. After the premiere they would move on to a fireworks party at the Villa Grimaldi and watch the Cannes night turn into a second day.

As the limousine crept forward, a chorus of fists drumming on its roof, I saw the fleshy figure of Pascal Zander lounging across the rear seat. Three young women, as blankly self-conscious as starlets, sat beside him, together trying to light his cigar. They waved like novice queens at the crowd, aware that they had crossed the threshold where celebrity and the illusion of celebrity at last fused for a few exhilarating hours.

A Chinese man carrying a camcorder strode through the spectators, searching for a target of opportunity. Followed by a Scandinavian woman with a clipboard, he took a short cut through the Blue Bar and brushed my shoulder, almost knocking me from my feet. I sat down clumsily, wincing over my inflamed knee. As Zander's limousine pulled away, I thought again how odd it was that I had to visit the Cannes Film Festival, and be assaulted by tourists, in the hope of meeting my wife.

In the months since Jane's panic attempt to leave Eden-Olympia I had seen less and less of her. We shared the same swimming pool, breakfast room and garage, but our lives were drawing away from each other. Jane had committed herself for good to the business park. Long hours of work, a diamorphine night and weekends with Simone Delage made up her world. I was still uneasy over the syrettes in her dressing table, but she had found professional success at Eden-Olympia. She had been profiled in the London medical press, and was completing the diagnostic tests that would soon link every employee in Eden-Olympia and Sophia-Antipolis.

At the same time, the most advanced system of preventive medicine in Europe had been unable to cure my knee injury. The rogue infection had flared up again, a hospital-bred bacterium that resisted antibiotics, rest and physiotherapy. This old barometer of my discontents was forecasting stormy weather. Taking pity on me as I limped around the house in the small hours, Jane made up a solution of muscle relaxant and painkiller. She taught me how to inject myself, and the modest doses were the only effective relief that any of the clinic's highly paid physicians had offered.

⋆ ⋆ ⋆

The helicopters clattered above the beach, cameras filming from open doorways. A small riot had started outside the Carlton. According to an American couple at the next table, a leading Hollywood star had promised to emerge from the front entrance, only to discover that a rival studio's production was advertised on a huge billboard above his head. He had turned back into the hotel and slipped out through a rear exit, leaving a rattled publicity woman to make his apologies. Even as she shouted through her megaphone a dozen hands were rocking a TV location van. A Cannes policeman sprawled across the windscreen like a stuntman, shouting to the hotel's security team as the crowd cheered him on.

Exhausted by the noise, I left the table to a middle-aged German tourist, who managed the feat of sitting in my chair before I could rise fully to my feet. I wiped my hands on his shoulder and limped to the toilets at the rear of the bar. I locked myself into a cubicle, and took the leather hypodermic wallet from my jacket. Leaning against the washbasin, I lifted my injured leg onto the lavatory lid and rolled my trouser to the knee. The surgical scars had faded, but the pain still nagged, a cry for help that sounded steadily from beneath the floorboards of my mind.

I broke the seal on the unlabelled phial and drew three ccs into the hypodermic. Avoiding the cluster of old puncture points, I injected the pale solution into the fold of smooth skin on the inner surface of my knee. I counted to twenty as the subcutaneous shot brought its slow but deep relief, pushing the pain further from me, like furniture moved to the far corners of a stage.

Letting my leg fall to the floor, I shouted through the door at an impatient woman rattling the lock. She stepped into another cubicle, and I sat across the washstand, my back to the mirror, letting the tap water run across my hands. As my chest warmed, I thought of Jane, dazzling as any film star in her minuscule black frock, the fur stole around her shoulders, walking into the Palais des Festivals with Alain and Simone Delage.

I, meanwhile, was stuck in a lavatory on the Croisette, like any junkie after a fix, and with scarcely a greater grip on reality. At Easter my cousin Charles had flown down to visit us, and we amicably agreed that I would give up the pretence of helping to edit the firm's publications. He enjoyed his stay, impressed by Jane's newfound role as international career physician, but puzzled by my transformation into a suntanned but distracted consort, forever listening to the ghosts in the garden. I told him nothing about the secret life of Eden-Olympia.

Meanwhile, my investigation into the Greenwood murders had stalled. Between myself and the truth stood an amiable bully with badly bitten fingernails. Although Wilder Penrose enjoyed my company, and generously allowed me to beat him at chess, I knew that he saw me as another of his experimental animals, to be stroked through the bars as I was fattened for yet another maze.

Trying to lead him on, I listened to him enlarge on his psychopathic credo. He had recruited a dozen more bowling clubs, and I hoped that he would soon overreach himself and drive his demented apocalypse into the buffers. He pressed me to join one of the therapy groups, and I finally gave in, intending to take careful notes of the victims and their injuries.

In the rear seats of cars stolen for the evening, I watched as the photographer – a financial analyst with a Japanese bank – recorded the ratissages on his camcorder. An empty mansion on Cap d'Antibes owned by an Egyptian property tycoon was broken into and thoroughly trashed. Another bowling team, made up of senior managers at Elf-Maritime, carried out a spectacular act of piracy in the Golfe-Juan marina, seizing a motor yacht owned by a family of Omani Arabs. They sailed the gaudy vessel to the Îles de Lérins, where it was beached and set alight. From the terrace of the Villa Grimaldi we watched the flames rise into the night. As sleek in their wetsuits as a chorus line of James Bonds, the corporate perpetrators raised their malt-whisky tumblers and toasted the cause of therapeutic psychopathy.

Gold, I soon noticed, was a special target of the bowling teams. I pretended to play lookout when a hapless Saudi broker was brutally beaten in the underground garage at the Noga Hilton. Sexual assaults provided a unique frisson, and older prostitutes received special treatment, for reasons locked deep in childhood pathology. I tried to forget that I had held open the lift doors in a Mandelieu tower block as a handsome Spanish whore who ran a two-room brothel fought to shield her infant daughter.

After this I almost broke with Penrose, warning him that his therapy programme was moving out of control. But he knew that neither I nor any other executives would go to the police. The camcorder footage incriminated us all, as he reminded me, and the radical therapy clearly worked. The members of the bowling teams glowed with health, and Eden-Olympia had never been so successful. The flow of adrenalin, the hair-triggers of fear and flight, had retuned the corporate nervous system and pushed profits to unprecedented heights.

Even I felt better. I sat in the lavatory cubicle in the Blue Bar, listening to the play of water on my hand. As the pain eased, I slipped into a reverie of Jane and our drive through Provence, in those months long ago that now seemed like years . . .

'*C'est stupide . . . Monsieur!*'

'Paul, are you in there? Don't die yet . . .'

I eased myself from the washbasin, woken by the raised voices. A fist pounded on the plywood panel. I unlatched the door as a Blue Bar waiter fell against me. He peered into the cubicle, searching the floor between my feet for any sign of an addict's gear.

Behind him stood Frances Baring, blonde eyebrows springing in alarm. She pressed her hands to my cheeks, staring into my still sluggish eyes.

'Paul? You're hiding in here? Is someone after you?'

'No. Why? Sorry, I fell asleep.'

'I thought, maybe . . .' She slipped a fifty-franc note into the waiter's hand. 'Monsieur is with me. Have a nice day . . .'

Frances took my arm and eased me out of the cubicle. The scent of her body, the touch of her hands, quickly revived me. She wore a white trouser suit and sunglasses, as if she had stepped from one of the gangster generals' helicopters. She leaned forward to kiss me, sniffing at my breath before our lips touched.

'Frances, relax . . .' I noticed the hypodermic wallet jammed behind the washbasin taps and stuffed it into my jacket. 'My knee's been creating hell – I gave myself a shot of Jane's painkiller and drifted off . . . thinking about you.'

'I hate that stuff. One day we'll be meeting in the local morgue. The barman said he'd seen you – an Englishman, *très méchant*.' Still unconvinced, she closed the cubicle door. 'Let's get you out of here.'

'I'm fine, no problems with the knee.' The sleep had refreshed me, and I felt almost euphoric. As we stepped into the crowded restaurant I pointed to the Croisette. 'God, it's dark.'

'It usually is. It's called night.'

Frances steered me to the stools by the bar. Glad to see her, I watched as she fumbled in her purse for cigarettes and lighter. I liked her quirky humour, her sudden moods of self-doubt when she gripped me tightly and refused to let me leave her bed. She was still trying to turn me against Eden-Olympia, but approved of my taking part in the ratissages, sometimes telling me of a mansion that might be robbed. In return, she asked me to introduce her to some of the pilots at the Cannes-Mandelieu airfield, an engaging crew of French, American and South African flyers who towed the advertising pennants above the beaches of the Côte d'Azur in their ageing Cessnas and met to drink at a Thai restaurant in La Napoule. She commissioned one of the Frenchmen to take aerial photographs of the Var plain near the Sophia-Antipolis science park, ostensibly as part of her property surveys, and later I found his flying jacket at her apartment. But Jane's anaesthetic took care of that pain too . . .

I kissed the pearl lipstick on her mouth, but she was distracted by the noise on the Croisette. She stabbed her cigarette into a wet pulp, and pushed away her martini.

'All this din,' she complained. 'Let's find somewhere quiet.'

'It's the film festival – everyone's enjoying themselves.'

'Awful, isn't it? You can get knocked down by the world's oldest hooligans.'

'Frances . . . ?' I pressed her hands to the bar. 'What is it? You're as nervous as a bird.'

She glanced into the mirror of her compact, scanning the restaurant behind her. 'I think I'm being followed.'

'I'm not surprised. You look like a movie star.'

'I mean it. That's why I haven't been in touch. There's someone watching me when I leave the office. I'm pretty sure it's one of Zander's security men.'

'What does he do?'

'Nothing. He sits in a parked car on the roof deck, near where David was killed.'

'Maybe he's holding a vigil?'

'Paul, I'm serious.'

'He's just doing his job. Frances, you're an important person in the property office. You help them with the . . . recreational side of things.'

'That's quite a euphemism. Write it down.' She frowned at the olive in her martini, as if suspecting that it might be bugged. 'At least I don't like doing it. You accept everything.'

'Not true. I'm waiting for Penrose to go over the edge. Then the whole balloon will burst and the police will have to act. I hate the racism and violence, but the ratissages are just an adult version of "ring the doorbell and run".'

'That's very tolerant, coming from someone as straitlaced as you. I'm glad no one rings my doorbell.' She laughed at this, trying to reassure herself, and then stared at me like a shady boxing manager setting up one of his fighters. 'Wilder Penrose impresses you, I can see that. Have you ever thought where it's going to lead? And where he's taking you?'

'Frances . . . he's not taking me anywhere. Stop working for them. Apply for a transfer. By the way, I assume you picked out the Arab yacht they set alight?'

'So vulgar. A floating brothel. I had a look round – it reeked of semen.' She revived, the flames almost reflected in her eyes. 'You should have joined in, Paul. You'd have fun beating up some rich Arab.'

'I doubt it.' I wanted to calm her, and took away her cigarettes. Lowering my voice, I said: 'You've been trying to use me ever since we met. Why?'

'Who knows? Revenge, anger, envy – invent a new deadly sin. We need one.' She moved closer to me, and took a cigarette from the packet in my hand. Casually, she said: 'There's going to be an "action" tonight. A really big one.'

'Ringing doorbells?'

'More serious than that. They've rented cars and an ambulance. Because of the film festival they've had to bring them in from Marseilles and Dijon.'

'That's a lot of trouble to go to. How do you know?'

'I booked the drivers' return air tickets. If there's an ambulance it means people will be hurt. I think they plan to kill someone.'

'I doubt it. Who?'

'Hard to say.' She stared at herself in the mirror behind the bar. 'It could be me. Or you. In fact, you're much more likely.'

'Hire cars and an ambulance? Return tickets to Dijon?'

'Why not? They must be tired of you poking around. You haven't discovered anything about David they didn't already know. You're no more part of Eden-Olympia than those African salesmen they're always roughing up. Your wife's practically moved in with one of their senior executives.'

'That's not true.'

'No? I'm sorry, Paul. I didn't mean that.' She smiled dreamily, like a clever child, and then seized her purse. 'I'm getting the Blue Bar blues. Let's get out of here and see some healthy, life-enhancing porn . . .'

We strolled arm in arm along the Croisette, stepping back when groups of limousine-chasers raced across the pavement, chattering into their mobile phones as they coordinated their celebrity hunt. I thought of Frances's talk of a special action. But I was too easy a target, a crippled ex-pilot barely able to pump the clutch pedal of his rebored Jaguar, with a wife who was a key member of the clinic.

But the threat nagged at me, as Frances had intended. She was forever playing with my emotions and loyalties, skilfully weaving them through the woof and warp of her own insecurities. Lying in bed beside me at Marina Baie des Anges, surrounded by the vast, curved night, she would watch me as I caressed her thighs, confused by the affection I felt for her. She had never understood the secret rationale of Eden-Olympia, and still assumed that its senior executives were giving in to a repressed taste for thuggery and violence.

'Paul?' She gripped my arm as I stopped to scan the traffic. 'You've seen something?'

I pointed to the central reservation, sealed off by railings to protect the palms from the graffiti artists. A stout man with reddish hair and a bottle nose stood on a patch of grass, staring over the crowd.

'The Riviera News manager . . .' Frances turned her back. 'Is that – ?'

'Meldrum. Do you want to talk to him?'

'No. He's watching us. He knows something is on tonight.'

'There is. You're in the middle of it.' I waited as the Australian jotted something into a notebook. 'He's a reporter, Frances. He's covering his beat.'

'Let's get away. Here, anywhere . . .' I could feel her shaking as she dragged me up the steps of a short-let apartment building. The flats had been rented out to small independent producers, and every balcony was draped with banners advertising the company's latest film.

'"Where Teachers Dare" . . . "Schoolgirl Killers" . . .' I read out. 'Manila, Phuket, Taiwan. What Meldrum calls one man, a boy and a dog operations . . .'

'The man holds the camera while the boy . . . Paul, are you interested?' Frances had calmed herself, and waited for me to reply. 'They're all on video. You sit on a bed and take your pick from six television sets.'

'Group sex, donkeys, water sports? Krafft-Ebing meets Video-8?'

'Please . . . this isn't Surbiton or Maida Vale. It's all very normal – paunchy men in their fifties having straight sex with fourteen-year-olds. Nothing pervy, thank you.' She took my arm like a helpful tour guide. '*Cahiers du Cinéma* says the porn movie is the true future of film.'

'In that case . . .'

We entered the lobby of the apartment building. Beyond the glass doors was the reception bureau, which resembled the registration office of a paediatric conference. Two middle-aged Asian women with the faces of retired croupiers sat at a baize-draped table, beside a display board covered with room numbers and film stills. Leaflets and advertisement flyers were stacked on a desk, showing a selection of well-groomed and smiling children barely on the edge of puberty, as if illustrating a seminar on rubella or whooping cough.

'Frances . . . hold on.'

'What is it? Spoilt for choice?'

'This isn't for me.'

'How do you know? Are you sure, Paul?'

'Absolutely. You've had me wrong from the beginning.'

'Fair enough.' She seemed relieved, but added offhandedly: 'David loved it here.'

'Greenwood? That surprises me.'

'It was a laugh. A huge joke. He was curious – in a way, he was working in the same field.'

'A joke?' I watched the Asian women. One of them was trying to smile, and a strange crevice appeared in the area of her mouth, a vent of hell.

I stepped into the Croisette and the safety of the television lights. A stretch limousine with Eden-Olympia pennants slowed to a halt, held up by the crowd that surged aimlessly along the pavement like a tide swilling to and fro among the piers of a tropical harbour. I could see clearly into the rear seat, where Jane sat between Alain and Simone Delage. All were in evening dress, Jane with Wilder Penrose's mink stole around her shoulders. She was staring at the sea, as if unaware of the film festival and lost in her thoughts of modem links and mass medical screenings. She was tired but all the more beautiful for it, and I felt proud of her and glad to be her husband, despite what Eden-Olympia had done to us.

On the jump seat sat Pascal Zander, eyes fixed on Jane's cleavage. He was aggressively drunk, gesturing in a coarse way at Alain Delage, who seemed bored by him. Simone held Jane's hand, trying to distract her from Zander, murmuring a commentary on the crowd into her ear.

When the traffic failed to move, Alain spoke to the chauffeur. The front passenger door opened and Halder stepped from the car, smartly dressed in dinner jacket and black cummerbund, gold cufflinks flashing at his wrists. He noticed me on the steps of the apartment building, and glanced at the display of film titles hanging from the balconies. Barely pausing, he raised his palms to the night air, as if puzzled by my choice of film fare for the evening.

'Paul, who was that?' Frances waved as the limousine moved off. 'I think I saw Halder . . .'

'Jane with the Delages and Pascal Zander. She seemed very happy.'

'Good. No one died of boredom during the film. They're off to the party at the Villa Grimaldi.'

'Zander looked drunk. Too drunk for a security chief.'

'People worry about him. They say he's going to be replaced. Pity me, Paul. I have to see him at the party. Those roving hands should be up there on the Noga Hilton with the samurai . . .'

I watched the tail lights of the limousine, and for a moment thought that Jane had turned to look back at me. 'The Villa Grimaldi? I'll come with you.'

'Did they send you a ticket?'

'I'll gate-crash.'

'You haven't seen the gates.' She stared gloomily at my stained shirt and leather sandals. 'I can get you in, but it's black tie.'

'They'll think I'm one of the security guards.'

'They're dressed like Cary Grant.' She pondered this sartorial impasse, still trying to integrate me into her scheme. 'We'll go back to Marina Baie des Anges. David's old dinner jacket is there. I think you're allowed to borrow it.'

'David's old tux . . . ?' I took her arm. 'Yes, I'd like to wear it. Something tells me it's going to fit . . .'

32

A Dead Man's Tuxedo

BEHIND US, MARINA Baie des Anges wrapped itself into the night, its curved towers enclosing a deeper darkness of sleep, dreams and seconal. We set off towards Antibes on the RN7, the beach of Villeneuve-Loubet to our left. A windsurfer tacked across the waves, watched by his wife and teenage son, sitting on the shingle slope below their parked car. As the sail caught the shifting air it seemed to vanish for a few seconds, then appeared again as if emerging from a defective space-time.

Frowning at the prospect of the Villa Grimaldi party, Frances leaned into the steering wheel, following the BMW's headlamps as they swerved across the steep camber. I lay back in the passenger seat and let the night air sweep across me, carrying away the last musty scents of Greenwood's dinner jacket.

The dead man's tuxedo was a tight squeeze, the seams straining against my armpits. Frances had taken the suit from the wardrobe in her bedroom, holding the garment to her shoulders and reluctant to share it with me. She sat on the bed and watched while I smoothed the bruised lapels. A scent of past time clung to the fabric, memories of medical society dinners in London, cigar smoke and long-forgotten aftershave that rose from the worn silk lining.

Yet I felt surprisingly comfortable in the dead doctor's hand-me-down. Gazing at myself in the wardrobe mirror, I sensed that I had become Greenwood and assumed his role. Frances was almost deferential, aware that through me her former lover had returned to her bedroom.

With one of her white yachting shirts and a black tie fashioned from a crepe hatband, I passed muster. We were leaving the flat when I noticed my leather sandals.

'Jesus, Frances – my feet!'

'So? You've got two of them.'

'Look at those toes – they're the size of lobsters.'

'It's a crowded party. Who's going to notice them?' Frances stared at my toes. 'They're prehensile . . . is that genetic?'

By chance, she found a pair of black espadrilles that I wrenched into shape. As we took the lift to the basement garage she touched the dinner jacket, trying to calm a fleeting ghost. For a moment she seemed to see my face for the first time.

My own memories of Greenwood were less pressing. The booster dose of painkiller that I injected in the bathroom had induced a pleasant torpor. The world could deal with itself, and make its own accommodation with the deranged doctor. When we reached Antibes, passing the harbour and the modest apartment building where Greene had spent his last years, I thought of the two Asian women, sitting like furies at the baize table, guarding their ugly sideshow to the film festival as Greenwood chuckled his way round the video-horrors.

We waited at the long traffic lights near the bus depot in Golfe-Juan. Under the sodium glare Frances smiled approvingly at me.

'You look so smart, Paul. Even your wife might fancy you.'

'I sleep in the children's room now. It's sunny and cheerful, like going back to infancy – Babar, Tintin and Rupert Bear watch over me . . .'

'The frieze? It's sweet. I helped David put it up.'

'Why, though? He wasn't married. It's an odd thing for a bachelor to do.'

'He had friends in London who came down.'

'The refuge at La Bocca – did any of the girls stay at the house?'

'With their uncles, now and then . . .'

'Migrant Arab labourers? It's hard to believe.' We were climbing the heights of Super-Cannes, along a smoothly paved road
that curved past palatial villas, lit like spectres by firework displays.
'This Alice obsession, lending these incomprehensible books to
the teenage girls. He was a one-man British Council, and about
as much use. Those tough teenagers can't have made head or tail
of them.'

'So why did he bother? Go on, Paul . . . you're thinking of
the Reverend Dodgson and his other interests.'

'It did occur to me.'

We reached the Villa Grimaldi and joined the queue of cars and
taxis waiting to enter the estate. In the darkness, the VIP guests
sat in their limousines like deposed minor royalty. Security men in
Eden-Olympia uniforms took Frances's invitation and waved her
through the gates into the drive, where she handed the BMW to
a squad of hyperactive valet-parkers.

Three marble terraces, the lowest enclosing a swimming pool,
looked out over a shelving lawn towards La Napoule Bay. Cannes
lay beneath us, a furnace of light where the Croisette touched the
sea, as if an immense lava flow was moving down from the hills
and igniting at the water's edge. The Palais des Festivals resembled
a secondary caldera, and the rotating strobes on its roof vented a
gaudy fountain above the Vieux Port.

Frances and I strolled forward, eyes stung by the flashes of
chemical colour from a firework display. Five hundred guests
packed the terraces, some dancing to the music of a marimba
band, others helping themselves to champagne and canapés. A
forced intimacy ruled the night, an illusion of good humour that
seemed part of a complex social experiment.

On the lowest terrace were the business park's more workaday
guests, the bureaucracy of local police chiefs, magistrates and senior
civil servants. They and their carefully groomed wives stood with

their backs to the Croisette, staring coolly at the actors, directors and film agents who occupied the middle terrace. I failed to identify any of the actors, aspiring newcomers who were still prepared to fraternize with their public but displayed the nervy jauntiness of celebrities forced to accept that no one recognized them or had seen their out-of-competition films. They in turn kept a careful watch on the upper terrace. Here an elite of film producers, bankers and investors endured the noise, a collective roar of inaudible voices. The Cannes Film Festival, like the Academy Awards in Los Angeles, momentarily confused them with the suggestion that film was about something other than money.

'The guests are here,' I shouted into Frances's ear. 'But where are the hosts?'

'This kind of party doesn't have hosts.' Frances ran a hand over my dinner jacket. 'Time for me to go to work, Paul. I hope you find Jane. If you don't, you can take me home . . .'

She plunged into the crowd, immediately equipping herself with an entourage of intrigued males. Finding my bearings, I realized that she was trying to avoid a far more serious admirer who had seen her arrive. Moving unsteadily down the steps from the upper terrace was Pascal Zander, helped by the ever-watchful Halder, mobile radio in hand. The security chief wore a dinner jacket and tie but seemed dishevelled, and had clearly been forced to dress in a hurry. He was sweating freely, and gazed around the terrace like a vaudeville performer who had emerged through a trap-door and realized he was on the wrong stage.

'Halder . . .' I caught his arm. 'Is Jane here?'

'Mr Sinclair . . . ?' Surprised to see me, Halder stared at my dinner jacket, eyes running along its worn seams and English cut. He searched my face, concerned that I was trying, unconvincingly, to impersonate someone else.

'Halder, my wife . . . ?'

'Dr Jane? She arrived two hours ago. I think she went home.'

'Was she tired?'

'It's possible. It was a long movie.' Halder's reply was evasive. 'She needed to . . . rest.'

'But she's all right?'

'I'm not a doctor, Mr Sinclair. She was fine.'

A heavy hand slapped my back. 'Of course she's fine . . .' Pascal Zander swung towards us and collided with Halder. Steadying himself, he swayed against me like a docking blimp. 'I saw her five minutes ago.'

'At the Villa Grimaldi? Good.'

'Not good for me.' Zander gave a tolerant shrug. 'You should see her, Mr Sinclair. She's a fine doctor.'

'I know she is.'

'You know?' Zander turned an unsteady eye on me, distracted by the dinner jacket I wore. 'Yes, you're her husband. I telephone her every day. We talk about my health.'

'Is anything wrong?'

'Everything is wrong. But not with my health. Jane looks after me, Mr Sinclair. She takes my urine, she tests my blood, she looks in my private places.'

'She's very thorough.'

'She's a serious woman.' Zander leaned against me, and whispered hoarsely into my ear. 'How can a man live with a serious woman? She lacks one thing – no bedside manner.'

He squeezed my shoulder in his large hand, then steadied himself and inhaled the night air. He was bored and drunk, but not as drunk as he pretended, and well aware that Halder was watching him like a guard dog on another master's leash. For all his craftiness, I was surprised that this corpulent beach Beria had been appointed Eden-Olympia's acting head of security. Tactical indiscretion was his forte.

'People at Eden-Olympia play too many games,' he confided, taking my arm and drawing me to the edge of the terrace, where the band and the fireworks were less noisy. A group of police chiefs' wives had begun to sashay to the music, dancing around their tolerant husbands, but Zander dismissed them with a wave. 'I have to be their amah, their nounou, calling them from the garden. When their noses bleed, I have to wipe them. When they soil their behinds, I clean them. They don't like me for that.'

'You know where they hide their toys?'

'Dangerous toys they're not old enough to play with. Wilder Penrose is turning them into children. That's not clever, Mr Sinclair. If someone went to Tokyo or New York and explained the games their people are playing here . . . what would they think about that?'

'I imagine they'd be concerned.'

'The good name of their companies . . . Nissan, Chemical Bank, Honeywell, Dupont. They would pay a lot to keep their good name.' Zander pointed to a group of magistrates standing nearby, judiciously silent as a waiter filled their champagne flutes. 'We should leave crime to the professionals. They're happy to work for us, but psychiatrists they don't trust. Psychiatry is for children who wet the bed . . .'

'Talk to Penrose. He'll be interested to hear it.'

'He has political dreams. In his mind he's a new Bonaparte. He thinks everything is psychology now. But his own psychology – that's the problem he doesn't face.' Zander fingered the lapels of my dinner jacket, as if intrigued by the stitching. 'You've worked hard, Mr Sinclair. You've found so much about your friend. The tragic English doctor . . .'

'Little you didn't know already.'

'I tried to help you. Was Halder useful?'

'As always. He could run a guided tour for the tourists. He's given himself a starring role in the last act.'

'That I heard. He's very ambitious – he wants my job.' He waved to Halder, who was watching him from across the swimming pool. 'A nice boy – he thinks he's German like I think I'm a Frenchman. We're both wrong, but my mistake is bigger. To the French he's a *nègre*, while I am an Arab . . .' He stared bleakly at the party, and then rallied himself, his awareness of his own corruptibility giving him confidence. 'We can help each other, Mr Sinclair. Now that you work for me.'

'Do I?'

'Naturally. Come and see me, I'll tell you more about Dr Greenwood. Maybe about your neighbours . . .'

He left me and swayed through the crowd, affable and devious in a way I found almost likeable.

Halder and I were not alone in keeping watch on the security chief. On a third-floor balcony of the Villa Grimaldi stood Alain Delage, fastening the cufflinks of his dress shirt as he gazed over the crowded terraces. Beside him was Olivier Destivelle, the elderly banker who had succeeded the murdered Charbonneau as chairman of the Eden-Olympia holding company. Together they followed Zander's progress as he wandered through the guests, slipping an arm around every woman who smiled at him. Destivelle spoke into a mobile phone, and he and Delage withdrew into the high-ceilinged room behind them. Despite Halder's assurance, I was certain that Jane was still somewhere within the Villa Grimaldi, as Zander had told me.

I climbed the steps to the upper terrace and strolled towards the entrance, where signs pointed to the cloakrooms. A flunkey in a brocaded uniform guarded the staircase, flicking the elastic bands of his white gloves.

'*Toilettes?*'

'*Tout droit, monsieur.*'

The door of the women's cloakroom opened, and a young German actress emerged, her mobile nostrils moving like hoses around her upper lip, hoovering up the last specks of powder. She exchanged quips with the flunkey, and let him admire her *décolletage.*

I walked to the staircase and climbed the deep maroon carpet. I had reached the half-landing when the flunkey turned from his inspection and shouted: '*Monsieur, c'est privé . . .*'

Careful not to break step, I called down: '*Monsieur Destivelle? Troisième étage?*'

He saluted and let me go, too bored to follow me up the stairs. I paused on the first floor, and strolled past the lavish public rooms with their gilt ceiling liners and empire furniture. In the dining room the tables were already laid with breakfast cutlery. A pantry door opened, and kitchen staff shouted above the blare of music from the terrace. A waiter sang to himself, setting silver cruets on a trolley, ignoring me when I returned to the staircase.

The next floor appeared to be disused, teak barriers shutting off the unlit corridors. I moved up the steps to the third floor, where the landing opened into a large reception suite, chandeliers glowing from the high ceiling. Voices, masculine and multilingual, sounded nearby. In a side chamber a lacquered table was laid with maps and aerial photographs, and I stopped to examine a detailed projection of the Var plain between Nice and Grasse. Ground leases marked out in red crayon defined the planned expansion of Eden-Olympia into a vast urbanization larger than Cannes itself.

In front of me, open connecting doors gave onto a formal drawing room. A television set stood on a blackwood table, watched by a man in evening dress sitting on a gilt chair. Without turning, he raised a hand and beckoned me into the room. I walked towards my reflection in the mantelpiece mirror, crêpe tie hanging from the soft collar of Frances's shirt like a poet's cravat.

'Come in, Paul . . . I was hoping you'd find me here.'

Wilder Penrose greeted me affably, lifting his huge body from the chair. As always, I was struck by how pleased he was to see me. He stood up and embraced me, hands patting the pockets of my dinner jacket as if searching for a concealed weapon. He tapped my cheek with his open palm, forgiving me for the mild subterfuge that had given me access to the villa. Once again I realized that my role was to play the naive and impressionable younger brother.

'Do join me, Paul.' He pointed with the remote control to a nearby chair. 'How's the party?'

'Hard work. I should have borrowed a wheelchair. Did the footman tell you that I was on the way up?'

'Security, Paul – we're obsessed by it. You walk in wearing an assassin's suit and ask for the chairman. You're lucky you weren't shot dead.'

'I'm looking for Jane. She's here somewhere.'

'She's resting in one of the bedrooms. I'll explain where to find her.' Penrose turned back to the television screen. 'Have a look at this footage before you go. Handheld cameras are so jerky, but you get a sense of what's happening.'

'Recent . . . therapy classes?'

'Of course. The teams are doing well.'

He pressed the remote control. Propelled by the fast-forward button, a sequence of violent images rushed past, a confused medley of accelerating cars, running feet, doors being hurled from their hinges, startled Arabs in alcoves and shocked women staring across dishevelled beds. The sound was turned down, but I could almost hear the screams and truncheon thuds. Headlights veered across an underground car park, where a trio of olive-skinned men lay on the concrete floor, pools of blood around their heads.

'Brutal stuff . . .' Penrose grimaced with distaste and switched off the video, relieved to see the blank screen. 'It's getting more difficult to steer the therapy classes. We've seen enough.'

'Don't stop on my account.'

'Well . . . I don't think you should watch too much. It's bad for your morale.'

'I'm touched. This must be the only censored film showing in Cannes. All the same, you're looking at some really nasty clips.'

'Context, Paul. You have to see it within its therapeutic frame. Routine heart surgery can easily resemble something out of a nightmare. Camcorder film is misleading – it's hungry for the colour red, so it turns everything into a bloodbath.' Aware that he was trying too hard to convince me, he said: 'It's in a good cause – Eden-Olympia and the future. Richer, saner, more fulfilled. And vastly more creative. A few sacrifices are worth it if we produce another Bill Gates or Akio Morita.'

'The victims will be glad to hear it.'

'Do you know, they might. Petty criminals, *clochards*, Aids-riddled whores – they expect to be abused. We're doing them a good turn by satisfying their unconscious expectations.'

'So it's also therapy for them?'

'Well put. I knew you'd understand. I wish everyone did.' For once, Penrose seemed distracted, openly gnawing at a thumb. 'Keeping a close eye on things can be tricky. I sense a change of direction. Too many of the teams are starting to treat the therapy classes as sporting events. I try to explain that I'm not interested in running a football league. It's their imaginations I want them to use, not their boots and fists.'

'Zander would agree with you. He thinks you're infantilizing them.'

'Zander, yes . . . his idea of crime comes with a secret Swiss account number. He can't understand why we're developing all this expertise and not putting it to good use. In some ways he's rather dangerous.'

'Doesn't he have a point? All games infantilize, especially when you're playing with your own psychopathy. You begin by dreaming of the *Übermensch* and end up smearing your shit on the bedroom wall.'

'You're right, Paul.' Solemnly, Penrose gripped my hand, nodding at the blank television screen. 'The teams have to work harder, and learn to fight their way into the darkest heart of themselves. I hate to do it, but I need to turn up the ratchet, until the nerve strings sing with anger . . .'

He turned to the window as a firework rocket whistled through the night air and exploded in a puffball of crimson light. A flush of animation touched his face and faded as the rocket spent itself and fell to earth. He seemed more driven than I first remembered him, frustrated by the sluggish reflexes of his senior executives and their flagging will to madness. Seated in this formal empire room, he was hemmed in by the caution of the executive mind. Though I hated everything he had done, and hated myself for failing to report him to the French authorities, I felt almost sorry for him. Mired in its mediocrity, the human race would never be insane enough for Wilder Penrose.

'Now, Paul . . .' He noticed me sitting beside him in Greenwood's dinner jacket. 'You're looking for Jane?'

'Halder saw her earlier. He said she's rather tired.'

'The film was a bit of an ordeal. Swiss bankers don't have the popular touch – the only people they meet are billionaires and war criminals. Jane still works too hard. She should join one of our new therapy groups for women.'

'Are there any?'

'Paul, I'm joking . . . or at least I hope I am.' He walked me to the door, an avuncular clubman with a favourite guest. 'In the case of women the system of imposed psychopathy is already in place. It's called men.'

I paused by the map table and its vision of a greater Eden-Olympia. 'This ratchet, Wilder – are the murders we saw part of it?'

'Murders?'

'The video you were playing. The three Arabs in the garage looked awfully dead.'

'No, Paul.' Penrose lowered his head, his eyes drifting away from me. 'I assure you, everyone recovered. As usual, large bundles of francs were handed over. Think of these people as film extras, paid for a few minutes' discomfort.'

'I'll try to. No murders?'

'None. Who put the idea into your head? Be careful with

298

Zander. He's an unhappy man, driven by powerful resentments. Some of his personal habits are disgusting. He may well be the only natural psychopath in Eden-Olympia.'

'And our very own police chief?'

'Sadly, there's a long tradition of the two roles coinciding. Senior policemen are either philosophers or madmen . . .'

The suites on the fourth floor were dark and unoccupied. Following Penrose's directions, I walked the long corridor, past the gilt-framed mirrors whose surfaces had been dulled by time. In the entrance to the west wing I noticed that a pair of carved oak doors stood ajar. I stepped through them, switched on a table lamp and found myself in a well-stocked gunroom. The barred cabinets were filled with shotguns and sporting weapons. Six Nato-issue automatic rifles occupied one cabinet, chained together through their trigger guards.

A notice-board leaned against an easel, listing the fixtures of the Eden-Olympia gun club. The names of the members, all senior executives at the business park, formed a set of rival leagues that I assumed were run independently of Wilder Penrose. Pinned to the board were photographs of well-set men in their fifties, clipped from the financial pages of a local Arab-language newspaper.

In a corner, behind one of the double doors, was a large department-store dumpbin, filled with what I first thought were gunnery-range targets in the form of animal cutouts. I held several of them to the light, and then recognized stuffed-toy versions of the dormouse, the Hatter and little Alice herself.

I laid the Alice back in the bin, and watched the eyelids swivel and close over the glassy stare, almost the first untroubled sleep I had seen in Eden-Olympia.

To the rear of the west wing, far from the terrace party and the fireworks, a waiter was moving a drinks trolley into the corridor. I stopped beside him, and scanned the debris of glasses and crushed napkins. Sharing a tumbler with a champagne cork was an empty syrette.

'Madame Delage?' I asked. 'Doctor Sinclair?'

'Monsieur? They sleep now.'

'Good. Like Alice . . .' I pressed a few coins into his hand, stepped past him into the suite and closed the door. A single standard lamp lit the empty sitting room, its glow warming the deep pile of a fur stole lying across an armchair.

A coarse masculine odour hung in the air, a blend of sweat and genital steroids, the unmistakable spoor of a man in rut. A bottle of Laphroaig stood on the mantelpiece, and I guessed that a passionate suitor had fortified himself for the rigours of the bed. Pools of malt whisky lay around the legs of a carriage clock, and stained a Palais des Festivals film programme.

The sound of running water came from the bathroom. I listened with my hand on the doorknob, uneager to catch Simone Delage in the act of clipping her toenails.

'Jane . . . ?'

She was sitting on the tiled floor between the bath and the bidet, knees drawn against her chest, her left hand trailing in the flow of water from the bath tap. She wore a man's black silk dressing gown that lay like a shadow across the white tiles. Her face was composed, but the blush of a hard slap still burned on one cheek. Propped in the bidet was the patent-leather handbag that served as her off-duty medical valise. Her hand covered the syringe lying on the porcelain rim.

'Paul?' She greeted me with a faint tremor of the lips. She raised her chin, focusing on my eyes and mouth, and then took my hands, as if she needed to assemble in stages a recognizable image of her husband. She seemed almost asleep, her voice slurred. 'Glad you came, Paul. I wasn't sure . . .'

'I had to come. I guessed you'd be here.'

'So many parties in Cannes tonight. We saw the Eden–Olympia film.'

'Any good?'

'Depressing. Everyone's so happy in Cannes and they make these depressing films. Did you see any?'

'One or two. Not the kind in competition.'

'Depressing?'

'Very.' I sat on the edge of the bath and turned off the tap. I pointed to the inner door. 'Is . . . ?'

'Simone? She's sleeping in the bedroom.' Jane tightened the dressing gown, her childlike shoulders swamped by the black silk. 'You look smart, Paul. I like the dinner jacket.'

'It was David's. It doesn't really fit.'

She nodded at this, and touched my sleeve. 'It suits you. Wear it all the time.'

'Frances Baring loaned it to me. God knows why she kept it.'

'So she won't forget David. He's everywhere still, isn't he?' She straightened her hair in the wall-mirror. 'Too many mirrors in this house. Paul, tell me how you escape inside them.'

'You don't need to escape. Just take things easier. Wilder agrees you work too hard.'

'Wilder agrees with you about everything. That way you do what he wants.' She smiled with the first affection I had seen since our decision to stay. 'Dear Paul. You crash-landed your plane here and can't climb out . . .'

I listened to the boom of rock music, a dull pulse like a weeklong headache. An odd smell caught my nostrils.

'Jane . . . was Zander here?'

'Zander?' She closed her eyes. 'Why ask?'

'I saw him on the terrace. The cologne he was using – I could smell it when I came in.'

'Nasty, isn't it? Reminds him of Beirut.' She felt the bruise on her cheek. 'It doesn't matter, Paul. High up here in Super-Cannes, nothing matters.'

I held her hand, chilled by the cold tap water, and noticed the torn skin on her wrist, blood clotting between the tendons. 'Did Zander do this?'

'I fell over. Zander was very drunk. He thinks he has serious problems at Eden-Olympia.'

'They want him out. He knows where the bodies are buried, and they've seen him sharpening his spade. What was he doing here?'

'Alain set up one of his little games. He didn't tell me Zander was going to play.'

'What happened?'

'They pushed him into the bedroom and locked the door.'

'Where were you?'

'In the bed.' Jane shrugged inside the dressing gown. 'He was too drunk.'

I sat on the floor and touched her bruised cheek. 'Jane, we should leave.'

'Now?' She gripped her bag, as if holding tight to a lifebelt. 'Can't leave, Paul. Taken my medicine.'

'All this diamorphine. You'll kill yourself.'

'I'm fine.' Jane squeezed my hand, the doctor reassuring an anxious relative. 'I know how much to take. That's what medical school is really for. All the doctors at the clinic need help to relax . . .'

'Let's pack tonight and set off for London. We can be in Lyons by morning. Jane, we've spent too long in Eden-Olympia.'

'I'll stay.' She spoke in a sleepy but firm voice. 'I'm really happy here. Aren't you? Talk to Wilder.'

'I have. He's downstairs, watching his pornographic films.'

'Lucky man. I have to cope with too much Belgian angst. Alain and Simone are quite prudish, in their own way.'

'They're degrading you.'

'I know. That's why I became a hippie, to see if I could cope with myself. Then all those caftans and dirty feet were a bit of a bore, so I turned into a doctor.'

'You kept the dirty feet.'

'And you still fell in love with me. I didn't wash for weeks. Now I have clean feet and I'm turning into a slut again. But I do my job and it doesn't matter.' Tired of me, she leaned her cheek against the tiled wall. 'Go, Paul. Just go . . . fly back to London.'

33

The Coast Road

FIREWORKS LEAPT INTO the night sky, ruby and turquoise umbrellas that formed huge cupolas over Super-Cannes, canopies fit for a caliph's throne. Like a hashish dream, they faded and rejoined the dark. Along the Croisette the flicker of flashbulbs marked the end of another premiere, and headlights glowed through the palm fronds as a motorcade left the Palais des Festivals. Forgotten above the crowds, the samurai on the roof of the Noga Hilton gestured with his sword at the beach restaurants, where the studio parties were in full swing.

I took a flute of champagne from a cruising waiter, and thought of Jane, asleep against the bidet in the fourth-floor suite. Despite my knee, I was strong enough to carry her to a taxi, pack her into the Jaguar and set off northwards with our passports. But once again I had hesitated, just as I had postponed my decision to report Wilder Penrose to the police. In part I resented Jane for no longer needing me. I knew that she would leave me at the first service station on the Paris autoroute and hitch a lift to Cannes without a backward glance. If anyone needed me now, it was Penrose and his faltering dream of social madness, a larger version of that plane crash from whose wreckage, as Jane had said, I had yet to free myself.

The band had turned up its amplifiers, filling the air with immense blocks of reverberating sound. The social stratification of the guests had at last collapsed. In a new-style peasants' revolt, the lawyers, civil servants and police officials had climbed the steps to the middle terrace, overwhelming the actors and film agents. As if expecting the worst, the bankers and producers on the upper terrace stood with their backs to the Villa Grimaldi, an *ancien régime* faced with the revolution it most feared, a rebellion of its indentured professional castes.

Frances Baring and Zander were alone on the lower terrace, dancing together by the swimming pool. Zander held his jacket like a matador's cape, urging Frances to lunge at him. Playfully, she let him chase her around the pool, watched by Halder, who sat on the diving board, his dark figure almost invisible against the night.

Seeing me, Frances waved her purse. She whispered something to Zander, ducked beneath his groping hands and ran from the pool. She embraced me, reeking of Zander's cologne.

'Paul . . . don't ever try dancing with a secret policeman. I'm probably pregnant. Do you mind if we go?'

'We'll leave now.' I was glad to see her, but turned to face Zander, who was searching for the sleeves of his dinner jacket. 'Just give me a moment.'

'What is it? Paul?'

'I need a word with Zander.' I flexed my shoulders. 'He's about to be the first policeman I've ever punched.'

'Why?' Frances held my arm. 'I was joking. You sound like a Victorian father. He scarcely touched me.'

'He touched Jane.' I waited while Zander strolled towards us, smiling with all his corrupt charm, as if our real evening together was about to begin. 'Frances, wait here . . . it won't take long.'

'Paul!' She shouted above the music, shaking her head when Halder caught up with the security chief. 'I'm too tired to watch you three brawling.'

'Right . . .' I saw Halder raise a slim hand in warning. I could

deal with Zander, but Halder would be too fast for me. 'We'll
go – I'll talk to Zander another time . . .'

'Is Jane all right?' Frances steered me down the path towards
the car park. 'What happened to her?'

'Nothing. Zander came on a little too heavily.'

'I'm sorry.' Frances handed her ticket to the valet-parkers, and
then gripped my arms. 'Forget about Zander. He doesn't matter.
None of it matters.'

'That's what Jane said. I almost believe it . . .'

We moved down the drive towards the gates, queueing behind
the Saudi ambassador's Cadillac. Trying not to think of Zander,
I realized that once again I had yielded to the greater status quo
that was Eden-Olympia. The business park set its own rules, and
had effectively switched off our emotions. Violence and aggression
were only allowed within the therapeutic regime administered by
Wilder Penrose, like rationed doses of a rare and dangerous medicine. Yet a brawl around the swimming pool of the Villa Grimaldi,
in full view of the assembled judges and police chiefs, with Halder
lightly hysterical and Zander wallowing in the deep end, would
have been a breakthrough of almost surrealist proportions, a genuine lunge for freedom. I was tempted to tell Frances to turn back.

'Paul . . .' She tapped my injured knee, waking me from my
reverie. 'Look up there . . .'

She pointed across the landscaped lawns to the conservatory
entrance of the Villa Grimaldi, where we had parked after the
Cardin Foundation robbery. Two immaculate black Mercedes
straddled the flowerbeds, as if delivered straight from a showroom.
Behind them was a commercial ambulance with curtained windows, its red-cross light switched off, the driver and his paramedic
asleep in the front seat.

Frances fumbled with the headlight switch, trying to read the
ambulance's numberplate.

'Toulon . . .' She seemed thrown by this. 'I told you they'd leased a lot of cars. Why bring an ambulance from Toulon?'

'Watch the Cadillac . . .' I held the wheel, avoiding the Saudi bumper. 'The ambulance is here for the party. Those elderly bankers have to be kept alive – as long as there's a pulse, the money flows.'

Frances stalled the engine, and clumsily restarted it. 'There's something on tonight, a ratissage . . .'

'Penrose would have told me. He's keen that I'm involved.'

'Only in the fun ones, the rugger club japes. This one is serious. Was Penrose here? He doesn't usually go to parties.'

'Frances, relax . . .' I moved her edgy hand from the gear lever, trying to calm her. 'He was upstairs, watching his videos. Nasty stuff – he's starting to prescribe some really violent therapy.'

'Then do something about it. At least six senior judges were at the party.'

'And several police commissaires. I appear in a lot of the video footage – I don't want to spend the next ten years in a Marseilles jail. Besides, they turn a blind eye. They won't admit it, but the French upper class are deeply racist.'

We left the gates of the Villa Grimaldi and set off along the high corniche. Despite her edginess, Frances drove at a leisurely pace, reluctant to change up from second gear. I lay back, and let the last traces of Zander's cologne blow away on the night air.

When we reached the Vallauris road Frances stopped at the green traffic lights. Without moving her head, she pointed to the rear-view mirror.

'Frances? Let's go.'

'There's a car following us.'

I gazed back at the darkened road, briefly lit by a salvo of fireworks. A car with dipped headlights approached us, drifting from the verge to the centre line as if the driver suffered from defective night vision.

'Paul?'

'It's all right. He's looking for someone's villa.'

'No. He's after us. The car has Eden-Olympia plates.'

The car, a grey Audi, was fifty yards behind us when the traffic lights turned to red. Frances let out the clutch and accelerated across the empty intersection, turning right towards Golfe-Juan. The Audi driver cruised through the red lights, and at the last moment swung round to follow us, his nearside wheel clipping the kerb.

I pointed to the first side road. 'Take a left here. He'll go by.'

We turned into an avenue of small houses with well-stocked gardens. The reflector discs of parked cars glowed in our headlights. The Audi had stopped, as if the driver was unsure where we had gone. Then he pulled off the Vallauris road and resumed his unhurried pursuit.

'Right,' I told Frances. 'He's tailing us. It's probably one of Halder's chums, keeping a routine watch over you. He's a real amateur – we'll soon lose him.'

'Him? It might be a woman.'

'Jane? She was too stoned to switch off the bath taps. Anyway, she doesn't care about us.'

Leaning against the door, I watched the Audi over my headrest. It swayed across the steep camber and its wing mirror struck a parked van. The driver caught himself and straightened out, but soon drifted from left to right across the road.

Below us, at the end of the avenue, was the RN7, the brightly lit coastal highway from Cannes to Golfe-Juan. We drove through the underpass, then paused at the junction. In the amber glare of the sodium lights I watched our pursuer stop thirty yards behind us. A hand emerged from the driver's window and tried to reset the broken wing mirror on its mount.

'Frances, you look exhausted . . .' Concerned for her, I tried to take the controls. 'Pull in here – I'll get out and talk to him.'

But Frances pressed on, joining the coast road towards Juan-les-Pins and Antibes. She gripped the wheel and glanced over her shoulder, as if fleeing from the night.

'Frances . . . slow down.'

'Not now, Paul. Our friend isn't alone.'

A few yards behind the stationary Audi were two large Mercedes limousines, similar models to those we had seen at the Villa Grimaldi. As the Audi followed us, they pulled out onto the RN7, moving nose to tail with their headlights dimmed. The Audi driver seemed unaware of his black escort, and was still grappling with the broken wing mount.

We passed the old Ali Khan house beyond the railway tracks, a crumbling deco ghost above the beach. A slip road crossed the railway line and led to the harbour and waterfront bars of Golfe-Juan. Frances accelerated and hurled the little BMW through the dark air, wheels almost losing their grip on the unlit macadam. At the last moment she braked as we reached the railway bridge. The Audi was now a hundred yards behind us, the driver irritated by the Mercedes trying to crowd him off the slip road. I saw a fist raised through the window, and his headlights flared when the tank-like limousine jolted his bumper.

'Brake now! Harder!' I leaned across Frances and switched off the lights. I forced the wheel from her hands and slewed the BMW across the beach road. We hurtled into the car park of Tétou's and came to a neck-jarring halt, startling the young attendant who was dozing in an open-topped Bentley.

The Audi sped past, its burly driver hunched over his wheel, followed by the two Mercedes, headlights on full beam, horns blaring as their drivers jockeyed like chariot-racers.

Too breathless to speak, Frances waved away the puzzled attendant. She lay back in the darkness, and stared at the diners in the beach restaurant across the road. She seemed stunned but relieved, as if she had completed an exhilarating fairground ride and was ready to rejoin the strolling crowd.

'Paul?' She smoothed her hair, aware that I was watching her with interest. 'What is it?'

'Nothing . . . Let's go. They're heading for the beach road to Juan. We'll follow.'

'Why? We've lost them, thank God. Those big cars look nasty.'

'They weren't after us. They were chasing the Audi. You were right all along – it's a ratissage . . .'

Watched by the perplexed attendant, we left the Tétou car park and drove into Golfe-Juan. Despite the film festival, most of the restaurants facing the marina had closed for the night. Guests were leaving a party aboard a motor yacht, tipsily making their way down a gangway, visitors to a white township that emitted an ivory light like a floating cemetery.

'They've gone.' Frances searched the darkness for a turning. 'We'll go back to the RN7.'

'They're up ahead. I want to see what happens.'

'Forget about it! Did you recognize the man in the Audi?'

'Some tired dentist on his way home.'

'He followed us. Why?'

'You, not us. A midnight blonde on her way back from the festival with her pimp. Our vigilantes must have seen him and didn't approve. He looked a little Maghrebian – they'll teach him a lesson in racial respect.'

Reluctantly, Frances drove along the darkened front. At the eastern edge of Golfe-Juan a new apartment complex stood on the site of the ceramics factory I had once visited with my parents. The Audi was circling a nearby roundabout, chased by one of the Mercedes. Almost rolling the limousine onto its side, the driver rammed the rear of the Audi. The second Mercedes blocked the exit of the return road to Golfe-Juan. Its headlights shone on a violent game, a private demolition derby played out beneath the palm trees. Shards of broken glass from the Audi's taillights lay on the road, spitting like embers of a fire as the tyres raked across them.

'Hold back for a second.' I tried to steady Frances, who seemed disoriented by the harsh collisions. 'He's decided to cut and run . . .'

The Audi swerved from the roundabout, struck the kerb and set off towards Juan-les-Pins. The two Mercedes hurtled after it, engines blowing with an elephant-like roar, headlights picking out their quarry.

'Frances . . . let's move.'

'Why?' She sat stiffly at the wheel, refusing to look at the windscreen. 'They're crazy, Paul . . .'

'They're trying to be crazy – that's the point. We need more evidence.'

'Evidence?' Frances hunted the gearbox until I rammed the lever through its gate. 'On top of everything else?'

'Just keep going.'

We followed the deranged motorcade as it moved along the beach road. Waves broke on the strip of sand, their foam sluicing through the debris of beer cans and forgotten rubber flippers where the ageing Picasso had once played with Dora Maar and his children. The rotating beam of the lighthouse at La Garoupe swept along the shore, illuminating the closed bar-cabins and the low sea wall.

Frances slowed when one of the limousines ran alongside the Audi, jostling it as the second Mercedes accelerated and braked, lunging at the rear bumper. On our left, across the railway line, was the apartment complex of Antibes-les-Pins. A single light shone above a balcony, where some insomniac neighbour of Isabel Duval sat alone in her high-security apartment. I searched the balconies, distracted by a rush of noise as the Nice to Paris express emerged from the darkness. It thundered past us in a roar of steel rails and sped away into the night.

Stunned by the sound, Frances lost control of the car as the black vacuum in the wake of the express sucked the BMW from her hands. She gripped the wheel and shouted: 'He's going to crash! Paul!'

'Where?'

She pointed to the road ahead, where brake lights flared in alarm. The Audi overran the stone kerb, struck the sea wall and whirled into the air before plunging onto the beach below.

I took the wheel from Frances's hands and steered the BMW onto the pedestrian walkway. The two Mercedes slewed around each other and stopped, for a moment vanishing into the darkness as they switched off their lights. We rolled to a halt beside a derelict bar, its wooden walls covered with fading posters for the Juan jazz festival. I turned off the engine and stepped onto the sea wall. Frances sat stiffly over the wheel, staring at the instrument panel. She touched the brake lever, as if convinced that her clumsy driving had led to the accident.

Leaving her, I walked down the beach and let the cold sea sluice across my feet, soaking the rope soles of the espadrilles. I ran along the dark sand, the night air cutting through the open seams of Greenwood's dinner jacket.

The Audi lay on its back in the shallow waves, flames lifting from the engine compartment. When the water retreated, I saw the driver's body trapped under the rear seat, an arm pressed to the passenger window. The dying flames flowed across the water that swilled around the car.

Two men in dinner jackets stepped from the first Mercedes, scaled the sea wall and walked to the water's edge, where one of them began to film the scene with a camcorder, waiting until the La Garoupe beam lit the stage for him. When I was twenty yards away he turned the camera and filmed me as I stood exhausted in the sodden espadrilles, my back to the lights of Golfe-Juan. I walked towards them, pointing to the trapped driver, but the two men climbed the beach and returned to their car.

'Paul! Help him!'

Frances ran along the sand, a high-heeled shoe in each hand, throat muscles working while she gasped at the night air. She strode into the waves and gestured with her shoes at the car.

'My God, they killed him . . .'

I held her as the waves broke around our knees, and steered her through the undertow onto the beach. A vehicle with a pulsing emergency light moved along the road from Golfe-Juan, slowing to a stop when it approached the burning car.

'Paul, it's the police . . . talk to them.'

'They aren't police.' I watched the occupants step from the vehicle. 'It's the ambulance you ordered. We saw it outside the Villa Grimaldi . . .'

We stood at the water's edge as the paramedics pulled the dead driver from the Audi. He was a large, fleshy man in his fifties, and his pallid skin seemed to have been immersed in the sea for days. His dinner jacket clung to one arm, lying beside him like the wing of a drowned bird. The paramedics turned him onto his back and began to work at his chest. On the collars of their white overalls were printed the name and telephone number of an emergency ambulance service in Toulon.

Looking down over their shoulders, I recognized the blanched features of Pascal Zander.

I stared into the security chief's eyes. Once so sharp and devious, they now gazed at nothing, the flat pupils like empty windows. All the memories of his professional life, the secret codes and misdemeanours, were being washed away by the sea. One of the paramedics, a blond young man with a surfer's physique, pointed to my feet, and I realized that I was standing on Zander's hand. I counted the pudgy fingers, their skin impressed with the sole pattern of my espadrilles, and realized that a few hours earlier they had probably fondled my wife's breasts.

Giving up their attempt to revive the dead man, the paramedics returned to the ambulance, where they lit cigarettes and spoke into their radio. I heard Frances gasp as she stood beside me, and turned to see her running along the beach to her car.

'Frances, wait! We'll call the police . . .'

Carrying her shoes, I set off towards the BMW. I was fifty yards away when I heard its engine begin to race. Frances waved me away, ran the car off the kerb and pulled out to pass the ambulance. In the pale light reflected from the waves I could see her face, almost stiff with shock. She swerved around the two Mercedes limousines and set off at speed towards Juan-les-Pins.

A mile away, beyond the Golfe-Juan marina, the siren of a police car seesawed through the night. The driver of the second Mercedes stepped from the car and opened the passenger door, beckoning to me. I stared at the dead man on the sand, at his overweight, deflating body. The floating sleeves of his dinner jacket semaphored as the waves swilled up the beach, signalling a death to the sea. I held Frances's shoes to my face, smelling the perfumed insoles and the fresh scent of brine.

The chauffeur waited while I climbed the sea wall to the Mercedes. He wore evening dress under his bowling jacket, and as I stepped up to him I saw his face and overlit eyes.

'Halder? What are you doing here?'

'Time to leave, Mr Sinclair.'

'You were driving the car? I thought you were guarding Zander . . .'

I pointed to the dead man on the sand, his exposed torso washed by the waves. Halder's face was expressionless. In the headlights of the approaching police car he resembled an accident bystander already bored by the tableau around him, the overturned Audi, a body and the waves. Too distracted to face me, he had distanced himself from any judgement on events.

'We're leaving, Mr Sinclair.' He gestured towards the open passenger door. 'It's best if you come with us.'

A strong hand reached from the rear seat and gripped my wrist. Too tired to resist, I watched myself step into the car.

'Paul . . .' Alain Delage drew me towards the jump seat. 'I'm glad we waited for you. I told Jane you'd join us.'

His composed face glowed in the police headlights. As I sat down he smiled with the ready sympathy of a rescuer reaching from a liferaft to help a survivor from the sea.

Facing me, squeezed together in the rear seat, were Jane and Simone Delage, the camcorder across their laps. Jane still wore her black silk dressing gown, and lay half-asleep against Simone's shoulder. Recognizing me, she raised a hand in welcome, and managed a faint flicker of her bloodless lips. I realized that I was still holding Frances Baring's shoes, and placed them on the floor at Delage's feet.

Half a mile behind us, the spotlight of the police car lit up the shacks along the beach. When Halder started the engine of the Mercedes I drummed on the glass behind his head.

'Alain – the police are on their way. We need to talk to them.'

'Not now, Paul.' Delage signalled to Halder. 'The ambulance men will tell them everything. It's been a long day for you . . .'

He sat back, larger and more confident than I remembered him. The overturned Audi had moved into the deeper water, and the paramedics returned to the beach. They knelt beside the dead security chief, taking a blood sample from his thigh. Zander's dinner jacket had at last detached itself from his arm. It floated off, working its way across the waves, sleeves moving in a wavering breaststroke, determined to reach the safety of the open sea.

We sped on into an even deeper night.

34

Course Notes and a Tango

'MR SINCLAIR, YOU'VE been most helpful.' Sergeant Jucaud paused at the door and tucked his notebook into his jacket. 'Pascal Zander was a close friend of the Cannes police.'

'As he often said – I'm glad to tell you all I know . . .'

I shook the young detective's hand and watched him walk back to his car. He paused by the Jaguar, admiring its lines, and knelt by the rear wing. Something out of the ordinary had caught his trained eye, perhaps an unpaid parking ticket snagged by the boot handle. With a small knife he teased a paint fleck from the chromium bumper, then raised it to the sunlight and waved reassuringly to me. The array of dents and scratches marking the Jaguar's venerable bodywork were too slight to suggest that the car had been involved in a serious collision. The miscreant paint fleck had probably come from Wilder Penrose's fibreglass door, still bearing its open wound like a duelling scar. Besides, as Sergeant Jucaud knew, I could hardly have reversed the Audi into the sea.

Careful to remain calm, and glad of the day's first injection, I returned the sergeant's salute. I waited until he had driven away, and then strolled back to the pool. I stared at my reflection in the water, trying to accept that I had spoken for twenty minutes to the sergeant and told him absolutely nothing about the true cause of Zander's death.

A publicity plane was carrying out its morning tour of Eden-Olympia, advertising a clay-pigeon range in the hills beyond

Grasse. I lay on the sun-lounger, feeling the guilt and pain ebb from my knee. A faint steam rose from the wet footprints Jane had left on the tiles. Looking at the tiny insteps, I thought of Frances Baring's shoes, with their scent of toes and midnight sea, now wrapped in a supermarket bag in the Jaguar's boot.

In the five days since Zander's death, Frances had not once returned to her office. Her secretary told me that she had taken a fortnight's leave, but her telephone at Marina Baie des Anges had been disconnected. I could still hear her cry of fear when she recognized Zander's body, and her panic as she ran blindly to her car. I needed to see her again, and somehow reassure her that Zander's death had been an accident. Already I had largely convinced myself.

A lethal evening had turned into an even stranger night. I remembered the drive back to Eden-Olympia, when I had been too stunned to demand that Halder stop the car and report the incident to the police. I stared into the night, at the closed filling stations and supermarkets, while Alain Delage flexed his thighs and the two women huddled together in the back of the Mercedes, a secure enclave in a world of violent men. Simone had watched Jane protectively, like a mother with a tired child, warning me away when I tried to take her hands.

As we reached Eden-Olympia I expected a detachment of French gendarmerie to be waiting for us. Too tired to join the others for a nightcap, I climbed the stairs to my bedroom and fell asleep with the light on. I woke an hour later, and heard the sprinklers playing on the cycad below my window. Dance music came from the lounge, the sweet strains and swoops of a 1940s tango. I went downstairs, still wearing David Greenwood's kelp-stained dinner jacket, and found that Jane had revived. She was dancing with Halder, one arm outstretched as he bowed her backwards across his thigh.

The Delages sat side by side in the armchairs, watching the dance like impresarios trying out a scene from a new musical, a tale of tragic love across the divide set in a shabby Buenos Aires dance hall. Halder moved with his light-footed grace, but he looked ill at ease, well aware that the dance might continue once the music had stopped. Alain Delage was filming the tango, and behind the camcorder his face bore the same expression that I had seen during the beating of the African trinket salesman.

I realized that a target was being primed. I stepped through the cigarette smoke and slipped my arm around Jane, who moved through a deep dream of her own and scarcely seemed to notice that her partner had changed. Responding to my clumsy steps, she smiled at me as if recognizing an old acquaintance who had strayed briefly into her life. But Halder bowed to me from the door, all too aware of the danger he had faced.

Alain Delage had taken over as Eden-Olympia's security chief, and Wilder Penrose's prize pupil was now his most eager collaborator. The introverted and mousy accountant so despised by Frances Baring had turned into a confident and well-adjusted sociopath.

I lay on the sun-lounger, listening to Jane's shower, and glad to have shared a late breakfast with her. Sergeant Jucaud had called at seven, delaying the start of her professional day and providing a small window of opportunity to revive a fading marriage. Sitting with us in the kitchen, the sergeant questioned me about Zander's 'state of mind', a euphemism for drunkenness. Analysis of the dead man's blood had indicated a high level of alcohol in his system. There were no witnesses to the accident, Jucaud told us, and it seemed likely that Zander had fallen into a stupor at the wheel of the Audi and met his death alone on the night sand.

Jane nodded her agreement, but I was surprised to learn that she had signed the death certificate. According to the official account, she was driving along the coast road and saw the paramedics beside the overturned car, stepped out and confirmed that Zander had died from severe head and chest injuries.

I listened to all this without comment. Sergeant Jucaud was a graduate of an elite police college, and certainly no part of any conspiracy between Eden-Olympia and the Cannes police. But one offhand remark unsettled me. Senior officers at the Villa Grimaldi had reported that I was one of the last people to speak to Zander, and had even seemed to threaten him.

Jane emerged from the terrace, dressed in a cream linen suit, hair tied with a black silk ribbon. She carried her coffee cup but barely needed the stimulant, moving in an easy, amphetamine stride. As always, I was amazed by how quickly she could recover her poise and energy. She waved cheerfully to the gardener, Monsieur Anvers, and threw her biscuit to a sparrow watching from the rose pergola. Once again I felt all my old affection for her, a warmth that transcended Eden-Olympia and everything that had happened to us.

At the same time, I could see how much she had changed. She had put on weight, and the skin of her face seemed grey and toneless. She often apologized for the bloody stools in the lavatory that she forgot to flush away, and blamed the constipating diamorphine. Without thinking, she tossed her coffee dregs into the swimming pool.

'Paul . . . do you think Jucaud was satisfied?'

'Our stories matched. You sounded very convincing.'

'They weren't stories. It was an accident.'

'Are you sure?'

'I was there.' Jane leaned her head back and let the sun play on her pallid skin. 'We were overtaking and he lost control. I didn't tell Jucaud because it would drag in everyone else.'

'That's thoughtful of you. Who was driving?'

'Alain, I think. Zander was very drunk. I could smell it on the beach.'

'I didn't like his cologne either. I'm surprised you could smell it from the car – you never left it.'

'I did.' Jane seemed genuinely indignant. 'Alain and Simone both said I went down to Zander with my valise.'

'I must have missed that. Did you see the accident?'

'More or less. It happened so quickly. The cars barely touched.'

'They didn't need to.' I watched the coffee grounds sinking through the water. 'Three tons of black Merc swerving after you . . . most people would do anything to get out of the way. Who was in the first car?'

'Yasuda and someone from Du Pont. And a chauffeur I haven't seen before.'

'He was good. That was highly skilled offensive driving. Alain probably brought in a police pursuit specialist.'

'Paul . . .' Jane stared into my pupils, as if suspecting that I had overdosed myself. 'You're getting obsessive again. First David, now this accident. It was tragic for Zander, but . . .'

'No one liked him?'

'He was too fleshy for me.' Jane grimaced, exposing the fine cracks in her make-up. 'Still, at least he was human.'

'Human enough to play Alain's games with you?'

'Paul, we agreed not to talk about that. It's my way of relaxing. Men get so nervous when we hitch up our skirts – they think mummy's going to have sex with the milkman.'

I took her discoloured hands, with their chipped nails. 'Jane, listen to me for once. Alain is dangerous. I watched his eyes while you were dancing with Halder. I saw something your telemetric links will never diagnose – the purest strain of plantation owner. The Belgian Congo under Leopold II, very nasty and very racist. Conrad wrote a novel about it.'

'It was a set book at school.'

'You actually read it?'

'The course notes. It was too frightening.' She stood up and straightened her skirt. 'I'm late for work. Paul, why don't you go back to London for a while?'

'I need to look after you.'

'That's sweet – I mean it. How is Frances? There haven't been any messages for days.'

'She's away. Zander's death shocked her badly.'

'Find her. You need her, Paul.'

'Should I marry her?'

'If you want to. I'd be happy for you . . .'

I walked Jane down to the drive and watched her as she reversed, admiring her wristy gear changes. She looked very elegant and cool in her linen suit, but I noticed a coffee stain on her sleeve. She treated me to the long smile and slow slide of the eyes that I remembered from our happy days. Our marriage would soon be over, but that made me all the more determined to save her.

My knee throbbed again, counting the hours as reliably as Big Ben. I sat on my bed in the Alice room, the hypodermic wallet on my lap, and listened to Jane's Peugeot leave the residential enclave and set off for the clinic. Its third gear screamed in the French mode that Jane had adopted. Top was a sign of weakness, of defensive driving reserved for the elderly and infirm, an evolutionary relic that had survived into a more advanced age. Jane belonged to an epoch that accelerated and braked, but never cruised.

Through the window I could see Simone Delage on her balcony, setting out her toiletries on the table like the pieces on a chessboard. A thick cosmetic cream covered her face, a mask that hid nothing. On the day after Zander's death we had met while we walked to our cars, but her expression was as depthless as the artificial lakes in Eden-Olympia. Only the presence of Jane brought a tremor of life to her impassive features.

Yet there was nothing prurient about her exploitation of Jane. She and Alain approached the freeports of sex like sophisticated tourists in a strange souk, exploring any alleyway that might offer an intriguing cuisine. To these educated travellers even human flesh would prompt no more than a mild query about the recipe. At Eden-Olympia they dined on the à la carte pathologies prepared for them by Wilder Penrose.

I knew that they saw me as a rather dull, voyeurist husband, enjoying my wife's infidelities. They had showed no surprise when I stepped through the cannabis smoke and took Jane from Halder's arms, assuming that I was sexually excited by the sight of them dancing together. By watching our wives have sex with strangers, we dismantled the mystery of exclusive love, and dispelled the last illusion that each of us was anything but alone.

I turned from Simone and considered my knee, as gnarled and rooted in itself as the bole of a lightning-scarred oak. I inserted the needle into the phial of painkiller and drew the pale fluid into the syringe. As I checked the meniscus my eyes strayed to the Alice characters on the wardrobe door. Carroll had furnished his young heroine with every manner of threats to her sanity, but she had survived them all with her unstoppable good sense.

Pondering this, I thought of Sergeant Jucaud's comment that I had been seen acting aggressively towards Zander. It had taken the detective five days to question me, which suggested that his information was part of a deliberate tip-off. He had pretended to admire the Jaguar, but had clearly been searching for signs of collision damage.

Was I being set up as Zander's killer? Months might pass, as I limped around the business park, my mind clouded by Jane's painkillers, a drugged lab animal being saved for a last injection, the final sacrifice when a scapegoat was needed. I could rely on Wilder Penrose to protect me, but Alain Delage might want me out of the way so that he and Simone could have Jane to themselves . . .

I searched the veins under my knee, a Mandelbrot pattern of shrivelled capillaries that mapped its own kind of addiction. Then I thought again of the ever-sensible Alice, swallowing her 'drink me' potion. I put down the hypodermic and held the phial to the light. The label was printed with my name, but 'inject me' might well have been stamped across it in bold letters.

My knee waited for relief, but for once I put away the syringe and fastened the leather wallet. I needed to be alert if I was to cope with Zander's death and the danger facing me, since other deaths would soon take place. I needed my infected ligaments and the metal pins clawing at my kneecap. I needed to think, and I needed pain.

35

The Analysis

THE SUPERMARKET ON the main concourse of Antibes-les-Pins was filled with a bounty of attractive merchandise: plates of charcuterie, olive breads, pyramids of a new super-detergent, dory and gurnard fresh enough for the surf to twinkle on their scales. But there were no customers. The residents of the high-security complex might have retreated so deeply into their defensible space that they had eliminated the need for food, bread and wine. The advertising displays in the estate office overlooking the roundabout on the RN7 had the look of museum tableaux, and the artist's impression of a concourse as crowded as the Champs-Elysées, lined with boutiques and thronged by high-spending customers, seemed to describe a forgotten twentieth-century world.

Only the cyber-café next door was serving any customers. The computer terminals facing the bar were out of use, but three bikers in metallized boots and Mad Max leathers sat at the outdoor tables. They formed a feral presence in the hyper-modern complex, like carrion-birds on a skyscraper cornice, filling an unplanned niche in the ecology of the future.

The supermarket might have been empty, but the retinal impact of its deserted aisles still surprised me. In the week since putting away the hypodermic syringe my senses had sharpened, as if an anaesthetized world had woken up and seized me in its grip. Reality had come into sudden focus, and for the first time in many months I was reaching into levels of my mind that had been closed like the floors of an empty telephone exchange. Each morning, after Jane left for the clinic, I drew a measure of painkiller from the phial that she prepared for me, then vented the pale liquid into the washbasin. Curiously, not only was my mind clearer, but the pain in my knee had eased. For once, Alice's example had not been the best to follow . . .

I saw Isabel Duval as soon as she entered the supermarket. Disguised in a headscarf and dark glasses, she hovered like an inexperienced shoplifter beside a display of gourmet cat food. She was pale and self-possessed, but glanced warily over her shoulder as if sensing a pursuer, only to realize that she had seen herself in a display mirror.

I was glad to meet her again. After speaking on the phone, I mailed the small package to her from a post office in Le Cannet, and expected her to take a month or more to deal with it. But she contacted me within the week.

'Madame Duval . . . you look well.' I held her hand before she could draw it away from me. 'It's good of you to help me.'

'Not at all . . .' She peered at me over her sunglasses, unsettled by my restless and eager manner. 'I'm happy to do what I can. You were David's friend.'

'Exactly. I'm still concerned for him. That's why I thought of you. There's a café next door – we'll be less conspicuous.'

We passed a shallow tank filled with lobsters, sidling around each other like airliners looking for a runway. I took Madame Duval's arm and steered her towards the entrance. She frowned at the bikers lounging in the sun, irritated by their presence on her doorstep.

'Mr Sinclair, these young men . . . are they messengers?'

'Let's hope not. I hate to think what the message might be.' We sat down at the empty tables, and I ordered mineral water from the waitress. 'Madame Duval, there's no reason why we shouldn't meet.'

'No?' She sounded doubtful.

'My wife was a colleague of David's, and you're one of the last people who knew him well. Now, you have the analysis with you?'

'As I promised.' She took off her glasses, her eyes turned inward as she thought about Greenwood. 'When we met, you were looking into the events around David's death. Can I ask if you found anything?'

'Nothing, to be honest. Everyone liked him.'

'That's good. He was an admirable doctor.' She ventured a sip of water. 'Time stands still at Antibes-les-Pins. But the dead go on opening doors in our minds.'

'Isabel, please – the analysis?'

'Forgive me.' She took an envelope from her handbag and drew out a sheet of typewritten paper. 'First, can I ask why you came to me?'

'I didn't want to involve the clinic. One never knows what complications might follow.'

'Any pharmacy would have arranged the analysis. There must be fifty in Cannes.'

'True. But I had no idea what was in the sample. An ordinary pharmacy might contact the police. It struck me that you would know of a suitable laboratory, one that would be . . .'

'Discreet?' Madame Duval shook her head, finding me a clumsy conspirator. 'What was the source of this phial?'

'I found it in the house.' Doing my best to lie fluently, I said: 'It was among David's old things. It might give a clue to his mood. If he suffered from diabetes . . .'

'He didn't. I contacted a small laboratory in Nice. David used them for special preparations before the clinic expanded. I may say that the chief pharmacist was surprised.'

'Why?'

'It's an unusual cocktail.' She put on her reading glasses and scanned the sheet. 'There were vitamins, B group and E, an anti-inflammatory preparation and a postoperative painkiller.'

'Good.' I thought of Jane putting together this potion, measuring the constituents like a mother preparing her baby's feed. 'Then it's in order?'

'Not exactly.' Madame Duval placed the sheet on the table, watching me warily as I fiddled with my mineral water. 'They were in very low concentrations, only fifteen per cent of the total. The remaining eighty-five per cent was made up of a powerful tranquillizer, amitryptiline. It's used as a long-term sedative in mental hospitals.'

I took the analysis from her and studied the French orthography with its vagrant decimal points. 'That sounds like a large dose.'

'Very. Assuming five ccs per day, the patient would find himself in a cloudy world like a steam bath. Nothing would bother him, either internally or from surrounding events.'

'It sounds useful.'

'For people under stress, or faced with a mental crisis they are unwilling to resolve.' Madame Duval provided a judicious pause. 'It's unusual to prescribe such a powerful tranquillizer for people in postoperative pain. Surgical patients are encouraged to move about, not sit in a chair all day.'

'There might be other reasons . . .' I took the analysis sheet and tucked it into my pocket. 'I'm grateful, Madame Duval. You've been a huge help.'

'I don't think so.' She steadied the table as my left knee bounced up and down. 'You're still happy at Eden-Olympia?'

'On the whole, yes.'

'It's a demanding place. Everything seems clear, but . . . at least pain sharpens the mind.'

I shook her hand warmly, glad that I did not have to spell everything out for this intelligent woman.

When we left the café the bikers were rearranging their legs around the open-air tables. Madame Duval stepped over an outstretched boot, but I waited for its owner to beat a loose heel plate against the pavement. As I leaned against the door I noticed a sandy-haired man with a straw hat in his hand, standing near a parked Renault. Printed notices intended to pacify the police and traffic wardens were peeling from the inner surface of the windscreen, hinting that the driver was a doctor or vet on urgent call. He turned his back to the café, and perused a map of the Côte d'Azur.

'Meldrum . . .' I recognized the Australian manager of Riviera News. He was watching Isabel Duval's reflection in the car's passenger window, and I guessed that he already knew who would follow her from the cyber-café.

I paid my respects to Madame Duval, and waited until she reached the entrance to her apartment wing. Walking to the car-park lift I saw that Meldrum was now sitting in the Renault fifty yards from the garage exit.

I rode the lift down to the lower level, where the Jaguar was parked. When I opened the driver's door a card fell to the floor at my feet. Someone had unlocked the door and then carefully closed it, trapping the card against the sill. Only one person had a spare set of the Jaguar's keys. I read:

Paul, leave the Jaguar here. My car is parked in the next aisle with the roof up. Keys under your seat. Try not to be seen as you drive out. We'll meet in the Church of La Garoupe by the lighthouse on Cap d'Antibes.

36

Confession

PRESIDING OVER THE gloomy silence, the gilded wooden statue of Our Lady of Safe Homecoming was barely visible in the darkness that filled the adjoining chapels of the modest church. Two women in bombazine dresses and dark headscarves sat in the front pew, lost in their thoughts of departed husbands or children. I bought a candle for ten francs, and carried the trembling flame down the side aisle. Dozens of votive offerings hung from the walls, memorials to disasters at sea, to air and road accidents, many illustrated with fading photographs and newspaper cuttings. Faces of the dead hung in brass lockets and plastic frames: a cheerful schoolgirl who had perished in a Nice ferry sinking, sailors who had died during a wartime naval action, fishermen from Antibes run down by a tanker, three scuba divers who had drowned within sight of the church that memorialized their deaths. Among the antique clutter of dusty silk flags and models of nineteenth-century steam yachts was a box with a transparent lid and a plasticine model of an air crash. A child's fingerprints were visible in the broken wings.

The door opened, throwing a brief light across this warehouse of grief. A woman in a wide-brimmed hat and black trouser suit closed the door behind her and searched the darkness.

'Frances?' Carrying the candle, I walked between the pews and held the flame to the woman's face. Shadows wavered across a nervous mouth and lowered eyes. 'Madame, excuse me . . . are you – ?'

'Paul? Good. We'll go outside.'

She pulled at the wooden door, flooding herself with light like a corpse in an opened coffin. Behind me, the two women rose from their seats and walked towards the exit. As they emerged into the sun I recognized Madame Cordier and Madame Ménard, the chauffeurs' widows I had last seen in the apartment at Port-la-Galère.

When they spoke to Frances they turned their backs to me, as if fearing that I might report them to the authorities at Eden-Olympia. After the briefest thanks they walked quickly to a waiting taxi in the car park.

Frances waved to them, but seemed too tired to look at me. Her hand fell under its own weight and hung by her side. She was thinner than I remembered, and hesitated before touching my shoulder, unsure whether I was still the person she had known. She held my hand for a moment, trying to remind herself that we had once been lovers. The ghosts of emotions past seemed to gather and dissolve in her troubled face.

'Frances . . . ? It's good to see you.'

'Wait. I can't breathe here.'

I followed her across the uneven ground outside the church, and we walked towards the fir trees that shielded the plateau of La Garoupe. A coin-in-the-slot telescope pointed towards the Antibes peninsula, a panorama of the Riviera from Super-Cannes to Juan-les-Pins, and from the crowded Antibes harbour beyond the Napoleonic battlements to the apartment city of Marina Baie des Anges. An airliner made its descent towards Nice Airport, its winged shadow trembling across the faces of the hotels that overlooked the glide path.

'Frances . . . try to relax. No one followed me.' I wanted to embrace her, but she stepped away from me and clasped the telescope with her hand. I knew that she was thinking of everything except myself. Tapping the telescope, she watched the taxi leave with the two widows.

'The chauffeurs' wives?' I asked. 'What were they doing here?'

'They wanted to see the chapel – it's dedicated to the souls of travellers. I collected them from the station at Antibes.'

'Did I spoil it for them?'

'I doubt it – why?'

'They looked at me . . .'

'They're very suspicious. Word gets around. You've been seen at some of the ratissages. They think you're part of Eden-Olympia.'

'I am.'

'That's why I'm here.' She managed a strained smile, reassuring herself that we were still close friends. 'Paul, I had to get away. That dreadful business with Zander. I ran to the nearest exit.'

'I felt the same.' I tried to find her eyes under the dipping brim of the straw hat. 'Where did you go?'

'Menton. A small hotel near the old town. There's a friend I had to see, a retired judge. I needed his advice.'

'I hope you take it. Everything at Eden-Olympia is starting to slide off the table.'

'Only now?' She studied me in a distracted way. 'You've had a long time to accept that.'

'Not true. I've been waiting for the right moment.'

'Waiting? That's too easy. You can wait for ever.'

We walked through the trees to the slip road beside the light-house, where I had parked the BMW. When she took the keys from me I noticed her frayed nails and raw fingertips.

'You're sure no one followed you?' she asked. 'The man outside the cyber-café?'

'Meldrum? No. He was keeping an eye out for the Jag. Journalists don't like to pay parking charges.'

We sat in the car, in the shadowy space under the roof, and Frances gripped the steering wheel as if to brace herself before a collision. Trying to calm her, I moved her hands to her lap.

'Frances, why would Meldrum want to follow me?'

'He probably smells a story. Someone at Antibes-les-Pins might have seen the accident. The apartments are close to the beach.'

'No one there ever looks at the sea. Besides, Meldrum works for Eden-Olympia. They own a large piece of the radio station.'

'Even so. If it pays him enough, he'll play both ends against each other. He wants a really big story he can sell to the news agencies. I think I can give him one . . .'

She nodded to herself and stared up at the lighthouse, patiently waiting for it to come to her aid and bathe the darkness of the Côte d'Azur in its searching rays. The weeks she had spent in Menton had made her both insecure and more resolute. I thought of the elegant but unconfident woman I had met at the orthopaedic conference, and realized that nothing had changed. We had started an affair, but our time together had been stolen from Eden-Olympia and would have to be returned.

I said: 'If Meldrum trailed me to Antibes-les-Pins he was very professional. I didn't see him.'

'You weren't looking. Some concierge will have tipped him off. A lot of high-powered people keep their girlfriends at Antibes-les-Pins.'

'But why were you there?'

'Isabel Duval told me she was seeing you. She didn't say why.'

'You're in touch with her?'

'I always have been. There are still one or two people I can trust.' She raised her chin, showing something of her old determination. 'I needed to see you, and I didn't want to use the phone or e-mail. Jane might have mentioned it to Wilder Penrose. Anyway, that old Jag is an easy car to trail. I had to meet the widows so I parked in the garage and used the spare keys to leave a message.'

'You were following me . . . ? For some reason, it feels odd.'

'Poor man. You're so naive, I think it's why you've survived.' A shadow of affection crossed her face. 'People have been following you since you came to Eden-Olympia. Once in a while try looking in the rear-view mirror.'

'I will. My mind's been rather foggy – too many painkillers. You'll be glad to hear I've given them up.'

'Good. You look a lot sharper. Who prescribed the pain-killers?'

'Jane. Her own special cocktail. Isabel Duval had them analysed for me. Mostly a strong tranquillizer.'

'She's keeping you sedated, so you won't ask too many questions. I like Jane, but . . . think about it, Paul.'

'I have.' I turned to face Frances. She had relaxed a little, no longer unsettled by my presence, and I guessed that she was ready to speak frankly to me. 'All right, Frances. Why are we here? It's an odd place to meet.'

'I wanted to see you. I even missed you. La Garoupe is far away from Eden-Olympia and all those big Mercs and gangster drivers. Besides, I was taking the widows here.'

'But why La Garoupe? Their husbands were shot dead in my garden, along with Jacques Bourget – not one of them, I'm ready to bet, by David Greenwood.'

'The widows know that. They wanted to see the shrine to Bourget's friend, a junior manager at Eden-Olympia.'

'The man who died in a hit-and-run accident? David was passing by and looked after him. It was quite a coincidence.'

'It wasn't an accident. Or a coincidence. David wouldn't talk about it but he felt very guilty. It was the early days of the ratissages and he hadn't realized what was happening. The chauffeurs were assigned to drive the cars and they didn't like what they saw. That's why they joined David, along with Jacques Bourget. They'd all seen men run down for fun, and wanted to expose what was going on.'

'By taking over a private TV station?'

'A lot of important conferences are held at Eden-Olympia. There's a direct link to TF1 and CNN. They were going to

333

broadcast a complete exposé and force the Interior Minister to act.'

'So you knew about the killings in advance?'

'No.' Frances took my hand and pressed it to her throat, as if to prevent herself from gagging. I could feel her larynx trembling, a sub-vocal rosary. 'I didn't know, believe me. But I guessed something was going to happen when David said he'd stored his rifle and ammunition with Philippe Bourget. I told him not to hurt anyone, but he wanted revenge.'

'For what they'd done to Bourget's friend?'

'No. He wanted revenge for what Eden-Olympia had done to him.'

Frances rapped the steering wheel with her fist, rousing herself to action. Chin raised, she stared through the windscreen at the Riviera coastline, a battle commander about to launch a beachhead but unsure of the underwater defences.

'Frances . . . what did Eden-Olympia do to David? He was happy here, running the refuge, lending his Alice library to the teenagers.'

'Alice? That's ironic.' Frances pushed up the brim of her hat. 'David wasn't happy. He hated himself, so much that it spilled over and he started to hate me.'

'Why did he kill all those people – Dr Serrou, Bachelet, Olga Carlotti? Frances, you know why.'

'Yes, I do.' She sounded almost offhand. 'I'm the only one who does. No one else is sure. Not even Wilder Penrose. That's why they used you.'

'They used me?'

'Yes, you. Paul Sinclair, the bored ex-pilot who'd lost his flying licence and was looking for a new way up into the clouds. Married to an oddball young doctor. The ultimate marital hot mix.'

'They knew nothing about me when they recruited Jane. I published aviation books.'

'But the headhunters passed on your background details, and

Eden–Olympia seized its chance. Penrose and Professor Kalman and Zander decided to conduct an experiment. They ran a special trial designed to explain what went wrong with David. You were their laboratory rat.'

'All I did was lie around the pool and smoke a little pot with Jane.'

'Just what they wanted. You had time on your hands, and they knew you'd soon be bored. Bored enough to take part in their weekend games. Why did they put you in David's house? Didn't that strike you as odd?'

'It did. Remarkably callous, in fact. So the house was part of the experiment?'

'Penrose wanted you to think about David. Where better to start than lying in David's bed? They knew you'd hear the gunshots as you made love to your child bride. Those murders sent a corporate shudder around the world. Everyone was aware something sinister had happened, and might happen again. Your job was to relive the whole nightmare. They cleaned the place up, but there were traces of David everywhere – the same bathroom, the same kitchen, the sun-loungers marked with his barrier cream. Penrose wanted you to take on David's role, and start to think like him. In case your mind wandered, they picked Señora Morales to be the housekeeper. One very garrulous Spanish lady. She'd seen Bachelet and Dr Serrou lying dead in Guy's bedroom, all the blood and drugs and Dominique in her erotic underwear. She was just bursting to fill you in with the background material.'

'So they opened the door to the maze and pushed me in. But how did Penrose know where I'd go?'

'He didn't. You started by nosing the air, and you didn't like the smell. You talked about going back to London. You were bored with Cannes and a wife who never stopped working. But then you found the bullets in the garden. Zander's men had missed them, but it was a blessing in disguise.'

'From then on I was hooked?'

'You were playing detective. But Penrose guessed that wasn't the only reason. You were starting to identify with David. You knew he'd changed since coming to Eden-Olympia. So you, too, wanted to change.'

'Did David take part in the actions? The attacks on blacks and Arabs in La Bocca?'

'No.' Frances grimaced into her cupped hands. 'He didn't like those at all. Penrose and Bachelet kept him in the dark. Anyway, he was developing a recreational side of his own.'

'What exactly? You were with him, Frances. What appealed to him – the rapes, the attacks on prostitutes?'

'He hated those.'

'Wilder must have talked to him. He can be very persuasive, setting out his Sadeian world, his do-it-yourself psychopathy kit.'

'We've all had the pep talk. Don't worry, David could see the benefits. Eden-Olympia was booming. But David didn't like the human cost.'

'Nor did I.'

'At first, Paul.' Frances stared bleakly at me. 'Then you changed. Now you don't take part but you go along for the ride. You're like all men – violence is your real turn-on, not sex. Penrose teased you, feeding you hints of a secret Eden-Olympia, letting you watch a little tasty truncheon work. Like that beating they gave the trinket salesman in the clinic car park. The whole thing was staged for you. They knew you'd go back to the Jaguar parked on the roof. Halder signalled when you'd left Jane and were on the way. They put the African and the Russian up against the wall and made sure you heard the screams.'

'I can still hear them. Nasty, but . . .'

'Effective? The raid on the Cardin Foundation really got you going – without all those wailing geishas we'd never have made it into bed.'

'Not true, Frances.'

'You practically came over the kitchen floor. All the while,

Penrose was drip-feeding his "explore your own pathology" message to you. And you wanted to hear it. Jane was too tired to have sex with you, but after a little pethidine she'd relax with Simone Delage. That was interesting, and you didn't mind too much.'

'Easy to say.'

'It intrigued you, for the first time you could stand back from yourself and enjoy a strange new feeling. And you were getting closer to David. Every time you stalled they laid down more scent. The appointments diary in David's computer. It didn't take you long to work out it was actually a target list.'

'Penrose supplied that?'

'Of course. Once you saw it, there was no stopping you. Then there was the Riviera News transcript of the special radio report.'

'By the rogue journalist who suddenly moved to Portugal?'

'He didn't exist. The report was never broadcast.'

'So who wrote the text?'

'I did. Zander and Penrose gave me a rough outline. They told Meldrum to hand it to you and hint at sinister goings-on.' Frances spoke matter-of-factly, as if explaining to a confused tourist how he had lost himself in a strange city. The release of this long-repressed material seemed to calm her, rage diffused into the cooling waters of truth. Before I could interrupt, she pressed on: 'I added a few interesting contact numbers – Isabel. Duval and the chauffeurs' widows. The first thing you did was drive out to see them. Once you'd actually met them you knew there was something wrong with the official story.'

'There was. The brainstorm explanation never made sense.'

'You started exploring the death route, feeling yourself into David's mind when he set off with his rifle. You were always talking about Lee Harvey Oswald, Hungerford and Columbine. So Zander told Halder to take you on a guided tour.'

'My very own Dealey Plaza. It was quite a day. The crime

photos showed the nasty little hobbies that people have at Eden-Olympia.'

'They *were* hobbies – assigned by Penrose as part of the therapy programme. That's why some of it looks so amateurish. Berthoud with his old-fashioned scales and smuggler's suitcase: he was acting out a fantasy of a drug-dealer and not doing it very well. Guy Bachelet with the stolen jewellery he couldn't be bothered to get rid of. The photos drew you in even deeper. You could see that Halder knew more than he let on.'

'He killed David. Did he shoot the hostages?'

'No. Zander led the execution squad. They arrested them outside the TV centre and took them back to the house. Then Kellerman shot them in the garden with David's rifle. Someone told me that Cordier and Bourget made a run for it and everything was botched. That's how you came to find the bullets.'

'So Halder was still on the garage roof?'

'They couldn't get him away from David's body. He was weeping all over him.' Frances pressed a fist to her mouth, forcing the blood from her blanched lips. 'Now he's using you to take his revenge. Be careful, Paul – you're a very small piece on Halder's board.'

'I know that.' I took her hand and kissed her wrist. 'Aren't you playing the same game, Frances? Did Zander and Penrose set up our meeting at the Palais des Festivals?'

'No. That was me. I'd had time to think about David. We'd split up very painfully. He more or less threw me out.'

'But why? I thought you were close.'

'Too close. That was the reason. I was frightened I'd lose him. So I showed him things about himself he didn't know.'

'Such as?'

'It doesn't matter now.' Frances stared fiercely at the hills beyond Cannes. 'Eden-Olympia corrupted David and destroyed him. He was the real victim on May 28. I watched him die in the gutter like an animal, crying in pain. After that I wanted to expose Wilder Penrose and Zander and Professor Kalman, but I needed hard evidence.'

'The photographs, the truth about the hostages . . . ?'

'Not hard enough. I'd been David's lover for months, my flat was full of his things. Zander wanted to frame me there and then. If Penrose hadn't stepped in I would have been charged as a co-conspirator. They'd have found me guilty.'

'Twenty years in a French prison. Or worse. Good for Wilder Penrose.'

'He knew I'd be useful. So I had to go along with them. I work in the property office, I know about all the lettings on the Côte d'Azur – which Omani millionaire is moving into a particular villa in Californie, which Turkish banker is buying a jewellery store in Villeneuve-Loubet or leasing warehouse space somewhere. I laid on the Cardin Foundation raid, and the marina hijacking at Golfe-Juan. Like it or not, I've been deeply implicated from the start. I wanted revenge for David, but there was nothing I could do.'

'Until Jane and I arrived?'

She opened my hand and studied my palm line, then closed it like a book she had decided not to read. 'Sorry, Paul, but that's true. They were using you, so I thought I'd do the same. I decided to build a maze of my own. Their maze was Eden-Olympia. Mine was the inside of your head.'

'And I was happy to play there?'

'You were a small boy again. Then I started to like you, which I hadn't bargained on. But that didn't affect my real goal.'

'Which was?'

'The same as Penrose's. I wanted to provoke you, to test you to destruction. I wanted to find your dirtiest little secret, and then work on it until you became disgusted with yourself and needed to explode. You'd go to the British Consul, talk to your MEP, take the story to Fleet Street.'

'It almost worked.'

'At first you were really coming along. You found those orthopaedic harnesses very perverse.'

'What man doesn't?'

'So true. There's nothing too weird to switch a man on sexually.
You'd worn a surgical harness when Jane first got you excited. But
then you threw everyone. You followed a child whore to the Rue
Valentin. Penrose and Zander couldn't believe their luck. You
looked like you wanted to fuck her.'

'No. Not in the sense you mean.'

'Don't worry, I understand.' Frances patted my head, as if I
were an elderly spaniel who had given dumb but loyal service.
'You were starting to miss Jane, and little Natasha reminded you
of your first love, the doctor's daughter in Maida Vale. Penrose
thought you were a full-blown paedophile, just waiting to climb
into the toy cupboard.'

'I let him down. How sad.'

'Never mind. You like girlish young women, that's all. The
paedo line didn't lead anywhere. I had a last go at the film
festival, hoping those Thai mammasans would stir you up with
some juicy kiddy-porn. But I could see it in their eyes – they
knew you weren't interested.'

'Sorry, Frances. I was looking for Jane.'

'You missed her, and being a voyeur was the next best thing.
You're curious to see Jane with other lovers – it liberates you
from all that old-fashioned jealousy you felt when your mother
was fondled by her men-friends. I'm only surprised you drew the
line at Zander.'

'A police chief? One has to have a few principles. He wanted
to fuck my wife so that Alain and Simone could watch.'

'I'm shocked. That is going too far.'

'Don't laugh. It was a close thing. Still, I didn't want him
dead. Frances . . . ?' She had turned away, covering her face as
a tourist coach turned into the car park. 'Has someone seen us?
Meldrum . . . ?'

'No. I was thinking of Zander and that terrible road . . . the water burning around the car.' Her voice fell away, and she turned almost searchingly towards me, as if I could reassemble her memories. 'Those nightmare headlights before the accident . . .'

'Frances, it wasn't an accident. They killed him.'

'Yes . . .' Blood flushed her cheeks, and she stared at herself in the driving mirror. Embarrassed, she opened the door and stepped out, then bent down and said to me: 'Yes, they killed him. But I helped them, Paul. I set it up for them . . .'

37

A Plan of Action

I FOUND FRANCES by the telescope, pacing to and fro under the trees, fingers tearing a pine cone she had picked from a branch. The black-clad women were walking towards the church, bereaved wives and mothers making their annual visit to the Virgin of La Garoupe.

Frances stared irritably at the women, unable to face this chorus of the undead. Aware of her blonde hair and tailored trouser-suit, she pulled at her buttons and scuffed through the gravel to the telescope. Leaning against the brass barrel, she stared across the bay to Golfe-Juan, searching for Zander's overturned car. I realized that she had chosen La Garoupe as our meeting place in order to punish herself.

'Frances, come on. Be honest, you loathed Zander . . .'

'Where is it?' She pushed me away, and tossed the pine cone from one hand to the other. 'A grey Audi – I can't see it.'

'It's in a police lab – they must be checking the brakes and steering.'

'Why? We can tell them all they need to know. Or will we, Paul? Somehow I doubt it . . .' She slapped the telescope, and her rings sent out a sharp metal cry that drew the eyes of the widows. 'Give me a coin – ten francs. The car must be there . . .'

I held her shoulders and steered her to the wooden bench on the observation platform. 'Let's rest here. There's nothing on the beach: I went back to have a look. Frances, we were two hundred yards away when it happened.'

'It was a set-up. Didn't you guess?' Her moment of panic had passed, and she spoke calmly. 'I was the decoy. While you were looking for Jane, I played the vamp with Zander. I told him to follow me back to Marina Baie des Anges.'

'And that's why he trailed us? He must have seen me in the passenger seat.'

'He didn't mind. I said you were a great fan of threesomes.'

'So all that roaming around Super-Cannes in the dark? The back streets near the Vallauris road . . . ?'

'I was giving everyone time to catch up. Alain Delage told me to take the coast road to Juan-les-Pins. Drink-drivers are always ending up in the sea.' She raised her arm and threw the pine cone down the slope, watching it bounce into the deep ferns. 'Believe me, I didn't think they planned to kill him.'

'So you knew nothing – don't blame yourself.'

'I should have known!' Disgusted with herself, she turned her eyes from the beach. 'Until then I could cope with Eden-Olympia. But the waves were on fire. Paul, that was a warning – these people have to be stopped, or others are going to die.'

'They'll pull back now. Delage took a risk in killing Zander. He was head of security.'

'Acting head. He knew too much, and that made him greedy. He had all the videotapes, and he'd started to put pressure on the smaller companies. He wanted huge share options built into his salary package. Besides, there was one other mark against him.'

'He was just another Arab? Still, Yasuda is Japanese. There are Hong Kong and Singapore Chinese in every boardroom. A Mexican CEO lives on my avenue.'

'But they're paid-up members of the new elite. They're the corporate chosen people. Zander ran a security firm in Piraeus before he came here. He was technical services, one up from the janitors. The top managements at Eden-Olympia are deeply racist, but in a new way. The corporate pecking order is all that counts. They know the world would collapse without them, and think they can get away with anything.'

'They probably can.'

'No!' Frances pulled at my shirt. 'Listen to me. Some of the therapy groups are starting to stockpile weapons. They're setting up "hunting lodges" near the immigrant housing estates in La Bocca and Mandelieu. Technically, they'll be safe depositories for pharmaceuticals and industrial diamonds, and the guards will be heavily armed.'

'But their real role will be to provoke the local criminals and layabouts?'

'And then take on the immigrant population as a whole. We're back in Weimar Germany, with a weekend Freikorps fighting the Reds. Sooner or later some corporate raider with a messianic streak will turn up, backed by all the natural gas in Yakut, and decide that social Darwinism deserves another go. Listen to Alain Delage and Penrose talking together and you know they're just waiting for him to arrive.'

'Dictators always step into an open jackboot. How many executives are involved in the therapy classes?'

'Something like three hundred. A lot are off on overseas trips, but most weekends at least a hundred take part. They're operating as far away as Nice and St-Raphaël. There's some grim stuff going on – nasty child porn, rapes of young Arab wives . . .'

'The police will step in.'

'They're looking the other way. Eden-Olympia is expanding. Destivelle and the holding company are buying thousands or hectares to the west of the D103, right up to the edge of Sophia-Antipolis.' Grimly, Frances gestured towards the open hinterland beyond the coast. 'The taxes paid by Eden-Olympia amount to billions of francs. They pay for new schools and colleges and sports stadia. That's why we're so popular. Wilder Penrose and Delage have to be stopped, along with their lunatic scheme. Not because it's crazy, but because it's going to work. The whole world will soon be a business-park colony, run by a lot of tight-lipped men who pretend to be weekend psychos.'

She stared fiercely at the beaches of Juan and Cagnes-sur-Mer, as if hoping for a tsunami to appear and wash the entire coastline into the sea. I remembered the bored and moody woman I had met at the Palais des Festivals, feigning an interest in me as she pondered how to take her revenge on Eden-Olympia. But Zander's death had driven her to the edge. For the first time she had looked down at her feet and was ready to jump.

'We'll stop them, Frances. But we need hard evidence. The testimony of Philippe Bourget and a couple of chauffeurs' widows won't be enough.'

'The evidence is there. All the ratissages are filmed. There must be a thousand tapes at the Villa Grimaldi. In Menton I went to see a retired judge I met when we bought his old house. He used to be vice-president of the Alpes-Maritimes Development Council, but fell foul of Jacques Médecin and his gangster cronies. They forced him to resign. He was very interested in what I told him.'

'Be careful, Frances. I need to think of Jane. I'll try to get her back to London.'

'She won't go. You know that.' Frances drummed her fists together, tired of my obtuseness. 'She's one of their main targets. They've given her this huge diagnostic project.'

'It's not a front. The system will work.'

'Naturally! It's a brilliant way of recruiting new entrants to the therapy classes. "Too many summer colds, feeling a little seedy? Try one of our special workouts, rubber truncheons provided." Jane is perfect for them.'

'She's pretty spirited.'

'Not any more. For God's sake, Paul, she's a heroin addict. They need a compliant doctor. One who'll supply all the hard drugs they want, ask no questions about strange bruises and find a hospital bed for any whore who gets hurt when some sadistic game goes wrong. They like a paediatrician who can deal with any underage girls and boys who catch VD. And it's always useful to have a doctor who'll sign death certificates when they're needed. Jane will do all that for them.'

'She's already started. She signed the attestation for Zander's death.'

'She saw what happened?'

'No. She was asleep in the back of Delage's Merc. Still, she was there.'

'That's why Alain brought her along. And she genuinely thinks it was an accident?'

'I'm not sure . . .' I watched the first of the old women leave the church and make their way back to their coach. 'Frances, there's one thing I've never understood. Why did David try to kill you?'

Frances stared me out, barely masking the self-contempt in her face. 'Did he?'

'You know he did. He was on his way to shoot you when he tried to get into the Siemens building.'

'Maybe he was looking for someone else. I can't say. I let him down.'

'That's hard to believe. You loved him, and yet he broke things off. A few weeks later he tried to kill you.'

'I wish he had. He knew I'd gone too far. I showed him a secret self he'd never seen before.'

'If not drugs, then what? Anything to do with the refuge?'

'Everything to do with it. All those nubile thirteen-year-olds, dying for sex and ready to go all the way for a new sound system. At first I thought I'd put the idea into his head, but it was there all along. The only thing it needed was a helping hand from Wilder Penrose. Then the whole horror of it stepped out of the daylight and stared David full in the face. Poor, sweet man, he was too honest.'

'Thirteen-year-olds? Are you saying that . . . ?'

'Yes!' Frances almost shouted at the widows, as if wanting to shock them out of their pious grief. 'I'm saying it. I encouraged him, the way I encouraged you. I loved David, and I wanted him to be happy. If a thirteen-year-old made him happy, why not? At first David didn't like it, so he went to see Penrose.'

'And Wilder said it was just what he needed? When did this start?'

'Six months before he died. It was a secret thing between us. We never talked about it, even though we knew it was going on.'

'Didn't the nuns try to stop him?'

'They didn't know. The girls soon grew up, there was a huge turnover. It all took place at Eden-Olympia.'

'At the house?'

'It started there. He'd bring one of the girls back for the weekend to help with her English. They'd read *Through the Looking-Glass* together, which they all thought was a scream. David fitted out one of the bedrooms for them. One thing led to another. Penrose told him not to feel guilty. Being true to himself did him good, and fired up his creativity. To begin with it was very innocent.'

'And then? It's not hard to guess.'

'Penrose said he knew a senior executive who'd like to help the girls with their English. Lewis Carroll was surprisingly popular among the CEOs. The girls could see the joke, but they liked their presents. They realized they were meeting some very important men.'

'So within a short time there was –'

'A full-scale paedophile ring.' Frances shook her head, as if despairing over a strange newspaper report. 'David organized everything. He distributed the Alice books and the lending library became the booking system. If you wanted to give an English lesson you picked your favourite copy. David arranged for the particular girl to be driven to you. Door-to-door service. Beats anything laid on for the Caliph of Baghdad.'

'The Alice books were the reservation system? That explains the

Russian who came to the house. He assumed I'd taken over, and offered me little Natasha. I wanted to get her to the police.'

'That confused a lot of people. Paedophiles we could cope with, but acting out of genuine selflessness? Far too original for Eden-Olympia.'

'But David cared for the orphans. Everyone said so. If you knew what was going on, why didn't you stop him?'

Frances stood up and gripped the telescope in her hands. She stared at the apartment houses at Antibes-les-Pins, as if wishing that she could hide herself for ever behind their cameras. She seemed exhausted by everything she had told me, but determined that I hear her out.

'Why? Because I was fond of him. I was like those affectionate wives who look the other way when their husbands stand a little too close to an attractive young man. Most of the time we met at my apartment. I didn't want to know.'

'But that wasn't enough to save you?'

'He blamed me. I was too tolerant, I was involved in the deep sickness of Eden-Olympia. The last time we met I could see the disgust he felt for me. I was his Hindley or Rosemary West, I'd turned him into this perverted librarian. He wanted to destroy all those sick people playing their deranged games – Wilder Penrose, our nail-biting Dr Death. Guy Bachelet, the security chief who ran the robbery circus. Olga Carlotti with her call-girl ring. Charbonneau and Robert Fontaine, with their racist plans. And the others.'

'Dominique Serrou? His partner at the refuge. Was she involved in the paedophile business?'

'She was the recruitment officer. She toured the foster homes around Cannes and Nice, looking for likely talent. Girls with abusive "uncles" or histories of VD.'

'A doctor? It's hard to believe.'

'She was vulnerable.' Frances raised her hands in a gesture of sympathy. 'A plain woman who knew she was getting older.

Every day dying a little inside. She saw Bachelet losing interest and moving away from her like a ship in a fog bank. She'd have paid any price to bring him back. Penrose convinced her the health of the senior executives depended on certain special therapies. She went along with it.'

'And that made her a target. So May 28 was David's attempt to clean the stables and wipe out the self-hatred he felt.'

'He wanted to kill the people who'd corrupted him. At least five or six had to die, to make the kind of splash that would reach the evening news and stay there.' Frances sat next to me and held my hands, her face as bleak as a tired child's. 'If it hadn't been for me he might have pulled it off. For a few seconds he lowered his guard, just long enough for Halder to kill him.'

'Frances, don't blame yourself. You didn't pull the trigger.'

'Maybe not.' She inhaled the pine-scented air, trying to rally herself. 'But I have to finish David's work. The madmen are still walking around Eden-Olympia. Paul, I need your help.'

'You have it. But it's hard to know what exactly we can do. People look at the Dow and the Nikkei and think everything is fine. Eden-Olympia is very powerful.'

'And over-confident. Penrose and Alain Delage think nothing can stop them. We need tapes of the special actions, the more violent the better. They incriminate everyone – the senior executives with the big companies, the security guards and off-duty local police.'

'And me. Don't forget that.'

'You're an observer. You sit in the back seat of the Merc while the heavy mob go in. We'll make copies of the tapes and send them to the head offices of Shell and Monsanto and Toyota.'

'That's more or less what Zander planned to do. The tapes are hidden away in the Villa Grimaldi. Security is tight.'

'We're not going to pick the locks.' Irritated with me, Frances kicked the ground. 'You're close to Penrose. He likes you, because you're so easily impressed. You half-believe his scary ideas. Go along with him, play more of a part in the ratissages.'

'Frances, I couldn't.'

'They won't expect you to rape some old whore. Just move into the front seat of the Merc. Help with the planning sessions, offer to look after the cameras. That should get you nearer the tapes. Find out the targets, especially the racist ones. We'll get our own film crew on the scene, some renegade BBC team. Sooner or later Penrose will make you his assistant. Like all great visionaries, he needs a disciple.'

'He does – you're right. The sad thing is, I think he's found one.'

'You?'

'Maybe.'

'Paul, what is it?'

'I'm thinking of Jane.'

'Good. She's Simone Delage's lover. Alain is at the heart of everything now. Use Jane to get closer to him.'

'I don't want to use her. She's my wife. I want to save her and get her back to London.'

'You will. Paul, it's the only way.'

'The only way to get her struck off the register. Plus a long spell in a French jail. I can't involve her.'

'Fair enough. But why so much husbandly concern?' Frances peered at me with a surprisingly cold eye. 'You've watched her turn into a heroin addict.'

'She's not an addict. Doctors work hard, and a lot of them take something to ease the stress. She talked it over with Wilder – it's all under control. You're asking me to incriminate her. Jane is –'

'It's not Jane! It's nothing to do with her.' Frances shook my shoulder, as if trying to rouse a dozing sleeper. 'You're thinking of Penrose. You don't want to damage him.'

'That's not true.'

'Part of you believes in his lunatic ideology. That's why you've been so passive from the start. They corrupted your wife and you sat back and watched. I always wondered why.'

'You say I'm a voyeur.'

'That's not the reason. You secretly think Penrose is right, and a new kind of world is being born here, based on psychopathology. You're deeply impressed by Eden-Olympia. These vast companies with their powerful executives, sitting in their glass atriums like so many minotaurs. Once a year there has to be a sacrifice of six maidens. Except that it isn't once a year. It's every weekend, in the back streets of La Bocca. Still, who cares if a few teenage whores disappear into the labyrinth?'

'I care. Frances, I can see the flaws in Wilder's scheme.'

'Can you?' She turned to stare at me, as if understanding me for the first time. 'I know him a lot better than you do.'

'I'm sure you do. Did you have an affair with him?'

'Nearly.' She nodded bleakly to herself, unsettled by the memory. 'He helped me after the divorce. I needed support, and he was generous with his time. Wilder Penrose can be very attractive.'

'And very dangerous?'

'He frightened me. One moment there was all that smiling charm, the gentle giant with the strange new take on the world. The next moment he was going to hit me. I laughed at him over something and he raised his fist. I got out fast.'

'He was a boxer. Like his father.'

'He wanted to be, but something went wrong. He started to tell me about it – a fight after a rowing-club party with a nightclub bouncer, an old pro with early signs of brain damage that Wilder spotted. The man couldn't see anything coming from his left side . . .'

'So Wilder gave him a beating. Did he injure the man?'

'Badly, but that wasn't it. He saw all the repressed violence inside himself, the kind of violence his father wouldn't have liked. So Wilder decided other people would be violent for him, and he looked around for a system that could make it happen. Psychiatry was tailor-made for him. Once he'd dreamed up his ideology he could sit back and watch his patients getting their faces bloodied, all these repressed executives like Alain Delage that he's turned into playgroup Nazis. Now Wilder sees himself as a new kind of messiah, and our role is to act out his fantasies for him. Zander was right about Wilder Penrose.'

'And that's why he was killed.' I took her arms and held her to me, feeling her heart as it beat against her breastbone. We left the observation platform and walked back to the BMW. 'Let's leave before anyone notices your licence number – these accident widows must have sharp eyes. Listen to me. David died for something I believe in. I want to put Eden-Olympia on trial. I want Wilder Penrose to take the stand and be our chief witness.'

PART III

38

The High Air

APPLAUSE EDDIED ACROSS the rows of guests, an approving murmur barely audible above the flapping of the canvas marquee. Sitting beside Penrose in the second row of gilt chairs, I watched Olivier Destivelle, chairman of the Eden-Olympia holding company, bowing his thanks. With a theatrical flourish he accepted a silver trowel, presented on a velvet-lined tray by an attractive aide in a sky-blue uniform.

In front of the platform was a short section of newly laid brick wall, the pointing between the courses still damp and creamy. Set into the wall was a marble plaque, celebrating the foundation of Eden-Olympia Ouest, better known in the international business community as Eden II.

Dressed in his morning suit, and as plumply convivial as a retired matinée idol, Destivelle held the silver trowel in his manicured hands. He beamed at the audience of notables as he plucked a scoop of fresh mortar from a trestle table. Distracted by the photographers' flashbulbs, the television lights and the distant drone of advertising aircraft, he raised the mortar in a proud gesture, his nostrils flicking at the scent of quicklime.

Penrose leaned back in his chair, treating me to a stage whisper. 'Is he recommending a new truffle pâté? He's poncing about like the maître d' at Maxim's. Lay it, Olivier, don't taste it.'

Already bored, Penrose loosened his tie. He took off the jacket of his dark suit, exposing his heavy shoulders and crumpled sleeves. Nibbling at a thumbnail, he ignored the glares of the sleekly dressed women around us, wives of the Riviera elite in their ribboned hats and couture gowns. Humming loudly to himself, he gazed over the greenfield site towards the Alpes-Maritimes.

Buoyed by the prospect of the new business park that would be his next ideas laboratory, Penrose had been in good humour during our drive to the ground-breaking ceremony. Collecting me from the house, he was handsomely at ease in his black silk suit, and adjusted the rear-view mirror so that he could watch himself turn the ignition key. He made no attempt to reset the mirror, and waved my worries aside.

'Paul, do we need a rear-view mirror?' he asked as we left the enclave. 'Nothing can overtake us, so why look back into the past?'

The future was a second Eden-Olympia, almost twice the size of the original, the same mix of multinational companies, research laboratories and financial consultancies. Hyundai, BP Amoco, Motorola and Unilever had secured their plots, investing in long-term leases that virtually financed the whole project. The site-contractors were already at work, clearing the holm oaks and umbrella pines that had endured since Roman times, surviving forest fires and military invasions. Nature, as the new millennium dictated, was giving way for the last time to the tax shelter and the corporate car park.

A line of tractors and graders waited by the forest edge, drivers sitting at their controls, like a squadron of tanks at a military display. The grass cover had been pared away, exposing the pale granitic marl to a few moments of sunlight before it was sealed away for ever under a million tons of cement.

'Progress, Paul, it's palpable . . .' When we left the car Penrose strolled to the refreshment tent, and gazed at the architect's model surrounded by a sea of canapés. Munching an anchovy, he smiled with pride at the landscaped office blocks, like a renaissance pope inspecting a model of his chapel and dreaming of the frescos he would never see. 'Look at it, Paul – the new Europe . . .'

'I hope not,' I commented. 'Eden II? It's another business park. You make it sound like Winthrop's City on a Hill.'

'It is, Paul, it is.' He seemed almost light-headed. 'A hundred cities on a hundred hills . . .'

A second round of applause rose from the guests as Olivier Destivelle patted the wet mortar into place. Within a year the ten-storey bulk of Eden II's administrative headquarters would tower above the plaque. As if signalling their approval, the massed engines of bulldozers and graders roared into life. Gearboxes rasped, metal tracks dug their cleats into the hard soil and a parade of yellow vehicles began.

Destivelle beamed at the lumbering parade, urging the spectators to applaud. But his eyes began to scan the sky. Half a mile to the north, a single-engined aircraft was heading towards us, towing a long green pennant like an agitated snake. It cleared a pine-covered hill, its fixed undercarriage almost scraping the canopy. The pilot flew on, scattered a flock of martins and set course for the phalanx of bulldozers, apparently intending to strafe them. Drivers watched over their shoulders, and already two of the huge vehicles had locked their scoops together.

But the pilot had a second target in his sights. When he was four hundred yards away he raised an arm over his windscreen and fired a signal flare from the open cockpit. The flare rose into the air, hovered above the refreshment tent and exploded in a globe of emerald light. It hung in the sky like a melting chandelier, and then fell into the car park, its green embers setting fire to the grass.

Already the first guests were rising from their seats, suspecting that this aerial display was not part of the official programme. Men buttoned their jackets as wives held their hats, coughing when fumes from the flare drifted through the marquee. A grim-faced Alain Delage, once again the harassed accountant, was calling to his aides, who sprang to life and began shouting into their mobile phones.

The pilot changed course, banked his wings and began a circuit of the site. Caught by the crosswind, his green banner had wrapped itself into a knot, turning the lettered slogan into an unreadable Möbius strip.

'Is that it?' Penrose made a two-fingered salute to the pilot. 'Not much of a show.'

'He hasn't got your resources. Wait, though . . .' I pointed to the fir-topped hills. The drone of competing engines made its Doppler run towards us. Three more publicity planes sped down the valley, towing their pennants and followed by a straggler who had joined the fly-past at late notice. I guessed that the pilots had joined the protest in a show of solidarity, leaving their allotted circuits of the Côte d'Azur to rendezvous above Sophia-Antipolis.

They flew towards us, shadows crossing the canvas roof above our heads, engines drumming against the hulls of the graders and bulldozers. The metal scoops amplified the mushy drone, a muffled anthem played by an involuntary steel band. Banners fluttered across the air, advertising a supermarket in Le Cannet, a kitchenware store and a sale of demonstration Renaults in Cagnes-sur-Mer. They crossed the D103 and set off for their beach patrols, rolling their wings in farewell.

The pilot with the green pennant circled the site, waiting until his companions had gone. A passenger sat in the open cockpit behind him, and as the sun struck the windscreen I caught a glimpse of blonde hair under an antique helmet and goggles. Satisfied, the pilot banked steeply and climbed into the sun, his wings shedding light into the air.

Groups of guests walked to their cars, while others sat among the overturned chairs. Olivier Destivelle stood by the plaque, pointing to the empty sky with his silver trowel. Alain Delage spoke to a senior police officer, but his men were distracted by the limousines jamming the car-park exits, horns blaring at each other.

'A slight cock-up . . .' Penrose swung his gilt chair in his hand, as if debating whether to climb into the sky. 'So much for security. Did you catch the slogan?'

'Used Renaults, a supermarket somewhere. Quite a threat.'

'Paul, be serious for once.' Penrose tried to wave away the pall of burnt aviation fuel. 'The pilot with the flare pistol. He was the organizer.'

'"Eden II – Extinction is For Ever." Mean anything?'

'Green nonsense.' Penrose shrugged and stared back at the sky, but I could see he was nettled. 'Still, the pilot made his point. Progress has been held back by a microsecond. A shame, though. It's an important day.'

Forgetting me, he set off for the refreshment tent. A few journalists were picking at the buffet tables as they spoke into their cassette recorders, but the television crews were climbing into their vans, ready to relay their footage to the evening news programmes.

Penrose listened to the last drone of the aircraft echoing through the valleys towards the coast. Barely able to control his irritation, he sucked the meat from a lobster claw. 'Paul, what sort of aircraft was it? Someone should have jotted down the registration number.'

'A Czech air force basic trainer. Slow, but fun to fly.'

'I bet. You recognized the pilot.'

'Four hundred yards away? Pilots don't sign their slipstreams.'

'I thought they did. Frances Baring may know him. She's chummy with the rodeo pilots at Cannes Airport.' Penrose held a smoked salmon fillet to his nose, smelling the pink flesh. 'You understand her, Paul. I'd hate to think she was involved in this nonsense.'

'She isn't. Wilder, she works hard for Eden-Olympia.'

'Everyone works hard – it proves nothing. People are impressionable, they snatch powerful emotions out of the air. The one thing Eden-Olympia doesn't need is its own Green movement. Why doesn't anyone want to save the planet's concrete?'

'I guess it can look after itself.'

'Can it?' Penrose turned to stare at me, as if I had conveyed a unique insight. He swallowed the canapé, took the glass of wine from my hand and gulped it back. 'Right, that was lunch. Let's go for a drive above Grasse. I need the high air to think in . . .'

The first signs of revolt had appeared, but not in a way that Wilder Penrose expected. As we set off for Grasse he watched the rear-view mirror, suspicious of any following cars. The pinpricks of the past weeks – the graffiti and vandalized cars in the Eden-Olympia garages – had begun to penetrate even the well-upholstered hide of the corporate elephant.

It was a pleasure to see Penrose in the role of quarry, for once. As Frances had predicted, the ratissages had grown more violent, but sooner or later the victims would turn on their attackers. One evening, in an immigrant neighbourhood, the residents would at last act together, corner a therapy class of senior executives and hold them until the television cameras arrived. Then the conspiracy would collapse and witnesses would come forward: the chauffeurs' widows, the girls at the refuge, brutalized whores and assaulted Arab workmen.

Yet, despite myself, I still admired Penrose, and the core truth of his bold but deranged vision. I hated the violence but remembered the brutal hazings at the RAF flight school, and how they had energized us all. Those fraternal beatings had been the closest we would ever come to tormenting our prisoners, part of the cruel but necessary pleasures of war. At Eden-Olympia, psychopathy was being rehabilitated, returned like a socialized criminal to everyday life.

For all his success, Penrose had been on edge in the two months since Zander's death. Often he knocked over his chesspieces as we played beside the pool. In the middle of a move he would leave the table and pace alone around the tennis court, then walk to his car without a word. At times he seemed to doubt that he was equal to the huge test of his talents posed by Eden II, and was searching for an even more radical leap of faith.

As we climbed the mountains above Grasse he patted my arm, treating me to the conspiratorial smile he turned upon waitresses and filling-station personnel who met his approval. He pointed to the rev counter, trembling in the red zone.

'Feel the power, Paul? When I'm bored you can take over.'

'As long as you're in control.'

'Who wants to be in control? Haven't I taught you anything?' He drummed a hand on the wheel. 'Those publicity planes – they spoilt the show.'

'No one noticed. They were glad to get back to the office. A kitchenware sale, some clapped-out cars . . .'

'You're wrong, Paul.' Penrose pointed to a billboard advertising a new hair spray. 'That's just the point. Reality is always a threat. I'm not worried by any rival ideology – there isn't one. But all these ads for aquaparks and swimming pools . . . they're the real enemy. They subvert everything. Frances probably arranged it deliberately.'

'Why should she?'

'To unsettle me. She's restless. You know that, Paul. She thinks she's a rebel, but doesn't realize that Eden-Olympia is the biggest rebellion of all.'

Frances would disapprove of my accepting a lift in Penrose's car. We met rarely now, and she said nothing of her plans to expose Eden-Olympia. Our hour together near the lighthouse at La Garoupe had been a closing of accounts. She had tried to use me again, hoping to trigger an outburst against Eden-Olympia, but I was too uncommitted for her. We met for dinner at the Vieux Port, and I told her that I was working my way into Penrose's confidence. She nodded, lit a cigarette and stared at the Arab yachts.

Meanwhile, the first graffiti and damaged surveillance cameras at Eden-Olympia seemed too feeble a protest to be her handi-work. The cryptic signs aerosolled across windscreens resembled teenage graffiti tags, and were soon scrubbed away by teams of maintenance men, but the stains of rebellion remained.

Curiously, I had become one of the first victims. Three days before the ground-breaking ceremony at Eden II, the Jaguar was brutally savaged. Vandals slashed the tyres and engine hoses, and wrenched the gear lever from its housing. Mr Yasuda was so impressed that he formally congratulated me, his wife bowing three paces behind him, under the impression that the Jaguar had served heroically in a ratissage of Pearl Harbor proportions.

But I no longer joined the bowling clubs on their outings, and distanced myself from the secret life of the business park. I moved from my Alice bed to a maid's room overlooking the tennis court. I said nothing to Jane about Greenwood's tragic end, and how her sometime lover had died in a paroxysm of self-disgust. At night, when I woke, I would step into Jane's bedroom and watch her as she slept, Simone's lipstick smudged across her mouth, the young woman I had loved, and one day, perhaps, would love again.

At the Col du Pilon, a few miles above Grasse, we parked by the observation point with its devil's view over the Var plain. Penrose filled his huge chest with the cold air, holding his breath as if only an over-oxygenated brain could envisage all the possibilities of his new kingdom.

'Spectacular, Paul? There are times when you feel the wind of history under your wings. You've watched the future break out of its egg. The Greenwich line of this millennium runs through Eden-Olympia.'

'All the same, it's time to go back to London. I have to persuade Jane.'

'But why?' Penrose turned his back to the sun, and concentrated all his professional sympathy on me, as if I had admitted to bed-wetting or shoplifting. 'Eden II is the only future we have.'

'Not for me.'

'We'll find you a job. You can start a publishing house for us, edit a monthly magazine.'

'Thanks, but everything looks less certain now. I couldn't take the risk.'

'You won't have to. You and Jane are safe, you're with us.'

'Along with those hundreds of senior executives arriving soon at Eden II? You're about to create a major crime wave.'

'Paul . . . the crime wave is already there. It's called consumer capitalism. Dear chap, I haven't asked you to defecate on the tricolour. A small social cost has to be borne, but we compensate the victims.'

'People like Zander?'

'That was an accident.'

'Wilder, I was there. It was an execution.' I lowered my voice as two elderly Chinese walked from their car and stood beside us at the observation rail. 'He knew about the paedophile ring and the jewellery raids, the strangled streetwalkers . . . I should have gone to the police.'

'They came to you. Sensibly, you said nothing.' Penrose raised his strong chin to the sun, inhaling the cool air. 'Who told you about the paedophile ring – Halder?'

'Not Halder.'

'I'm glad. He's too ambitious to be disloyal. We think very highly of Halder.'

'Good. Alain Delage shouldn't play games with him.'

'Does he? That's unpleasant. I'll tell him to pick another

deprived group – English tourists, say. If Halder didn't talk to you, who did? Frances Baring?'

'She's said nothing.'

'You spend a lot of time with her. She must talk about something. She's always had friends outside Eden-Olympia – an attractive woman in the property office, who visits a lot of very rich people. Some of them have axes to grind, and carry weight in Paris and Brussels.'

'She's never talked to me. Besides, she knows nothing.'

'She knows more than you think. I worry about Frances. For her, the clocks stopped on May 28 . . .'

He broke off as the drone of a publicity plane rose from the valley below. He snatched at the air, trying to seize the miniature aircraft, no larger than a gnat against his outstretched hand.

'Those planes. Paul, don't you find them annoying? Like all the graffiti at Eden-Olympia – a fifty-million-dollar office building and a few francs' worth of paint turn it into something from the Third World.'

'When Eden II opens you'll have larger problems on your mind.'

'You're right, Paul. It's an enormous challenge. Still, we have to press on. The therapy classes unsettle you, but they've proved their worth.'

'For the moment. Too many people know that something nasty happens after dark at Eden-Olympia. Sooner or later, the authorities will act.'

'Of course they will. It's a gamble we had to take.' Penrose took my arm, moving me closer to the observation rail. He had perspired heavily during the aerial protest at Eden II, and the wind lifted a stale scent of unease and frustration from his damp shirt. 'I don't want you to worry, Paul. Forget about going back to London. I need you here – you're one of the few people I can trust. You've seen the truth of what we're doing, and that's why you've never betrayed the therapy programme.'

'I'm an observer. Frances tells me I'm too dull and normal for Eden-Olympia.'

'Normal? Careers have foundered trying to define what that means. Be careful, we've moved into a world where it's dangerous to be normal. Extreme problems call for extreme solutions. As it happens, the therapy programmes aren't needed now. We're scaling them back.'

'Are you sure?' Penrose's offhand tone surprised me. 'Why? Are they getting out of control?'

'No, but Eden II changes everything. What worked so well for a small group of elite professionals can't be applied to a huge population. Eden II will employ 20,000 people. I don't want to start a race war – or not yet. That Green pilot was a warning. Besides, we have to look ahead. A titanic battle is about to begin, a Darwinian struggle between competing psychopathies. Everything is for sale now – even the human soul has a barcode. We're driven by bizarre consumer trends, weird surges in the entertainment culture, mass paranoias about new diseases that are really religious eruptions. How to get a grip on all this? We may need to play on deep-rooted masochistic needs built into the human sense of hierarchy. Nazi Germany and the old Soviet Union were Sadeian societies of torturers and willing victims. People no longer need enemies – in this millennium their great dream is to become victims. Only their psychopathies can set them free . . .'

He drove cautiously down the hillside towards Grasse, allowing other cars to overtake us, waving them on with a large hand. He seemed tired but at peace. I realized that he had conducted a private experiment, taking himself up to a high place and offering himself the kingdoms of the new earth. He had accepted the offer, and was already working out his strategy for dealing with the huge possibilities that Eden II brought with it.

When we reached Eden-Olympia he scarcely noticed the fresh graffiti aerosolled across the glass doors of the administration building.

He dropped me at the house, gripping my arm as I stepped from the car.

'I'm glad you came, Paul. You've helped me a great deal.'

'I hope not.'

'There's a small thing you can do. I'm worried about Frances. Some of my medical records have gone missing.'

'The videotapes?'

'Exactly. They're highly confidential; we wouldn't want them in the wrong hands. Do tell Frances that the therapy programmes are coming to an end.'

'She'll be glad to hear it.'

'Good. When are you next seeing her?'

'Tonight. I'm picking her up at Marina Baie des Anges. She'll be impressed.'

'Invite her out to dinner. Explain that it may take a little time. She's obsessed with David Greenwood, and nothing else matters to her. That's dangerous for us.'

'It makes sense. She loved the man.'

'So did I.' Penrose's smile slipped from his face. He stared at his hands, then pulled back his sleeves and exposed the scars on his forearms. 'It's true, Paul. I owe him my life.'

'You were on the target list, along with Berthoud. If he'd seen you he would have killed you.'

'He did see me. I never told you.' Penrose nodded to himself. 'He shot Berthoud through the glass door, stepped forward and saw me bleeding on the floor in the corridor. I can still remember his eyes. He wasn't in the least mad, you know.'

'Then why didn't he kill you? He certainly planned to. You were the architect of everything he hated.'

'I know.' Penrose gripped the steering wheel, listening to the throaty quaver of the sports car's engine. 'I've thought about it ever since. He wanted me to face what I'd done. For a few moments he was completely sane . . .'

39

A New Folklore

KURT WEILL'S 'SURABAYA JOHNNY' boomed from the CD player propped against the pillows. Jane swayed around the bedroom, a lurid figure in a spangled crimson minidress and stiletto heels. A frizz of lacquered black hair rose in a retro-punk blaze from her forehead, above kohled eyes and a lipsticked mouth like a wound.

I sat among the debris of discarded underwear, admiring Jane's stamina and panache. Overwork and pethidine had coarsened her face, and she seemed a decade older than the young woman who had driven me down to Cannes.

'Jane, I love the costume. You look wonderfully . . . I'd say decadent, if that wasn't so passé.'

'Tarty.' She cocked a hip and pointed a carmined fingernail at my eyes. 'Miss Weimar, 1927.'

'The Delages will love it. You're going out with them?'

'On the town.' She began to bump and grind, and tripped over a pair of thigh-length boots. 'Hell, too many feet in this room. Where's my gin?'

'By the phone.' A full tumbler stood on the bedside table. 'Save it for later.'

'I'm the doctor here.' She swayed and smiled, as if recognizing me across a noisy room. 'Stop worrying, Paul. The human body's capacity for painkillers is almost unlimited.'

'How much pain are you in?'

'None. Wonderful, isn't it? Dr Jane is in control.'

'I hope Dr Jane isn't driving. Where are the Delages taking you?'

'Dinner at . . . somewhere terribly smart. They'll pretend I'm a *poule* they picked up in the street. Then an open-air costume party.'

'And you're going as . . . ?'

'Can't you guess?'

She vamped around me, sitting on my lap and moving away before I could embrace her, a dizzying slide of silk and flesh. 'How was the ground-breaking ceremony?'

'Impressive. All the top brass were there. A plane pulling a Green banner dropped a small bomb on us.'

'How funny. And how sad. Nothing can stop Eden-Olympia. Wilder must have been thrilled.'

'A bit subdued. The Wild West phase is over. Life will be a lot quieter here. Any chance of you taking a long break?'

'Paul . . .' Jane glanced at me through the mirror, sympathetic but distant, like a mother watching a handicapped child. 'Go back to London? For what? Some health centre in Clapham?'

'Why put it like that? We'd be together again.'

'They need me here. The project is expanding.'

'Good. But they need you for other things.'

'Such as?' Jane switched off the CD player. 'Selling stolen pharmaceuticals? Doing female circumcisions for rich Sudanese?'

'It doesn't work like that. They're more subtle.'

'Paul . . . where drugs and sex are concerned, no one is that subtle.' She walked over to me and placed her hands on my cheeks. 'You've spent too long here. Take Frances to London with you. Now it's my turn to fly . . .'

I watched her hunt through a drawer and pick out her most garish handbag. She embraced me fiercely before she left. When I winced, uneasy with this bogus affection, she looked at me with sudden concern.

'Paul? Is your knee acting up? Start taking your shots again. You were happier then.'

'That was the problem.'

'Are you seeing Frances tonight?'

'We're having dinner at Tétou. There's some good news to celebrate.'

'Give her my love. And use my car. Sorry about the Jag. All this graffiti everywhere. Alain thinks the wrong people are getting into Eden-Olympia.'

Later, as I drove the Peugeot along the RN7 to Villeneuve-Loubet, I listened to the echoes of Lotte Lenya inside my head and remembered Jane's advice. With or without Frances Baring, I would soon be back in London. As Eden II spread its parks and artificial lakes across the Var plain a more workaday future would arrive. The winding-down of Penrose's therapeutic programme marked a defeat for him and the triumph of the contingent world, the inescapable reality of corridor rivalries and executive washrooms, the relativities of status and success. After a long day at Eden II, the notion of psychopathy would seem almost folkloric in its quaintness.

40

The Bedroom Camera

'FRANCES, THERE'S GOOD news . . .'

Using the spare key, I let myself into her apartment at Marina
Baie des Anges. The standard lamp in the hall shone onto a clutch
of financial journals, but the other rooms were in darkness. Her
car keys lay in the silver tray on the hall stand. I opened the door
into the kitchen, and caught an odd odour in the air, a medley
of cheap aftershaves that were almost familiar.

'Frances . . . ? I've booked Tétou.'

Was she in bed with another man, perhaps the pilot of the
Green protest plane? An image formed in my mind of her lying
naked beside her lover, both frozen with embarrassment, the man
reaching for his shoes beneath the bed and coming up with one
of my lost sandals . . .

I eased open the bedroom door. Frances lay asleep across the
pillows, an arm stretched out like a child's. In the light of the
nearby balconies I could see her white teeth, lips drawn in a
sleeping smile. The shower ran in the bathroom, a soft patter
like distant rain.

Careful not to wake her, I stepped across the darkened room. I
sat on the bed beside her, trying to stop the mattress from sighing
under my weight. My hand touched the linen sheet, then flinched
from a patch of wetness. The sodden fabric of the under-blanket
was still warm, as if soaked with a sticky soup.

'Frances . . . ?'

Her eyes were open, but the pupils were unfocused. The beam

of the La Garoupe lighthouse swept the marina, and I stared down at Frances's bruised face, at her open mouth with its broken teeth and the blood on her forehead. The beam touched her eyes, animating them for the last time, like a passing headlight shone through the windows of an empty building.

'Jesus . . . God . . .' I fumbled with the switch of the bedside lamp and flicked it on, only to find that the bulb was missing. I left the bed and stepped to the door, searching the shadows for the wall switch.

A hand gripped my wrist, forcing my fingers against the wall. A slim but athletic man in an Eden-Olympia uniform stepped from the hall and pinned me against the fitted wardrobe. I wrenched myself from him, and raised a fist to strike his face, but he clamped his hand over my mouth, trying to calm me.

'Mr Sinclair . . . take it easy. I'm with you.'

'Halder?' As the lighthouse beam crossed the room I recognized the security guard. I reached again for the switch but Halder knocked away my arm.

'Leave it, Mr Sinclair. They're watching the apartment – once the lights go on they'll be up here in seconds.'

'Who? Halder . . . ?'

'The people waiting for you. They knew you were coming.'

'Frances . . .' I stepped towards the bed and stared down at her disjointed arms. Blood covered her breasts in a bodice of black lace. I held her wrist, feeling the loose tendons almost torn from the bones in her struggle, and searched for a pulse.

'Frances, please . . . Halder, she's still breathing. Call an ambulance. There's a chance . . .'

Halder steadied me in his strong hands. 'She's dead, Mr Sinclair. She died half an hour ago.'

'Wait. How did she die?' I let her hand fall onto the blood-stained pillow, pulled back the sheet and stared at her broken body. Around her waist was the zebra-striped dress. A man's crumpled dinner jacket lay between her legs, silk facings torn from its lapels by a pair of frantic hands.

'It's Greenwood's. Halder, someone wore it while they killed her . . .'

I stepped back, and almost knocked over a metal tripod standing by the bedside table. My foot crushed a piece of brittle plastic.

'A video? Good God, what were they doing here?'

'Making a film.' Halder took a lightbulb from his pocket and placed it on the table. 'A film of a very ugly kind.'

'The dress from La Bocca?'

'A costume. I don't think she wanted to wear it. She put up a real fight. Now, let's go. If they find you here they'll kill you as well. Then say you murdered her.'

'Hold on. Were you here when they . . . ?'

'No. I arrived ten minutes ago. The front door was off the latch. They didn't know you had a spare set of keys. I'm sorry, Mr Sinclair. She was dead when I found her.'

'How did she die?'

'The . . . lover . . . used a knife. It's in the shower, having the prints washed away. They'll say you made your snuff movie and were washing the knife when they broke in.'

'They?'

'People working for Eden Olympia – under Alain Delage's orders.'

'And if we leave now?'

'They'll call it a burglary that went wrong. They can deal with you another time.'

I picked up the dinner jacket and laid it across the dead woman's shoulders, David Greenwood's final embrace. Halder waited as I stared at Frances for the last time, brushing away the clumps of blonde hair from her scalp that covered the pillow. When the La Garoupe beam turned between the apartment buildings her bruised face seemed to switch itself on and off. The quirky lips had flattened themselves against her teeth, and her features were those of a child of ten. As she grew cold she became younger, slipping away from herself and withdrawing into a greater darkness, carrying in her broken hands the only memories she would take with her into the night.

The doors of the elevator closed, and Halder turned towards me, staring at the blood on my hands as if trying to convince himself that I had taken no part in Frances's death. His slim face was as narrow as an axehead, and his eyes were aroused, roving above his flared nostrils. I was still dazed by the spectacle of the dead woman and the camera tripod beside the bed, and pushed Halder away when he tried to wipe the blood from my chin.

The doors opened at the ground floor, where a dozen residents waited to board the lift. They moved forward, then stopped when they saw me surrounded by a gallery of blood-stained figures multiplied by the mirrors. A woman with a small child shrieked at me, a reflex of panic, and a security man in the lobby strode towards us.

Halder pumped the buttons, and held the doors together when the guard drummed on the echoing metal. 'Mr Sinclair . . . we have to clean you up. You'll never get out of here.'

He pressed the emergency button, waited for the doors to open and seized my arm. We emerged onto the floor above the mezzanine. We crossed the landing to a service door, closed it behind us and made our way down a metal staircase used by the maintenance staff. Beyond a freight lift were the swing doors at the rear of a restaurant.

We stepped into the clatter of the kitchen, momentarily blinded by the haze of fat and steam. Everyone was shouting at once as scullions hauled racks of plates and cutlery. In the butchery a sous-chef bent over a work table, picking his fillet steaks as the carver in a bloodied apron sliced at the leaking red muscle.

A side of lamb hung from the wall, and Halder seized my hands and pressed them to the marbled flesh.

'Halder . . . ?'

'Move it around, feel the flesh . . . there's a security man nosing about.'

Halder walked away from me, sidestepping a line of metal trolleys. Exhausted, I rested against the waxy meat when the security guard emerged from the pantry doors and scanned the crowded work space. His gaze touched me briefly as I pretended to wrestle with the carcass, my bloodied hands gripping the foreknuckles. He spoke to Halder, who pointed to the rear staircase and the freight lift.

A few minutes later, in the staff washroom behind the cold store, Halder watched from the door while I cleaned the blood from my arms and face. Reluctantly I washed away the last traces of Frances that clung to my skin. The swirling water in the deep stone sink carried the dark grains of her blood into the rushing vortex.

Halder turned off the taps and stuffed paper towels into my hands. He was tense but poised, like a gymnast powdering his palms as he prepared to seize the parallel bars.

'That's enough.' He pushed me from the sink as the last blood rilled away. 'Where's your car?'

'On the slip road near the garage exit. Jane's small Peugeot — someone trashed the Jag.'

'I did. It was too easy to follow.' He kicked back the door and propelled me towards the freight lift. 'They would have used it as part of the frame. I'm parked in the basement — we'll go down and wait there. The guard who saw you in the lobby must have called the police.'

'Halder, I need to find Jane.'

'I know.' Halder stared at me while the huge lift, almost as large as an aircraft carrier's, sank towards the basement. 'It's taken you a long time, Mr Sinclair . . .'

*   *   *

We sat in the front seat of the Range Rover, watching the cars leave and enter the garage. I could smell the detergent on my hands, and tried to remember the scent of the young woman who lay dead in her bedroom, far above me in the curving night.

'Mr Sinclair?' Halder steadied me when I swayed against the door. 'Hold on for a few minutes. We'll get you out of here.'

'I'm all right.' I pointed to the exit, and the sounds of a motorcycle siren. 'What about the police? They'll be looking for the man who killed Frances.'

'They don't know about it yet. You're safe, Mr Sinclair. And Frances . . .'

'The people outside the lift – several of them saw me.'

'They saw a man with blood on his face. A food mixer might have blown up. No one will identify you.'

'A pity.' I held my hands away from me, repelled by them and their past. 'Poor woman – why did they need to kill her?'

'She was going to cause trouble. Frances Baring had important friends, and some of them weren't happy about Eden-Olympia.'

'Everything is winding down – the special actions, the robberies and raids. Penrose is calling them off.'

'That's not true.'

'I talked to him this afternoon. He explained everything – they realize now they were going too far, it was all out of control. That's why I came here – I wanted to tell Frances it was over.'

'It isn't over. Penrose was leading you on.' Halder spoke quietly but firmly, no longer afraid to point out my self-delusions. 'There are more raids scheduled for the next month than ever before. Penrose and Delage are thinking about Eden II, they want to try out large-scale actions. They're planning racist attacks in Nice, La Napoule and Cagnes-sur-Mer. I've seen the programme at the Villa Grimaldi – it looks like an advent calendar.'

'Armed attacks?'

'Shotguns, pumps, semi-automatics. The bullets have Ahmed and Mohammed written on them. Key security personnel wear sidearms outside Eden-Olympia.' Halder opened his jacket to expose a holster clipped to his belt. 'They're stockpiling weapons at the Villa Grimaldi.'

'I've seen them. The CRS will close the whole place down tomorrow.'

'They'll never be called in. Besides, most people secretly approve. You've listened to Penrose. He dresses up in fancy talk what everybody will tell you in a pied-noir bar. Have a few pastis too many after a football match and give some Arab a good kicking – it fires you up. Your wife finds you more of a man and you work better the next day. Same thing for all those top executives.'

'Then why did Penrose say he was ending the programmes?'

'He wanted you here. Then they could deal with you and Frances at the same time. A classic crime passionnel. Or even a sex game that went wrong. You know how the English are . . .'

'And Jane?'

'They don't see her as a problem. She's already one of them, though she doesn't know it.'

'I need to find her.'

'Right. And then?'

'We'll head for the airport, drive into Italy, anything to get her away from here. She and the Delages are going to a street party somewhere. Ask the night staff at the clinic to page her.'

'Too risky. Anyway, we know where she'll be. The street party is in the Rue Valentin.'

'So . . .' I thought of Jane's lurid costume. 'The whore's garb – like Antoinette and her milkmaids.'

'Mr Sinclair? You aren't making sense.'

'You didn't see what she was wearing. How do you know all this?'

'Delage wanted me to go along. I like Dr Jane, but too much for what he had in mind. Anyway, Penrose earmarked a different job for me.'

'Be careful – they used you to kill Greenwood. Sooner or later they'll give you another target.'

Halder turned the ignition key and listened to the sound of the engine. 'They already have, Mr Sinclair.'

'Me?' I pressed my head against the window, almost hoping that I could break the glass. 'That's why you were in Frances's apartment. You were waiting there, ready to kill me. Why didn't you?'

'Because I like you.' Halder stared at his instruments. 'And I like Dr Jane. Besides, you're more useful to me alive. You're the one person they never predicted, the kind they can't really handle.'

'Too dull, too normal?'

'Something like that. There are things Eden-Olympia can't cope with – the key that breaks in the lock, the toilet that backs up, the druggy woman you fall in love with. The every-day world where the human race still lives. It never arrived at Eden-Olympia.'

'And you're going to bring it there?'

'Exactly. Trashed cars, a few house fires and office break-ins. Eden-Olympia can fight off a billion-dollar takeover bid, but a little dog shit on the shoe leaves it helpless.'

'So the graffiti, the Green slogans – you're behind them?'

'Along with a few friends. I'm climbing to the top, Mr Sinclair, in my own way . . .'

We drove past the parked cars to the exit ramp. When we reached the slip road I pointed to a small crowd dispersing on the steps below the main lobby. I recognized the woman with the child who had shouted at me. Still agitated, she watched resentfully as two traffic policemen remounted their motorcycles. Clearly they had been unimpressed by the story of a blood-stained man in the lift.

'So they haven't found Frances?'

'Not yet. They're still waiting for you, Mr Sinclair.'

As we turned onto the slip road I gripped the steering wheel, forcing Halder to brake. The traffic policemen sat astride their cycles, talking to a sharp-faced man in a camel-hair jacket and patent-leather shoes.

'Alexei . . . what's he doing here?'

'Who?' Halder squinted into the rear-view mirror. 'The man with the cycle cops?'

'Alexei – a small-time Russian crook. He came to the house after we arrived. I saw him in the Rue Valentin, renting out an eleven-year-old girl.'

'He works for Eden-Olympia now. His name is Golyadkin, Dmitri Golyadkin.'

'He said Alexei.'

'Alice, Mr Sinclair. He thought you'd taken over the library . . .'

I watched the Russian talking to the policeman, apparently discussing his illegally parked car. But his eyes never left the balcony far above him. Despite the smart clothes, he looked cheap and unsavoury, like the smell of his body as we wrestled on the grass.

Then I remembered the coarse odour of a man's sweat in Frances's kitchen.

'Golyadkin? Did he kill Frances?'

'I hate to say it, but maybe he did. Alain Delage finds him useful. He has a bunk in the guardroom at the security building. I'll deal with him later for you . . .'

41

The Streetwalker

THE PROMENADE OF the night had begun in the Rue Valentin. I turned the Peugeot into a side street, the Avenue des Fleurs, and waited for Halder to park his Range Rover behind me. Groups of Arab and eastern European men smoked their cigarettes, while the young French whores clicked their heels and stared for inspiration into the night air. The older women in their sixties gazed at each other from their street corner, shifting from one tired ankle to the other like stoical commuters.

I left the car and walked back to the Range Rover.

'Frank, can you see her?'

'Not yet, Mr Sinclair. She'll be here soon.'

Halder seemed unsettled, his eyes avoiding the exposed thighs of the transvestites who ambled past like Olympic oarsmen in drag. He pulled a blue trenchcoat from the rear seat and buttoned it over his jacket. Together we walked down the Rue Valentin. Nothing appeared to happen, but a busy invisible commerce was taking place. One of the bored French whores leaned forward on her stilettos and began to walk at a brisk pace. Ten steps behind her a young Arab followed with quick strides, like a messenger with an urgent telegram. Cars cruised the kerb, drivers staring ahead but communicating by some sixth sense with the pimps who stood with their backs to the road. Everyone trafficked in time, sex displaced into blocks of darkness, thirty-minute cages of the night where pleasure flared and was gone like a shooting star. Somewhere in this third-rate hell were Jane and her street party.

'At least there are no children,' I said. 'What is it?'

'Careful, Mr Sinclair . . .' Halder stepped around me and nodded to a cobbled side alley. A black Mercedes was parked against a wall, the aerial of a radio telephone rising from the rear deck.

'Frank? The car in the alley? What's special about it?'

'It's the Delages'.' Halder surveyed a film poster above a shuttered tabac. 'They're standing in the doorway next to the car.'

'There's nothing there . . .'

'Right by the Merc.' Halder lowered his head and let his eyes drift along the street. Away from Eden-Olympia he was a black man in a trenchcoat, with no secure place in the corridors of the night. At any moment the dark air could open like a trap and release a spasm of hate and violence.

Over Halder's shoulder I saw the Delages. They were leaning against each other in a doorway, her head against his chin, like clandestine lovers.

'They're watching the damned Mercedes. No one's going to steal it. Where's Jane?'

'It's all right, Mr Sinclair.' Concerned for my safety, Halder steered me from the path of an aggressive transvestite who shouldered past, looking down at us with an expression of contempt. 'I'll take over . . . she's here.'

A rear door of the Mercedes opened, and a young prostitute in high-heels and a sequinned shift dress stepped onto the cobbles. She swayed against the open door, and closed it clumsily with her elbow. Tired by the effort, she leaned on the window, staring into her own fatigue. She seemed drugged by more than narcotics, but turned towards the Delages and made a brief, parodic curtsy. As she straightened her skirt I saw the sequins glitter in the streetlights.

'Jane . . . ?' I spoke loudly enough for her to hear me, but she was smiling in an unfocused way at the men who passed the alley.

'Frank, I can see her. What's she playing at? It looks like a stage act.'

'I don't think it is . . .'

'No?' I stepped on a discarded cigarette that glowed near my feet. As its embers flared and died, the air around me seemed to lighten. My anger had passed, and I felt responsible for myself for the first time in months. 'Wait here while I bring the Peugeot. I want to get her away before the action starts.'

'Move fast, Mr Sinclair.'

The Delages stood in the doorway beside the Mercedes, arms around each other, watching Jane like concerned foster parents at an amateur-dramatic performance where their much-loved ward was making her début. Simone followed Jane with her familiar devoted gaze, showing the same shy affection that I had noticed at their first meeting. Alain nodded to her, unsure of Jane but still confident in her, the senior bureaucrat glad to put aside his distractions to encourage a family friend, willing her to succeed. Looking across the night air at this dangerous couple, I imagined their Roman predecessors, administrators of colonial Provence, sitting in the arena at Nimes and watching a favourite slave bravely meet her end. Wilder Penrose's feat was not to have driven the Delages mad but to have made them appear sane.

Halder caught up with me and held my arm as I stepped into the Peugeot. 'Mr Sinclair . . . I can get her for you. They've always wanted me to . . .'

'Thanks, but you'll be their target for ever. They can write me off as a spoilsport husband.'

I stopped the Peugeot outside the entrance to the alley. Jane was still leaning against the Mercedes, handbag swinging like a signalman's lamp. Her eyes stared at nothing, but every few seconds she seemed to wake as she forced herself to breathe. She failed to recognize me, or her car, and gestured towards the interior of the limousine, inviting me to her boudoir. The

Delages nodded from the doorway, not realizing who I was, faces hidden inside the collars of their coats.

A young Frenchman in black trousers and white shirt stopped beside the Peugeot. A smell of stale cooking fat clung to his clothes, and I guessed that he was an off-duty waiter ready to spend his tips. He surveyed Jane like a seasoned racegoer, intrigued by the combination of this back-alley novice and her powerful car. Assuming that the Delages were her pimps, he strolled towards Jane, nodding with approval at her waif-like body.

I left the Peugeot and strode towards the alley. The Delages were watching the rear seat of the Mercedes, where Jane and her client sat together, as close but as distant as strangers on a scenic railway. The Frenchman unzipped his fly. With one hand he hunted through his wallet, while the other held Jane's thigh, trying to keep her attention as she lay rigidly against the headrest, a passenger frozen in the last seconds before a collision.

'Paul . . . over here.' Seeing me, Alain Delage beckoned me to the doorway and made room for me beside Simone. 'I'm delighted you came. We thought . . .'

He was pleased to see me, glad that I had made the effort to turn up, a valued co-investor. Simone drew me into the doorway, stepping back to allow me the best view. Pressed against her, I noticed that she wore no scent or make-up, as if cleansing her senses and preparing her palate for this most savoury of dishes.

I pulled away from them and leaned against the roof of the Mercedes. Calmly, I said: 'I'm glad I came. What exactly is going on?'

'Paul?' Alain was surprised by my studied but aggressive tone. 'It's Jane – she said she told you. She wanted to try it out . . .'

'It's interesting for her.' Simone took my arm reassuringly. 'Like all wives . . .'

Inside the Mercedes the Frenchman had his wallet between his teeth. He gripped Jane's wrists, trying to restrain her as she struggled against him, small fists striking the roof of the car. When I opened the door he swore and released Jane. He stuffed his wallet into a hip pocket and sprang from the rear seat with a shout of anger. He tried to strike me, but I caught his arm and threw him heavily across the bonnet. He swayed to his feet, thought better of attacking me and strode off, gesticulating at a streetlamp.

The Delages watched as I drew Jane from the car. They seemed disappointed but resigned, accepting that I had committed a modest social gaffe, an investor so caught up by the drama that he had mounted the stage to rescue the leading actress. Already Simone had opened the rear door and was brushing the seat, sweeping away the loose sequins from Jane's dress.

Jane embraced me as we stood by the Peugeot, a shocked child waking from a bad dream. She touched the bruise on her cheek and tried to wipe the lipstick from her mouth. Under the make-up her face was toneless, and I sensed that she still failed to grasp what had happened to her.

'Paul, you came . . .' Her hands gripped my shoulders. 'Something went wrong. It didn't feel like a game any more.'

I held her close to me, closer than I had held her since arriving at Eden-Olympia. 'Jane, dear – it never was a game . . .'

She was asleep when I parked behind Halder's Range Rover. He stood by the door and watched me brush the hair from her face. She woke briefly and stared into my eyes with a kind of dazed surprise, as if I were an old friend from her medical school who had strayed into a blind corner of her life.

Halder surveyed the passing cars, the elderly drivers and broad-shouldered transvestites. The Delages had driven off in the Mercedes, resigned to their spoilt evening. Halder's gaze included me in its candid sweep, and I realized that he held me responsible for everything that had happened to Jane.

'She's all right, Mr Sinclair. You can take her home to London.'
He looked down at the Peugeot's keys that I had placed in his
hand. 'You'd like me to drive?'

'Yes. But not back to Eden-Olympia.'

'That's very wise. You're in danger there.'

'I know. It took me a long time to realize it. Frank, I want
you to head for Marseilles. Get Jane to the British Consul.'

'Marseilles? That's an all-night drive.'

'Good. You'll be out of the way. Jane will wake up in a few
hours. Stop for coffee somewhere. Tell her everything we know –
about Frances Baring's death, the child-sex ring, why Greenwood
shot all those people, Wilder Penrose and his therapy classes. Find
the British Consul, and Jane can claim she lost her money and
passport. He'll issue her with some kind of *laissez-passer*. Make
sure she gets on a plane back to England.'

'And you, Mr Sinclair?'

'I'll join her in London. First, I have a few jobs to do here. I
need your Range Rover.'

'All right, if you're sure. I'll say it was stolen.'

'And your pistol. Don't worry, I've had weapons training.'

Halder's hand moved to his holster. He stared at me through
the passing headlamps, unclipped the holster from his belt and
handed the weapon to me.

'Mr Sinclair, you're taking a big risk.'

'Maybe. But there are people who have to be stopped. You
know that, Frank. You've known it from the day you killed
Greenwood.'

'Even so . . .' Halder took off his trenchcoat and slipped out
of his uniform jacket. He waited as I zipped it over my shirt. 'Be
careful. They'll be looking for you.'

'They expect me in the Peugeot with Jane. I need to move
around Eden-Olympia. Whatever happens, I'll say nothing about
you. One day you'll be security chief of Eden II. You'll make a
better job of it than Pascal Zander.'

'I will.' He walked me back to the Range Rover. 'What exactly are you planning to do?'

'Tie up some loose ends. It's best that you don't know.'

Halder handed me his electronic key card. 'This will get you through all the doors in Eden-Olympia. When I come back from Marseilles I'll leave the Peugeot at Nice Airport. They'll think you flew to London. Take care, Mr Sinclair . . .'

I watched him drive away with Jane in the Peugeot. She slept in the passenger seat, her face white and unresponsive, younger even than the teenage physician I had first met at Guy's, an exhausted Alice who had lost her way in the mirror world.

42

Last Assignment

LIGHT TOUCHED THE wings and tail-fins of the parked aircraft, warming the cold metal as the first hint of dawn appeared between Cap d'Antibes and the Îles de Lérins. I sat in the front seat of the Range Rover, and watched the darkness retreat across the dew-moist grass, stealing away like a thief between the hangars and fire engines. Above my head the night seemed to falter, then tilted and withdrew in a rush behind the Esterel. The scent of aviation spirit crossed the airfield as mechanics fuelled a twin-engined Cherokee for an early flight.

Parked beyond the perimeter wire, the aircraft had kept me company during the night. Unable to sleep, I listened to the traffic along the autoroute, Paris-bound tourist buses and lorries from Italy loaded with courgettes and vacuum cleaners and mobile phones. Meanwhile, my damaged Harvard sat in the storage hangar at Elstree, the caked soil embedded in its engine. Flight was an element missing from Eden-Olympia, the certainties of wind-speed, gravity and lift. Absent, too, was the need to explore any interior space, to pioneer the mail routes inside our heads. Only Wilder Penrose had furnished us with an atlas of destinations, a black geography sketched on his prescription pads, populated by menageries of perverse creatures like Simone and Alain Delage.

The scent of Jane's dress clung to my hands, and reminded me of our embrace in the Rue Valentin. She would have arrived in Marseilles, and be sitting with Halder in a café near the Old Port, embarrassed by her whore's frock as she listened to him unfold the secret history of Eden-Olympia. By nine o'clock she would be rousing the British Consul, and soon after be on her way to the airport. While she flew back to London, high above the Rhône valley, Frances Baring would still lie on her bed at Marina Baie des Anges, the zebra dress around her waist and Greenwood's dinner jacket across her legs. And no doubt the film of her death was being hawked by Dmitri Golyadkin around the villas of Super-Cannes . . .

A Mobylette passed me, engine clacking, its slim-shouldered rider in a large safety helmet. Fishing tackle was tied to the pillion seat in a green canvas bag. Searching for the sea, he circled the next roundabout and drove back towards me, then cut the engine and stopped outside the showroom of Nostalgic Aviation. After dismounting, he pushed up his visor, and I recognized Philippe Bourget, brother of the murdered hostage.

When I stepped from the Range Rover he stared in surprise at the blue uniform jacket I was wearing, as if expecting to be arrested.

'Paul Sinclair? That's a relief. For a moment, I thought . . .'

'I'm glad you came.' I held his hands, surprised by how cold they were. 'When I phoned last night you weren't sure.'

'Well . . . at the last moment there are always doubts. I've thought about it for many months.' He watched me warily, not wholly convinced that I was the man he had met at Port-la-Galère. He pointed to the Range Rover. 'You're alone?'

'Yes. No one will know I called you.'

He took off his helmet and held it under his arm. His schoolmaster's face was paler than I remembered, and I guessed that he had not slept since my call. Reassured that I was in command of myself, he placed the helmet on the seat of the Mobylette and untied his fishing tackle. He paused to blow on his fingers, taking a little too long to warm them.

'Monsieur Bourget?'

'I need a minute. It's a large decision, I can't visualize all the consequences.' He spoke in a low voice, as if clearing his conscience. 'Last night I listened carefully to what you said.'

'It's all true – the murder of my friend, the stockpiling of weapons . . .'

'I decided it was time to act. We've heard many stories – violent attacks in La Bocca, rapes of immigrant women. And everyone is bought off. It's a kind of weekend fascism, where the stormtroopers clean up afterwards.'

'But the blood-stains remain. You've spoken to the chauffeurs' widows?'

'No. It would upset them. They will testify for you if it's necessary. The investigation into their husbands' deaths is now closed. The magistrate said they were hostages and they're content to believe that. But it's not right, Mr Sinclair.'

'That's why I'm going to act.'

'By yourself? Is that wise? I can come with you.'

'No. Three dead hostages is enough.'

'You're going to Eden-Olympia? How will you get in? There's good security.'

'It's Sunday morning. I have the Range Rover and a special pass.' Trying to reassure this worried schoolmaster, I said: 'I'll arrest a few key people and take them to the TV centre. There's a link to TF1 in Paris.'

'A public confession? Good. That's the best justice available today.' He unpacked the long canvas shroud containing his fishing rod. 'I don't like afternoon television, but I'll be watching. Good luck, Mr Sinclair.'

He shook my hand and managed a smile of encouragement, and then left me before he could reveal his doubts.

I watched him putter away, his face hidden inside his helmet. Without looking back, he waved for a last time. The Cherokee's engines were warming up, too loud to let me think, and I stepped into the rear seat of the Range Rover. I unclipped the canvas shroud and looked down at the pump-action shotgun. A pack of large-bore shells, the heavy duck-load with which Hemingway had blown out his brains, was taped to the stock. Jacques Bourget's weapon would take his revenge.

Twenty yards away was the showroom of Nostalgic Aviation, with its collection of memorabilia, ejection seats and radial engines, an Aladdin's Cave of possibilities far more potent and enduring than anything Wilder Penrose could offer. Looking at the forties flying helmets, I thought of the blonde-haired passenger sitting behind the Green pilot who had strafed the Eden II ceremony. She had worn a pair of antique goggles, bought or borrowed from Nostalgic Aviation, a tribute to her beauty and quirky tongue from one of her pilot-admirers. I only wished that I could have flown Frances Baring towards the sun . . .

It was 6.45. Even the most sympathetic British Consul would take his time, and it would be noon before Jane could board a scheduled flight to London. The news of what was about to happen at Eden-Olympia would not break until the evening, when whoever was left to run the business park finally decided to call in the police.

With luck, or without it, I would make my case on the international news, the bodies of the guilty laid out behind me like hunting trophies. Within a few days, if Jane flew back to the south of France, she would see me in custody and later be the first witness for the defence. A host of others would follow: Isabel Duval and the chauffeurs' widows, Señora Morales and Philippe Bourget, the wives and brothers of Arab labourers who met their deaths in the dark streets of La Bocca, Japanese film technicians flown in from Tokyo, jewellery store managers in Nice, retired prostitutes and waiters from the Villa Grimaldi. To save the embarrassment of the local police and judiciary, and to preserve the dream of Eden II, a deal would be done with my defending counsel, and if necessary a Presidential pardon would be arranged.

I loaded the shotgun, and then stowed it under the rear seat. By the time I reached Eden-Olympia my targets would still be asleep. I would start with Alain and Simone Delage, drowsy after their late night in the Rue Valentin. Jane had told me that Simone kept a small chromium pistol in her bedside table, so she would be the first. I would kill her while she slept, using Halder's handgun, and avoid having to stare back into her accusing eyes. Then I would shoot Alain as he sat up, drenched in his wife's blood, moustache bristling while he reached for his glasses, unable to comprehend the administrative blunder that had led to his own death.

The Delages slept with their air-conditioning on, and no one would hear the shots through the sealed windows. Wilder Penrose would be next, ordered from his bed at gunpoint and brought down to the bare white room where he had set out his manifesto. He would be amiable, devious and concerned for me to the end, trying to win me with his brotherly charm while unsettling my eyes with the sight of his raw fingernails. I admired him for his hold over me, but I would shoot him down in front of the shattered mirror, one more door to the Alice world now closed for ever. Destivelle and Kalman would follow, and the last would be Dmitri Golyadkin, asleep in his bunk in the security building. I would reach the TV centre in time for a newsflash on the early-afternoon news, but whatever happened I knew that Eden-Olympia would lead the bulletins. This time there would be questions as well as answers.

I listened to the Cherokee taxi towards the runway, then stop and begin its take-off checks. Its propellers threw the morning light back into the sun, and the high drone of its engines seemed a warning call to the people of the Riviera, rousing them from their torpor.

I started the Range Rover, reversed outside the showroom of Nostalgic Aviation and set off through the airport access roads to the coastal highway. The Cherokee moved down the runway, rose confidently into the air and made a wide turn over the sea towards the heights of Super-Cannes. I watched it disappear beyond Eden-Olympia and Sophia-Antipolis, its passengers briefing themselves for their board meetings at Sandoz and Ciba, Roche and Rhône-Poulenc, the pharmaceutical companies who blessed the deepest sleep of the townsfolk and tourists lying behind their shuttered balconies. The beaches beside the coastal road were littered with forgotten film magazines and empty bottles of suntan cream, the debris of a dream washed ashore among the driftwood. I drove on, thinking of Jane and Frances Baring and Wilder Penrose, ready to finish the task that David Greenwood had begun.